# FIELD OF 13
# &
# SHATTERED

*Also by Dick Francis in Pan Books*

THE SPORT OF QUEENS
(autobiography)

LESTER: The Official Biography

DEAD CERT
NERVE
FOR KICKS
ODDS AGAINST
FLYING FINISH
BLOOD SPORT
FORFEIT
ENQUIRY
RAT RACE
BONECRACK
SMOKESCREEN
SLAY-RIDE
KNOCK DOWN
HIGH STAKES
IN THE FRAME
RISK
TRIAL RUN
WHIP HAND
REFLEX
TWICE SHY
BANKER
THE DANGER
PROOF
BREAK IN
BOLT
HOT MONEY
THE EDGE
STRAIGHT
LONGSHOT
COMEBACK
DRIVING FORCE
DECIDER
WILD HORSES
TO THE HILT
10LB PENALTY
SECOND WIND

DICK FRANCIS
OMNIBUS ONE:
Long Shot, Straight,
High Stakes

DICK FRANCIS
OMNIBUS TWO:
Forfeit, Risk, Reflex

DICK FRANCIS
OMNIBUS THREE:
Slay-Ride, Banker, Proof

DICK FRANCIS
OMNIBUS FOUR:
Enquiry, Rat Race, Smokescreen

SID HALLEY OMNIBUS:
Odds Against, Whip Hand,
Come to Grief

Dick Francis has written over forty-one international best-sellers and is widely acclaimed as one of the world's finest thriller writers. His awards include the Crime Writers' Association's Cartier Diamond Dagger for his outstanding contribution to the crime genre, and an honorary Doctorate of Humane Letters from Tufts University of Boston. In 1996 Dick Francis was made a Mystery Writers of America Grand Master for a lifetime's achievement and in 2000 he received a CBE in the Queen's Birthday Honours list.

Dick Francis

# FIELD OF 13
# &
# SHATTERED

PAN BOOKS

*Field of 13* first published 1998 by Michael Joseph.
First published by Pan Books 1999
*Shattered* first published 2000 by the Penguin Group.
First published by Pan Books 2001

This omnibus edition published 2005 by Pan Books
an imprint of Pan Macmillan Ltd
Pan Macmillan, 20 New Wharf Road, London N1 9RR
Basingstoke and Oxford
Associated companies throughout the world
www.panmacmillan.com

ISBN 0 330 44091 8



1 3 5 7 9 8 6 4 2

A CIP catalogue record for this book is available from
the British Library.

Printed and bound in Great Britain by
Mackays of Chatham plc, Chatham, Kent

# FIELD OF 13

My thanks to a whole host of researchers:

MARY
MERRICK FELIX
JOCELYN

ANDREW
JEFFREY JENNY
LAWYERS GALORE

# PROLOGUE

## Notes on the Racecard

Tell me a story, and tell it strong and quick.

Tell it so I go to sleep at bedtime. No bloody corpses, no horrors, no hung, drawn and quartered heroes.

Can't promise that there won't be any deaths. Still, bodies were not my brief.

Amuse, enthuse, raise the protest, sink the fearsome terror. Pull wide a window, watch the play within. Close the curtains. Try the next house, look into the fridge there, tumble its ice cubes down sleepy necks.

Thirteen assorted flavours. Recipes second to size. Never mind the contents, feel the length. Three thousand best words, here please, and eight thousand or so there. Newspapers and magazines like to cut the tale to fit the space. (Don't get me wrong, I enjoy the game.) So some of the excursions are longer and some are short. Some have tight belts, others float.

Some date from way back, some are recent. Meet a few old friends here. See if new acquaintances shake hands.

If one has to be plain, eight of these thirteen stories were originally commissioned by various publications who kindly dictated only length, not content. The other five stories are new, their length – and content – my choice.

*

When the field of thirteen runners were assembled and ready to parade to the start, there arose as in all of life the question, 'Who Goes First?' Should the book lead off with the first story written? Did primogeniture rule?

Leave it to chance, we said in the end, so we held an impromptu draw.

'We', in this instance, meant four of us gathered contentedly for a before-lunch drink. 'We' are my wife Mary, my son Felix, my literary agent Andrew Hewson and myself.

We wrote the titles of the thirteen stories on thirteen sticky-back labels and folded them up carefully, and put them into a splendid glass champagne cooler that had been given to my wife and me by Phyllis and Victor Grann as a house-warming present for our apartment beside the Caribbean Sea. (Mrs Phyllis Grann is the President of PenguinPutnam Inc., who publish D. Francis in the USA.)

The four of us took turns to stir the folded labels in the cooler and pick one out.

Each choice was unfolded, read, and sticky-backed in order onto a board. Thirteen labels . . . three picks each, with the thirteenth and last left to me.

We drew light-heartedly. To be honest, we thought we'd want to fiddle around with the result. But to our amazement it came out pretty well as we would have chosen, so we left it unchanged.

The stories appear in *Field of 13* exactly in the order that their titles came out of the champagne cooler . . . and yes, after that, we put champagne into the cooler . . . and drank to the Draw . . . what else would one expect?

# THE DRAW


| | |
|---|---|
| RAID AT KINGDOM HILL | 1 |
| DEAD ON RED | 17 |
| SONG FOR MONA | 52 |
| BRIGHT WHITE STAR | 88 |
| COLLISION COURSE | 103 |
| NIGHTMARE | 142 |
| CARROT FOR A CHESTNUT | 156 |
| THE GIFT | 187 |
| SPRING FEVER | 220 |
| BLIND CHANCE | 243 |
| CORKSCREW | 266 |
| THE DAY OF THE LOSERS | 305 |
| HAIG'S DEATH | 324 |

# RAID AT KINGDOM HILL

*Time has an uncanny way of laughing at fiction. The goings-on of a bomb-scare at Kingdom Hill – an imaginary racecourse – were invented for the summer entertainment of readers of* The Times *newspaper in 1975. Years later the major fantasy was put into fact: a bomb hoax halted the running of the 1997 Grand National Steeplechase at Aintree.*

*There has been a great change in security and the value of money since Tricksy Wilcox had his brainwave. At Kingdom Hill and throughout* Field of 13, *money and usages have been millenniumized.*

Thursday afternoon, Tricksy Wilcox scratched his armpit absent-mindedly and decided Claypits wasn't worth backing in the 2.30. Tricksy Wilcox sprawled in the sagging armchair with a half-drunk can of beer within comforting reach and a huge colour television bringing him the blow-by-blow from the opening race of the three-day meeting at Kingdom Hill. Only mugs, he reflected complacently, would be putting in a nine to five stint in the sort of July heatwave that would have done justice to the Sahara. Sensible guys like himself sat around at home with the windows open and their shirts off, letting their beards grow while the sticky afternoon waned towards evening.

In winter Tricksy was of the opinion that only mugs struggled to travel to work through snow and sleet, while sensible guys stayed warm in front of the TV, betting on the jumpers; and in spring there was rain, and in the autumn, fog. Tricksy at thirty-four had brought unemployment to a fine art and considered the idea of a full honest day's work to be a joke. It was Tricksy's wife who went out in all weathers to her job in the supermarket, Tricksy's wife who paid the rent on the council flat and left the exact money for the milkman. Eleven years of Tricksy had left her cheerful, unresentful, and practical. She had waited without emotion through his two nine-month spells in prison and accepted that one day would find him back there. Her dad had been in and out all her childhood. She felt at home with the minor criminal mind.

Tricksy watched Claypits win the 2.30 with insulting ease and drank down his dented self-esteem with the last of the beer. Nothing he bloody touched, he thought gloomily, was any bloody good these days. He was distinctly short of the readies and had once or twice had to cut down on necessities like drink and fags. What he wanted, now, was a nice little wheeze, a nice little tickle, to con a lot of unsuspecting mugs into opening their wallets. The scarce ticket racket, now that had done him proud for years, until the coppers nicked him with a stack of forged duplicates in his pocket at Wimbledon. And tourists were too fly by half these days, you couldn't sell them subscriptions to non-existent porn magazines, let alone London Bridge.

He could never afterwards work out exactly what gave him the great Bandwagon idea. One minute he was peacefully watching the 3 o'clock at Kingdom Hill, and the next he was flooded with a breathtaking, wild and unholy glee.

He laughed aloud. He slapped his thigh. He stood up and jigged about, unable to bear the audacity of his thoughts sitting down. 'Oh Moses,' he said, gulping for air. 'Money for old rope. Kingdom Hill, here I come.'

Tricksy Wilcox was not the most intelligent of men.

Friday morning, Major Kevin Cawdor- Jones, Manager of Kingdom Hill Racecourse, took his briefcase to the routine meeting of the Executive Committee, most of whom detested each other. Owned and run by a small private company constantly engaged in boardroom wars, the racecourse suffered from the results of spiteful internecine decisions and never made the profit it could have done.

The appointment of Cawdor-Jones was typical of the mismanagement. Third on the list of possibles, and far less able than one and two, he had been chosen solely to side-step the bitter deadlock between the pro one line-up and the pro two. Kingdom Hill in consequence had acquired a mediocre administrator; and the squabbling executives usually managed to thwart his more sensible suggestions.

As a soldier Cawdor-Jones had been impulsive, rashly courageous, and easygoing, qualities which had ensured that he had not been given the essential promotion to Colonel. As a man he was lazy and likeable, and as a manager, soft.

The Friday meeting as usual wasted little time in coming to blows.

'Massive step-up of security,' repeated Bellamy, positively. 'Number one priority. Starting at once. Today.'

Thin and sharp featured, Bellamy glared aggressively round the table, and Roskin as usual with drawling voice opposed him.

'Security costs money, my dear Bellamy.'

Roskin spoke patronizingly, knowing that nothing infuriated Bellamy more. Bellamy's face darkened with fury, and the security of the racecourse, like so much else, was left to the outcome of a personal quarrel.

Bellamy insisted, 'We need bigger barriers, specialized extra locks on all internal doors and double the number of police. Work must start at once.'

'Race crowds are not hooligans, my dear Bellamy.'

Cawdor-Jones inwardly groaned. He found it tedious enough already, on non-race days, to make his tours of inspection, and he was inclined anyway not to stick punctiliously to the safeguards that already existed. Bigger barriers between enclosures would mean he could no longer climb over or through, but would have to walk the long way round. More locks meant more keys, more time-wasting, more nuisance. And all presumably for the sake of frustrating the very few scroungers who tried to cross from a cheaper to a dearer enclosure without paying. He thought he would very much prefer the status quo.

The tempers rose around him, and the voices also. He waited resignedly for a gap. 'Er . . .' he said, clearing his throat.

The heated pro-Bellamy faction and the sneering pro-Roskin clique both turned towards him hopefully. Cawdor-Jones was their mutual let-out; except, that was, when his solution was genuinely constructive, when they both vetoed it because they wished they had thought of it themselves.

'A lot of extra security would mean more work for our staff,' he said diffidently. 'We might have to take on an extra man or two to cope with it . . . and after the big initial outlay there would always be maintenance . . . and . . . er . . . well, what real harm can anyone do to a racecourse?'

This weak oil stilled the waters enough for both sides to begin their retreat with their positions and opinions intact.

'You have a point about the staff,' Bellamy conceded begrudgingly, knowing that two extra men would cost a great deal more than locks, and that the racecourse couldn't afford them, 'but I still maintain that tighter security is essential and very much overdue.'

Cawdor-Jones, in his easygoing way, privately disagreed. Nothing had ever happened to date. Why should anything ever happen in future?

The discussion grumbled on for half an hour, and nothing at all was done.

Friday afternoon, Tricksy Wilcox went to the races having pinched half of his wife's holiday fund from the best teapot. The trip was a recce to spy out the land, and Tricksy, walking around with his greedy eyes wide open, couldn't stop himself chuckling. It did occur to him once or twice that his light-hearted single-handed approach was a waste: the big boys would have had it all planned to a second and would have set their sights high in their humourless way. But Tricksy was a loner who avoided gang life on the grounds that it was too much like hard work; bossed around all the time, and with no pension rights into the bargain.

He downed half pints of beer at various bars and wagered smallish amounts on the Tote. He looked at the horses in the parade ring and identified those jockeys whose faces he knew from TV, and he attentively watched the races. At the end of the afternoon, with modest winnings keeping him solvent, he chuckled his way home.

Friday afternoon, Mrs Angelisa Ludville sold two Tote tickets to Tricksy Wilcox, and hundreds to other people whom she knew as little. Her mind was not on her job, but on the worrying pile of unpaid bills on her bookshelf at home. Life had treated her unkindly since her fiftieth birthday, robbing her of her looks, because of worry, and her husband, because of a blonde. Deserted, divorced and childless, she could nevertheless have adapted contentedly to life alone had it not been for the drastic drop in comfort. Natural optimism and good humour were gradually draining away in the constant grinding struggle to make shortening ends meet.

Angelisa Ludville eyed longingly the money she took through her Tote window. Wads of the stuff passed through her hands each working day, and only a fraction of what the public wasted on gambling would, she felt, solve all her problems handsomely. But honesty was a lifetime habit; and, besides, stealing from the Tote was impossible. The takings for each race were collected and checked immediately. Theft would be instantly revealed. Angelisa sighed and tried to resign herself to the imminent cutting off of her telephone.

Saturday morning, Tricksy Wilcox dressed himself carefully for the job in hand. His wife, had she not been stacking baked beans in the supermarket, would have advised against the fluorescent orange socks. Tricksy, seeing his image in the bedroom mirror only as far down as the knees, was confident that the dark suit, dim tie and brown felt trilby gave him the look of a proper race-going gent. He had even, without reluctance, cut two inches off his hair, and removed a flourishing moustache. Complete with outsize binoculars case slung over his shoulder, he smirked at his transformation with approval and set out with a light step to catch the train to Kingdom Hill.

On the racecourse Major Kevin Cawdor-Jones made his race-day round of inspection with his usual lack of thoroughness. Slipshod holes in his management resulted also in the police contingent arriving half an hour late and under strength; and not enough racecards had been ordered from the printers.

'Not to worry,' said Cawdor-Jones, shrugging it all off easily.

Mrs Angelisa Ludville travelled to the course in the Tote's own coach, along with fifty colleagues. She looked out of the window at the passing suburbs and thought gloomily about the price of electricity.

Saturday afternoon at 2.30 she was immersed in the

routine of issuing tickets and taking money, concentrating on her work and feeling reasonably happy. She tidied her cash drawer ready for the 3 o'clock, the biggest race of the day. The extra long queues would be forming soon outside, and speed and efficiency in serving the punters was not only her job but, indeed, her pride.

At 2.55 Cawdor-Jones was in his office next to the weighing-room trying to sort out a muddle over the casual workers' pay. At 2.57 the telephone at his elbow rang for about the twentieth time in the past two hours and he picked up the receiver with his mind still on the disputed hourly rates due to the stickers-back of kicked-up chunks of turf.

'Cawdor-Jones,' he said automatically.

A man with an Irish accent began speaking quietly.

'What?' said Cawdor-Jones. 'Speak up, can't you? There's too much noise here . . . I can't hear you.'

The man with the Irish accent repeated his message with the same soft half-whisper.

'*What?*' said Cawdor-Jones. But his caller had rung off.

'Oh my God,' said Cawdor-Jones, and stretched a hand to thc switch which connected him to the internal broadcasting system. He glanced urgently at the clock. Its hands clicked round to 2.59, and at that moment the fourteen runners for the 3 o'clock were being led into the starting stalls.

'Ladies and gentlemen,' said Cawdor-Jones, his

voice reverberating from every loudspeaker on the racecourse. 'We have been warned that a bomb has been planted somewhere in the stands. Would you please all leave at once and go over into the centre of the course while the police arrange a search.'

The moment of general shock lasted less than a second: then the huge race crowd streamed like a river down from the steps, up from the tunnels, out of the doors, running, pelting, elbowing towards the safety of the open spaces on the far side of the track.

Bars emptied dramatically with half-full glasses overturned and smashed in the panic. The Tote queues melted instantaneously and the ticket sellers followed them helter-skelter. The stewards vacated their high box at a dignified downhill rush and the racing press pell-melled to the exit without hanging round to alert their papers. City editors could wait half an hour. Bombs wouldn't.

The scrambling thousands deserted all the racecourse buildings within a space of five minutes. Only a very few stayed behind, and chief of these was Kevin Cawdor-Jones, who had never lacked for personal courage and now saw it as his duty as a soldier to remain at his post.

The under-strength band of policemen collected bit by bit outside the weighing-room, each man hiding his natural apprehension under a reassuring front. Probably another bloody hoax, they told each other. It was always a hoax. Or nearly always. Their officer took charge of organizing the search and told the civilian Cawdor-Jones to remove himself to safety.

'No, no,' said Cawdor-Jones. 'While you look for the bomb, I'll make quite sure that everyone's out.' He smiled a little anxiously and dived purposefully into the weighing-room.

All clear there, he thought, peering rapidly round the jockeys' washroom. All clear in the judge's box, the photo-finish developing room, the kitchens, the boiler room, the Tote, the offices, the stores . . . He bustled from building to building, knowing all the back rooms, the nooks and crannies where some deaf member of the staff, some drunk member of the public, might be sitting unawares.

He saw no people. He saw no bomb. He returned a little breathlessly to the open space outside the weighing-room and waited for a report from the slower police.

Around the stands Tricksy Wilcox was putting the great Bandwagon idea into sloppy execution. Chuckling away internally over the memory of his Irish impersonation (good enough for entry to Equity, he thought), he bustled speedily from bar to bar and in and out of the other doors, filling his large empty binoculars case with provender. It was amazing, he thought, giggling, how careless people were in a panic.

Twice, he came face to face with policemen.

'All clear in there, Officer,' he said purposefully, each time pointing back to where he had been. Each time the police gaze flickered unsuspectingly over the brown trilby, the dark suit, dim tie, and took him for one of the racecourse staff.

Only the orange socks stopped him getting clean away. One policeman, watching his receding back view, frowned uncertainly at the brilliant segments between trouser-leg and shoe and started slowly after him.

'Hey—' he said.

Tricksy turned his head, saw the Law advancing, lost his nerve, and bolted. Tricksy was never the most intelligent of men.

Saturday afternoon at 4 o'clock, Cawdor-Jones made another announcement.

'It appears the bomb warning was just another hoax. It is now safe for everyone to return to the stands.'

The crowd streamed back in reverse and made for the bars. The barmaids returned to their posts and immediately raised hands and voices in a screeching sharp chorus of affronted horror.

'Someone's pinched all the takings!'

'The cheek of it! Taken our tips, and all!'

In the various Tote buildings, the ticket sellers stood appalled. Most of the huge intake for the biggest race of the meeting had simply vanished.

Angelisa Ludville looked with utter disbelief at her own plundered cash drawer. White, shaking, she joined the clamour of voices. 'The money's gone.'

Cawdor-Jones received report after report with a

face of anxious despair. He knew no doors had been locked after the stampede to the exit. He knew no security measures whatever had been taken. The racecourse wasn't equipped to deal with such a situation. The Committee would undoubtedly blame him. Might even give him the sack.

At 4.30 he listened with astounded relief to news from the police that a man had been apprehended and was now helping to explain how his binoculars case came to be crammed to overflowing with used treasury notes, many of them bearing a fresh watermark resulting from the use of a wet beer glass as a paper-weight.

Monday morning, Tricksy Wilcox appeared gloomily before a magistrate and was remanded in custody for seven days. The great Bandwagon idea hadn't been so hot after all, and they would undoubtedly send him down for more than nine months this time.

Only one thought brightened his future. The police had tried all weekend to get information out of him, and he had kept his mouth tight shut. Where, they wanted to know, had he hidden the biggest part of his loot?

Tricksy said nothing.

There had only been room in the binoculars case for one-tenth of the stolen money. Where had he put the bulk?

Tricksy wasn't telling.

He would get off more lightly, they said, if he surrendered the rest.

Tricksy didn't believe it. He grinned disdainfully and shook his head. Tricksy knew from past experience that he would have a much easier time inside as the owner of a large hidden cache. He'd be respected. Treated with proper awe. He'd have status. Nothing on earth would have persuaded him to spill the beans.

Monday morning, Major Cawdor-Jones took his red face to an emergency meeting of his Executive Committee and agreed helplessly with Bellamy's sharply reiterated opinion that the racecourse security was a disgrace.

'I warned you,' Bellamy repeated for the tenth self-righteous time. 'I warned you all. We need more locks. There are some excellent slam-shut devices available for the cash drawers in the Tote. I'm told that all money can be secured in five seconds. I propose that these devices be installed immediately throughout the racecourse.'

He glared belligerently round the table. Roskin kept his eyes down and merely pursed his mouth, and Kingdom Hill voted to bolt its doors now that the horse was gone.

Monday evening, Angelisa Ludville poured a double gin, switched on the television and put her feet up. Beside her lay a pile of stamped and addressed envelopes, each containing a cheque clearing one of her dreaded debts. She sighed contentedly. Never, she thought, would she forget the shock of seeing her empty till. Never would she get over the fright it had given her. Never would she forget the rush of relief when she realized that everyone had been robbed, not just herself. Because she knew perfectly well that it was one of the other sellers whose take she had scooped up on the scramble to the door. She had thought it plain stupid to lift the money from her own place. She couldn't know that there would be another, more ambitious thief. It would have been plain silly at the time to steal from her own place. And besides, there was far more cash at the other window.

Monday evening, Kevin Cawdor-Jones sat in his bachelor flat thinking about the second search of Kingdom Hill. All day Sunday the police had repeated the nook-and-cranny inspection, but slowly, without fear, looking not for a bang but a bank. Cawdor-Jones had given his willing assistance, but nothing at all had been found. The money had vanished.

'Tricksy must have had a partner,' said the police officer in charge morosely. 'But we won't get a dicky bird out of him.'

Cawdor-Jones, unsacked from his managership, smiled gently at the memory of the past few days. Cawdor-Jones, impulsive and rashly courageous, had made the most of the opportunity Tricksy Wilcox had provided.

Cawdor-Jones, whose nerve could never be doubted, had driven away unchallenged on Saturday evening with the jackpot from the Tote.

He leaned over the arm of his chair and fondly patted his bulging briefcase.

# DEAD ON RED

*Although first published here,* Dead on Red *is set in the past (in 1986 and 1987, to be exact) partly because the regulations regarding the carriage of handguns from mainland Europe to England were tightened as part of the 1988 Firearms Act.*

Emil Jacques Guirlande, Frenchman, feared flying to the point of phobia. Even advertising posters featuring aeroplanes, and especially the roar of stationary jet engines at airports, raised his heartbeat to discomfort and brought a fine mist of chill sweat to his hairline. Consequently he travelled from his Paris home by wheels and waves on his worldwide entrepreneurial missions, the more leisurely journeys in fact suiting his cautious nature better. He liked to approach his work thoughtfully, every contingency envisaged. Panicky reactions to unforeseen hitches were, in his orderly consideration, the stupidity of amateurs.

Emil Jacques Guirlande was a murderer by trade, a killer uncaptured and unsuspected, a quiet-mannered man who avoided attention, but who had by the age of thirty-seven successfully assassinated sixteen targets comprising seven businessmen, eight wives and one child.

He was, of course, expensive. Also reliable, inventive and heartless.

Orphaned at seven, unadopted, brought up in institutions, he had never been warmly loved for himself, nor had ever felt deep friendly affection for any living thing (except a dog). Military service in the army had taught him to shoot, and a natural competency with firearms, combined with a developing appetite for power, had led him afterwards to take employment as a part-time instructor in a civilian gun club, where talk of death reverberated in the air like cordite.

'Opportunities' were presented to Emil Jacques through the post by an unidentified go-between he had never met, but only after careful research would he accept a proposition. Emil considered himself high class. The American phrase 'hit man' was, to his fastidious mind, vulgar. Emil accepted a proposition only when he was sure his customer *could* pay, *would* pay, and wouldn't collapse with maudlin regrets afterwards. Emil also insisted on the construction of unbreakable alibis for every customer likely to be an overwhelming suspect, and although this sounded easy it had sometimes been the overall stop or go factor.

And so it was on a particular Tuesday in December 1986. The essential alibi looking perfect, Emil committed himself to the task and carefully packed his bags for a short trip to England.

Emil's English, functional rather than ornate, had sustained him so far through three English killings in four years. Tourist phrase-book gems – ('*Mon auto ne marche pas*'; 'My car's broken down') – had both kept him free from the damaging curiosity of others and also allowed him to abort his mission prudently if he felt unsafe before the act. He had, indeed, already twice retreated at a late stage from the present job in hand: once from bad weather, once from dissatisfaction with the sickness alibi proposed.

'*Pas bon*,' he said to himself. 'No good.'

His client, who had paid a semi-fortune in advance, grew increasingly impatient at the delays.

On the Tuesday in December 1986, however, Emil Jacques, as satisfied with the alibi as he could be, having packed his bag and announced an absence from the gun club, set off in his inconspicuous white car to drive to Calais to cross the wintry waters of the English Channel.

As usual, he openly took with him the tools of his trade: handguns, ear defenders, multiple certificates proving his accreditation as a licensed instructor in a top-class Parisian club. He carried the lot in a locked metal sponge-lined suitcase, in the manner of photographers, and as it was still years before the banning of handguns in England, his prepared tale of entering competitions passed without question. Had he run into trouble on entry, he would have smiled resignedly and gone home.

Emil Jacques Guirlande, murderer, ran into no trouble on this Tuesday in December 1986. Unchallenged at Dover, he drove contentedly through the hibernating fields of southern England, peacefully reviewing his wicked plan.

On British racecourses that year the steeplechasing scene had been sizzlingly dominated by the improbable trainer–jockey allegiance of a long-haired descendant of true gypsies with the aristocratic nephew of an historic house.

Gypsy Joe (more accurately, John Smith) felt and displayed the almost magical affinity with animals that ran like a gene river in his people's blood. To please Gypsy Joe, thoroughbreds dug into their own ancient tribal memory and understood that leading the herd was the aim of life. The leader of the herd won the race.

Gypsy Joe gave his horses judiciously the feed and exercise that best powered their hearts, and whispered mysterious encouragements into their ears while he saddled them for races. He was successful enough by ordinary standards and grudgingly admired by most of his peers, but for Joe it was never enough. He searched always – and perhaps unrealistically – for a rider whose psyche would match what he knew to be true of his horses. He searched for youth, courage, talent, and an uncorrupted soul.

Every year he watched and analysed the race-riders new on the scene while he busied himself with his regular runners, and not for five years did he see what he wanted. When he did see it, he wasted no time in publicly securing it for his own.

So Gypsy Joe rocked the jump-racing fraternity in the late spring of 1986 by offering a riding contract to a light-hearted amateur who had ridden in races for precisely one season and had won nothing of note. All the amateur had to do in order to accept the unusual proposal was to take out a professional licence at once.

Red Millbrook (he had red hair) had listened to the telephoned offer from Gypsy Joe in the same general bewilderment that soon raised eyebrows from the Jockey Club mandarins to critical clusters of stable-lads in local pubs.

Firstly, few retainer contracts of any sort were offered to jockeys in steeplechasing. Secondly, Gypsy Joe already regularly employed two long-time professionals (without contracts) whose results were widely considered satisfactory, as Gypsy Joe lay fifth on the trainers' races-won table. Thirdly, Red Millbrook, not long out of school, could be classed as an ignorant novice.

With the assurance of youth, the 'ignorant novice' applied for a licence at once.

Red Millbrook, thus newly professional, met Gypsy Joe face to face for the first time when he walked with curiosity into the parade ring before the April Gold Cup at Sandown Park. Gypsy Joe, at forty and full of bullish confidence, knew he was inviting sneers for letting this almost untried lordling loose on a testing track in a big-news event on a horse he'd never even sat on. Adverse comments in various racing papers had already lambasted Joe for passing over both of his two useful, faithful – and fuming – stable jockeys and 'throwing away the chance of a Golden Cup for the sake of a publicity stunt'. Gypsy Joe trusted his instincts and was not deterred.

Young Red Millbrook, meeting Gypsy Joe in the parade ring, thought him a big untidy long-haired shambles of a man and rather regretted the impulsive promise he'd signed, which was to ride always where and when bidden by the trainer.

The two ill-assorted future allies tentatively shook hands with television thousands watching, and Red Millbrook thought the tingle that ran through him was due only to the excitement of the occasion. Gypsy Joe, however, smiled to himself with satisfaction, and was perhaps the only onlooker not surprised when his runner clung on for the Gold by half a length.

It wasn't that Red Millbrook had ever in his short life ridden badly: he had in fact spent all his adolescent spare hours on horseback, although those spare hours had been purposefully limited by parentally imposed education. His titled father and mother could summon pride in an *amateur* jockey for a son, but shied away wincing at the word *professional.* Like a tart, his mother groaned.

Red Millbrook thought his new professional status a step up, not down. Anxious to put on a reasonable show at Sandown, he took a fierce determination to the starting gate, and over the first fence awoke to an unexpected mental alliance with the horse. He had never felt anything like it. His whole body responded. He and the horse rose as one over each of the string of jumps constructed and spaced to sort out the fleetest. He as one with the horse swept round the final bend and stretched forward up the last testing hill. He shared the will and the determination of his animal partner. When he won, he felt, not amazement, but that he had come into his natural kingdom.

In the winner's unsaddling enclosure Gypsy Joe and Red Millbrook smiled faintly at each other as if they had joined a private brotherhood. Gypsy Joe knew he'd found his man. Red Millbrook embraced his future.

*

Up on the stands the two passed-over stable jockeys watched the race and the win with increasing rage. One of them would normally have been on the horse, and he – Davey Rockman – felt his fury thoroughly justified.

Gypsy Joe was a rough customer to work for (Davey Rockman considered), but his horses ran often, were well schooled, and had kept him – Davey – in luxury and girlfriends for the past five years. Davey Rockman's appetite for women, once the scandal of the racecourse, had long been accepted as the norm; and conversely 'The Rock's' dark good looks were known powerfully to attract anything female. Davey Rockman's anger at the loss of the money he would have earned by winning the big prestigious race was minor compared with the insult to his sexual pride.

It didn't once occur to him that had he, and not the usurper Red Millbrook, been riding the horse, it might not have won.

Nigel Tape, the stable's regular second-string jockey, burned with loyal resentment on 'The Rock's' behalf. Nigel Tape, destined never himself to shine as a star, habitually basked in his position of side-kick to 'The Rock', always echoing the same frustrations, the same triumphs, the same unrealistic gripes. He felt all of Davey Rockman's legitimate indignation at having been replaced, and magnified the umbrage to vindictive proportions. Davey 'The Rock' felt flattered by Nigel

Tape's almost fanatical devotion and didn't see its dangers.

On the Monday after the April Gold Cup, Gypsy Joe surveyed the glowering faces of his two long-term jockeys as they drove into his stable-yard for the morning exercise and training session.

He said to them flatly, in businesslike tones, 'As you've probably realized, Red Millbrook will be my first retained jockey from now on. You, Davey, have the option of staying on here as schooling jockey, which you're good at, and riding the occasional race, or of course if you prefer it you can try for chief stable jockey with a different trainer.'

Davey Rockman listened in bitter silence. His status as Gypsy Joe's first jockey had been comfortably high in the jump-racing world. The demotion the trainer was handing out not only meant a severe permanent drop in face and in income, but also the virtual end of his attractiveness to skirts. He habitually used the power of his position to dominate women. He liked to slap them about a bit and make them beg for passion. He felt superior. He strode about often in his jockey boots, counting them a symbol of virility.

Finding a job with comparable standing was hardly an option: there weren't enough good stable-jockey jobs to go round. Davey Rockman looked straight at Gypsy Joe's uncaring determination to downgrade him and felt the first surge of murderous hate.

Nigel Tape asked aggressively, 'What about me, then?'

'You can go on as before,' the trainer told him.

'Picking up crumbs? It's not fair.'

'Life is never fair,' Gypsy Joe said. 'Haven't you noticed?'

Gypsy Joe's ancient instincts proved spectacularly right. Red Millbrook and Gypsy Joe's horses galvanized each other on track after track while the main part of the jump-racing programme waned towards summer. The cheers for one win barely died away before they rose for another. The owners of the horses were ecstatic: new owners offered horses every day. By the time the next ten-month-long season warmed up in August, the trainer had rented a lot of extra stabling and the jockey was whistling to himself in happy fulfilment as he drove his car from success to success. Through September and October and November it seemed he could do no wrong. He led the jockeys' list.

His parents became reconciled to his 'tart'ness and boasted about him instead, but his two elder sisters, unmarried, grew jealous of his fame. He still lived in the family house in London which his sophisticated mother much preferred to clomping round weekend fields and battling mildew in a damp old cottage. Red settled for her London comfort while planning to buy a house of his own with his winnings, though not one necessarily on Gypsy Joe's doorstep. The lives of jockey and trainer remained as separate as before their partnership had fused at Sandown, but the vibrations between them remained unchanged. They smiled always the same understanding smile, but they never drank together.

Red Millbrook – friendly, uncomplicated, generous-hearted – mixed little with the other jockeys, who tended to be in awe of his dazzling skill, and he cheerfully ignored the ill-will he saw blazing in Davey Rockman's eyes, and the identical copycat resentment in Nigel Tape's. Owing to the multiplication of the horses in the stable, Davey Rockman, Red Millbrook blithely reflected, still rode a fair amount of races, even if not on the winning cream of the string, and even if not with the same stunned and genuflecting coverage in the press. It wasn't his fault, he assured himself, that Gypsy Joe had singled him out and given him such a great and satisfying opportunity.

He was unaware that it was the disastrous collapse of his vigorous sex life that most infuriated The Rock; and The Rock on his part failed to realize that it was his bitter constant grumbling that put women off. For the first time in his life girls flocked round Red Millbrook, who thought their approaches amusing: and his amusement further inflamed his seething dispossessed rival.

In December, when Davey Rockman broke some

small bones in his foot in a racing fall, Red Millbrook sent him a message of sympathy. The Rock thought it an insult and didn't reply.

Red Millbrook kept his car in the London street outside his parents' house and drove from there each day to wherever he was due to race. Normally he set off northwards on a road which took him through tall black railings into the grassy expanse of Hyde Park. There were paths there and clumps of evergreen bushes, and benches for the rest of tired walkers. Also there were several sets of traffic lights, both to aid pedestrians crossing and to allow traffic to turn right in a complicated pattern. Almost always one of the sets of lights would be red against Red Millbrook. Patiently he would wait for the green while his radio filled the car with music.

On one Friday morning in December, while he waited, humming, at the stop light, a man approached his stationary car and tapped on the passenger-side window. He was dressed as a tourist and carried a large street map, to which he hopefully pointed.

Red Millbrook pressed a button and obligingly opened the electrically controlled window. The tourist advanced the map politely into the car.

'Excuse me,' said the tourist, 'which way to Buckingham Palace, please?'

He had a foreign accent, Red Millbrook thought

fleetingly. French, perhaps. The jockey leaned towards the window and bent his head over the map.

'You go—' he said.

Emil Jacques Guirlande shot him.

Truth to tell, Emil Jacques enjoyed killing.

He took pride in being able to bring death so quickly and cleanly that his prey hadn't even a suspicion of the need for fear. Emil Jacques considered he would have failed his own high standards if ever he'd seen eyes widen with desperate fright or heard just the beginning of a piteous plea. Some assassins might take pleasure in their victims' terror: Emil Jacques, for a murderer, was kind.

Red Millbrook had looked exclusively at the map held half open in Emil Jacques' left hand. He hadn't had time to see the Browning 9mm pistol with its efficient long silencer slide smoothly out from within the map's lower folds. Emil's right hand had a speed and sweetness of touch with a gun that no magician could have bettered.

The fire-hot bullet instantly destroyed Red Millbrook's brain. He felt nothing, knew nothing, made no sound. The faint 'phut' of the Browning lost its identity in the beat of the radio's music.

Without hesitation Emil Jacques withdrew his map, the pistol again hidden in its folds. He made a gesture of thanks in case of onlookers and walked casually away.

He went unhurriedly along a path and round a clump of bushes, and he had gone quite a long way when he heard car horns blaring behind him. The red lights, he knew, had turned to green, but one car was unmoving, obstructing the traffic. By the time irate drivers had discovered the blood and skull splinters and had screamed with hysterics, Emil Jacques was leaving the park to rejoin his car; and by the time the Metropolitan Police were hurriedly setting up an incident room to investigate the crime, Emil Jacques, driving carefully, was halfway to Dover on his way back to France.

Not bad, he thought. Not bad in the end, though it had been difficult to set up.

In late October, when he'd been offered the job, he had made his usual unarmed reconnaissance, had learned the pattern of life of his target and had noted the opportunity presented by the multiple traffic lights at the one particular entrance to Hyde Park. With a stopwatch, he'd driven over and over his target's normal daily route until he knew to the second the maximum and minimum times a car might have to stand and wait for red to turn green. Red Millbrook left home at varying times but almost always took the Park way to avoid traffic. Once in every four days or fewer, he was stopped by the lights. Every time the lights stopped him, he sat defenceless before them in his car. Killing him there was wholly possible, Emil Jacques decided, if he were quick.

He practised at home with map and gun through his own car window until he could bring off the attack routine within seconds. He then accepted the offered proposition and in November, when he had received his agreed up-front payment, he crossed from Dieppe to Newhaven (for a change) and drove through customs with his handgun suitcase declared and cleared.

Almost at once things went wrong. Red Millbrook left London and went to Scotland for a two-day race meeting at Ayr, afterwards dawdling southwards, staying with friends and owners while he rode them winners all over the north. Emil Jacques fretted helplessly in London and felt vulnerable, and when Red Millbrook did finally return to his parents' house, the weather turned brutal with gales and hailstorms and long bursts of rain; the sort of weather no tourist would walk about in, asking directions with a map.

Finally Emil Jacques read a racing newspaper carefully, and with the help of his English–French dictionary, realized that the promised ill-health alibi of his customer was no longer secure. Uneasily aware also that the small hotel's receptionist was beginning to want to flirt with the quiet guest with the French accent, Emil Jacques aborted his mission entirely and cautiously went home.

It was three weeks later, when the weather was cold but sunny on a Friday morning in December, that Red Millbrook stopped at the traffic lights and died.

*

The outrage that shook the racing world surprised Emil Jacques in France. He hadn't realized how intensely the British people revered their sporting heroes, and he was unexpectedly shaken to hear that he (the assassin) would be lynched (at least) if found. A fund was being set up, contributed to in a flood of sentiment at every racecourse gate, offering a tempting price on the killer's head.

Emil Jacques Guirlande sat at his customary inconspicuous corner table in the café near his apartment and painstakingly, word by word, translated the eulogies paid to the dead young prodigy in the English racing press. Emil Jacques pursed his lips and suppressed regret.

The patron, a bulky man with a bulging apron and heavy moustache, paused at Emil Jacques' side and added his own opinion. 'Only a devil,' he said, pointing at Red Millbrook's attractive picture, 'would kill such a splendid fellow.' He sighed at the villainy of the world, adding, 'And there's a letter for you, Monsieur.' He gave Emil Jacques a conspiratorial leer and a nudge in the ribs and produced an envelope from beside the till. The patron believed the letters he occasionally passed to his most constant customer were notes of assignation made secretly by sex-starved ladies looking for fun.

Emil Jacques always accepted the letters with a wink, never disillusioning his host: and in this way, at the end of a three-cut-off go-between chain he received messages and sent them. The envelope that evening duly delivered the remainder of the agreed price for the Millbrook job: no wise man or woman ever risked withholding what they owed to a killer.

It could have been expected that the sharp Metropolitan Police Force superintendent in charge of finding Red Millbrook's murderer would never attain soul-mate heights with Gypsy Joe Smith. Gypsy Joe was a man of instinct with a great accountant. Instinct won the races, the accountant made his client rich. Gypsy Joe operated on a deep level of intuition. The policeman and the accountant worked on fact and logical deduction.

The superintendent thought all racing people to be halfway crooks and Gypsy Joe held the same belief about the police. The superintendent took a sceptical view of Gypsy Joe's intense and genuine grief. Gypsy Joe wondered how such a thick-brained super had reached that rank.

They engaged like bulls in Gypsy Joe's stable office, fiercely attended also by a local high-ranking detective who seemed chiefly concerned about 'patch'.

'Who cares whose patch he died on,' Gypsy Joe bellowed. 'Put your stupid heads together and find out who did it.'

Separately and finally the two high-rankers did put their not-so-stupid heads together, but without any sudden blaze of enlightenment. They extensively interviewed the two women who'd stopped at the lights behind Red Millbrook's car, and who'd tooted at him when the lights went green, and had gone to yell at him, and had found his slumped bloody body and would never sleep dreamlessly again.

They had seen no one, they said. They had been talking. There weren't many people in Hyde Park. It was winter.

Emil Jacques had left no clues in Red Millbrook's car: no fingerprints, no fibres, no hairs. The bullet, hopefully dug out of the chassis, matched nothing on anyone's record, nor ever would. Careful Emil Jacques never killed anyone with a gun he'd used for the purpose before. For all of everyone's efforts, the case remained unsolved.

The Metropolitan Police superintendent changed his mind about Gypsy Joe and unwillingly began to respect him. This was the man, he realized, standing with him in his windy stable-yard, who was least likely in the world to have harmed the dead jockey, and that being so, he could ask his help. He didn't believe in second sight or fortune telling, but really one never knew ... And Gypsy Joe had plucked Red Millbrook out of the air: had seen his undeveloped genius and given it springing life. Supposing ... well, just supposing the gypsy's insight could do what good detection methods couldn't.

The superintendent shook his head to free himself

from such fancies and said pragmatically, 'I've asked around, you know. It seems most of the jockeys were screwed up with envy of Red Millbrook and the bookmakers hoped he'd break his neck, but that's different from actually killing.' He paused. 'I'm told the person who hated him most was his second fiddle, David Rockman, your former number one.'

'He couldn't have done it,' Gypsy Joe asserted gloomily. 'His alibi's perfect.'

'He couldn't have done it,' the superintendent nodded, 'because at the relevant time he was hobbling round the hospital here on crutches, getting physiotherapy for his broken foot.'

'And his glued-on trusty, Nigel Tape, couldn't have done it either, because he was here under my very eyes, riding my horses on the exercise gallops when Red . . .' Gypsy Joe stopped short, his throat constricting. The waste and destruction of the soaring talent he'd set free on his horses brought Gypsy Joe daily nearer to tears than he would have thought possible. He knew he would never find another Red Millbrook: a match like that to his horses happened only once in a trainer's lifetime.

When the superintendent had gone, Gypsy Joe's hatred for Red Millbrook's killer continued to burn like a slow relentless furnace in his dark gypsy soul. He would *know*, he thought. One day, in the unexplained way that things became clear to him, he would know who'd killed Red Millbrook, and he would know what to do.

His horses, meanwhile, had to run in their intended races. The owners telephoned demanding it. Life had to go on. Davey Rockman's fractured foot mended like magic and Gypsy Joe, with misgivings he didn't wholly understand, allowed his former number one to retake his earlier place.

The horses missed Red Millbrook. They won races, but not joyously in droves. The glory days were over. Some racegoers cheered; some wept. Gypsy Joe despaired.

It was at the memorial service for Red Millbrook's life that The Rock made his revealing mistake. In the church, oblivious to Gypsy Joe standing grimly and unsuspected behind him, Davey Rockman turned his head to Nigel Tape and *smirked.*

Gypsy Joe saw first the evil in the curve of the sneering lips, and felt pierced only with simple disgust. But by evening and through the night the deeper knowledge that he sought arrived.

In the morning he telephoned the Metropolitan Police superintendent.

'A *paid* murderer?' the super repeated doubtfully. 'Contract killers are very rare, you know. It's unlikely that this is one.' He thought to himself that most murders were domestic – family affairs – impulsive, and he knew most were solved. Often drugs were the dynamics of unexplained deaths, but not this time, he didn't think. There was no smell of it. And no suggestion of political assassination, which was normally flamboyant and led to arrest, either on the scene itself, or soon after.

'Which leaves you where?' asked Gypsy Joe.

'Looking at the currents inside the Millbrook family. We think the young man knew his killer. We think whoever shot him tapped on the window and the young man, recognizing the person, lowered the window to talk. The sisters are no sweet cookies . . .'

'I don't believe it.' Gypsy Joe was positive. 'The Millbrook family didn't kill him. I saw violent destructive hatred in Davey Rockman's eyes at yesterday's memorial service. You are underestimating the violence of hate. Nearly everyone does. I saw him *gloat* over Red's death. I'm certain he had him killed. I'll go after him and stir things up.'

The superintendent, doubting and believing in turns, not sure after all that gypsy insight could be relied on, told his informant weakly, 'Take care, then, there's a murderer about.'

Gypsy Joe took the warning seriously but walked his big frame and his outsize personality into the path of everyone he thought might show him a line to crime. No one exactly gave him directions to an assassin but at length, when his quest had become the talk of every racecourse, someone with a snigger told him to look under his own nose. Nigel Tape, he eventually discovered, had a brother who'd once done time for receiving stolen cars. Hardly helpful, he thought. A pussy-cat when he was looking for a lion.

With nothing therefore but implacable suspicion to fuel him, Gypsy Joe began asking Davey 'The Rock' questions. Endless needling questions, on and on and day by day.

'How did you find a killer? Who did you ask?'

'How did you pay him? Did you send him a cheque?'

'He'll blackmail you, won't he? He'll want more and more.'

On and on.

He shredded Davey Rockman's nerves, but kept on offering him rides in races. The questions tormented The Rock, but he needed the fees. His hands began shaking. Gypsy Joe, everywhere, accused in his ear, 'Murderer.'

'I didn't do it,' The Rock yelled, frantic.

Gypsy Joe, regardless, repeated 'Murderer' again and again, and allowed his jockey no peace.

Davey Rockman and Nigel Tape went to Warwick races together, Nigel Tape driving his own leased car and hoping The Rock would pay his share of the petrol. Gone were the days, it seemed, when The Rock grandiosely paid all of their joint expenses as a matter of course. The Rock, Nigel Tape morosely considered, wasn't any longer the hero he'd worshipped all these years.

The Rock's saturnine good looks had rapidly lost their taut appeal since the smooth tanned skin on his jaw and cheekbones had loosened and greyed. The bravado of the riding boots no longer strode with self-confident near-arrogance from weighing-room to parade ring. The maestro no longer masterfully slapped his calf with his riding whip. Onlookers used to the swagger of pre-Red Millbrook days hardly recognized the dimmed round-shouldered slinker as the wolf of the tracks, the sexual predator that had set alarmed mothers scurrying protectively after their chicks.

The Rock, under Gypsy Joe's pitiless barrage, had more than halfway crumbled.

'He's sure I did it,' The Rock moaned. 'He never leaves me alone five minutes. He wants to know who killed his precious boy and I can scream and scream that I don't know and he just goes on asking.'

Nigel Tape glanced sideways at the wreck of his friend. He – and every pair of eyes on the racecourse – could clearly see the atrophy of The Rock's vivid character, let alone his riding skill. Horses in his hands were going soft.

'You can't tell him who killed Red Millbrook because you don't know.' Nigel Tape's voice was edging from reasonableness to exasperation. He'd said the same thing a dozen times.

'I tell him over and over I don't know,' The Rock complained. 'He thinks I just walked up to someone who has a gun and said, "Shoot Red Millbrook for me." He's so simple he's pathetic.'

Gypsy Joe, neither simple nor pathetic, watched his jockey's spineless performances that afternoon and was obliged to apologize to his owners.

For all his persistent inquisition of The Rock, Gypsy Joe hadn't learned who'd killed Red Millbrook. He began to believe that the jockey truly didn't know whose hand had actually held the gun. He didn't change his certainty of The Rock's basic guilt.

At the end of an unproductive three hours of also-rans, the trainer told his jockey that good owners were harder to replace than good riders (Red Millbrook excepted). He'd given Davey Rockman every chance, he said, but the owners were bitterly complaining and enough was enough, so goodbye. The Rock, speechless, burned behind his eyes with incandescent malice and saw no fault in himself.

'What about me?' demanded Nigel Tape. 'Do I get The Rock's job? First jockey to the stable?'

'No, you don't. You haven't the drive. If you want to, you can carry on as before.'

'It isn't fair,' Nigel Tape said.

On their drive home from the races, The Rock violently swore to revenge himself for the public disgrace of losing his job.

'Get that gunman for me,' The Rock said. 'Tell him I need him again.'

Nigel Tape drove erratically in troubled silence. Fair haired, with sun-bleached eyebrows, the pale shadow of Davey The Rock painfully felt his long allegiance weakening. He had quite liked Red Millbrook, he belatedly realized, and Gypsy Joe hadn't been bad to work for, all these years. A steady job, better than most . . .

'Do it,' The Rock insisted. 'Tell your brother to fix it again.'

'It'll cost you,' Nigel Tape said weakly.

'Get on with it,' he was told.

Nigel Tape's ex-jail-bird car-thief brother knew a man who knew a man who was in touch with a man who knew someone in the elimination business. In early February 1987, the patron of Emil Jacques' local café produced from beside his till a pale pink envelope that smelled sweetly of carnations.

The patron smiled widely, nudging Emil Jacques in the ribs. Emil Jacques smelled the scent and with many a wink stowed the billet-doux away to read in private.

Emil Jacques later stood at the window of his splendid lofty apartment and thoughtfully watched the small boats busy below on the Seine. The pink envelope had contained only a postcard-sized black and white photograph of Gypsy Joe, with his name, address, age and occupation written in pencil on the back. Underneath, in small letters, he read, 'David Rockman, jockey'.

Owing to his careful and successful slaughter of British steeplechasing's brightest boy, Emil Jacques had begun to take a passing interest in the sport. He bought occasionally from news-stands British racing newspapers and persevered with them to the extent that he needed a French–English dictionary less and less. His English, in racing terms, became increasingly idiomatic.

He was tempted by the prospect of killing Gypsy Joe.

Normally he refused two terminations within the same small social or business circle, reckoning the duplication doubled his risk. Also two killings instigated so soon by the same client sent fierce warning shivers down his spine. David Rockman, jockey, however, had paid him promptly for Red Millbrook's death and presumably knew that at least a similar sum would be expected again.

Emil Jacques cared nothing about his clients' motives or inner psychological forces which could be roughly categorized, he thought, as greed, lust or hate. He cared only that he did his job cleanly, got safely clear and banked the proceeds later in his secretive way. He cared nothing personally for Red Millbrook or Gypsy Joe Smith. Emil Jacques Guirlande was always a true mercenary, a cold soldier for hire.

He decided that it would be safe enough to reconnoitre at least the Gypsy Joe prospect. Consequently, with small bag packed (no guns) he crossed the Channel with his car, uncomfortably sea-sick for once because of a sudden maritime winter storm. Early February snow fell and lay obstinately over southern England, bringing horse racing to a halt, the weather again conspiring to prolong Emil Jacques' target's life.

Emil Jacques could make only sporadic checks on Gypsy Joe's daily existence without drawing comment on himself, but he learned the trainer's morning routine of travelling up by Land Rover to the white-dusted Downs and watching the long string of horses cantering past for exercise up an all-weather sand track. He listened to the stable-lads' chat in the local pubs in the evenings and absorbed their graphic language, along with the general flow of stable life.

He learned that Gypsy Joe's devotion to his horses included a late-night visit to each of them, to see that all were comfortable and at peace, and on silent shoes one evening he approached the stable-yard and stopped at an undiscovered distance, watching.

Gypsy Joe came out of his house alone at ten o'clock and made his rounds, finally leaving his much loved horses safe until morning. At ten the following evening he made his rounds again, and at ten the next evening, again.

It was there, in the tranquil yard, Emil Jacques decided, that one night soon a quiet death would spit out of the dark.

During the night of Emil Jacques' decision, a thaw turned England brown and green, and next day Gypsy Joe took his runners to Sandown Park races.

The two months since Red Millbrook's murder had in no way lessened Gypsy Joe's furious grief, and he couldn't help remembering that it was here on this testing track that the red-haired boy's dormant genius had first fully awakened. While he watched his February runners do moderately well with a jockey-replacement, Gypsy Joe mourned the past and vowed to continue his pursuit of Davey The Rock. However long it took him, he would reduce the guilty villain to breakdown and confession.

Davey Rockman, that afternoon, had been engaged (by a minor trainer) to ride only one race. He finished second to last with his mind not on the job. He spent his time glaring at Gypsy Joe in unabated hate, hopping up and down for an answer to the demand he'd passed to Nigel Tape's brother.

Emil Jacques Guirlande, correctly positive that neither man would know him, went with inner amusement to Sandown Park races and stood close to both.

Gypsy Joe, his quarry, gave a cursory glance at the neat youngish undistinguished racegoer reading his racecard six feet away and felt none of the supernatural shudder of foreboding that his ancestry would have expected. Gypsy Joe looked at Red Millbrook's murderer and didn't know him.

An hour later, on the stands before the fifth race, Emil Jacques rubbed sleeves with Davey The Rock and listened to him complaining acidly to Nigel Tape about merciless trainers, the slow post and the spitefulness of ungrateful whores.

Emil Jacques, disliking him, decided to increase his fee sharply.

When the proposal reached Davey The Rock three days later he screeched with fury; the swollen payment demanded up-front would swallow the rest of his savings. But Gypsy Joe's campaign of accusation was driving him to drink and madness, and he would do anything – *anything* – he thought, to get rid of the remorseless whispers in his ears. 'Murderer. Murderer. Admit you let loose a murderer.'

Davey Rockman sent every advance cent asked for, leaving nothing in reserve. He was foolishly risking that the murderer would not come looking for the rest after the deed was done.

A week later, at the beginning of March, the patron of the café passed two letters – nudge nudge – to his lucky customer with the busy sex life. The customer winked and smiled and began to think of moving to a different mail box.

Emil Jacques took his letters home. One, a thick sort of package, contained the whole of Davey The Rock's hard-earned savings. The other proposed the almost immediate assassination of a politician in Brussels, death to occur within ten days, before a crucial vote.

Emil Jacques stood by his high window and looked down on the Seine. Caution warned him that Brussels was too soon. His anonymity, he reckoned, depended in part on the infrequency of his operations.

He had survived Red Millbrook's murder easily, but the hunt would be redoubled after Gypsy Joe's. The enlarged fee might make that death worthwhile, but a further murder in Brussels, his third in little over three months, that quick murder might give him an identity in police consciousness. The last thing he wanted, he thought grimly, was to be 'Wanted'.

All the same, the Brussels proposal included the offer of a magnificent fee for a prompt performance, and he was, he considered, the BEST.

The following day therefore he banked Davey Rockman's savings, put in a morning's teaching with new guns at the gun club and in the afternoon and evening drove across Belgium to Brussels. He would reconnoitre the Brussels job, he decided, and would give his yes or no before crossing to England to terminate Gypsy Joe. He would be careful, he thought, and go one step at a time.

He spent three too-slow days in Brussels stalking his politician round the bazaars of the European Commission, finding to his growing dismay that his quarry was seldom alone and even in the gents' was thoroughly guarded. What was worse, there was a fond wife and a pack of bright children with little sharp eyes. Children were a hazard for sensible murderers to steer wide of.

Emil Jacques, impatient and under pressure, unusually sent an acceptance by post of the Brussels proposition without clearly planning his ambush in advance, confident he would think of a good one in plenty of time. Meanwhile, as he waited for the Brussels up-front money to arrive, he would finish off Gypsy Joe: he would spend the weekend in England, earning the Rockman fee. He set off on this plan but almost at once things again began to go wrong. Even before he'd even left the city, his car broke down. ('*Mon auto ne marche pas.*') Emil cursed.

It was Friday morning. He was told his car would be repaired by Monday lunchtime. Emil Jacques blasphemed.

He went into a travel agent's office to study his options and found himself at the desk of a smiling motherly middle-aged madame who took a liking to her youngish customer and made endless helpful suggestions.

Monsieur wanted to spend the weekend in England? Well, of course, he must *fly*.

Sabena, Belgium's airline, had frequent flights every day to Heathrow.

Madame gestured to a poster on the wall advertising a fantail of huge aeroplanes, all taking off.

Emil Jacques Guirlande shuddered and began to sweat.

Monsieur could rent a car at Heathrow. She, Madame, would arrange it.

Emil Jacques took a heroic grip on his neurosis and said he would go by sea, by car ferry, as he had intended. Madame said the delay obviously meant that he would miss the boat he'd planned to take, but he could go later by a different route and she, Madame, could arrange a rental car to meet him at Dover.

Emil Jacques agreed.

Beaming with pleasure, Madame busied herself on the telephone while her customer wiped his forehead.

She told him kindly that soon he would be able to travel to England by tunnel. The excavation would be starting this year, 1987. Wasn't that splendid? In one instant Emil Jacques progressed from fear of flying to tunnel claustrophobia.

Madame gave him tickets and reservations and a boarding pass for his preference for water.

She said, 'I'm afraid the crossing takes four and a half hours, but I've booked a rental car to be ready for you at Dover. So sorry about your troubles with your own.'

Emil Jacques, still smothering his trembles, paid her with feeble smiles and prudent cash and, following her directions, travelled by train to the Channel coast. He carried with him his metal suitcase and an overnight grip, and he reassured himself over and over again that if this unsettling departure from his normal approach to slaughter looked at all risky he would return to see to Gypsy Joe at a later, calmer date.

He boarded the ferry, along with about four hundred and fifty other passengers, many of whom had come across from England on a day-trip to shop and were going home laden with bags labelled 'Duty Free'. Emil Jacques found a seat in the bar and ordered mineral water, and tightly gripped his metal suitcase between his feet.

The ferry moved off from its berth on Friday 6 March 1987 at five past six in the evening. At six twenty-four the ship cleared the harbour's outer mole and accelerated towards the open sea.

Four minutes later she sank.

*Extract from the official account of the accident, published by Her Majesty's Stationery Office.*

On the 6th March 1987 the Roll on/Roll off passenger and freight ferry *Herald of Free Enterprise* sailed from Number 12 berth in the inner harbour at Zeebrugge at 18.05 G.M.T. The *Herald* was manned by a crew of 80 hands all told and was laden with 81 cars, 47 freight vehicles and three other vehicles.

Approximately 459 passengers had embarked for the voyage to Dover. The *Herald* passed the outer mole at 18.24. She capsized about four minutes later. During the final moments the *Herald* turned rapidly to starboard and was prevented from sinking totally by reason only that her port side took the ground in shallow water. The *Herald* came to rest with her starboard side above the surface. Water rapidly filled the ship below the surface level with the result that not less than 150 passengers and 38 members of the crew lost their lives.

The *Herald* capsized because she went to sea with her inner and outer bow doors open.

The bow doors were open because they had not been closed after the cars and other vehicles had been loaded for the passage to Dover. No one had checked the doors were shut.

The ferry filled and capsized fast in thirty seconds.

The hull, showing above the water, had been painted a brilliant red.

Red as traffic lights.

Redder than Red Millbrook's hair.

RED.

In England at six twenty-five on 6 March Davey The Rock, in self-pitying tears, borrowed enough from Nigel Tape to get drunk. Broke, out of work, starved of sex and frightened to disintegration of a half-paid murderer, The Rock blamed everyone else.

When the *Herald* capsized, Emil Jacques' gun-laden metal suitcase slid away inexorably from between his feet. He stretched to catch it, and fell from a height, and the last thing the murderer who feared flying saw was the wall of water that drowned him.

At ten o'clock that evening, while the cold North Sea still swirled in eddies through the settling wreck, Gypsy Joe left his house and made his quiet normal rounds of his stableful of dozing horses; as he would safely do the next night, and the next night, and the next.

The stars were bright.

Not knowing why, Gypsy Joe felt at peace.

# SONG FOR MONA

*There are crimes that aren't punishable by imprisonment or fines. There's no official offence called Grievous* **Mental** *Harm. Malice aforethought can apply to more than murder – but malice can be nonplussed by goodwill.*

Song for Mona *is a new story about an old old sin.*

Joanie Vine accompanied her mother to the races and loathed every minute of it. Joanie Vine was ashamed of the way her mother dressed, spoke and lived; that is to say, she recoiled with averted eyes from the weathered tweed trilby above the tightly belted raincoat; winced at the loud unreconstructed vowels and grammar of a Welsh woman from the valleys, and couldn't bring herself to identify to others her mother's occupation as a groom of horses.

Joanie Vine accompanied her mother to the first day of the Cheltenham Festival – one of the most prestigious jump meetings of the year – solely because it was her mother's sixtieth birthday, and Joanie Vine aimed to receive admiring plaudits from her friends for her magnanimous thoughtfulness. Even before the first race she'd decided to lose her mother as soon as possible, but meanwhile she couldn't understand why so many people instinctively smiled at the ill-dressed woman she had automatically relegated to one step behind her heels.

Mona Watkins – Joanie Vine's mother – bore her daughter dutiful love and wouldn't admit to herself that what Joanie felt for *her* was close to physical hatred. Joanie didn't like Mona touching her and wriggled away from any attempt at a motherly hug. Mona, if she thought about it, though she didn't often because of the regret it caused her, could blame Joanie's progression from adolescent rebellion to active dislike on the advent in the local amateur dramatic society of a certain plump self-satisfied thirty-year-old smooth-tongued Peregrine Vine, assistant to auctioneers of antiques and fine arts.

Peregrine, Joanie had informed her mother, came from a 'good family'. Peregrine, who spoke upper-class English with no lilt or inflection of Wales, soon had Joanie copying him. Joan (he never called or referred to her as Joanie) had grown tall and big bosomed and beautiful, and Peregrine, although his parents had hoped for an heiress, willingly agreed to Joanie's terms of marriage before sex. He saw the ultimatum as morality, not leverage.

Joanie, by then living away from home and queening it in a flower shop, told Peregrine and his parents that her mother was 'eccentric' and a 'recluse', and didn't want to meet them. Peregrine and his parents resentfully believed her.

Joanie didn't invite her mother to the wedding. Joanie not only didn't ask her but didn't even tell her that her only child would be heading up the aisle in full bridal fig. Joanie deliberately denied her mother her big day of maternal pride and happiness. She sent her a postcard view from Venice: 'Married Peregrine last Saturday, Joanie.'

Mona stoically propped the Doge's Palace on her mantleshelf and toasted the match in beer.

It wasn't until months later that Peregrine met Joanie's earthy mother, and experienced at first hand the clothes, the voice and the occupation: the lot. He was, as Joanie had known he would be, horrified. His instinct, like Joanie's own, was to keep the embarrassment hidden. They moved to the next town. Peregrine advanced in his career and Joanie joined a showy tennis club. Their social aspirations soared.

Mona, living as always in the two-up two-down terraced cottage that had once been Joanie's home, continued to ride her creaky old bicycle morning and evening to work in a children's riding school, where she looked after a row of hard-worked ponies. One evening she cycled into the stable-yard to find the riding-school owner dead on the ground of a heart attack, several children screaming and the stables on fire.

Mona coped: saved the ponies, quietened the children, called the fire brigade, covered the frightening body with her old raincoat and became a bit of a heroine on television and in the press.

'Mona Watkins, mother of Mrs Joan Vine, well-known wife of prestigious auctioneer, Peregrine.'

Mona, standing in her cottage doorway, cheerfully announced on screen in her broad Welsh accent that she was 'ever so proud of my daughter Joanie, look you.'

*Horrors. Cringe.*

It was in an attempt to prove publicly that Joanie valued her mother that she had announced grandiloquently that she would take her to the races to celebrate her sixtieth birthday.

One morning after her day at the races Mona Watkins hummed tunelessly to herself as she groomed the chestnut champion show-jumper now in her care.

Shc hummed with the flutter of the lips that prevented most of the dust from the chestnut's shiny coat going down into her lungs. She hummed in the old way of centuries of ostlers and, like them, from time to time, she spat.

She very much liked her new employers who had actively sought her out in consequence of the publicity given to the riding-school fire. Out of work for three weeks since the ponies had been dispersed and sold, she had opened her cottage door one day to a summons on the knocker and had found on the pavement outside a man and a woman whom she recognized with incredulity as the Olympic Gold-Medal rider Oliver Bolingbroke and his platinum-album-selling Country and Western singer wife, American and friendly Cassidy Lovelace Ward.

Once, the month-long courtship and impulsive marriage of these two had been cynically categorized by the media as mere attention-seeking. Four years of steady devotion later, the world found it hard to think of one without the other.

The luminous pair had come in a black stretch limousine that had magnetically drawn many of the drab street's inhabitants out of their front doors; and they were carefully accompanied by a black uniformed chauffeur and a wary bodyguard whose watchful gaze swung around like a radar beam searching for a blip.

'Mrs Mona Watkins?' Oliver Bolingbroke enquired.

Mona speechlessly opened her mouth and nodded.

'Can we come in?'

Mona backed into her tiny front room and her visitors followed. They saw a way of life utterly alien to their own carefree prosperity but were also instantly aware of order, cleanliness and pride. Mona gestured them to her two fireside chairs and numbly closed her door.

Oliver Bolingbroke, tall, lean and wealthily civilized, made a slow visual traverse of the pink rose-bud wallpaper, the linoleum on the floor, the peacock blue satin cushions on the rusty-brown chairs, the unlined floral curtains at the window. No money and no taste, he thought, but that didn't mean no heart. He was good at estimating worth. He had also checked on Mona's reputation as a groom and had heard nothing but praise. She was uncouth, he'd been warned. One would go to her in trouble, but not for advice on manners.

'My husband has show-jumpers,' the singer straightforwardly said. Dressed in ordinary jeans with a topping of a huge cream hand-knitted sweater, Cassidy Lovelace Ward, with tousled blonde curls and soft pink lipstick, looked both informal and purposefully glamorous, a combination that Mona, in her forthright way, had no trouble at all feeling at home with. Mona took to Cassidy on a level far below surface gloss. Cassidy, sensing it, was, to her surprise, flattered. What both women saw unconsciously in the other was goodness.

Oliver Bolingbroke and his wife explained that they had recently bought a house with stables for three of his best horses a few miles out of town. Mona, who had seen the item in the local newspaper, nodded. The Bolingbrokes travelled a good deal, they said. Mrs

Bolingbroke made tours and gave concerts. While they were away, they required a groom to live in quarters they were building in the stables. When Oliver Bolingbroke took his horses to distant or foreign competitions, he would require their familiar groom to travel with them.

Mona, they said, though not young, would suit them well.

'I want to keep my little house,' Mona said at once, meaning, 'I want to keep my independence.'

'Of course,' Oliver agreed. 'When can you start?'

So Mona hummed as she groomed the champion chestnut show-jumper (and the solidly muscled grey and the agile ten-year-old star of them all, the Olympic Gold-winning bay) and she talked to her charges in the homey way she'd used on the ponies – and on many a horse before them – but somehow these three, as she had sadly had to acknowledge to herself, tended to look at her down their medal-winning noses, as if she were their servant, not their friend.

Mona, instinctively wise, forgave them as sorrowfully as she bore no malice towards Joanie and Peregrine Vine.

Those two, finding (despite the Cheltenham races ploy) that their sanctimonious status was being irretrievably damaged by sneers and sniggers within their chosen precious circle, moved away yet again to another town and rose again in caste without having to mention at all that Joan's mother worked knee-deep in horse manure. (Horse shit, Mona called it.) Peregrine became a chief auctioneer and patronized his clients. Joanie joined a charity committee of local ladies and helped to organize plushy fund-raising balls.

As weeks and months passed, Mona grew increasingly devoted to her employers while remaining merely dutiful to their horses. Oliver Bolingbroke found no fault or lack in the fitness of his three mounts as he schooled them patiently hour by hour: on the contrary, he felt inspired and reassured by their innate arrogance. Never before, he thought gratefully, had he employed as groom anyone who would preserve his mounts' essential bloody-mindedness. No other groom had ever sent his horses out to competitions with such a determination to win.

Oliver Bolingbroke retained his reputation as one of the best horsemen in the country and kept quiet about Mona's excellence for fear a competitor would entice her away.

Cassidy Lovelace Ward paid a decorator to make attractive the bed-sitting room, bathroom and kitchen that had been fitted into an unused end of the stable block, but Mona, uncomfortable with even minimum luxury, preferred a creaky journey by bicycle morning and evening from her two-down two-up independence. Cassidy without irritation let her do as she liked.

Cassidy herself went routinely by limousine to studios in London where music, not horses, occupied most hours of her week. She rehearsed; she made recordings. She patiently submitted to costume fittings. She accepted without resistance the chauffeur and bodyguard required by her cautious insurance company. She repressed a thousand snappy words.

Oliver drove himself to horse shows in a sturdy dark red four-wheel-drive Range Rover, sending Mona on ahead with the horses. Oliver signed endless autograph books, fretted when he didn't win and suffered all the angst of a perfectionist.

In spite of their public fame, both Oliver and Cassidy valued private time together, not just, it must be admitted, for endless love, but for the freedom of shouting at each other in bad-tempered rows. They yelled at each other not about money or from any resentment of the other's fame, but mostly from too much tension in their work. Tiny frustrations would set them off. Doors were slammed. Vases were thrown. Anyone overhearing them would have nodded sagely: the unlikely marriage was over.

But it wasn't. The sulks evaporated into steam. Oliver stamped about. Cassidy played her piano fortissimo. Eventually they laughed. The roller-coaster screeching emotions, however, had caused their cook to leave, and they'd never replaced her. They ate instead from takeaways. They had nutritionists swooning but Oliver soared clear over double-oxers, and Cassidy outsang the birds.

Mona walked into an especially vicious row one

evening to tell Oliver the grey had heat in a tendon. Mona, astounded, stood stock still in surprise with her mouth open, listening to the noise.

'Don't just bloody stand there,' Oliver shouted at her. 'Make us some bloody supper.'

'She's not the sucking cook,' Cassidy yelled.

'She can put a couple of sucking eggs together, can't she?'

So Mona made omelettes. Mona made three omelettes at her employers' invitation and ate with them at the kitchen table. Oliver at length grinned at her and finally laughed.

No arrangement was actually formalized, but from time to time after that Mona cooked while the other two yawned and unwound and saw less and less to quarrel about. Mona with her wrinkled country face, her uncompromising accent, with the smell of stables that clung about her clothes, all the unpolished components somehow bled away the artificiality of her employers' lives and gave them a murmuring peace that lasted to bedtime.

Mona thought of them as fractious horses needing her soothing arts. Their fame in the outside world came to mean little to her: they were Oliver and Cassidy, her people. Oliver and Cassidy, on their side, could hardly imagine life without her. The three of them settled contentedly into a routine that suited them all.

*

Joanie Vine and Peregrine decided not to try for children, and among Joanie's many and jumbled reasons there was definitely the miserly pleasure that Mona would be deprived of being a grandmother. Never would she – Joanie – have to explain Mona away to inquisitive and talkative offspring.

Peregrine didn't like babies, toddlers, teenagers, adolescents or any stage in between. Peregrine heard boys being rude to their fathers and delicately shuddered. Peregrine couldn't understand how people could let themselves in for the worries of medical problems, school fees, drug taking and lying accusations of sexual abuse. Peregrine liked a peaceful house, gracious entertaining and money.

Ever more pompous, Peregrine also succeeded in forgetting for weeks at a time his lovely wife's true origins. Joanie invented a set of aristocratic forebears and convinced herself they were real.

Each of the five souls, Peregrine, Joanie, Oliver, Cassidy Lovelace and Mona Watkins lived for one long summer in personally satisfactory equilibrium. Each in his or her own way enjoyed success. Oliver collected champion's rosettes and armfuls of cups. Cassidy's new album hit platinum again. Mona, glowing with reflected pride in the horses, spent light-heartedly on new tyres for her bicycle. The chestnut, the big grey and the whippy bay did her proud.

Peregrine's auctions became social events: Sotheby's and Christie's paid attention. Joanie, tall and truly arresting in sumptuous (rented) ball-gowns, graced the colour pages of heavy shiny magazines.

Mona, artlessly proud of her daughter, snipped out the multiplying pictures and kept them in a box along with many clippings extolling Cassidy's silver voice and Oliver's equine golds.

Mona wrote a shakily literate note to Joanie describing her happy life with the Bolingbrokes, including the cooking sessions in the kitchen. Joanie tore up the letter and didn't reply.

Because of her undaunted pride, which Joanie didn't deserve, Mona strapped her box onto her bicycle carrier one day when she rode to work and showed the contents to Cassidy.

'This is your daughter?' Cassidy asked, surprised.

'Isn't she beautiful?' Mona beamed.

'It says here,' Cassidy read, 'that she's related to the Earls of Flint.'

'That's just her way,' Mona explained forgivingly. 'She was plain Joanie Watkins by birth. Her dad was a stable-lad, same as me. Got killed on the gallops, poor old boy.'

Cassidy told Oliver about the pictures and out of curiosity Oliver wrote to Peregrine – care of Peregrine Vine and Co., Quality Auctioneers – and invited him and his wife to lunch.

Joanie at once told Peregrine she didn't want to go, but then reconsidered. To have met – to have *lunched* – with Oliver and Cassidy Bolingbroke would give her splendid name-dropping opportunities. Mona's existence could safely and totally be ignored.

Mona wished Oliver had consulted her first, but in both men curiosity overcame doubt. On the appointed day, the Vines in their Mercedes drove into the large stable-yard where the Bolingbrokes and Mona awaited them.

Oliver knew at once that he'd made a serious mistake when he heard Joanie superciliously call her mother 'Mona', and saw her frostily repel Mona's attempt at an embrace, but with worldly civility he ignored the awkward moment and swept everyone into the drawing-room for a drink before food. Peregrine, Oliver noted with a wince, ran a practised glance over the furniture, assessing its worth.

Mona, hanging back, was firmly collected by Cassidy linking an arm through hers. Cassidy too realized the occasion to be a disaster. Mona's reluctance had been right.

Mona, doing her best, wore clean corduroy trousers and a white blouse pinned above the top button by her ultimate in *soigné* dressing, a small pearl brooch. Cassidy melted with pity for her, and plunged, like Oliver, into regret.

After stilted minutes of conversation between the two men (chiefly about the difference in sales routine of commodes and colts) Cassidy grimly but with surface gaiety moved her guests into the dining-room where places at table in silver and crystal had been laid for five.

Joanie said without thinking, 'So you're expecting another guest?'

'No,' replied Cassidy puzzled, 'just us.'

'But surely,' Joanie's eyebrows rose, 'Mona will be eating in the kitchen, as usual.'

Even Joanie saw, in the sudden frozen immobility of her hosts, that she'd committed the worst sort of social-climbing blunder. She said helplessly, 'I mean . . . I mean . . .' but her assumption and its expression were plain and couldn't be undone.

Peregrine nervously cleared his throat, thinking numbly for something – anything – to say.

Oliver, by far the fastest thinker, stirred and laughed and exclaimed, 'Cass, my dear, what a splendid suggestion of Joanie's. Let's all eat with Mona in the kitchen, as we usually do. Let's all pick up our plates and napkins and glasses and carry them through to the kitchen.'

He collected together the things laid for him at the head of the table and gestured to the others to follow him. Then, cheerfully mustering his troops, he led the way, head high, through the swing door giving on to the spacious, homely room where, indeed, he and Cassidy familiarly ate with Mona.

The lunch, none the less, was an overall ordeal. No one regretted the Vines' early departure, cheese uneaten on the side plates and coffee undrunk. Oliver apologized to Mona before the Vines' Mercedes had cleared the front gates, but Mona, ever quick to pardon, worried about the debacle least of all.

Cassidy Lovelace Ward led a double existence, as performer and wife. At first she had indeed been powerfully sexually attracted by Oliver's looks, bearing and skill on a horse. She knew, being no novice in life, that it was her own feelings for Oliver that had roused a similar response in him. The media, cynically observing the physical magnetics, should not have been wrong in prophesying rapid boredom and farewells but, to their mutual surprise, horseman and singer slowly became deep and trusting friends.

Cassidy, when they met, had been almost constantly on tour across her homeland, singing the Mississippi River songs of Nashville, Tennessee. She travelled by bus with manager, musicians and backing group. Props, scenery, lights, dresser and wardrobe followed along. The whole enterprise depended on her for genius, energy and pulling power, and indeed she could, like all great performers, light up from inside and take her audience flying.

The process exhausted her. Oliver had almost fallen over her one night as she sat on a wicker chest, a wardrobe skip, outside the great touring bus that would presently take her overnight to the next town, to the next rehearsal, the next hungry, roaring, applauding multitude of fans.

Oliver's presence had been the result of someone's bright idea that Cassidy could for that one evening's performance ride out on stage in Western clothes, cowboy boots, white ten-gallon hat and clinking spurs. The manager, horse-illiterate, had engaged a lively show-jumper for her, not a lethargic nag. Oliver, house-guest of the horse's owner, had been good-naturedly thrown in with the package and asked to look after the lady. Thanks to his condensed instruction, Cassidy's debut on horseback had gone well.

'Come with me,' she said. 'We can rent a horse in every town.'

He sat beside her on the wicker skip and said, 'It's not my sort of life.'

'Too honky-tonk, is that it?'

She had finished the tour and gone to live Oliver's sort of life in England: and when that life hadn't been enough she'd amalgamated the old ways with the new, and still glittered on stage in crystal fringes and brought crowds breathless to their feet. Music pulsed in her always. She saw life's dramas in chords. On the afternoon of the appalling lunch party Cassidy played Chopin's lament for Poland passionately on her piano and promised herself that one day she would get Joanie Vine to value her remarkable mother.

Oliver, passing, understood both the music and Cassidy's meaning.

He said, however, 'Why don't you write a song yourself, especially for Mona? You used to write more.'

'Audiences like the old songs.'

'Old songs were new once.'

Cassidy made a face at him and played old songs because she had no inspiration for the new.

Mona comforted Cassidy and Oliver, both of whom were downcast by their blighted hospitality and dumbfounded by Joanie's brutal contempt for her mother.

Mona resignedly said she'd been used to it ever since Joanie hadn't asked her to her wedding. Oliver and Cassidy would have throttled Joanie, if she'd still been there.

'Don't think about her,' Mona told them. 'I expect I couldn't give her enough when she was little. I hadn't much money, see. I expect that's it. And anyway,' she added, no fool where it mattered, 'I'm not going to spoil her life now, am I, by walking into those grand balls she puts on and saying I'm her mam, now am I? I wouldn't thank you to do that, either. Let her be, if she's happy, that's what I say.'

'You're a saint, Mona,' Oliver said.

It took a little while, several weeks in fact, for Oliver, Cassidy and Mona to feel comfortable again about supper in the kitchen, and meanwhile the Bolingbrokes' quarrels broke out as before with fierce shouting rows and airborne ornaments. Mona, hearing Oliver's voice heavily finding fault and Cassidy's screaming defiance, walked sturdily into the kitchen after work one evening and stood there disapprovingly with her hands on her hips.

Her arrival silenced the combatants for about ten seconds, then Oliver growled, 'What the hell do you think you're doing in here?'

'Sucking eggs?' Mona suggested.

'Oh God,' Cassidy began to giggle. Oliver strode disgustedly out of the room but presently returned with a grin and three glasses of whisky. Mona made omelettes, and Cassidy told her that the quarrel had been about a long tour she – Cassidy – was about to make in America. She would be away from home for two months and Oliver didn't like it.

'Go with her, boy-o,' Mona said.

With peace and reason they formed a plan. Oliver would fulfil his showing and eventing obligations for the first month and travel with Cassidy for the second month, returning home with her in November. Mona would then move into the living-quarters in the stable, to look after the place, and, for the month he was away, Oliver would engage a secondary groom to help her.

'It's all so simple,' Oliver sighed. 'Why did we fight?'

While the Bolingbrokes were still engaged on cheese and thinking about Häagen Dazs, their long-time lawyer called in (by forgotten appointment) to secure their signatures on complicated trust fund arrangements.

Oliver went to the front door to welcome him and brought him into the kitchen, where his urbanity, like Oliver's, at once understood the inner worth, ignoring the outer rustic uncouthness, of the third individual at the table.

Mona, in her heavy Welsh accent, instantly offered to leave. The lawyer, with all of Oliver's civility, begged her not to. A witness to the signatures was essential. Mona cleared away the supper and wrote her name on dotted lines.

'And now,' the lawyer said light-heartedly, 'now, Mrs Watkins, how about some arrangements for you, too?'

Mona, bewildered, asked about what.

'A will?' the lawyer suggested. 'If you haven't made a will, let's do it now.'

'Yes, indeed,' urged Oliver, who had wanted to reward Mona for her signature without insulting her. 'Everyone should make a will.'

'I did talk about it once,' Mona said. 'Peregrine wanted me to leave everything to Joanie.'

The lawyer smoothly brought a printed basic will form from out of his loaded briefcase and smilingly entered on it, to her dictation, Mona's name and address.

Then, ball-point poised, he asked her for her beneficiaries.

'What?' Mona asked.

'The people you want to inherit your individual things after your death.'

'Like my bicycle,' Mona nodded. 'Well . . .' She paused. '. . . well, Joanie wouldn't want my old bike. I'd just ask Cass or Oliver to give my old bike to someone as needs it. What if I just ask them to do as they like with my old bits and pieces?'

The lawyer wrote, 'Cassidy Lovelace Ward' in the slot for 'sole beneficiary' and he and Oliver accompanied Mona on her bicycle down to the local pub on her way home and got two strangers there to witness Mona's signature, thanked by pints of beer.

Cassidy supposed the least she could do for Mona was to distribute her 'old bits and pieces' as Mona would have liked, but hoped not to have to do it. Oliver came smiling back from the pub and took his wife to bed in splendid humour.

When the time came, Cassidy went on her lengthy tour in America. Oliver, though lonely, won a European Equus Grand Prix and was chosen as Sportstar of the Year. Mona, travelling with Oliver to look after the horses, thought she'd never been happier.

At the end of the first half of Cassidy's tour, Oliver punctiliously settled Mona into the small apartment in the stables block and checked that the stand-in groom (a time-weathered nagsman even older than Mona) would arrive (on his own bike) every day to help exercise the horses. Mona with confidence sent Oliver off to join Cassidy and began to be seduced during the next few weeks by the refrigerator full of food, by the colour television, and by not having to put coins in a meter to pay for electricity to cook with, or to keep warm. Mona in her independent two-up two-down carefully paid rent for everything. She saved a little each week into a Christmas Club for 'rainy days'. She had managed all her life on little.

Oliver, talking to Cassidy in America as they relaxed at the end of her sell-out triumphs before starting the long legs home, suggested that they should increase Mona's wages when they got back.

'We already pay her over the top for a groom.'

'She's worth more,' Oliver said.

'OK, then.' Cassidy yawned. 'And you need another horse . . . The brave big grey's too old now, didn't you say?'

Mona, half a world away, mucked out the heavy clever grey and sadly knew Oliver would sell him soon. He had reached fifteen and the spring was leaving his hocks.

Mona felt feverish and unwell as she worked on the grey, but paid no attention. Like all healthy people, she didn't know when she was ill.

Eyeing her flushed face the next morning, the old nagsman said *he* would do the horses, and *she* was to go off on her bicycle to see the doctor. Mona felt unwell enough to do as he said, and learned with relief that what was wrong with her was flu.

'There's a lot of it about,' the overworked doctor said. 'Go to bed, drink a lot of fluids, you'll soon feel better. Flu's a virus. I can't give you a prescription to cure it, as antibiotics don't work against a virus. Take aspirin. Keep warm. And drink a lot of water. Let me know if you cough a lot. You're a healthy woman, Mrs Watkins. Go to bed, rest and drink water and you'll be fine.'

Mona slowly cycled back to the Bolingbrokes' yard and reported the diagnosis to her helper.

'You go on to bed then right now,' he insisted. 'Leave the horses to me.'

Mona thankfully undressed into her warm night-gown and crawled between her sheets. The cycle ride had made her feel much worse. She remembered she should take aspirin, but she hadn't any. She dozed and smilingly relived the faultless rounds of Oliver's European Equus Grand Prix.

The old nagsman felt too shy and embarrassed to enter Mona's little apartment, as her bed – in its bed-sitting room – was barely six feet from the outer door. He opened the door and spoke with her morning and evening though, through a slender crack, and when she seemed no livelier after three days he cycled to see the doctor himself.

'Mrs Watkins? Flu takes time, you know.' He turned pages in a meagre file. 'I see she has a daughter, down here as "next of kin", Mrs Peregrine Vine. Let's enlist her help.'

Kind man that he was, he phoned Joanie himself to save the old nagsman's pocket.

'*Flu!*' Joanie exclaimed. 'I'm sure Mona's perfectly all right, if you are looking after her.'

The doctor frowned. 'She could do with some simple nursing. Change her sheets. Make her cups of tea. Give her orange drinks, or even beer. Things like that. It's very important she drinks a lot. If you can—'

'I can't,' Joanie interrupted. 'I have committee meetings all day. I can't put them off.'

'But your mother—'

'It's too inconvenient,' Joanie said positively. 'Sorry.'

The doctor, shaking his head over his abruptly disconnected receiver, wrote Joanie's phone number on one of his business cards and gave it to the nagsman.

On the following day the nagsman telephoned Joanie himself and told her that Mona was neither better nor worse, but needed her daughter's company, he thought.

'Why doesn't Cassidy Bolingbroke look after her?' Joanie asked. 'She likes her well enough.'

The nagsman explained that Mrs Bolingbroke was on her way home from America, but wasn't expected back for two more days.

'Two days? That's all right then,' Joanie said, and put the phone down. She felt, in fact, relieved. The thought of nursing her mother, of having to make physical intimate contact with that old flesh, revolted her to nausea.

Mona, not unhappy, lay like a log in bed without any appetite for food or drink. She supposed vaguely that she would soon be better: meanwhile she'd sleep.

When the Bolingbrokes returned, Cassidy went into Mona's room, which she found hot, fetid and airless, with Mona herself bloated and drifting in and out of consciousness on the bed. Cassidy did what she could for her, but in great alarm she and Oliver sent for the doctor. Anxiously he came at once and, having spent time with Mona, summoned an ambulance and repeated over and over to Cassidy and Oliver, 'But I *told* her, I *insisted* she should drink fluids. She says she hasn't drunk anything for a week. She hasn't had the energy to make a cup of tea.' There was despair in his voice. 'I will have to alert Mrs Vine that we have a serious situation here . . . may I use your phone?'

Joanie, predictably, saw no reason for panic and said she was sure her mother was in good hands. The doctor raised his eyes to heaven and, despite everything that could be done, despite dialysis and drip and Cassidy's prayers, Mona drifted quietly away altogether and died late that night in hospital from total kidney failure.

The hospital informed Joanie Vine of the death, not the Bolingbrokes. It was the doctor who told Oliver.

'So unnecessary, poor lady. If only she'd drunk fluids. People don't understand or realize the danger of dehydration . . .'

He was excusing himself, Oliver thought, but Mona had undoubtedly ignored his advice.

Oliver and Cassidy sat in the kitchen and grieved for their vital missing friend.

It was when the old nagsman told them about the doctor and himself phoning Joanie without results that the Bolingbrokes' grief turned to fury.

'Joanie *killed* her.' Cassidy clenched her fists in outrage. 'She literally killed her.'

Oliver more objectively thought Joanie hadn't meant to: hadn't known how her neglect would turn out. No court would convict her, even of involuntary manslaughter, let alone murder. No case would ever be brought.

Oliver, suddenly remembering Mona's simple will, decided to consult her next-door two-up two-down neighbour at once about what to do with Joanie's 'bits and pieces', that she'd bequeathed to Cassidy. If the neighbour would welcome them, they would have found a good home. Leaving Cassidy upset in the house, he drove his Range Rover into town and found a van of Peregrine's firm – 'Peregrine Vine and Co., Quality Auctioneers' – parked outside Mona's little cottage, with overalled workmen busily carrying out her pathetic goods and furniture, to load them for removal.

Mona's neighbour, wearing curlers in her hair, bedroom slippers on her feet and a floral apron over her dress, stood shivering out in the November street, futile protest obvious in every muscle.

Oliver stopped the exodus and talked to the neighbour.

'Mona had not been dead six hours,' she said indignantly, 'when Joanie herself came to pick through her mother's things. It's my belief she didn't find what she came for. She was slamming things about and she drove off furious. That's why they're clearing out the house so fast now. Like hyenas, they are. Mona left her rent book with me, see, and the rent money for when she's been away at your place. You don't think that's what they want, do you? It's not very much. What shall I do about the rent?'

Oliver said he would see to the rent, and everything else. On his ultra-light mobile phone, he reached Peregrine and explained to him the existence and provisions of Mona's will. 'So please instruct your men, my dear fellow,' he said with courteous but inflexible authority, 'to unload the van.'

Peregrine thought it over briefly and did as Oliver asked. He had sent the van at Joanie's insistence, but she hadn't explained the need for speed: it wasn't as if Mona's things were valuable, far from it. Joan (confided Peregrine to Oliver, man to man) sometimes got the bit between her teeth. She would be livid though, he privately realized, when she learned Mona had bequeathed her tatty old rubbish to someone else.

'About Mona's funeral,' Oliver said, 'Cassidy and I would like to attend. We were very fond of her, as you know.'

Peregrine asked which day would suit them.

'Any day except this coming Wednesday,' Oliver replied. 'Cassidy is flying to Scotland for a concert on that day and I have a lunch-time speaking engagement which I cannot shift.'

'It was Mona's own fault she died,' Peregrine said, suddenly defensive. 'Joan offered to go and look after her, you know, but Mona didn't want her. She phoned several times and told Joan to stay away. Very hurtful, Joan says.'

Oliver said thoughtfully, 'There isn't a telephone in that room where Mona was ill. It was very cold outside in the stable-yard, I believe, and it's quite a step to any door into our house, which was unheated while we were away.'

'What do you mean?'

'Where did Mona phone from?'

Peregrine's silence lasted long enough for him to change the subject to photos of Joan in childhood. If Oliver found any . . .

'I'm certain,' Oliver assured him smoothly, 'that Cassidy will give Joanie everything Mona would have liked her to have.'

'Funeral any day but Wednesday,' Peregrine confirmed, sounding almost friendly. 'I'll let you know.'

*

When Oliver reached home Cassidy was no longer hunched over the kitchen table but had moved to the drawing-room where she could let out her feelings on her piano.

Oliver sat quietly on the broad staircase from where he could listen to her without being seen. Cassidy sang a new song, a raw song, a song without many words, a song of sorrow in flats and minor intervals.

All good songs, she'd told Oliver once, were of love or longing or loss. Cassidy's new song vibrated with all three.

She stopped playing abruptly and, finding Oliver on the stairs, sat down beside him.

'What did you think?' she asked.

'Brilliant.'

'It hasn't a name yet . . .'

'But you wrote it for Mona,' Oliver completed.

'Yes.'

With Oliver beside her, Cassidy took her half-defined melody next day to the musicians in her studio in London, where her often gloomy lyrics writer, captivated, gave it words of universal sadness and universal hope. Cassidy sang it heartbreakingly softly, under her breath. Everyone in the studio heard platinum in her throat.

Cassidy, always bone-weary after creative sessions, slept in the limousine going home with her head on Oliver's shoulder. Oliver spent the time making tentative plans that he supposed Mona might not have approved of. When, once the limousine had departed and Cassidy had yawned off to rest, the old nagsman (no longer quite so temporary) told Oliver that he'd heard Mona was to be cremated in two days' time, on Wedneday, Oliver's intentions firmed to rock.

'Wednesday!' he exclaimed. 'Are you sure?'

'They said so, down the pub.'

Oliver called three undertakers before finding the one dealing with Mona.

'Mrs Watkins? Yes, Wednesday.'

Oliver asked questions. The answers were 'a basic cheap package funeral', and 'Yes, most any other day would have been possible as the short form of committal took little time, but the next of kin had specifically wanted Wednesday.'

Oliver's slow burning plan caught inner fire.

Joanie was depriving her dead mother of one last dignity, the honour of having the celebrities she'd worked for attend her coffin.

Oliver and Cassidy sent a big wreath of lilies. Mona's next-door neighbour told them later that Joanie had left it to one side, ignored. Joanie had announced to the few mourners present that the Bolingbrokes simply hadn't bothered to come.

Mona's ashes had been scattered on a rose-bed in the crematorium gardens, with no memorial plaque. Joanie, privately exulting in liberation, could now reinvent her awkward parent and bestow posthumous respectability on 'a charming horse-woman of the old school', as Peregrine unctuously put it.

Although Oliver and Cassidy might choose to live a mostly private life, both of them were of course aware that to the public they were stars. Both had indeed worked hard to reach star status and each intended to keep it as long as possible. Oliver, after Mona's parsimonious funeral, decided to use his formidable power to the limit, whether Mona would have wanted him to, or not.

With Cassidy's agreement, Oliver went to see the committee organizing the great annual horse spectacular, the five-day Christmas Show at Olympia, with five performances in the afternoon and five more in the evening.

Aside from the top jumping contests, in which he would anyway be taking part, he, Oliver Bolingbroke, as European Equus Grand Prix winner and Sportstar of the Year, would also be leading the finale of each of the ten performances in the prestigious Ride of Champions. The parade indeed could barely take place satisfactorily without him. Oliver Bolingbroke, in short, was a force to whom the committee was bound to listen. He proposed an extra dimension to the end of all ten performances.

They listened.

Their eyes widened. Eventually they nodded.

Oliver shook their hands. Then he went home and patiently taught his intelligent old grey a whole load of new tricks.

Cassidy's manager wrote contracts by the dozen. Her musicians distilled sparkling sounds. Factories pressed hot tracks. Cassidy's new song of love and loss and longing slid into the recognition cortex of the nation.

Oliver invited Joanie Vine to take part in a televised tribute to her mother. Joanie's hysterics nearly choked her. Peregrine tried for an injunction to stop Oliver's project but could offer no credible grounds. 'The Life of Mona' filled the glossy magazine that reprinted Joanie's ball-gowns and put them alongside views of the dingy two-up two-down. Peregrine suffered sniggers, albeit hidden behind hands.

Every seat of the great Olympia Stadium was filled for the first of the five afternoon performances. People sat illegally in the aisles. News had got around. All ten shows were sold out.

Oliver's voice in silent darkness announced that this performance, given free, was dedicated to the memory of his top-flight groom, Mona Watkins, a homespun Welshwoman from the valleys. Her care and understanding of what it took to prepare a European-class horse had been without equal.

'I owe her,' he said, 'so ladies and gentlemen, here, in her memory is her friend, my wife Cassidy Lovelace Ward, with a Song for Mona.'

The darkness suddenly vibrated with music from vast speakers pouring out a huge wattage of sound from high up round the arena, delivering the sweet clear theme carefully taught in advance so that the song was known, recognized, hummable.

A single spotlight flashed on, slicing through the tingling air, lighting with throbbing dramatic impact the big grey horse standing motionless in the entrance to the ring. Astride the horse's back sat Cassidy, dressed in silver leather, Western style, with glittering fringes, silver gauntleted gloves and a white ten-gallon hat. The rig that had galvanized the Mississippi brought spontaneous cheering to London.

Cassidy and the grey horse circled the ring with banks of rainbow lights making stained-glass-window colours on the silver and white, with prisms flashing on the sparkling fringes. Every few paces the grey circled fast on his hocks, standing tall with Cassidy clinging, clearly enjoying himself, the old show-jumper in a starring role; and the crowd, who knew who he was from a page-long introduction in the programme, laughed and cheered him until, back at the start, Cassidy swept off her outsized hat and shook free her silver-blonde curls.

Oliver had worried slightly that the glitz that had triumphed in Tennessee might strike too brassy a note for a horse-show audience in England, but he needn't have feared. Cassidy's people were expert professionals – musicians, lighting crew, electricians, all, and they'd promised – and were delivering – an unforgettable excitement.

At the end of the multicoloured circuit Cassidy rode to the centre of the ring and slid off the horse's back, handing the reins to Oliver, who waited there in the dark. Then in one of the transformations that regularly brought gasps and a stamping of feet, Cassidy shed her riding gear in a shimmering heap and, revealed in a white, full-skirted, crystal-embroidered evening dress, climbed shallow steps to a platform where a microphone waited.

Cassidy took the microphone and sang the Song for Mona with Mona in her mind, a song of a woman who longed for the love she remembered but had lost. Cassidy sang not of Mona by name, but of all lonely people searching for a warm new heart. Cassidy sang the song twice: once quietly, murmuring, plaintive, and then with full voice, glorious, flooding all Olympia, beseeching and arousing the Fates, calling on hope.

She sustained the last long true soaring note until it seemed her lungs must burst, then from one second to the next the barrage of super-sound from the speakers fell silent. The white spotlights folded their beams, as Cassidy, shedding the glittering dress in the lights' dying rays, left just a heap of glimmer while she slipped out of the ring in black.

She returned briefly to wild applause in a black cloak with a sparkling lining. She waved in thanks with raised arms, and was gone. The old magic that had worked so well in Nashville had spread its wings and flown free at Olympia.

Sentimental, some critics complained; but sentimental songs reached the hearts of millions, and so it was with Cassidy's Song for Mona. By the end of the ten live performances at Olympia, the long-lasting melody was spilling from CDs and radios everywhere on its way to classic status.

Joanie and Peregrine, with gritted teeth, watched the cheering show the evening it was televised. Such a pity, the studio announcer deplored with regret, that top auctioneer Peregrine Vine and his socialite wife Joan, who was Mona Watkins' only daughter, had been unable to attend any of the performances.

Joanie fell speechless with bitter chagrin. Peregrine wondered if it were possible to start again in yet another town: but the Song for Mona was sung everywhere, from concerts to karaoke. Peregrine looked at his beautiful selfish wife and wondered if she were worth it.

A while after the glories of Olympia, Oliver and Cassidy cooked in their kitchen and ate without quarrelling. Although they were used to Mona's absence, her spirit hovered around, it seemed to them, telling them to break eggs, not plates.

Probate completed, Cassidy had duly given all Mona's 'bits and pieces' (including the pearl brooch and the bicycle) to the hair-curlered neighbour who lovingly took them in, and it was only occasionally that either of the Bolingbrokes wondered what Joanie had so urgently sought on the morning her mother died.

'You know,' Cassidy said over the mushroom omelettes, 'that old box Mona brought with pictures of Joanie in her ball-gowns . . . there were pictures of us in it, too.'

Oliver lifted down the neglected box from a high shelf on a dresser and emptied it onto the table.

Under the clippings of Joanie and themselves they found two folded pages of a Welsh country town newspaper, now extinct; old, fragile and brown round the edges.

Oliver cautiously unfolded them, careful not to tear them, and both of the Bolingbrokes learned what Joanie Vine had been frantic to conceal.

Centre front page on the first sheet was a picture of a group of three people: a younger Mona, a child recognizably Joanie, and a short unsmiling man. Alongside, a headline read: '*Local man pleads guilty to child rape, sentenced to ten years.*'

*Idris Watkins, stable-lad, husband of Mona, and father of Joan, confessed to the crime and has been sentenced without trial.*

The second brown-edged fragile page ran a story but no pictures:

'*Stable-lad killed in a fall on gallops.*

*Idris Watkins, recently freed after serving six years of*

*a ten-year sentence for child rape, died of a fractured skull, Thursday. He leaves a widow, Mona, and a daughter, Joan, 13.*'

After a silence, Oliver said, 'It explains a lot, I suppose.'

He made photocopies of the old pages and sent the copies to Joanie.

Cassidy, nodding, said, 'Let her worry that we'll publish her secret and ruin her social-climbing life.'

They didn't publish, though.

Mona wouldn't have liked it.

# BRIGHT WHITE STAR

*A country magazine,* Cheshire Life, *sent me a letter.*

*'Write us a story,' they said.*

*I asked, 'What about?'*

*'About three thousand words,' they replied.*

*It was winter at the time, and by car I drove frequently up and down a hill where a tramp had once lived in a hollow. So I wrote about a tramp in winter.*

*This story describes how to steal a horse from an auction.*

*Don't do it!*

The tramp was cold to his bones.

The air and the ground stood at freezing point, and a heavy layer of yellowish snow-cloud hung like a threat over the afternoon. Black boughs of stark trees creaked in the wind, and the rutted fields lay bare and dark, waiting.

Shambling down a narrow road the tramp was cold and hungry and filled with an intense unfocused resentment. By this stage of the winter he liked to be deep in a nest, sheltered in a hollow in the ground in the lee of a wooded hill, roofed by a lavish thatch of criss-crossed branches and thick brown cardboard, lying on a warm comfortable bed of dry dead leaves and polythene sheeting and sacks. He liked to have his wood-fire burning all day near his threshold, with the ashes glowing red all night. He liked to live snug through the frost and the snows and the driving rains, and kick the whole thing to pieces when he moved on in the spring.

What he did not like was having someone else kick his nest in as they had done on that morning. Three of them – the man who owned the land where he had settled, and two people from the local council, a hard-eyed middle-aged man and a prim bossy woman with a clipboard. Their loud voices, their stupid remarks, echoed and fed the anger in his mind.

'I've told him every day for the past week that I want him off my land . . .'

'This structure constitutes a permanent dwelling and as such requires planning permission . . .'

'In the town there is a hostel where vagrants can sleep in a dormitory on a one-night basis . . .'

The council man had begun pulling his branch-and-cardboard roof to pieces, and the other two had joined in. He saw from their faces that his smell offended them, and he saw from the finicky picking of their fingers that they didn't like touching what he had touched. The slow burning anger had begun in his mind then, but as he detested contacts with other humans and never spoke if he could avoid it, he had merely turned and walked away, shapeless in his bundled clothes, shuffling in his too-big boots, bearded and resentful and smelly.

He had walked six miles since then, slowly.

He needed food and somewhere to shelter from the coming snow. He needed a nest, and fire. His rage against mankind deepened with every leaden step.

In London on the same afternoon the Director of the Racecourse Security Service looked morosely out of the Jockey Club office window at the traffic in Portman Square. Behind him in the comfortable brightly lit room Mr Melbourne Smith was complaining, as he had done either in person or on the telephone every day for the past two weeks, about the lax security at the November Yearling Sales, from which someone had craftily stolen his just-bought and extremely expensive colt.

Melbourne Smith poured so much money into the British bloodstock industry that his complaints could not be ignored, even though strictly it was a matter for the police and the auctioneers, not the Jockey Club. Melbourne Smith, fifty, forceful, a wheeler-dealer to his fingertips, was as much outraged that anyone should dare to steal from *him* as by the theft itself.

'They just walked out with him,' he said for the fiftieth injured time. 'And you've done bloody little to get him back.'

The Director sighed. He disliked Melbourne Smith intensely but hid it well under a bluffly hearty manner. The Director, with a subtle and inventive mind behind a moustached and tweeded exterior, wondered just what else he could do, short of praying for a miracle, to find the missing colt.

The trail, for a start, was cold, as Melbourne Smith had not discovered his loss for more than a month after the sales. He had bought, as usual, about ten of the leggy young animals who would race the following summer as two-year-olds. He had arranged to have them transported, as usual, to the trainer who would break them in, handle them and saddle them and ride them and accustom them to going in and out of starting stalls. And, as usual, in due course he had gone to see how his purchases were making out.

He had been puzzled at first by what should have been his prize colt. Puzzled, and then suspicious, and then explodingly furious. He had paid a fortune for a well-grown aristocratic yearling and he had received instead a spindly no-hoper with a weak neck. Between his purchase and the changeling there were only two points in common: the body colour, a dark bay, and the large white star on the forehead.

'It's a scandal,' Melbourne Smith said. 'I'll spend my money in France, next year.'

The Director reflected that the theft of racehorses was exceedingly rare and that the security at the sales was more a matter of behind-the-scenes paperwork than of bars and bolts: and normally the paperwork was security enough.

Every thoroughbred foal had to be registered soon after birth, the certificate not only giving parentage and birth date but also skin colours and markings and where exactly on the body the hairs of the coat grew in whorls. The markings and whorls had to be carefully drawn onto regulation outline pictures of side, front and rear views of horses.

Later on, when the foal was grown up and ready to race, a second chart of his markings had to be filled in by a veterinary surgeon and sent off to the registry. If the foal certificate and the later certificate matched, all was well. If they didn't, the horse was barred from racing.

The foal certificate of the yearling Melbourne Smith had bought definitely did not match the changeling he had been landed with. The colour and the white star were right, but the whorls of hair were all in different places.

The Director had set his assistant the mammoth task

of checking the changeling against the 20,000 foal certificates in that year's registry, but so far none of them had matched. The Director thought that the changeling, whom he had seen, was very likely a half-bred hunter, which hadn't been eligible for Stud Book entry in the first place, and of whom there would be no official record anywhere.

'That gate check is a laugh,' grumbled Melbourne Smith.

The men on the sales paddock gates, the Director admitted to himself, were there only to check that there was an auctioneers' exit chit for each horse, and that the horse bore the same number, stuck onto its rump, as was written on the chit. They were not there to check whether anyone had sneakily changed the numbers on the horses. They were not at fault because the number 189 which had walked out accompanied by chit 189 had been a weedy-necked no-hoper, and not Melbourne Smith's expensive aristocrat. It was no good asking them (although the Director had) under exactly what number the expensive aristocrat had actually made his exit. They couldn't possibly know, and they didn't.

The Director had discovered in some respects how the substitution had been made, and guessed the rest.

At the sales, the horses up for auction were housed in stable blocks. Horse number 1 in the catalogue was allotted box number 1 and had number 1 stuck on his hip. Number 189 would be found in box 189 and have

189 on his hip. Coming and going along all the rows of boxes would be the customers, assessing and prodding and deciding whether or not to bid. As each horse was sold, its former owners returned it to its box and left it there, and from there the new owners would collect it. Sellers and buyers, in this way, quite often never met.

The lad who had come with 189 had taken it from the sale ring back to its box, and left it there. Melbourne Smith's lad had collected the horse from box 189 and sent it to the trainer, and it had been the changeling.

The exchange, with so many horses and people on the move, could be (and had been) done without anyone noticing.

The Director supposed that the thieves must have entered their changeling for the sales, and put a ridiculously high reserve on it, so that no one would buy it. He reckoned that the changeling must have been one of the unsold lots between numbers 1 and 188, but the auctioneers had looked blank at the thought of remembering one among so many, so long ago. They auctioned hundreds of horses every week. They didn't enquire, they said, where the merchandise came from or where it went. They kept records of the horses that had found no takers, but presumed that their owners had taken them back.

'And this publicity campaign of yours,' sneered Melbourne Smith, 'lot of hot air and no results.'

The Director turned wearily away from the window

and looked at the newspaper which lay open on his desk. In a week short of headlines the editors had welcomed the story he had persuasively fed them, and no reader could miss the 'Where is he?' pictures of the missing treasure. The tabloids had gone for the sob-stuff. The 'serious' dailies had reproduced the foal certificate itself. Television newscasters had broadcast both. Two days' saturation coverage, however, had produced no results. His 'phone at any time' number lay silent.

'You get him back,' Melbourne Smith said furiously, finally leaving, 'or I send all my horses to France.'

The Director thought of his wife and children who were preparing for a party that evening and would greet his return with excited faces and smiling eyes. I'll not think of that damned yearling for two days, he thought: and meanwhile he gave in and prayed intensely for his miracle.

'What I need,' he said aloud to his peacefully empty office, 'is a white star. A bright white star, stationary in the sky, shining over a stable, saying, "Here I am. Come here to me. Come here and find me."'

God forgive me my blasphemy, he thought; and went home at four o'clock.

In the country on that afternoon Jim and Vivi Turner spread out four newspapers on the kitchen table and studied them over mugs of tea.

'They won't find him, will they?' Jim said.

Vivi shook her head. 'A bay with a white star . . . common as dirt.'

Their minds wandered to the aristocratic yearling rugged up outside in their tumbledown twenty-box stable, but it was five weeks or more since they had stolen him, and time had given them a sense of safety.

'And anyway,' Vivi said, 'these papers are two days old, and nothing's happened.'

Jim Turner nodded, reassured. He would never have brought it all off, he knew, without Vivi. It was she who had said that what they badly needed, to get him going as a trainer, was one really good horse. The sort, let's face it (she said), that no one was going to send to a newly retired jump jockey who had never risen above middle rank and who had been suspended twice for taking bribes.

As Jim Turner would take a bribe any time anyone offered, the two suspensions had been mild. He himself wouldn't have minded retiring to a job as a head lad in a big stable, where the chances for bribery grew like berries ripe for plucking. Vivi had wanted to be a trainer's wife, not a head lad's, and you had to hand it to her – the girl had brains.

It was Vivi, with her sharp eyes, who had seen how they could steal a top yearling from the sales. It was Vivi, a proper little Lady Macbeth, who had egged Jim on when he faltered, who had herself engineered the exchange in box 189; she who had taken the aristocrat and Jim who had left the changeling.

Vivi, deciding that they should use a half-bred unregistered throw-out as their entry to the sales, had bought one from a knacker's yard for peanuts; a bay with a white star, common as dirt. There would be bound to be one a bit like him at the sales, she'd said. They would swap him for anything great that came after him in the catalogue; and, sure enough, number 189 had been perfect.

Vivi, planning ahead, would send Jim up north in the spring with all their savings to buy a cheap thoroughbred two-year-old, a bay with a white star, that looked at any rate passable. Then Jim would get the vet to fill in the new horse's markings certificate which would match its foal certificate in the registry; and Jim Turner, racehorse trainer, would have in his stable a bay with a white star checked and registered and free to race.

Jim and Vivi knew, as the Director did, that young horses changed as they grew older, like children into men, so that there would be little chance of anyone recognizing the aristocrat by sight. It could race for ever in its new identity, and no one would ever know. Vivi couldn't see how anything could go wrong, and never thought of the long-term tenacity of the Director, who was already pondering wearisome sporadic whorl-checks of white-starred bays for years to come.

'In the summer,' Vivi said, 'we'll smarten the place up a bit. Lick of paint. Tubs of flowers. Then in autumn when the colt starts winning and people take notice, we'll have a place new owners won't mind coming to.'

Jim nodded. Vivi could do it. She was real bright, Vivi was.

'And you'll be on the map right enough, Jim Turner, and none of those snooty cows of trainers' wives will look down on us ever again.'

There was a sudden metallic clatter just outside the back door and, immediately intensely alarmed, they both stood up jerkily and went outside.

A shambling, untidy figure stood there, with his hands fumbling through the household refuse in their dustbin, turning already to back away.

'It's a tramp!' Vivi said disbelievingly. 'Stealing our rubbish.'

'Get off,' Jim said, advancing roughly. 'Go on, get off.'

The tramp retreated a few steps, very slowly.

Jim Turner dived back into his kitchen and snatched up the shotgun with which he deterred rabbits.

'Go on,' he shouted, coming out again and pointing the barrels. 'Clear off and don't come back. I don't want muck like you round here. Bugger off.'

The tramp went slowly away towards the road, and the Turners, righteously reassured, returned to their warm kitchen.

The landowner spent the afternoon regretting what he'd done in the morning. It was not a good day, he belatedly realized, for turning a man out of his home, even if his home was a hole in the ground.

When they'd pulled the nest to pieces, the two council workers and himself, he had found in the ruins a plastic bag full of cigarette ends. He wasn't an imaginative man, but it came to him that everything the tramp had, his home and his comforts, he had taken away. He had looked up at the sullen sky, and shivered.

During the afternoon he walked lengthily round his land, half looking for the tramp, to quieten his own conscience; but it was almost with surprise that he finally saw him walking towards him along one of his boundary roads.

The tramp shambled slowly, and he was not alone. At his shoulder, as slowly following, came a horse.

The tramp stopped, and the horse also. The tramp held out a horse cube on a grimy palm, and the horse ate it.

The landowner looked in puzzlement at the two of them, the filthy man and the well-groomed horse in its tidy rug.

'Where did you get that?' said the landowner, pointing.

'Found it. In the road.' The tramp's voice was hoarse from disuse, but the words were clear. They were also not true.

'Look,' said the landowner awkwardly, 'you can build that house of yours again, if you like. Stay for a few days. How's that?'

The tramp considered it but shook his head, knowing

that he couldn't stay, because of the horse. He had freed the horse from its stable and taken it with him. They would call him a thief and arrest him. In his past he had compulsively absconded from institutions, from children's homes and then the army, and if he couldn't face the walls of a doss house, still less could he face a cell in the nick. Cold and hunger and freedom, yes. Warmth and food and a locked door, no.

He turned away, gesturing unmistakably to the landowner to take the horse, to put his hand on its head-collar and do what was right. Automatically, almost, the landowner did so.

'Wait,' he said, as the tramp retreated. 'Look ... take these.' He pulled from his pocket a packet of cigarettes and held them out. 'Take them ... please.'

Hesitating, the tramp went back and accepted the gift, nodding his acknowledgement of something given, something received. Then again he turned away and set off down the road, and the long-threatened snow began to fall in big single floating flakes, obliterating his shaggy outline in the dying afternoon.

Where will he go? the landowner wondered uncomfortably: and the tramp thought without anxiety that he would walk all night through the snow to keep warm, and in the morning he would find shelter, and eat, as usual, what others of their plenty had thrown away. The tramp's earlier festering anger, which had flared up and focused on Jim Turner, had by now burned away, and all he felt, as he put distance safely behind him, was his normal overwhelming desire to be alone.

The landowner looked at the horse and the white star on its forehead, and shook his head sardonically at the thought which came to him. All the same, when he'd shut the horse into a stable behind his house, he fished out the day before yesterday's newspapers, and looked at the tabloid's headline 'Find the Bright Star' and at the foal certificate facsimile in the 'serious' daily. And then he tentatively telephoned the police.

'Found a horse, have you, sir?' said a cheerful sergeant's voice robustly. 'And you're not the only one, I'll tell you that. There's horses all over the village, here. Some fool opened all the boxes at Jim Turner's place and let them all out. It might be a tramp. Turner says he chased one out of his yard earlier. We're looking for that one as lived on your land. But it's dark and it's snowing and I'm short of men, of course, as today's Christmas Eve.'

*Christmas Eve.*

The landowner felt first a burst of irritation with the tramp, and then, like a stab, understood that he wouldn't have set loose the horses if he hadn't been turned out of his own home at Christmas. He decided not to tell the sergeant that he'd seen the tramp with the horse now in his own stable, nor which way the tramp had gone.

'I'll tell Jim Turner to come and fetch that horse,

sir,' said the sergeant. 'He'll be glad to have it back. In a proper tizzy, he is.'

'Er . . .' said the landowner, slowly, not wanting to be thought a fool, 'I don't know if you've read the papers about that stolen horse, Sergeant, but I think instead of returning this one to Jim Turner immediately, we might try that "phone at any time" number for reaching the Director of the Racecourse Security Service.' He paused. 'I don't suppose that the Director believes in Christmas miracles, but the horse I have here in my stable is a young bay colt with a bright white star on his forehead . . . and whorls in all the right places . . .'

# COLLISION COURSE

*No murder here. No blood.*

*PREJUDICE, sure, and PRIDE, OK, but this isn't Austen Bonnet and Bennet land; this is today's out-of-work newspaper editor versus a brash operator putting his foot in it.*

With a mug of strong black coffee at his elbow the editor of the *Cotswold Voice* sat at his desk in his shirt sleeves and read the splashy column that would lead the newspaper's racing pages the next day, unless he vetoed it. The words were a blur. His mind spun from being sacked.

Twice a week, Tuesdays and Saturdays, from uninspiring factory-type premises on an industrial park west of Oxford, the *Cotswold Voice* fed a stream of lively newsprint into the towns and villages along the Cotswold hills.

On Tuesdays the slant was towards news, comment and interpretation and on Saturday to sport, fashion and general knowledge competitions. Something for everyone, the paper announced. Something for mums, dads, kids and aunties. Births, deaths and 'wanted' ads. Lots of verve. Horoscopes, scandal . . . All a succulent worm for a hawk.

The present editor of the *Cotswold Voice*, twenty-nine years old when he'd been surprisingly appointed, had in four short years doubled the paper's circulation while himself being reasonably mistaken for the office gofer.

Short and thin, he had exceptionally sharp eyesight, acute hearing and a sense of smell that could distinguish oil on the north wind and sheep on the west. His accent was a mixture of Berkshire, Wiltshire and the University of Cambridge. He could read at light-speed, his brain a sponge. He'd been christened Absalom Elvis da Vinci Williams, and he could lose his cool like a bolt of lightning. His staff, who recognized power when they felt it, walked round him warily, and at his bidding called him Bill.

The editor – Absalom Elvis et cetera Williams – scanned the racing pages' leader over again. Concentrate, he told himself. Don't leave with a whimper.

He read:

*'Coronary cases, don't read on. Others, give your valves aerobic work-outs while couch-potatoing it Saturdays p.m. Snap a can. Feet up? Down to the start, and they're off!'*

The work was technically perfect; neat typing, double spacing, an impeccable paper printout of a computer disk. This racing correspondent never scattered his pages with messy amendments.

A wade through another couple of florid paragraphs encouraging heart-thumping indolence finally revealed the core of the guff to be advice on buying shares in syndicated racehorses.

Bill Williams frowned. Syndicated racehorses were hardly hot news. What made this spiel different was that the meat of it explained that the syndicated horses, when acquired, would not be sent to an established trainer, but would form the nucleus of a new stable with a new trainer, one Dennis Kinser.

The *Voice* assured its readers the scheme was an exciting financial prospect. Buy, buy, and – er – buy.

The editor picked up the pulse-stirring article and walked unhurriedly down the lengthy editorial floor to where his chief racing writer awaited a verdict. The whole busy room was noticeably quiet owing to the editor, during his first weeks in office, having had the last of the crash-tinkle tap-tap typewriters pensioned off and the squeaky functional vinyl flooring covered in dark blue sound-absorbing carpet tiles. The frenetic hyperactivity common to newspapers had died with the clatter, but productivity had nevertheless soared. The older hands yearned for a return to noise.

The editor sat on a rolling stool drawn up beside the racing writer's desk and, floating the typed pages in front of him, asked without belligerence, 'What's all this really about?'

'Well . . . syndicates.' The racing writer, lazy, middle-aged, heavily moustached, showed more energy on the page than off it.

'This Dennis Kinser,' the editor asked, 'have you yourself met him?'

'Well . . . no.'

'Where did you get the story?'

'From the agent who's putting the syndicates together.'

'Do you know him?'

'No. He phoned.'

The editor drew a blue-pencil line through the multiple advice to buy and buy, and initialled the rest of the column for publication. There was little of more pressing interest: it was August, the month of newspaper and racing doldrums.

'Follow up the story,' he said. 'Do a personality piece on Dennis Kinser. Get a picture. If there are no bigger stories and no one scoops you, we'll run it next Saturday.'

'What if he's a fraud?'

'Frauds are news,' the editor said. 'Be sure of the facts.'

The racing writer winced, watching the editor walk away. Bone idle, the racing writer had once written a cuttingly satirical 'eye-witness' account of a much looked forward to parade of champions that had in fact been cancelled by heavy rain. The editor's fury had frightened the racing writer into diarrhoea and the shakes. This time, he morosely supposed, he would actually have to get off his backside and track down the wannabe trainer. (The racing writer thought in journalese, much as he wrote.) The only bright area on his constricted horizon was that after next Saturday the editor would be out on holiday for a week. The racing writer could get away with much sloppier reporting, he cosily reflected, when the sharp little blue-pencil bastard wasn't creeping around demanding actual physical *work*. The racing writer liked to gather his information via the telephone, sitting down. He picked up the receiver and talked to the syndicate-arranging agent.

Bill Williams went back to his desk and drank his left-over lukewarm coffee, his thoughts as stark and black as the liquid. The *Voice* had belonged to a dynasty whose kindly head had recently died. The descendants, wanting to divide the cash, had sold their biggest asset to a multi-faceted company as just one more local rag in their commercial chain. Individualism, the new men did not want. Maximum profit, they did. As far as possible, their array of provincial papers would all speak economically as one. Consequently, they would appoint their own rubber-stamp editor for the *Voice*. It was fortunate that ex-editor Williams was due for a week off. He could clear his desk and not come back.

Bill Williams had known the dynasty family would one day sell and that he would move on. He'd known there was a new brutality abroad in the cut-throat newspaper world. Knowing hadn't prepared him for the abruptness, the ferocity, or the total lack of even a shred of courtesy from any side. There had been no handshakes, no apology, certainly no good wishes, simply a blunt dismissal message among his private e-mail.

From the general peace in the long room he realized that the new owners had so far told no one else about the change of regime. It suited him fine. His last three issues – Saturday, Tuesday and Saturday – would be the best he could do. And after that . . .

Toughening his mind, he pulled onto his screen the names of all newspapers published in London, together with their owners. He had served his time in the provinces – like the horses going up and down on the outside ring of a roundabout, and he reckoned he had earned a hand on the levers. If he didn't tell the ringmasters he was free out there and willing, he thought, mixing his metaphors cheerfully, how would they know?

He phoned and wrote letters and e-mail and sent copies of the *Voice* all over the place. His CV was impressive, but the ringmasters seemingly were deaf.

From a conglomerate known for treating their journalist staff badly, he did at least get one firm offer to meet. Dinner for four at a place of Williams' choosing. Outside London, they stipulated. Williams to pay.

It was by then Thursday of his last week at the *Voice*. Once the Saturday paper was on the street, he would be done. Philosophically he accepted the conglomerate's reverse invitation and made a booking for a table in a restaurant beside the River Thames south of Oxford. His food column writer had raved about the place for a month.

The *Voice*'s racing writer, after a series of telephone enquiries, had finally located the hopeful Dennis Kinser and, not yet aware that the 'blue-pencilling bastard' of an editor would be chasing him no more after Saturday, he had actually stirred himself to drive sixty miles for a face-to-face enlightenment.

When he tried, the racing writer's assessment of people and horses tended to be stingingly accurate, which was why Bill Williams put up with him. The racing writer saw faults and said so, and was often enough proved right.

He saw faults in Dennis Kinser that others might have thought virtues, the first of them being overweening confidence in himself. Kinser's aim in life *began* at reigning as champion trainer: after that, the world.

The racing writer listened to the cockiness with weary disillusion and made shorthand notes on spiral-bound pages as if tape-recorders hadn't been invented. He would have described Kinser as an envy-driven bumptious self-important snake-oil salesman had he not been sure the little blue-pencil devil would let him get away only with 'ambitious'.

Dennis Kinser at thirty had developed a game-plan for his life which involved a swift future shinny up the celebrity ladder to a first-name clap-on-the-shoulder familiarity with any well-known achiever. He would pay restrained respect to every inherited title. He would do favours that required favours in return. He needed a first public toehold for this upward mobility and the *Cotswold Voice* sports pages' leading article would give it to him.

He told the racing writer with faintly defiant pride that as he'd been too heavily built to make it to the top as a jump jockey he had spent six years as a stable-lad, 'doing his two' and living in squalor in a hostel.

'Was that part of the game-plan?' the racing writer asked.

'Sure,' Kinser said, lying.

The racing writer wrote on his notepad, 'The time to make friends with this guy is NOW.' He said, 'What do you intend to do next?'

Kinser told him exhaustively. He would beguile the

owners of the horses he'd looked after to send him some to train. Their horses had won, he would smilingly assure them, because of his knowledgeable care. Then he would publicize and glamorize the syndicates and welcome all part-owners warmly. He would be given a trainer's licence because he'd completed all three of the British Racing School's official courses – in horse, business and people management.

'Top-class manipulator,' the racing writer noted and in the evening wrote one of his very best pieces for the *Voice*, giving Kinser the benefit of the self-made doubt.

Bill Williams, still the editor on the next day, Friday, walked down the quiet editorial floor carrying the sparkling pages and sincerely complimented his racing writer. Then he called his staff together and unemotionally told them that a different editor would be running the paper from Sunday.

Bill Williams, whose odd-ball father had burdened him with Absalom, Elvis and da Vinci, had spent his council house and comprehensive-school years hiding his brains in order not to be bullied. His teachers declared him puzzlingly dumb: not stupid themselves, they saw flashes of stifled brilliance and went into an 'I thought so all along' mode when A. E. da V. Williams, insisting against their moderating advice on aiming for the top and trying for Cambridge, had won scholarships all over the place with a subsequent clutch of Firsts and Doctorates in his fist.

As an undergraduate A. E. da V. Williams had founded and edited *Propter* which, like *Granta* before it, had quickly become the most prestigious of all academic university newsprint publications. Dr Williams, MA, PhD, distinguished at twenty-seven, turned down a lectureship, left Cambridge and academe behind and humbly free-lanced as a roving journalist with comment pieces and reviews until the *Cotswold Voice* dynasty liked his style and took him on as an editorial gamble.

His fast temper mostly controlled and internalized by inclination and habit, Bill Williams spent his holidays (and much of his life) alone. Unlike many solitary people, though, he bubbled not far below the surface with a self-deprecating sense of humour that stopped him taking himself too seriously: which was why, in the August of what he now thought of as the 'Summer of the Lost Voice', he decided not to change the restful plans he'd had for his week off, but to rent a punt high up the River Thames, as he'd intended, and steer it down with the current to Oxford.

He thought pragmatically that since he had arranged the dinner meeting with the unsatisfactory conglomerate to take place at a restaurant lower down the river from Oxford, and since he had no job to hurry back to, he would extend his water journey in time and distance, and rest-cure his bruised expectations while mentally rehearsing how to cajole juice from conglomerate flint.

At Lechlade, the town at the highest navigable point on the Thames, the boatyard had allocated one of its newly refurbished punts to Mr Williams, in consideration of his having paid extra for the best. The varnish on the solid wood was rich and dark and there was new blue velvet upholstering the wide comfortable reclining seat that would extend down to be a mattress for sleeping on.

From each end a canopy could unfold, meeting in the middle to keep out the night and the rain, and the boatyard also provided mooring ropes, a gas lamp, rowlocks and oars for alternative manoeuvrability, a six-foot pole with a hook on the end of it, and a twelve-foot punt-pole for propelling the eighteen-foot flat-bottomed boat along on top of the water.

Bill Williams had learned to punt on the Backs, the backwater system of the river at Cambridge, and felt peacefully at home on the rudderless engineless craft, much preferring to punt than to row. With deep contentment he smelled the new varnish and tested the weight, flexibility and balance of the long pole. He asked questions that reassured the boatyard people and bought a few basic provisions from their handy shop. They seldom had customers who travelled as far down river as this one proposed to, but they willingly agreed to keep his car safe while he was away, and to retrieve him and their boat whenever he'd had enough.

Among the essential comforts their customer took with him were a sleeping bag, binoculars, swimming shorts, pens and writing paper, clean clothes, a battery razor and ten books. Stowing all these safely, he stripped off his sweater, and in T-shirt, jeans and trainers jumped lightly onto the poling platform at one end of the boat. He looked young and unimportant and not in the slightest like the editor of any newspaper, let alone the vivid and successful *Cotswold Voice*.

He poled his flat craft along with an ease that had the boatyard staff nodding in approbation, and they watched him until he was out of sight round the first slow bend. Bill Williams, looking back across the fields to the small town with its church spire shining in afternoon sunlight, felt an enormous sense of release. There was nothing to clutch him, no crisis to demand his return to his desk: he had even deliberately not brought with him his mobile phone with its brigade of charged-up batteries, normally the first objects of his packing.

Two days earlier his Saturday edition – his last – had been a triumph, sold out. He'd used all the crowd-pleasing ideas he would in past years have spread over the autumn and with breath-shortening delight he'd sat in a pub window across the road from a large newsagent and in the early evening watched copy after copy of the Saturday *Voice* being carried away. Word of mouth in action, he'd thought. Absolutely bloody marvellous.

Quiet and contented on the river on Monday as the

long August dusk lengthened, Bill Williams steered his unaggressive boat to a stretch of sweet-smelling bank, and tied a mooring rope to a sapling willow. The little sounds of water birds snuggling down for the night in a patch of reedbed, the whisper of the faintest of wind movement in dead and dry grass stems along the bank, the faint chuckle of the current as the river gently bypassed his inert boat, all the tiny natural things obliterated for a while the clamour of the raucous outside world that had to be dealt with and lived in, and if possible changed for the better. Long ago, to his surprise, young Dr A. E. da V. etc. had come to the self-knowledge that if a cause were just, he would kill for it.

Death on the Thames that week came no nearer than river-rage, with motorway bad manners spilling over into raised voices and shaken fists. The punt was slow. Fast fibreglass cruisers filled with holidaymakers in a hurry swept past with boom boxes thumping. Anglers sitting half-hidden on stools along the bank (patiently waiting to hook the uneatable) cursed the silent punt for dragging their lines. Lock-keepers stifled impatience while the boat with no rudder but a trailing punt-pole manoeuvred difficult eddies at the entrances and exits of the locks.

Bill Williams, expert though he was, attracted abuse.

On the credit side he watched the sunsets after the busy river was quiet, and listened to geese honking on the meadows above Oxford, and ate at an inn with peacocks on the roof and once, half disbelieving, caught the bright blue flash of the wing of a rare kingfisher on the hunt.

He lived down among the moorhens with snapdragons and floppy poppies growing wild beside him. He floated eyeball to eyeball with bad-tempered hissing swans and was looked down on superciliously by alarmed herons who plucked up their feet fastidiously and stalked away.

By the time Bill Williams reached the public mooring at Oxford his mind was filled with amusement and his arms were fit and strong from swinging and leaning on the punt-pole. He had written a leading article (from habit) and read nine of his books.

He went ashore for food, and from a public phone called up the message service he used in his rare absences. Most of the messages were from disgruntled *Voice* readers as usual. There were no offers or even expressions of interest from any people who could give him a job.

In Oxford he bought as usual every local and London newspaper he could lay his hands on, and went back to the boat.

It was a Tuesday. He had been travelling down the river for eight undemanding days and would easily, in two days more, reach the restaurant for his dinner meeting with the conglomerate-proprietors. Much now, it seemed, depended on their assessment of him. He read their papers first.

There were two of them, the *Blondel News* and the *Daily Troubadour*, each split into two sections, with sport, art and finance coming second.

He knew of course that as broadsheets both papers took responsibility seriously and seldom bared a breast. He knew also that the fierce in-fighting with others in the circulation war had meant they'd sprouted offshoots of glitz on Sundays. He considered that that Tuesday's edition of the *Troubadour* was boring; and he found the same story (identical paragraphs) unforgivably printed on two different pages. He felt not in the least downhearted but more like taking the *Troubadour* by its complacent sloth and giving it a colossal shake.

Later, moored comfortably downstream in the dappled shade of a graceful willow, he read, with carefully throttled emotion, that day's – Tuesday's – *Cotswold Voice*. The previous week's two editions, read in pubs upstream, had both partly carried his own recognizable imprint. This Tuesday's issue, the third of the new owners' reign, had wholly reverted to the shape of the old *Cotswold Voice*, before young da V. Williams got his hands on it.

Bill Williams sighed.

The racing writer of the *Cotswold Voice* was missing the little creeping blue-pencil bastard something chronic (as he put it).

He'd been immediately told by the new editor, a

large man with a bullying manner, that in future the *Voice* would use a centrally written opinion piece as their leader on the racing page. The present racing writer would take second lead, and yes – grudgingly – as there still seemed to be no great fresh news, he could do a follow-up piece this week about Dennis Kinser and his syndicates, always supposing the *Voice* itself had succeeded in launching the Kinser training career. After that, the racing writer would do no more features, but concentrate on tipping winners.

Aggrieved, the racing writer phoned Dennis Kinser, and he and Dennis Kinser between them, prompter and prompted, concocted a totally false account of the new trainer being flooded by applications to take horses from excited would-be syndicate owners, thanks to the enthusiastic support of the *Cotswold Voice*.

The new editor nodded over the piece sagely and initialled it for publication. The ex-editor shook his head, and, knowing his racing writer and reading his Saturday gush in an up-river bar, didn't believe a word of it.

Bill Williams floated down in two days from Oxford to the meeting-place, a restaurant by the river – imaginatively named Mainstream Mile – and in late afternoon sunshine tied his mooring ropes tidily to the pier provided. He agreed at once with his food columnist's statement that, from the water at least, the dining-room of Mainstream Mile was one of the most attractive on the Thames, with tables set on terraces behind a sheet of glass, so that diners could have a grandstand view of river traffic.

There was a short patch of rose garden between the building and the river, with a path winding upwards from the pier. Down the path, as Bill Williams stood on the pier, stretching and relaxing in his jeans and T-shirt after his completed journey, a young dark-suited man bounced with a self-satisfied air and told the visitor to leave at once as he was not welcome.

'I beg your pardon,' Bill Williams said, thinking it a joke. 'What do you mean, leave?'

'The dining-room is fully booked for tonight.'

'Oh,' Bill Williams laughed, 'that's all right then. I booked a table for tonight two weeks ago.'

'You cannot have done!' The young man began to lose his bounce. 'It is impossible. We do not accept boats.'

Incredulously, Bill Williams looked around him. He said, 'This restaurant is called Mainstream Mile. It is on the bank of the Thames. It has a proper pier, to which you see I am properly moored. How can you say you don't accept boats?'

'It is the rule of the house.'

Bill Williams lost more than half of his temper. 'You go and tell the house,' he said forcefully, tapping the young man's chest with his forefinger, 'that I booked a table here two weeks ago, and no one said anything about not accepting boats.'

The editorial floor of the *Cotswold Voice* knew better than to argue with a Williams righteous rage. The young man backed off nervously and said, 'What name?'

'Williams. Four people. Eight o'clock. I am meeting my three guests in the bar here at seven-thirty. You go back and tell that to the house.'

Mrs Robin Dawkins drove north-westwards from London in a bad mood made worse by the dipping sun shining straight into her eyes.

Beside her sat F. Harold Field with Russell Maudsley behind her, belted into the rear seat. Mrs Dawkins had wanted the company chauffeur, not herself, to be at the wheel of the firm's Daimler for this aggravating expedition, but had been outvoted on the good grounds that the chauffeur's discretion leaked freely if offered enough cash.

Mrs Robin Dawkins, Mr F. Harold Field and Mr Russell Maudsley collectively owned the newspaper conglomerate, the Lionheart News Group. All were hard-eyed bottom liners. All were fifty, astute and worried. The circulation of all newspapers had dropped owing to television, but theirs more than most. Boardroom rows were constant. Each of the three proprietors strongly disliked the other two, and it was the feuding between them that had led to the last disastrous choice of editor for the *Daily Troubadour*.

Mrs Robin Dawkins thought it completely pointless

interviewing a thirty-three-year-old from the boondocks, and only desperation had persuaded her onto this road.

The Lionheart News Group's Daimler reached the Mainstream Mile restaurant at seven-thirty-five and the proprietors walked stiffly into the bar. There were several sets of people sitting at little tables with no one approximating Mrs Robin Dawkins' idea of a newspaper editor in sight. Her glance swept over the young man standing to one side, holding a file-folder, and it was with depression that she realized, as he came tentatively towards her, that this, the personification of a waste of time, was the person they'd come all that way to meet.

F. Harold Field and Russell Maudsley shook his hand, introducing themselves, and both were dismayed by his youth. In dark trousers, white shirt and navy blazer he looked right for a summer Thursday evening dinner by the Thames, but wrong for their idea of bossing a news room. Bill Williams, more anxious than he would admit about his job prospects, was also disconcerted by the restaurant's ongoing hostility towards him, for which he saw no logical reason. Why ever should he not arrive in a punt?

In the bar Bill Williams seated his guests at a small table and ordered drinks, which were a long time coming. The bar filled up with people and then began to empty again as the head waiter in a formal dinner jacket began distributing menus and taking orders and leading guests away to seat them in the dining-room. Other guests: not the Williams party.

Irritated at being overlooked, Bill Williams asked the head waiter for menus, as he passed by with smiling customers in tow. The head waiter said, 'Certainly,' frowning, and took five minutes over returning.

Mrs Robin Dawkins seethed at the off-hand treatment and waited, fuming, for her host to assert himself. Bill Williams twice insisted that the head waiter seat them for dinner, but he and his guests were last out of the bar and last in the dining-room, and were allocated the worst table, in a corner. Bill Williams came near to punching the smugness off the head waiter's face.

Unbelievable, Mrs Robin Dawkins thought. The food she ordered came late and cold. F. Harold Field and Russell Maudsley tried to assess this Williams boy's capacity to run a newspaper, which was what they had come for, but were distracted by the restaurant staff's ungracious service at every turn.

Bill Williams, with bunched but helpless fists, furiously demanded an improvement in the waiters' manners and didn't get it. When Mrs Robin Dawkins requested coffee, she was told it was available in the bar.

Every table in the bar was by that time filled. Mrs Robin Dawkins headed straight out of the exit door to the car park without looking back. F. Harold Field and Russell Maudsley judiciously shook their heads at Bill Williams and vaguely said they would let him know.

Bill Williams thrust into F. Harold Field's arms the file-folder he'd been nursing all evening, and F. Harold Field, though looking at it as if he thought it contained dynamite, held on to the file, gingerly at first, and then strongly gripped it, and followed Mrs Dawkins and Russell Maudsley out to their car.

'I told you so,' Mrs Robin Dawkins ground out, thrusting out her jaw and driving fiercely away, 'a wimp of a boy who couldn't organize a sandwich.'

F. Harold Field said, 'I got the impression that Williams would have hit that head waiter if we and everyone else hadn't been watching.'

'Nonsense,' Mrs Dawkins contradicted, but F. Harold Field knew what he'd seen. He fingered the file that had been pushed into his arms and decided to read the contents in the morning.

Bill Williams returned to the dining-room, which was now empty of guests and being set up for the morning, and demanded to see the head waiter. None of the busy under-waiters hurried to help him, but one finally told him that the head waiter had gone home, his work finished for the night.

Bill Williams, rigid with unvented anger, stood as if planted immovably and insisted on seeing whoever was now in charge. The waiters shuffled a bit from foot to foot. People on boats were supposed to go quietly, not look as if at any minute they'd have the whole crew of them walking the plank at the end of the pier.

Perhaps he'd better see the management, one of them eventually and weakly suggested.

'At once,' Bill Williams said.

The management, located in a small room down a passage behind the bar, turned out to be an imposing woman in a flowing red and gold kaftan counting money. She was sitting behind a desk. She did not invite Bill Williams to sit in the chair across from her, but he did, anyway. She looked down her long thin nose.

She said, sounding as if such a thing were impossible, 'I'm told you have a complaint.'

Bill Williams forcefully described his ruined evening.

The management showed no surprise. 'When you booked a table,' she said, not disputing that the table had been booked, 'you should have said you would be arriving on a boat.'

'Why?'

'We do not accept boats.'

'Why not?'

'People on holiday on boats behave badly. They break things. They're noisy. They dirty our lavatories. They have wild children. They complain of our prices.'

'I booked a table in the ordinary way,' Bill Williams said with slow, distinct and heavy emphasis, 'and I am angry.'

The truth of that statement reached the management heavily enough to send a tremble through the kaftan, but she licked her lips and obstinately repeated, 'You should have said you were coming on a boat. When you booked the table you should have said it. Then we would have been prepared.'

'When I booked the table, you didn't say, "How will you be arriving?" You didn't say, "Will you be arriving in a Rolls-Royce?" "Will you be arriving on a tractor?" "On a bicycle?" "On foot?" My three guests came in a Daimler and you treated them as if they were here to steal your forks.'

The management tossed her head, compressed her lips and stared blindly at her wronged and steaming customer. She wanted him to go away. She had no appetite for a fight.

Bill Williams, who did have such an appetite, felt the militancy drain away in the management and, as always when he had won, his own hostility weakened. Lowering one's guard is lethal, he'd been often warned, but he'd never got the knack of kicking the fallen foe. He rose abruptly from the management's chair and sought the fresh night air and the path through the rose garden and the blue upholstered mattress in the punt.

He changed his clothes, folded back the punt's anti-rain canopies and lay in his sleeping bag looking up at the dry clear sky. He knew he'd lost any chance of editing the *Daily Troubadour*. He spent the night not sleeping but ceaselessly revolving in memory the humiliations heaped on him undeservedly and his own failure to make a public fuss. And would the public fuss have won him the *Troubadour*? Would it not more likely have passed into snigger-raising mythology, whereas now, if he read Mrs Robin Dawkins right, the evening would merely give her an 'I told you so' weapon in her internecine wars?

He fantasized about an appropriate revenge, doubting his ability to carry it out. As ex-editor he couldn't get the food columnist to do a demolition job: the same columnist that had given the recently opened restaurant a ten-star rave. As Mr Ordinary Citizen, he might fume without costing Mainstream Mile a fraction of his sleepless night.

Dawn brought him no sweet dreams. Full daylight found him putting the punt shipshape, though there was no joy left in his journey. In the next town downstream he would summon the Lechlade people to collect their boat.

Down the path through the rose garden came the same dark-suited waiter as before, though this time without the bouncing smirk.

'The management,' he said, 'invite you to take coffee ashore.'

'Coffee?'

'Served in the bar.'

He turned away and departed without waiting for a response.

Bill Williams didn't know, in fact, what response to make. Was coffee an olive branch? An apology? He felt far from accepting either. Could coffee, though, be a preliminary to the cancelling of his credit card slip? Had the management decided he shouldn't have to pay for their appalling treatment?

The management had not. It wasn't in any case the money that had infuriated Bill Williams, since his abrupt removal from the *Voice* had cost the new owners several noughts. He entered the restaurant intending to accept a refund grudgingly, but was offered not a cent.

He went into the bar, which was shuttered and dark at breakfast time. A waiter slowly came in and put on one of the small tables a tray bearing a cup and saucer, a cream jug, sugar, and a china pot of coffee.

And that was all. In cold disbelief Bill Williams drank two solitary cups of admittedly good strong coffee. No one came into the bar. No one said anything at all.

If the coffee were an olive branch, it was also an insult.

When he'd finished the second cupful Bill Williams rose from his small table and, going across the room, opened the exit door which led through a small vestibule to the car park outside. Over the entry door of every place in Britain licensed to sell alcoholic drink there has to be displayed by law the name of the licensee. Bill Williams, without a clear plan of retaliation, went to see at least the name behind the affront.

The name over the entrance door of Mainstream Mile was Pauline Kinser.

Kinser. A coincidence, but odd. Bill Williams turned back into the bar and found it, this time, not empty. The management lady from the previous evening stood there, flanked by four of her staff. They stood stiffly, bodyguards, but also vigilant that she shouldn't blame them for their behaviour.

'Are you,' Bill Williams asked the woman slowly, 'Pauline Kinser?'

She reluctantly nodded.

'Do I get an apology for last night?'

She said nothing at all.

He asked, 'Do you know anyone called Dennis?'

Bill Williams was aware only of deepening silence. Pauline Kinser's eyes stared at him darkly, wholly devoid of any admission of fault. He shook with a primitive impulse to slam her against the wall and frighten her into speech but was constrained not by clemency but by the thought of handcuffs.

Pauline Kinser felt relieved to see her difficult customer return to his punt and move off down river, and she believed she'd heard the last of him. She didn't even mention what she thought of as 'the unpleasantness' when her nephew Dennis Kinser drove in for one of their frequent business meetings. Dennis Kinser, always golden tongued, had first persuaded his unmarried aunt to sell her house to start the restaurant and then had raised a mortgage on it to set himself up as a racehorse trainer. His Aunt Pauline baulked at putting the proceeds of her house directly into a racing stable as she didn't like horses. Apart from that, in her eyes Dennis could do no wrong. Dennis it was who had chosen the comfortable chairs in the restaurant dining-room and the handsome tableware, Dennis who had engaged a chef of renown, Dennis who had dressed her in kaftans, Dennis who had enticed newspaper columnists to visit and dazzled them with excellence, and Dennis, too, who had made the rule of no boats.

'Restaurants in London turn away people they don't want,' he'd told his aunt. 'And I don't want vulgar hire boats clogging up our pier and attracting the hoi polloi.'

'No, Dennis,' his aunt said staunchly, seeing the sense of it.

Her nephew heard about the customer in the punt from the waiters in the kitchen and, vaguely troubled by their evasive self-justifications, he asked his aunt what had happened.

Dennis Kinser was only moderately dismayed. However badly he'd been wronged, one disgruntled diner couldn't ruin a brilliantly successful enterprise.

'This punt guy,' he said, looking through ledgers, 'he really had booked a table?'

'Yes, he had.'

'Then you should have served him decently, same as everyone else.'

'But you said no—'

'Yeah, yeah, but use some sense.'

Pauline Kinser's reservations book lay open on the desk. Dennis Kinser, glancing at it, asked, 'Which booking came from the man in the punt?'

'That one.' His aunt pointed. 'The first one for yesterday. Williams, four people, eight o'clock. We took his phone number too, of course.'

Dennis Kinser glanced at the phone number and his whole body lurched. He knew that number. He couldn't believe it. *Wouldn't* believe it. He tugged his aunt's phone roughly towards him, pushed the buttons and listened to the woman answering saying, '*Cotswold Voice*, good morning.'

Half speechless, Dennis Kinser asked to be connected to the racing writer who, as usual, was leaning back in his chair cleaning his nails.

'Williams?' the racing writer said. 'Sure, of course I know him. He used to be our editor. Bloody good at it too, though I wouldn't tell him. It was thanks to him you got all that publicity for your racing syndicates and such. He sent me to interview you, that day we had the photographer for the pics. What do you want him for?'

'I . . . er . . . I just wondered.' Dennis Kinser's throat felt glued together.

'Don't mess with him,' the racing writer said with half-solemn warning. 'He may look small and harmless but he strikes like a rattlesnake when he's angry.'

Swallowing, feeling light-headed, Dennis Kinser spoke next to the food columnist who'd given his Aunt Pauline the puff that had sent her soufflés soaring.

'Williams?' the food man said. 'He used to like me to do recipes. The new editor's got a chips and ketchup complex. Bill Williams asked me – well, he was probably joking, but he asked me where to take three business people to dinner who could make or break his whole future, so I said your aunt's place, and I know he phoned up straight away.'

Dennis Kinser put down the receiver with his whole brain repeating 'Oh my God', 'Oh my God', like a mantra.

'What's the matter?' his aunt asked. 'You've gone white.'

'That man Williams . . .' Dennis Kinser sounded strangled. 'What did you say to him to put things right?'

Pauline Kinser wrinkled her forehead. 'I gave him some coffee.'

'Coffee! And an abject apology? And his money back? And the grovel of the century?'

Confused, she shook her head. 'Just coffee.'

Her nephew, frightened, screamed at her, 'You stupid bitch. You bloody stupid bitch. That man will find a way of bankrupting us both. He writes for newspapers. And I owe him ... God, I owe him ... and he'll ruin us for last night.'

His aunt said mulishly, 'It's all your fault. It was you who said to turn away boats.'

In London that afternoon the Lionheart News Group held a monthly progress meeting consisting of the three warring proprietors, the business managers of all the Group's many newspapers and periodicals, and sundry financial advisers. No editors or journalists were ever invited to this sort of affair: to Mrs Robin Dawkins – acting as Chairman – they were merely the below-stairs hired help.

Mrs Dawkins treated the urgent need for a replacement editor for the *Daily Troubadour* – fourth on the agenda – as if she were lacking a butler. As long as he knew his place and was metaphorically good at keeping the silver untarnished, she could overlook an afternoon fondness for port. The dismayed managers tactfully tried to point out that the present editor's fondness for afternoon port was three-quarters of the trouble.

Russell Maudsley forcefully reported that Absalom Williams, ex-editor of the *Cotswold Voice*, whom they had at first considered, need not now be borne in mind, and F. Harold Field declared with even more emphasis that Absalom Williams at thirty-three was too young, had too many academic degrees and couldn't insist on getting his own way.

Several of the managers held their breath, not least a competent but thwarted woman from the *Daily Troubadour* who knew from experience that when Field and Maudsley agreed *against* a course of action Mrs Robin Dawkins would suddenly be *for*. As the majority shareholder she would *insist*, and the two men would shrug and give in.

The *Daily Troubadour* manager knew that most great editors hit the top in their middle thirties: that like orchestral conductors they either did or didn't have the flair. She listened to Mr Field complaining to Mrs Dawkins that moreover Williams couldn't even write, and then she read a portion of only one of the photocopied sheets that F. Harold had been lackadaisically distributing all round the table from a folder, and felt the instant impact of the fizzing Williams talent on the page. Not write? This was Gettysburg stuff.

Looking up, she saw F. Harold Field watching her. He smiled. He *wants* this Absalom, she thought.

That same afternoon Dennis Kinser's first explosive rage against his aunt had deepened painfully like mustard-gas burns. He sat leaning his elbows on her desk with his head in his hands, seeking a way out of a quicksand of debt.

His aunt grumbled repetitively, 'It was *you* who said no boats.'

'Shut *up*.'

'But—'

'Bugger the boats,' Dennis Kinser said violently, and his aunt, regally distinguished in a blue, silver and purple kaftan of Dennis's choosing, retired hurt and wept in the tiny sitting-room that held all that was left of her former home. She'd given Dennis everything else. She couldn't bear his anger. She didn't like horses. She hated the man in the punt.

Dennis Kinser's wheeler-dealing relied entirely on Mainstream Mile flourishing as the rave of the region. In spite of the *Voice* racing writer's golden superlatives there hadn't so far been enough promises of response to the couch potato gambling syndicates to fill even a short row of boxes, let alone the whole sparkling stable he craved. To bamboozle the horse-racing licensing department into believing that he had the qualifying dozen horses in his yard, he'd invented a few and brought in others limping from their retirement fields; and in a burst of typical hubris he'd promised to sponsor a two-mile hurdle at Marlborough races – the Kinser Cup. Fame would follow. Rich owners, impressed, would eat at his restaurant and send him horses galore. Fame and riches attracted fame and riches. He'd seen it. He, Dennis Kinser, would have both.

His trouble was, he was in too much of a hurry. He had that very morning sent out press releases to every publication even distantly aware that racing existed. His invitations to every influential pen couldn't be retrieved from the Royal Mail. He would in effect be shouting 'Look at me, I'm great', and the rattlesnake in the punt could print and publish, 'Look at him, he's a fraud', and the write-ups he'd get would be mocking instead of admiring.

Dennis Kinser groaned aloud.

Bill (Absalom Elvis etc.) Williams bought a copy of the *Cotswold Voice* the next day, Saturday, and winced his way from the headlines onwards.

On the racing page, his racing writer, now demoted to halfway down the space available, was happy to let readers know that their very own syndicate-forming trainer was sponsoring a race at Marlborough the following Saturday. 'Be there!' encouraged the *Voice*. 'Kinser can win.'

'Race to Mainstream Mile!' admonished the food column. 'A brilliant Kinser double!'

As he had always done to dilute disappointment and make frustration bearable, Bill Williams stretched for a ball-point and paper and wrote the knots out of his system.

He wrote with vigour, and unforgiving fire. He wrote from the sharp memory of humiliation and from an unappeased lust for revenge. He ridiculed Pauline Kinser for the pretension of her kaftans and the snobbery of her no-boats ban. He savagely pulverized the multiple lies of the make-believe glamorous racing stable and he jeered at Dennis Kinser himself for being a conceited humbug, a fast-talking trickster, a self-deluding sham. It was a piece designed and calculated to trample and destroy. It would probably never see public print.

One of Dennis Kinser's gaudy press releases ended up in the Lionheart News Group's little-used office of F. Harold Field. F. Harold, his hand hovering over the shredder, caught a glimpse of the words 'Mainstream Mile' and briefly glanced at the come-hither.

'Warm Welcome', he read, and smiled grimly. Not his lasting impression of the head waiter.

'Hurdle race sponsored by trainer Dennis Kinser, co-owner of Mainstream Mile. Buffet lunch. Restaurant chef. Chance to buy a share in a Syndicate!'

Hm . . . F. Harold Field, who liked a flutter, decided to go.

Bill Williams, Dennis Kinser and F. Harold Field collided at Marlborough racecourse.

During the past week the August days had been edged out by the chill of early September dawns.

During that week Bill Williams wrote five opinion and comment pieces and sent them all to the prestigious London broadsheets that had published him pre-*Voice.* They were enthusiastic on the telephone, but no one needed an editor.

During that week Dennis Kinser finally received from the syndicate fixer one half-paid-for but talented hurdler complete with an entry in the Kinser Cup. Dennis the ex-stable lad did know how to train horses and turn them out looking good. When the syndicate horse paraded before the Cup, its coat shone in the sun.

Dennis Kinser spent the rest of his week borrowing money and sucking the restaurant dry.

During that week F. Harold Field visited the Lionheart Group's managers one by one and left a pro-Williams consensus in his wake. Russell Maudsley nodded. Mrs Robin Dawkins, still believing her colleagues intended a thumbs down, said contrarily, 'I think you're wrong to ditch him, Harold.'

Waving his conspicuous invitation, F. Harold made his way from his (chauffeur-driven) Daimler up to the large private box where Dennis Kinser, though now running on an empty gas tank, was trying to buy himself a glittering future by the widespread indiscriminate application of champagne.

Dennis Kinser, not knowing by sight half the freeloaders guzzling his bubbles, gave F. Harold a wide hello and with an extravagant gesture put an arm familiarly round his guest's shoulders. A hard-headed businessman impervious to soft soap, oil and honey, F. Harold Field intensely disliked the too intimate unwanted pressure of the arm, but without shaking himself free he turned his well-groomed head to look Dennis Kinser in the eye and asked him straightly what Williams, the sometime editor of the *Cotswold Voice*, could possibly have done to be treated so insufferably by the management and staff of Mainstream Mile.

To F. Harold Field this was no idle question: he needed to know what would stir A. E. de V. Williams to clenched fists, and, beyond that, what would stop him from using them. F. Harold regularly judged people by their rages: sought the cause and watched the performance. When not overruled by Mrs Robin Dawkins (as he had been the last time they'd chosen an editor) F. Harold Field seldom made mistakes.

Dennis Kinser removed his arm from his guest's shoulders with sick speed. All week he'd been unable to sleep or eat with physical ease. Each day he'd expected to hear the rattlesnake and be pierced by the fangs. But this, he thought in bewilderment, this solid grey-suited taxpayer didn't match the racing writer's verbal identikit. This couldn't be the lean mean man in the punt.

F. Harold Field flatly said, 'As Williams' guest I was treated like dirt, and I don't know why. Give me a reason why all the papers and periodicals I co-own in the Lionheart Group shouldn't blow your house down.'

'But . . . b–but,' Dennis Kinser stuttered, aghast at this new abyss, 'he came in a boat.'

'He . . . *what*?'

Dennis Kinser abruptly left-wheeled and crashed into the gentlemen's retreat. He had taken days of drugs to control the bacteria in his gut, but nothing it seemed could anaesthetize the cataclysm he saw ahead.

F. Harold Field, still unsatisfied, went down (on the

non-reappearance of his host) to watch the horses as they plodded round the parade ring. Dennis Kinser's extravagant Cup lay two races ahead. F. Harold Field filled in time by winning modest third-place money on the Tote.

Bill (Absalom etc.) Williams drove to Marlborough races having read far too much all week about the Kinser glories. Kinser this and Kinser that . . . Kinser's horses, Kinser the trainer, Kinser on the Thames. Every racing page seemed to have paid in advance for a free lunch. The *Cotswold Voice* published a sunny encouragement, but the racing writer himself lounged at home to tele-watch with a couple of cans.

On the basis of 'know thine enemy', Bill Williams went to Marlborough races to learn what Dennis Kinser looked like. He saw the ballyhoo but not the man himself, who remained in pain in the gents'. Instead he came unexpectedly face to face with the Lionheart decision maker who had shaken his head as a death-toll over any dreams of *Troubadour* days.

F. Harold Field had expected more than silence from his Absalom Williams host. He'd seen the clenched fists. He now sought the cause bluntly.

'Why did you want to hit that restaurant's head waiter? And why didn't you?'

Bill Williams explained, 'He was insulting me on the management's say so. You don't shoot the messenger because of the message.'

He dug into a pocket and handed F. Harold a copy of the raging axe he'd taken on paper to Dennis Kinser. F. Harold Field glanced at it and started reading, eyebrows slowly rising towards hairline.

'Don't give that paper to anyone but Kinser,' Bill Williams said. 'I didn't write it for publication.'

Dennis Kinser, looking pale, came down to the parade ring before the Kinser Cup and put on a bravado performance as owner, sponsor and general king, all designed to grab media attention. Side by side, Bill Williams and F. Harold Field watched from afar and felt nauseated.

Twenty minutes later their nausea increased geometrically, as the syndicate horse, hooves flying, won the Kinser Cup.

Dennis Kinser's exultation and expanding arrogance filled the television screens of the nation. He announced he was the top trainer of the future and, inside, he believed it. Winning the race meant the exit of at least half of his money troubles, and surely, now, the rich and famous would flock to his stable.

It was while he preened himself in front of countless camera lenses that F. Harold Field gave him Bill Williams' lightning bolt.

The applauding crowds faded away towards the next race. Success on racecourses was ephemeral.

Dennis Kinser stood reading the explosive page in his hand and he faced his two ill-treated customers feeling that although he'd won the world he was going to lose it. Lose it over a bloody *punt.* It wasn't *fair.* He'd worked so hard . . .

In aggressive despair, he said bitterly to Absalom Elvis da Vinci Williams, 'What will you take not to publish this article?'

'Blackmail?' Bill Williams asked, surprised.

Dennis Kinser stuttered. 'Take the horse? Will that do you?'

'It's not yours to give,' Bill Williams said.

'What then? Money? Not the restaurant . . .' Panic rose in his voice. 'You can't . . . you can't do that . . .'

Bill Williams watched the real fear rising and thought it revenge enough.

'I'll take,' he said slowly, 'I'll take an apology, and my money back . . . and a notice in your bar and printed on your menu saying that people on boats are welcome, especially if they have booked a table in advance.'

Dennis Kinser blinked, swallowed, wavered, clenched his teeth and finally nodded. He didn't like it – he hated to be defeated – but compromise was better than destruction.

F. Harold Field stretched a hand forward, plucked the sheet of paper out of Dennis Kinser's hands and tore it up.

He said to Bill Williams, 'Come and see me in my office at the *Troubadour* on Monday.'

# NIGHTMARE

Nightmare *was commissioned by* The Times *in April 1974. (Three thousand words, please.)*

Nightmare, *set loosely in horse country, USA, explains how to steal a valuable brood mare and her unborn foal.*

*Don't do it!*

For three years after his father died Martin Retsov abandoned his chosen profession. To be successful he needed a partner, and partners as skilled as his father were hard to find. Martin Retsov took stock of his bank book, listed his investments, and decided that with a little useful paid employment to fill the days he could cruise along comfortably in second gear, waiting for life to throw up a suitable replacement.

A day's travel put him a welcome distance from the scene of his unhappier memories, although they themselves journeyed along with him, as inescapable as habit. Thoroughbred Foodstuffs Inc. gave him a month's trial as a salesman and when the orders swelled everywhere in his wake, a permanent post. Martin Retsov relaxed behind the wheel of the company car and drifted easily around his new area, visiting stud farms and racing stables and persuading their managers that even if Thoroughbred Foodstuffs were no better than anyone else's, at least they were no worse.

The customers of Thoroughbred Foodstuffs saw a big man in his late thirties with a rugged, slightly forbidding face and a way of narrowing his eyes to dark-lashed slits. The frank, open and sincere stock-in-trade expression of a salesman was nowhere to be seen, nor was there any obvious honey in his voice. The one factor which brought out the handshakes, the fountain pens and the cheque books was his formidable knowledge of horses. He could sum up a horse in a glance and make helpfully constructive suggestions in a throwaway fashion, never taking credit although it was due.

'I expect you've tried remedial shoeing,' he would say casually, or 'Don't you find vitamin B12 injections help build bone?' Second time around he was greeted as a trusted friend.

He prospered.

All the same he was in trouble. There was no peace in his sleep. When he slept, he woke always from a nightmare, his heart thumping, his skin prickling with cold instant sweat. Always a dream variation on the same theme – the violent untimely death of his father. Sometimes he saw the face, dead but still talking, with blood gushing out of the mouth. Sometimes he saw the wheel, the great fat black sharp-treaded tyre biting into the soft bulging belly.

Sometimes he felt he was inside his father's body, slipping and falling behind the loaded motor horsebox and having the life crushed out of him in one great unimaginable explosion of agony. Sometimes, but not so often, he saw the face of the other man who had been there, the callous man in the dark clothes, looking coldly down at his dying father and giving him no comfort, saying not a word.

Every morning Martin Retsov stood wearily under the shower, rinsing the stickiness from his body and wishing he could as easily sponge his subconscious mind. Every day, sliding into the car, he shed his night self and looked to the future. He saw foals born, watched them grow, traced their fortunes at auction and beyond. He could have told the trainers, better than they knew themselves, the breeding, history, career and fate of every horse he reached with Thoroughbred Food.

After nearly three years he had made many acquaintances – she was not a man to make friends. He knew every horse over a wide stretch of country and hundreds that had been sold out of it. He was the most efficient salesman in his company. And even his nightmares were at last becoming rarer.

One evening in early spring he picked up Johnnie Duke. A hitchhiker, a tall thin fair-haired youth looking not much above twenty, wearing faded jeans and an old leather jacket and carrying a few extra clothes in a canvas hold-all. Martin Retsov, in an expansive mood, took him to be a college kid on vacation and agreed to drop him forty miles down the road in the next town.

'Haven't I seen you before?' he asked, half puzzled, as the young man settled into the front seat beside him.

'Shouldn't think so.'

'Well . . .' He thought it over. 'Yeah, I've seen you. Day or two ago. Where would that be?'

The young man took his time over answering. Then he said, 'I hitch up and down this road pretty regular. Maybe you saw me thumbing.'

Martin Retsov nodded several times. 'Yeah, yeah. That's it.' He relaxed in his seat, glad to have resolved the small mystery. He liked to be sure of things. 'That's where I've seen you. On the road. More than once.'

The young man nodded briefly and said he was glad Martin had stopped for him because he had a date with his girl.

'I don't often stop for hitchers,' Martin Retsov said,

and thought with amusement that three easy years must have softened him.

They drove amicably together for five miles and passed alongside the white railed paddocks of a prosperous stud farm. Martin Retsov cast a rapid assessing eye over the small groups of animals grazing the new spring grass but kept his thoughts unspoken.

It was Johnnie Duke who said, 'It's odd you never get a piebald thoroughbred.'

'You know about horses?' Martin Retsov asked, surprised.

'Sure. I was raised with them.'

Martin Retsov asked him where, but the young man evasively said he'd had some trouble back home and left in a hurry, and he didn't exactly want to talk about it. Martin Retsov smiled. He dropped Johnnie Duke in the next town and drove on towards his destination, and it was only when he stopped to fill up his tank that the remains of the smile vanished as smartly as investors in a depression.

Johnnie Duke had stolen his wallet. Retsov kept it in the inside pocket of his jacket, and his jacket, owing to the efficiency of the heater, had been lying on the back seat of the car. He remembered Johnnie Duke putting his hold-all on the floor behind the front seats, and he remembered him leaning over to pick it up. His rugged face hardened to something his customers had never seen, and the eyes slitted as narrow and glittery as ice chips. The sum of money he had lost was small compared to the affront to his self-respect.

For several days he drove round his area actively searching for Johnnie Duke, remembering details about him from their drive together. The hesitation when Martin had said he'd seen him before. The refusal to say where he'd come from. The slickness with which he'd spotted and extracted the wallet. Martin Retsov searched for him with a hard face but without success and finally, after two or three weeks, he accepted the fact that the young man had gone away to another district where irate victims in cars were not looking for him sharp-eyed.

Regularly once a month Martin Retsov called at the furthest stud farm in his area, and it was as he left there, early one evening, that he again saw Johnnie Duke. Standing by the roadside, lifting his thumb, hesitating perhaps when he saw Retsov's car.

Martin drove up fast beside him, braked to a wheel-locked standstill, opened his door, and stood up smoothly outside it. For a big man he moved like oiled machinery, precise and efficient; and he held a gun. 'Get in the car,' he said.

Johnnie Duke looked at the barrel pointing straight at his stomach and turned pale. He swallowed, his larynx making a convulsive movement in his neck, and slowly did as he was told.

'I'll pay back the money,' he said anxiously, as Martin Retsov slid onto the seat beside him. The gun was held loosely now, pointing at the floor, but both were aware that this could change.

'I should hand you over to the police,' Martin Retsov said.

The young man dumbly shook his head.

'Or you could do a little job for me instead.'

The young man looked at Martin Retsov's slitted eyes and visibly shivered.

'Is this blackmail?' he asked him.

'I'll pay you, if you're any good.'

'Doing what?'

'Stealing horses,' Martin Retsov said.

He made his plans as meticulously as in the old days with his father, untraceably buying a two-horse trailer and a car to pull it; and hiding them away in a city lock-up garage. He decided against the large type of motor horsebox he had used with his father, mostly because of the nightmares about those wheels. Besides, he was not sure if his new apprentice would be suitable for long-term planning. They would do one trial run – a test, Martin Retsov thought, before he offered a steady partnership for the future.

Johnnie Duke had greeted Martin Retsov's announcement of his chosen profession with a huge relieved grin.

'Sure,' he said. 'I can steal horses. Which ones?'

'It's not so easy round here,' Martin Retsov said. 'Training stables and stud farms have good security arrangements.' But he knew them all; he had been assiduously studying them for three years.

He gave Johnnie Duke a list of things to buy and some money for himself, and two days later they inspected together the resulting mole-grip wrench and bolt cutters.

'There is no time to waste,' Martin Retsov said. 'We will go ahead tomorrow night.'

'So soon?'

Martin Retsov smiled. 'We are taking two brood mares. One is near to foaling. We want her safely away before that happens.'

Johnnie Duke looked at him in long surprise. 'Why don't we take good fast racers?' he said.

'They're too easily identified. Tattoo marks and registrations see to that. But foals, now. Newborn foals. Who's to say which is which? So we take a top-class mare, now in foal by the best sire, and we drive her a long way off and sell her at the end of the journey to some owner or trainer who is glad to get a fabulously bred foal for a fraction of what it would cost him at auction.

'The star foal is swapped soon after birth with any other one handy, and is registered and tattooed in its new identity. Its new owner knows what he's really got, so after racing it he keeps it for stud. Some of my clients in the past have made millions out of these foals. I always collect a small percentage.'

Johnnie Duke listened with his mouth open.

'This is not casual thieving,' Martin Retsov said with a certain pride. 'This is like stealing the Mona Lisa.'

'But what happens to the brood mare afterwards? And to the other foal?'

'Some of my clients have consciences. For these, for a consideration, I collect the mare and foal and dump them in any convenient field. If the owner of the field is honest, she gets identified and sent home.'

Johnnie Duke did not ask what happened when the client had no conscience. He swallowed.

'Do you already have a buyer for the two we're taking tomorrow?' he asked.

'Of course. You don't steal a Leonardo da Vinci on spec.' Martin Retsov laughed at the idea, showing a strong row of teeth. 'When we've got the mares I'll tell you where to go. You will go alone. And you will bring back the money.'

Johnnie Duke was again surprised. 'Can you trust me?' he asked.

'I want to find out.'

The following evening at dusk they collected the newly bought car and hitched on the trailer. Martin Retsov had difficulty manoeuvring the two linked vehicles in the small courtyard which enclosed the lock-up garage, and Johnnie Duke, trying to be helpful, went to the rear of the trailer to report how much space there was for reversing.

'Get away from there,' Martin Retsov said sharply. 'Get away at once.' He stood up out of the car and Johnnie Duke saw that he was shaking.

'I was only . . .' he began.

'You are never to go behind the trailer. Understand? Never.'

'Well, all right. If you say so.'

Martin Retsov took several deep breaths and wiped the palms of his hands on his trousers. He was horrified at the strength of his own reaction. Three years, he thought, had hardly blunted the terror at all. He wondered whether, if his nerves were so jumpy, it might not be better to abandon the whole project. He wondered whether the fact that it had taken him three years to get back to his business meant that deep down he was afraid to get back.

He licked his lips. His heartbeat settled down. This time there would be no ambush when he took the horses. That last time his potential client had betrayed him to the police, but this time it was perfectly safe. This client had bought three top-grade foals in the past and had been delighted to hear he could now have two more. Martin Retsov eased himself back into the car, and Johnnie Duke climbed in beside him.

'What's the matter?' Johnnie asked.

'I saw an accident once. Man fell behind a horsebox.'

'Oh.'

Martin Retsov shut his mouth on the untellable details, but they rolled on inexorably through his mind. The ambush. Police spotlights suddenly shining out before his father was safe up beside him in the horsebox's cab. He'd had to reverse a yard or two to get a clear run at the only space left between the police cars and the fence. He'd thrown the lever, stamped on the accelerator, shot backwards – he would never forget his father's scream. Never.

Just one scream, cut short. He'd jumped from the cab and seen the tyre cutting into the belly, seen the blood pouring out of the dying mouth . . . and the other man, the policeman, standing there looking down and doing nothing to help.

'Help him!' Retsov had said frantically.

'Help him yourself.'

He leaped back to the cab, climbed panic-stricken into the driving seat, knowing even as he pushed at the gear lever with a disembodied hand that his father was dead.

Dead. Past help, past saving, past everything.

He rolled the horsebox forward off the crushed body and he kept on going. He took the police by surprise. He drove the horsebox at 65 for two miles, and long before they caught up he had abandoned it and taken to the woods.

The police had not known his name, which he prudently never divulged to his clients. All the police had was one quick sight of him *in extremis*, which was not enough, and evasion and escape had in the end proved the smallest of his personal problems.

He had never forgotten the face of the policeman who had looked down at his father. A senior policeman, wearing authority and insignia. He saw him too often in his uneasy dreams . . .

Martin Retsov shook off the regretted past and applied his concentration to the theft in hand. He had expected to feel the old anticipation, the old excitement, the pleasing racing of the pulse. He felt none of these things. He felt old.

'Come on,' said Johnnie Duke. 'Or it will be light again before I deliver the goods.'

Martin Retsov nodded unwillingly and committed them both to the enterprise. Half an hour later when they pulled up in a dark side road he had succeeded in thrusting his soul's shadows back into their closet and was approaching the next half-hour with cool, calm practicality.

They stepped quietly from the car and let down the ramp of the trailer. The night closed around them – small sounds, light sighing wind, stars showing in sparkling bunches between greyly drifting clouds. Traffic on the high road half a mile away swept past now and then, more a matter of flashing lights than of noise. Martin Retsov waited for his eyes to grow used to the dark, then he put his hand lightly on the young man's arm.

'This way,' he said. His voice was a gentle whisper and when he moved his feet were soundless on the grass verge. Johnnie Duke followed him, marvelling at the big man's silence and easy speed.

'Where are we?' Johnnie whispered. 'Whose horses are we taking?'

'Never you mind.'

They came to a gate, padlocked. The bolt cutter made it easy. They slid through into the field. Martin Retsov whistled gently in the dark, a seductive gypsy trill in the teeth.

He pulled out a handful of Thoroughbred horse nuts and called persuasively into the blackness ahead.

'Come on, then, girl. Come on.'

There was a soft warm whinny and movement somewhere out beyond sight. Then they came, slowly, enquiringly, moving towards this human voice. They ate the nuts held out to them and made no fuss when the two men took hold of their headed collars.

'You go ahead,' Martin Retsov said softly to Johnnie Duke. 'I'll be right behind you.'

They went sweetly, the two great mares big with four-legged assets. Out of the gate and down the road to the transport. Easy as ever, thought Martin Retsov, once you knew what to take. Johnnie Duke led his mare into the trailer and fastened her there.

And that was when the nightmare began again. That was when the lights shone out, blinding Martin Retsov's adjusted sight. That was when the man stepped out to confront him. The same man. The face from the dreams. The same callous face, dark clothes, high-rank insignia.

'Martin Retsov,' he was saying, 'I arrest you . . .'

Martin Retsov was not listening. He was thinking wildly that it simply couldn't be true. This particular client would never betray him. Never.

The police took the mare from his unresisting charge and put handcuffs round Martin Retsov's wrists.

'How did you get here?' he asked blankly.

'We've been looking for you for three years,' said the policeman with smug satisfaction. 'A few weeks ago we found you. But we had no conclusive evidence against you, so we've been keeping you in sight ever since.'

Johnnie Duke came out of the trailer, and Martin Retsov thought it was hard on the boy, being caught on his first job. The cold policeman walked over to him, looking pleased.

He brought out no handcuffs. He patted Johnnie on the shoulder.

'Well done, Sergeant Duke,' he said.

# CARROT FOR A CHESTNUT

*Out of the blue in 1970 I was invited by the prestigious American magazine* Sports Illustrated *to write a short story for them – length and subject matter to be my own choice. I hadn't at that time ever attempted a short story but the result,* Carrot for a Chestnut, *must have seemed OK to their editors, because they invited me to stay in Lexington with the* Sports Illustrated *team assembled there to cover the 1972 Kentucky Derby. I was commissioned to write a Derby-day story for the Kentucky Derby issue the following year.*

Chick stood and sweated with the carrot in his hand. His head seemed to be floating and he couldn't feel his feet on the ground, and the pulse thudded massively in his ear. A clammy green pain shivered in his gut.

Treachery was making him sick.

The time: fifty minutes before sunrise. The morning: cold. The raw swirling wind was clearing its throat for a fiercer blow, and a heavy layer of nimbo-stratus was fighting every inch of the way against the hint of light. In the neat box stalls round the stable-yard the dozing horses struck a random hoof against a wooden wall, rattled a tethering chain, sneezed the hay dust out of a moist black nostril.

Chick was late. Two hours late. He'd been told to give the carrot to the lanky chestnut at four o'clock in the morning, but at four o'clock in the morning it had been pouring with rain – hard, slanting rain that soaked a man to the skin in one minute flat, and Chick had reckoned it would be too difficult explaining away a soaking at four o'clock in the morning. Chick had reckoned it would be better to wait until the rain stopped, it couldn't make any difference. Four o'clock, six o'clock, what the hell. Chick always knew better than anyone else.

Chick was a thin, disgruntled nineteen-year-old who always felt the world owed him more than he got. He had been a bad-tempered, argumentative child and an aggressively rebellious adolescent. The resulting snarling habit of mind was precisely what was now hindering his success as an adult. Not that Chick would have agreed, of course. Chick never agreed with anyone if he could help it. Always knew better, did Chick.

He was unprepared for the severity of the physical symptoms of fear. His usual attitude towards any form of authority was scorn (and authority had not so far actually belted him one across his sulky mouth). Horses had never scared him because he had been born to the saddle and had grown up mastering everything on four legs with contemptuous ease. He believed in his heart that no one could really ride better than he could. He was wrong.

He looked apprehensively over his shoulder, and the shifting pain in his stomach sharply intensified. He had a fierce urge to defecate. That simply couldn't happen, he thought wildly. He'd heard about people's bowels getting loose with fear. He hadn't believed it. It couldn't happen. Now, all of a sudden, he feared it could. He tightened all his muscles desperately, and the spasm slowly passed. It left fresh sweat standing out all over his skin and no saliva in his mouth.

The house was dark. Upstairs, behind the black open window with the pale curtain flapping in the spartan air, slept Arthur Morrison, trainer of the forty-three racehorses in the stables below. Morrison habitually slept lightly. His ears were sharper than half a dozen guard dogs', his stable-hands said.

Chick forced himself to turn his head away, to walk in view of that window, to take the ten exposed steps down to the chestnut's stall.

If the guv'nor woke up and saw him . . . Gawd, he thought furiously, he hadn't expected it to be like this. Just a lousy walk down the yard to give a carrot to the gangly chestnut. Guilt and fear and treachery. They bypassed his sneering mind and erupted through his nerves instead.

He couldn't see anything wrong with the carrot. It hadn't been cut in half and hollowed out and packed with drugs and tied together again. He'd tried pulling the thick end out like a plug, and that hadn't worked either. The carrot just looked like any old carrot, any old carrot you'd watch your ma chop up to put in a stew. Any old carrot you'd give to any old horse. Not a very young, succulent carrot or a very aged carrot, knotted and woody. Just any old ordinary *carrot*.

But strangers didn't proposition you to give any old carrot to one special horse in the middle of the night. They didn't give you more than you earned in half a year when you said you'd do it. Any old carrot didn't come wrapped carefully alone in a polythene bag inside an empty cheese-biscuit packet, given to you by a stranger in a car park after dark in a town six miles from the stables. You didn't give any old carrot in the middle of the night to a chestnut who was due to start favourite in a high-class steeplechase eleven hours later.

Chick was getting dizzy with holding his breath by the time he'd completed the ten tiptoed steps to the chestnut's stall. Trying not to cough, not to groan, not to let out the strangling tension in a sob, he curled his sweating fingers around the bolt and began the job of easing it out, inch by frightening inch, from its socket.

By day, he slammed the bolts open and shut with a smart practised flick. His body shook in the darkness with the strain of moving by fractions.

The bolt came free with the tiniest of grating noises, and the top half of the split door swung slowly outwards. No squeaks from the hinges, only the whisper of metal on metal. Chick drew in a long breath like a painful, trickling, smothered gasp and let it out between clamped teeth. His stomach lurched again, threateningly. He took another quick, appalled grip on himself and thrust his arm in a panic through the dark, open space.

Inside the stall, the chestnut was asleep, dozing on his feet. The changing swirl of air from the opening door moved the sensitive hairs around his muzzle and raised his mental state from semiconsciousness to inquisitiveness. He could smell the carrot. He could also smell the man: smell the fear in the man's sweat.

'Come on,' Chick whispered desperately. 'Come on, then, boy.'

The horse moved his nose around towards the carrot and finally, reluctantly, his feet. He took the carrot indifferently from the man's trembling palm, whiffling it in with his black mobile lips, scrunching it languidly with large rotations of jaw. When he had swallowed all the pulped-up bits, he poked his muzzle forward for more. But there was no more, just the lighter square of sky darkening again as the door swung shut, just the faint sounds of the bolt going back, just the fading smell of the man and the passing taste of carrot. Presently he forgot about it and turned slowly round again so that his hindquarters were towards the door, because he usually stood that way, and after a minute or two he blinked slowly, rested his near hind leg lazily on the point of the hoof and lapsed back into twilight mindlessness.

Down in his stomach the liquid narcotic compound with which the carrot had been injected to saturation gradually filtered out of the digesting carrot cells and began to be absorbed into the bloodstream. The process was slow and progressive. And it had started two hours late.

Arthur Morrison stood in his stable-yard watching his men load the chestnut into the motor horsebox that was to take him to the races. He was eyeing the proceedings with an expression that was critical from habit and bore little relation to the satisfaction in his mind. The chestnut was the best horse in his stable: a frequent winner, popular with the public, a source of prestige as well as revenue. The big steeplechase at Cheltenham had been tailor-made for him from the day its conditions had been published, and Morrison was adept at producing a horse in peak condition for a particular race. No one seriously considered that the chestnut would be beaten. The newspapers had tipped it to a man and the bookmakers were fighting shy at 6–4 on. Morrison allowed himself a glimmer of warmth in the eyes and a twitch of smile to the lips as the men clipped shut the heavy doors of the horsebox and drove it out of the yard.

These physical signs were unusual. The face he normally wore was a compound of concentration and disapproval in roughly equal proportions. Both qualities contributed considerably to his success as a racehorse trainer and to his unpopularity as a person, a fact Morrison himself was well aware of. He didn't in the least care that almost no one liked him. He valued success and respect much more highly than love and held in incredulous contempt all those who did not.

Across the yard Chick was watching the horsebox drive away, his usual scowl in place. Morrison frowned irritably. The boy was a pest, he thought. Always grousing, always impertinent, always trying to scrounge up more money. Morrison didn't believe in boys having life made too easy: a little hardship was good for the soul. Where Morrison and Chick radically differed was the point at which each thought hardship began.

Chick spotted the frown and watched Morrison fearfully, his guilt pressing on him like a rock. He couldn't know, he thought frantically. He couldn't even suspect there was anything wrong with the horse or he wouldn't have let him go off to the races. The horse had looked all right, too. Absolutely his normal self.

Perhaps there had been nothing wrong with the carrot ... Perhaps it had been the wrong carrot, even ... Chick glanced around uneasily and knew very well he was fooling himself. The horse might look all right but he wasn't.

Arthur Morrison saddled up his horse at the races, and Chick watched him from ten nervous paces away, trying to hide in the eager crowd that pushed forward for a close view of the favourite. There was a larger admiring crowd outside the chestnut's saddling stall than for any of the other seven runners, and the bookmakers had shortened their odds. Behind Morrison's concentrated expression an itch of worry was growing insistent. He pulled the girth tight and adjusted the buckles automatically, acknowledging to himself that his former satisfaction had changed to anxiety. The horse was not himself. There were no lively stamping feet, no playful nips from the teeth, no response to the crowd; this was a horse that usually played to the public like a film star. He couldn't be feeling well, and if he wasn't feeling well he wouldn't win. Morrison tightened his mouth. If the horse were not well enough to win, he would prefer him not to run at all. To be beaten at odds-on would be a disgrace. A defeat on too large a scale. A loss of face. Particularly as Morrison's own eldest son Toddy was to be the jockey. The newspapers would tear them both to pieces.

Morrison came to a decision and sent for the vet.

The rules of jump racing in England stated quite clearly that if a horse had been declared a runner in a race, only the say-so of a veterinary surgeon was sufficient grounds for withdrawing him during the last three-quarters of an hour before post time. The Cheltenham racecourse veterinary surgeon came and looked at the chestnut and, after consulting with Morrison, led it off to a more private stall and took its temperature.

'His temperature's normal,' the vet assured Morrison.

'I don't like the look of him.'

'I can't find anything wrong.'

'He's not well,' Morrison insisted.

The vet pursed his lips and shook his head. There was nothing obviously wrong with the horse, and he knew he would be in trouble himself if he allowed Morrison to withdraw so hot a favourite on such slender grounds. Not only that, this was the third application for withdrawal he'd had to consider that afternoon. He had refused both the others, and the chestnut was certainly in no worse a state.

'He'll have to run,' the vet said positively, making up his mind.

Morrison was furious and went raging off to find a steward, who came and looked at the chestnut and listened to the vet and confirmed that the horse would have to run whether Morrison liked it or not. Unless, that was, Morrison cared to involve the horse's absent owner in paying a heavy fine?

With a face of granite Morrison resaddled the chestnut, and a stable-lad led him out into the parade ring, where most of the waiting public cheered and a few wiser ones looked closely and hurried off to hedge their bets.

With a shiver of dismay, Chick saw the horse reappear and for the first time regretted what he'd done. That stupid vet, he thought violently. He can't see what's under his bloody nose, he couldn't see a barn at ten paces. Anything that happened from then on was the vet's fault, Chick thought. The vet's responsibility, absolutely. The man was a criminal menace, letting a horse run in a steeplechase with dope coming out of its eyeballs.

Toddy Morrison had joined his father in the parade ring and together they were watching with worried expressions as the chestnut plodded lethargically around the oval walking track. Toddy was a strong, stocky professional jockey in his late twenties with an infectious grin and a generous view of life that represented a direct rejection of his father's. He had inherited the same strength of mind but had used it to leave home at eighteen to ride races for other trainers, and had only consented to ride for his father when he could dictate his own terms. Arthur Morrison, in consequence, respected him deeply. Between them they had won a lot of races.

Chick didn't actually dislike Toddy Morrison, even though, as he saw it, Toddy stood in his way. Occasionally Arthur let Chick ride a race if Toddy had something better or couldn't make the weight. Chick had to share these scraps from Toddy's table with two or three other lads in the yard who were, though he didn't believe it, as good as he was in the saddle. But though the envy curdled around inside him and the snide remarks came out sharp and sour as vinegar, he had never actually come to hate Toddy. There was something about Toddy that you couldn't hate, however good the reason. Chick hadn't given thought to the fact that it would be Toddy who would have to deal with the effects of the carrot. He had seen no further than his own pocket. He wished now that it had been some other jockey. Anyone but Toddy.

The conviction suddenly crystallized in Chick's mind as he looked at Toddy and Morrison standing there worried in the parade ring that he had never believed the chestnut would actually start in the race. The stranger, Chick said to himself, had distinctly told him the horse would be too sick to start. I wouldn't have done it, else, Chick thought virtuously. I wouldn't have done it. It's bloody dangerous, riding a doped steeplechaser. I wouldn't have done that to Toddy. It's not my fault he's going to ride a doped steeplechaser, it's that vet's fault for not seeing. It's that stranger's fault, he told me distinctly the horse wouldn't be fit to start . . .

Chick remembered with an unpleasant jerk that he'd been two hours late with the carrot. Maybe if he'd been on time the drug would have come out more and the vet would have seen . . .

Chick jettisoned this unbearable theory instantly on the grounds that no one can tell how seriously any particular horse will react to a drug or how quickly it will work, and he repeated to himself the comforting self-delusion that the stranger had promised him the horse wouldn't even start – though the stranger had not in fact said any such thing. The stranger, who was at the races, was entirely satisfied with the way things were going and was on the point of making a great deal of money.

The bell rang for the jockeys to mount. Chick bunched his hands in his pockets and tried not to visualize what could happen to a rider going over jumps at thirty miles an hour on a doped horse. Chick's body began playing him tricks again: he could feel the sweat trickling down his back and the pulse had come back in his ears.

Supposing he told them, he thought. Supposing he just ran out there into the ring and told Toddy not to ride the horse, it hadn't a chance of jumping properly, it was certain to fall, it could kill him bloody easily because its reactions would be all shot to bits.

Supposing he did. The way they'd look at him. His imagination blew a fuse and blanked out on that picture because such a blast of contempt didn't fit in with his overgrown self-esteem. He could not, could *not* face the fury they would feel. And it might not end there. Even if he told them and saved Toddy's life, they might tell the police. He wouldn't put it past them. And he could end up in the dock. Even in jail. They weren't going to do that to him, not to *him*. He wasn't going to give them the chance. He should have been paid more. Paid more because he was worth more. If he'd been paid more, he wouldn't have needed to take the stranger's money. Arthur Morrison had only himself to blame.

Toddy would have to risk it. After all, the horse didn't look too bad, and the vet had passed it, hadn't he, and maybe the carrot being two hours late was all to the good and it wouldn't have done its work properly yet, and in fact it was really thanks to Chick if it hadn't; only thanks to him that the drug was two hours late and that nothing much would happen, really, anyway. Nothing much would happen. Maybe the chestnut wouldn't actually *win*, but Toddy would come through all right. Of course he would.

The jockeys swung up into their saddles, Toddy among them. He saw Chick in the crowd, watching, and sketched an acknowledging wave. The urge to tell and the fear of telling tore Chick apart like the Chinese trees.

Toddy gathered up the reins and clicked his tongue and steered the chestnut indecisively out onto the track. He was disappointed that the horse wasn't feeling well but not in the least apprehensive. It hadn't occurred to him, or to Arthur Morrison, that the horse might be doped. He cantered down to the post standing in his stirrups, replanning his tactics mentally now that he couldn't rely on reserves in his mount. It would be a difficult race now to win. Pity.

Chick watched him go. He hadn't come to his decision, to tell or not to tell. The moment simply passed him by. When Toddy had gone, he unstuck his leaden feet and plodded off to the stands to watch the race, and in every corner of his mind little self-justifications sprang up like nettles. A feeling of shame tried to creep in round the edges, but he kicked it out smartly. They should have paid him more. It was their fault, not his.

He thought about the wad of notes the stranger had given him with the carrot. Money in advance. The stranger had trusted him, which was more than most people seemed to. He'd locked himself into the bathroom and counted the notes, counted them twice, and they were all there, just as the stranger had promised. He had never had so much money all at once in his life before . . . Perhaps he never would again, he thought. And if he'd told Arthur Morrison and Toddy about the dope, he would have to give up that money, give up the money and more . . .

Finding somewhere to hide the money had been difficult. The bundle of used notes had turned out to be quite bulky, and he didn't want to risk his ma poking around among his things, like she did, and coming across them. He'd solved the problem temporarily by rolling them up and putting them in a brightly coloured round tin which once held toffees but which he used for years for storing brushes and polish for cleaning his shoes. He had covered the money with a duster and jammed the tin back on the shelf in his bedroom where it always stood. He thought he would probably have to find somewhere safer, in the end. And he'd have to be careful how he spent the money – there would be too many questions asked if he just went out and bought a car. He'd always wanted a car . . . and now he had the money for one . . . and he still couldn't get the car. It wasn't fair. Not fair at all. If they'd paid him more . . . Enough for a car . . .

Up on the well-positioned area of stands set aside for trainers and jockeys, a small man with hot dark eyes put his hand on Chick's arm and spoke to him, though it was several seconds before Chick started to listen.

'. . . I see you are here, and you're free, will you ride it?'

'What?' said Chick vaguely.

'My horse in the Novice Hurdle,' said the little man impatiently. 'Of course, if you don't want to . . .'

'Didn't say that,' Chick mumbled. 'Ask the guv'nor. If he says I can, well, I can.'

The small trainer walked across the stand to where Arthur Morrison was watching the chestnut intently through the race glasses and asked the same question he'd put to Chick.

'Chick? Yes, he can ride it for you, if you want him.' Morrison gave the other trainer two full seconds of his attention and glued himself back on to his race glasses.

'My jockey was hurt in a fall in the first race,' explained the small man. 'There are so many runners in the Novice Hurdle that there's a shortage of jockeys. I just saw that boy of yours, so I asked him on the spur of the moment, see?'

'Yes, yes,' said Morrison, 90 per cent uninterested. 'He's moderately capable, but don't expect too much of him.' There was no spring in the chestnut's stride. Morrison wondered in depression if he was sickening for the cough.

'My horse won't win. Just out for experience you might say.'

'Yes. Well, fix it with Chick.' Several other stables had the coughing epidemic, Morrison thought. The chestnut couldn't have picked a worse day to catch it.

Chick, who would normally have welcomed the offer of a ride with condescending complacency, was so preoccupied that the small trainer regretted having asked him. Chick's whole attention was riveted on the chestnut which seemed to be lining up satisfactorily at the starting tape. Nothing wrong, Chick assured himself. Everything was going to be all right. Of course, it was. Stupid getting into such a state.

The start was down the track to the left, with two

fences to be jumped before the horses came past the stands and swung away again on the left-hand circuit. As it was a jumping race, they were using tapes instead of stalls, and as there was no draw either, Toddy had lined up against the inside rails, ready to take the shortest way home.

Down in the bookmakers' enclosure they were offering more generous odds now and some had gone boldly to evens. The chestnut had cantered past them on his way to the start looking not his brightest and best. The bookmakers in consequence were feeling more hopeful. They had expected a bad day, but if the chestnut lost, they would profit. One of them would profit terrifically – just as he would lose terrifically if the chestnut won.

Alexander McGrant (Est. 1898), real name Harry Buskins, had done this sort of thing once or twice before. He spread out his fingers and looked at them admiringly. Not a tremble in sight. And there was always a risk in these things that the boy he'd bribed would get cold feet at the last minute and not go through with the job. Always a gamble, it was. But this time, this boy, he was pretty sure of. You couldn't go wrong if you sorted out a vain little so-and-so with a big grudge. Knockovers, that sort were. Every time.

Harry Buskins was a shrewd middle-aged East End Londoner for whom there had never been any clear demarcation between right and wrong, and a man who thought that if you could rig a nice little swindle now and then, well, why not? Tax was killing betting, you had to make a quick buck where you could, and there was nothing quite so sure or quick as raking in the dough on a red-hot favourite and knowing for certain that you weren't going to have to pay out.

Down at the post the starter put his hand on the lever and the tapes went up with a rush. Toddy kicked his chestnut smartly in the ribs. From his eyrie on top of the stand the commentator moved smartly into his spiel. 'They're off, and the first to show is the grey . . .' Arthur Morrison and Chick watched with hearts thumping from different sorts of anxiety, and Harry Buskins shut his eyes and prayed.

Toddy drove forward at once into the first three, the chestnut beneath him galloping strongly, pulling at the bit, thudding his hooves into the ground. He seemed to be going well enough, Toddy thought. Strong. Like a train.

The first fence lay only one hundred yards ahead now, coming nearer. With a practised eye Toddy measured the distance, knew the chestnut's stride would meet it right, collected himself for the spring and gave the horse the signal to take off. There was no response. Nothing. The chestnut made no attempt to bunch his muscles, no attempt to gather himself on to his haunches, no attempt to waver or slow down or take any avoiding action whatsoever. For one incredulous second Toddy knew he was facing complete and imminent disaster.

The chestnut galloped straight into the three-foot-thick, chest-high solid birch fence with an impact that brought a groan of horror from the stands. He turned a somersault over the fence with a flurry of thrashing legs, threw Toddy off in front of him and fell down on top and rolled over him.

Chick felt as if the world were turning grey. The colours drained out of everything and he was halfway to fainting. Oh God, he thought. Oh God. *Toddy.*

The chestnut scrambled to his feet and galloped away. He followed the other horses towards the second fence, stretching out into a relentless stride, into a full-fledged thundering racing pace.

He hit the second fence as straight and hard as the first. The crowd gasped and cried out. Again the somersault, the spreadeagled legs, the crashing fall, the instant recovery. The chestnut surged up again and galloped on.

He came up past the stands, moving inexorably, the stirrups swinging out from the empty saddle, flecks of foam flying back now from his mouth, great dark patches of sweat staining his flanks. Where the track curved round to the left, the chestnut raced straight on. Straight on across the curve, to crash into the rail around the outside of the track. He took the solid timber across the chest and broke it in two. Again he fell in a thrashing heap and again he rocketed to his feet. But this time not to gallop away. This time he took three painful limping steps and stood still.

Back at the fence Toddy lay on the ground with first-aid men bending over him anxiously. Arthur Morrison ran down from the stands towards the track and didn't know which way to turn first, to his son or his horse. Chick's legs gave way and he sagged down in a daze on to the concrete steps. And down in the bookmakers' enclosure Harry Buskins' first reaction of delight was soured by wondering whether, if Toddy Morrison were badly injured, that stupid boy Chick would be scared enough to keep his mouth shut.

Arthur Morrison turned towards his son. Toddy had been knocked unconscious by the fall and had had all the breath squeezed out of him by the chestnut's weight, but by the time his father was within one hundred yards he was beginning to come round. As soon as Arthur saw the supine figure move, he turned brusquely round and hurried off towards the horse: it would never do to show Toddy the concern he felt. Toddy would not respect him for it, he thought.

The chestnut stood patiently by the smashed rail, only dimly aware of the dull discomfort in the foreleg that wouldn't take his weight. Arthur Morrison and the veterinary surgeon arrived beside him at the same time, and Arthur Morrison glared at the vet.

'You said he was fit to run. The owner is going to hit the roof when he hears about it.' Morrison tried to keep a grip on a growing internal fury at the injustice of fate. The chestnut wasn't just any horse – it was the best he'd ever trained, had hoisted him higher up the stakes-won list than he was ever likely to go again.

'Well, he seemed all right,' said the vet defensively.

'I want a dope test done,' Morrison said truculently.

'He's broken his shoulder. He'll have to be put down.'

'I know. I've got eyes. All the same, I want a dope test first. Just being ill wouldn't have made him act like that.'

The vet reluctantly agreed to take a blood sample, and after that he fitted the bolt into the humane killer and shot it into the chestnut's drug-crazed brain. The best horse in Arthur Morrison's stable became only a name in the record books. The digested carrot was dragged away with the carcass but its damage was by no means spent.

It took Chick fifteen minutes to realize that it was Toddy who was alive and the horse that was dead, during which time he felt physically ill and mentally pulverized. It had seemed so small a thing, in the beginning, to give a carrot to the chestnut. He hadn't thought of it affecting him much. He'd never dreamed anything like that could make you really sick.

Once he found that Toddy had broken no bones, had recovered consciousness and would be on his feet in an hour or two – the bulk of his physical symptoms receded. When the small trainer appeared at his elbow to remind him sharply that he should be inside changing into colours to ride in the Novice Hurdle race, he felt fit enough to go and do it, though he wished in a way that he hadn't said he would.

In the changing-room he forgot to tell his valet he needed a lightweight saddle and that the trainer had asked for a breast girth. He forgot to tie the stock round his neck and would have gone out to ride with the ends flapping. He forgot to take his watch off. His valet pointed everything out and thought that the jockey looked drunk.

The novice hurdler Chick was to ride wouldn't have finished within a mile of the chestnut if he'd started the day before. Young, green, sketchily schooled, he hadn't even the virtue of a gold streak waiting to be mined: this was one destined to run in the ruck until the owner tired of trying. Chick hadn't bothered to find out. He'd been much too preoccupied to look in the form book, where a consistent row of noughts might have made him cautious. As it was, he mounted the horse without attention and didn't listen to the riding orders the small trainer insistently gave him. As usual, he thought he knew better. Play it off the cuff, he thought scrappily. Play it off the cuff. How could he listen to fussy little instructions with all that he had on his mind?

On his way out from the weighing-room he passed Arthur Morrison, who cast an inattentive eye over his racing colours and said, 'Oh yes . . . well, don't make too much of a mess of it.'

Morrison was still thinking about the difference the chestnut's death was going to make to his fortunes and he didn't notice the spasm of irritation that twisted Chick's petulant face.

There he goes, Chick thought. That's typical. *Typical.* Never thinks I can do a bloody thing. If he'd given me more chances ... and more money ... I wouldn't have given ... Well, I wouldn't have. He cantered down to the post, concentrating on resenting that remark, 'don't make too much of a mess of it,' because it made him feel justified, obscurely, for having done what he'd done. The abyss of remorse opening beneath him was too painful. He clutched at every lie to keep himself out.

Harry Buskins had noticed that Chick had an unexpected mount in the Novice Hurdle and concluded that he himself was safe, the boy wasn't going to crack. All the same, he had shut his bag over its swollen takings and left his pitch for the day and gone home, explaining to his colleagues that he didn't feel well. And in truth he didn't. He couldn't get out of his mind the sight of the chestnut charging at those fences as if he couldn't see. Blind, the horse had been. A great racer who knew he was on a racetrack starting a race. Didn't understand there was anything wrong with him. Galloped because he was asked to gallop, because he knew it was the right place for it. A great horse, with a great racing heart.

Harry Buskins mopped the sweat off his forehead. They were bound to have tested the horse for dope, he thought, after something like that. None of the others he'd done in the past had reacted that way. Maybe he'd got the dose wrong or the timing wrong. You never knew how individual horses would be affected. Doping was always a bit unpredictable.

He poured himself half a tumbler of whisky with fingers that were shaking after all, and when he felt calmer he decided that if he got away with it this time he would be satisfied with the clean-up he'd made, and he wouldn't fool around with any more carrots. He just wouldn't risk it again.

At the starting post Chick lined up in the centre of the field, even though the trainer had advised him to start on the outside to give the inexperienced horse an easy passage over the first few hurdles. Chick didn't remember this instruction because he hadn't listened, and even if he had listened he would have done the same, driven by his habitual compulsion to disagree. He was thinking about Toddy lining up on this spot an hour ago, not knowing that his horse wouldn't see the jumps. Chick hadn't known dope could make a horse blind. How could anyone expect that? It didn't make sense. Perhaps it was just that the dope had confused the chestnut so much that although its eyes saw the fence, the message didn't get through that he was supposed to jump over it. The chestnut couldn't have been really blind.

Chick sweated at the thought and forgot to check that the girths were still tight after cantering down to the post. His mind was still on the inward horror when the starter let the tapes up, so that he was caught unawares and flat-footed and got away slowly. The small trainer on the stand clicked his mouth in annoyance, and Arthur Morrison raised his eyes to heaven.

The first hurdle lay side-by-side with the first fence, and all the way to it Chick was illogically scared that his horse wouldn't rise to it. He spent the attention he should have given to setting his horse right in desperately trying to convince himself that no one could have given it a carrot. He couldn't be riding a doped horse himself . . . it wouldn't be fair. Why wouldn't it be fair? Because . . . because . . .

The hurdler scrambled over the jump, knocked himself hard on the timber frame, and landed almost at a standstill. The small trainer began to curse.

Chick tightened one loose rein and then the other, and the hurdler swung to and fro in wavering indecision. He needed to be ridden with care and confidence and to be taught balance and rhythm. He needed to be set right before the jumps and to be collected quickly afterwards. He lacked experience, he lacked judgement and he badly needed a jockey who could contribute both.

Chick could have made a reasonable job of it if he'd been trying. Instead, with nausea and mental exhaustion draining what skill he had out of his muscles, he was busy proving that he'd never be much good.

At the second jump he saw in his mind's eye the

chestnut somersaulting through the air, and going round the bend his gaze wavered across to the broken rail and the scuffed-up patches of turf in front of it. The chestnut had died there. Everyone in the stable would be poorer for it. He had killed the chestnut, there was no avoiding it any more, he'd killed it with that carrot as surely as if he'd shot the bolt himself. Chick sobbed suddenly, and his eyes filled with tears.

He didn't see the next two hurdles. They passed beneath him in a flying blur. He stayed on his horse by instinct, and the tears ran down and were swept away as they trickled under the edge of his jockey's goggles.

The green hurdler was frightened and rudderless. Another jump lay close ahead, and the horses in front went clattering through it, knocking one section half over and leaving it there at an angle. The hurdler waited until the last minute for help or instructions from the man on his back and then in a muddled way dived for the leaning section, which looked lower to him and easier to jump than the other end.

From the stands it was clear to both the small trainer and Arthur Morrison that Chick had made no attempt to keep straight or to tell the horse when to take off. It landed with its forefeet tangled up in the sloping hurdle and catapulted Chick off over its head.

The instinct of self-preservation which should have made Chick curl into a rolling ball wasn't working. He fell through the air flat and straight, and his last thought before he hit was that that stupid little sod of a trainer hadn't schooled his horse properly. The animal hadn't a clue how to jump.

He woke up a long time later in a high bed in a small room. There was a dim light burning somewhere. He could feel no pain. He could feel nothing at all. His mind seemed to be floating in his head and his head was floating in space.

After a long time he began to believe that he was dead. He took the thought calmly and was proud of himself for his calm. A long time after that he began to realize that he wasn't dead. There was some sort of casing round his head, holding it cushioned. He couldn't move.

He blinked his eyes consciously and licked his lips to make sure that they at least were working. He couldn't think what had happened. His thoughts were a confused but peaceful fog.

Finally he remembered the carrot, and the whole complicated agony washed back into his consciousness. He cried out in protest and tried to move, to get up and away, to escape the impossible, unbearable guilt. People heard his voice and came into the room and stood around him. He looked at them uncomprehendingly. They were dressed in white.

'You're all right, now,' they said. 'Don't worry, young man, you're going to be all right.'

'I can't move,' he protested.

'You will,' they said soothingly.

'I can't feel . . . anything. I can't feel my feet.' The panic rose suddenly in his voice. 'I can't feel my hands. I can't . . . move . . . my hands.' He was shouting, frightened, his eyes wide and stretched.

'Don't worry,' they said. 'You will in time. You're going to be all right. You're going to be all right.'

He didn't believe them, and they pumped a sedative into his arm to quiet him. He couldn't feel the prick of the needle. He heard himself screaming because he could feel no pain.

When he woke up again he knew for certain that he'd broken his neck.

After four days Arthur Morrison came to see him, bringing six new-laid eggs and a bottle of fresh orange juice. He stood looking down at the immobile body with the plaster cast round its shoulders and head.

'Well, Chick,' he said awkwardly, 'it's not as bad as it could have been, eh?'

Chick said rudely, 'I'm glad you think so.'

'They say your spinal cord isn't severed, it's just crushed. They say in a year or so you'll get a lot of movement back. And they say you'll begin to feel things any day now.'

'They say,' said Chick sneeringly. 'I don't believe them.'

'You'll have to, in time,' said Morrison impatiently.

Chick didn't answer, and Arthur Morrison cast

uncomfortably around in his mind for something to say to pass away the minutes until he could decently leave. He couldn't visit the boy and just stand there in silence. He had to say *something*. So he began to talk about what was uppermost in his mind.

'We had the result of the dope test this morning. Did you know we had the chestnut tested? Well, you know we had to have it put down, anyway. The results came this morning. They were positive ... *Positive.* The chestnut was full of some sort of narcotic drug, some long name. The owner is kicking up hell about it and so is the insurance company. They're trying to say it's my fault. My security arrangements aren't tight enough. It's ridiculous. And all this on top of losing the horse itself, losing that really great horse. I questioned everyone in the stable this morning as soon as I knew about the dope, but of course no one knew anything. God, if I knew who did it I'd strangle him myself.' His voice shook with the fury which had been consuming him all day.

It occurred to him at this point that Chick being Chick, he would be exclusively concerned with his own state and wouldn't care a damn for anyone else's troubles. Arthur Morrison sighed deeply. Chick did have his own troubles now, right enough. He couldn't be expected to care all that much about the chestnut. And he was looking very weak, very pale.

The doctor who checked on Chick's condition ten

times a day came quietly into the small room and shook hands with Morrison.

'He's doing well,' he said. 'Getting on splendidly.'

'Nuts,' Chick said.

The doctor twisted his lips. He didn't say he had found Chick the worst-tempered patient in the hospital. He said, 'Of course, it's hard on him. But it could have been worse. It'll take time, he'll need to learn everything again, you see. It'll take time.'

'Like a bloody baby,' Chick said violently.

Arthur Morrison thought, a baby again. Well, perhaps second time around they could make a better job of him.

'He's lucky he's got good parents to look after him once he goes home,' the doctor said.

Chick thought of his mother, forever chopping up carrots to put in the stew. He'd have to eat them. His throat closed convulsively. He knew he couldn't.

And then there was the money, rolled up in the shoe-cleaning tin on the shelf in his bedroom. He would be able to see the tin all the time when he was lying in his own bed. He would never be able to forget. Never. And there was always the danger his ma would look inside it. He couldn't face going home. He couldn't face it. And he knew he would have to. He had no choice. He wished he were dead.

Arthur Morrison sighed heavily and shouldered his new burden with his accustomed strength of mind.

'Yes, he can come home to his mother and me as soon as he's well enough. He'll always have us to rely on.'

Chick Morrison winced with despair and shut his eyes. His father tried to stifle a surge of irritation, and the doctor thought the boy an ungrateful little beast.

# THE GIFT

The Gift *is the story published in* Sports Illustrated*'s Kentucky Derby issue of 1973. The magazine renamed the story 'The Day of Wine and Roses', referring both to the blanket of real flowers thrown over the withers of the Derby-winning horse, and to the fictional alcohol flowing on the pages.*

The Gift *given to Fred Collyer, though, was worth far more than roses.*

When the breakfast-time flight from LaGuardia was still twenty minutes short of Louisville, Fred Collyer took out a block of printed forms and began to write his expenses.

*Cab fare to airport, $40.*

No matter that a neighbour, working out on Long

Island, had given him a free ride door to door: a little imagination in the expenses department earned him half as much again (untaxed) as the *Manhattan Star* paid him for the facts he came up with every week in his Monday racing column.

*Refreshments on journey*, he wrote, *$25.*

*Entertaining for the purposes of obtaining information, $30.50.*

To justify that little lot he ordered a second double bourbon from the air hostess and lifted it in a silent good-luck gesture to a man sleeping across the aisle, the owner of a third-rate filly that had bucked her shins two weeks ago.

Another Kentucky Derby. His mind flickered like a scratched print of an old movie over the days ahead. The same old slog out to the barns in the mornings, the same endless raking over of past form, searching for a hint of the future. The same inconclusive workouts on the track, the same slanderous rumours, same gossip, same stupid jokes, same stupid trainers, shooting their goddam stupid mouths off.

The bright-burning enthusiasm which had carved out his syndicated by-line was long gone. The lift of the spirit to the big occasion, the flair for sensing a story where no one else did, the sharp instinct which sorted truth from camouflage, all these he had had. All had left him. In their place lay plains of boredom and perpetual cynical tiredness. Instead of exclusives, he nowadays gave his paper rehashes of other turf writers' ideas, and a couple of times recently he had failed to do even that.

He was forty-six.

He drank.

Back in his functional New York office, the Sports Editor of the *Manhattan Star* pursed his lips over Fred Collyer's last week's account of the Everglades race at Hialeah and wondered if he had been wise to send him down this week as usual to the Derby.

That guy, he thought regretfully, was all washed up. Too bad. Too bad he couldn't stay off the liquor. No one could drink and write, not at one and the same time. Write first, drink after; sure. Drink to excess, to stupor, maybe. But *after*.

He thought that before long he would have to let Fred go, that probably he should have started looking around for a replacement that day months back when Fred first turned up in the office too fuddled to hit the right keys on his computer. But that bum had had everything, he thought. A true journalist's nose for a story, and a gift for putting it across so vividly that the words jumped right off the page and kicked you in the brain.

Nowadays all that was left was a reputation and an echo: the technique still marched shakily on, but the personality behind it was drowning.

The Sports Editor shook his head over the Hialeah clipping and laid it aside. Twice in the past six weeks

Fred had been incapable of writing a story at all. Each time when he had not phoned through they had fudged up a column in the office and stuck the Collyer name on it, but two missed deadlines were one more than forgivable. Three, and it would be all over. The management were grumbling louder than ever over the inflated expense accounts, and if they found out that in return they had twice received only sodden silence, no amount of for-old-times'-sake would save him.

I did warn him, thought the Sports Editor uneasily. I told him to be sure to turn in a good one this time. A sizzler, like he used to. I told him to make this Derby one of his greats.

Fred Collyer checked into the motel room the newspaper had reserved for him and sank three quick mid-morning stiffeners from the bottle he had brought along in his briefcase. He shoved the Sports Editor's warning to the back of his mind because he was still sure that drunk or sober he could outwrite any other commentator in the business, given a story that was worth the trouble. There just weren't any good stories around any more.

He took a taxi out to Churchill Downs. (*Cab fare, $24.50*, he wrote on the way; and paid the driver eighteen.)

With three days to go to the Derby the racecourse looked clean, fresh and expectant. Bright red tulips in tidy columns pointed their petals uniformly to the blue sky, and patches of green grass glowed like shampooed rugs. Without noticing them Fred Collyer took the elevator to the roof and trudged up the last windy steps to the huge glass-fronted press room which ran along the top of the stands. Inside, a few men sat at their laptop computers knocking out the next day's news, and a few more stood outside on the racetrack-side balcony actually watching the first race, but most were engaged on the day's serious business, which was chat.

Fred Collyer bought himself a can of beer at the simple bar and carried it over to his named place, exchanging Hi-yahs with the faces he saw on the circuit from Saratoga to Hollywood Park. Living on the move in hotels, and altogether rootless since Sylvie got fed up with his absence and his drinking and took the kids back to Mom in Nebraska, he looked upon racecourse press rooms as his only real home. He felt relaxed there, assured of respect. He was unaware that the admiration he had once inspired was slowly fading into tolerant pity.

He sat easily in his chair reading one of the day's duplicated news releases.

'Trainer Harbourne Cressie reports no heat in Pincer Movement's near fore after breezing four furlongs on the track this morning.'

'No truth in rumour that Salad Bowl was running a temperature last evening, insists veterinarian John Brewer on behalf of owner Mrs L. (Loretta) Hicks.'

Marvellous, he thought sarcastically. Negative news was no news, Derby runners included.

He stayed up in the press room all afternoon, drinking beer, discussing this, that and nothing with writers, photographers, publicists and radio newsmen, keeping an inattentive eye on the racing on the closed-circuit television, and occasionally going out onto the balcony to look down on the anthill crowd far beneath. There was no need to struggle around down there as he used to, he thought. No need to try to see people, to interview them privately. Everything and everyone of interest came up to the press room sometime, ladling out info in spoon-fed dollops.

At the end of the day he accepted a ride back to town in a colleague's Hertz car (*cab fare, $24.50*), and in the evening, having laid substantial bourbon foundations in his own room before setting out, he attended the annual dinner of the Turfwriters' Association. The throng in the big reception room was pleased enough to see him, and he moved among the assortment of press-men, trainers, jockeys, breeders, owners and wives and girlfriends like a fish in his own home pond. Automatically before dinner he put away four doubles on the rocks, and through the food and the lengthy speeches afterwards kept up a steady intake. At half after eleven, when he tried to leave the table, he couldn't control his legs.

It surprised him. Sitting down, he had not been aware of being drunk. His tongue still worked as well as most around him, and to himself his thoughts seemed perfectly well organized. But his legs buckled as he put his weight on them, and he returned to his seat with a thump. It was considerably later, when the huge room had almost emptied as the guests went home, that he managed to summon enough strength to stand up.

'Guess I took a skinful,' he murmured, smiling to himself in self-excuse.

Holding on to the backs of chairs and at intervals leaning against the wall, he weaved his way to the door. From there he blundered out into the passage and forward to the lobby, and from there, looking as if he were climbing imaginary steps, out into the night through the swinging glass doors.

The cool May evening air made things much worse. The earth seemed literally to be turning beneath his feet. He listed sideways into a half circle and instead of moving forwards towards the parked cars and waiting taxis, staggered head-on into the dark brick front of the wall flanking the entrance. The impact hurt him and confused him further. He put both his hands flat on the rough surface in front of him and laid his face on it, and couldn't work out where he was.

Marius Tollman and Piper Boles had not seen Fred Collyer leave ahead of them. They strolled together along the same route, making the ordinary social phrases and gestures of people who had just come together by chance at the end of an evening, and gave no impression at all that they had been eyeing each other meaningfully across the room for hours, and thinking almost exclusively about the conversation which lay ahead.

In a country with legalized bookmaking, Marius Tollman might have grown up a respectable law-abiding citizen. As it was, his natural aptitude and only talent had led him into a lifetime of quick footwork which would have done credit to Muhammad Ali. Through the simple expedient of standing bets for future racing authorities while they were still young enough to be foolish, he remained unpersecuted by them once they reached status and power; and the one sort of winner old crafty Marius could spot better even than horses was the colt heading for the boardroom.

The two men went through the glass doors and stopped just outside with the light from the lobby shining full upon them. Marius never drew people into corners, believing it looked too suspicious.

'Did you get the boys to go along, then?' he asked, standing on his heels with his hands in his pockets and his paunch oozing over his belt.

Piper Boles slowly lit a cigarette, glanced around casually at the star-dotted sky, and sucked comforting smoke into his lungs.

'Yeah,' he said.

'So who's elected?'

'Amberezzio.'

'No,' Marius protested. 'He's not good enough.'

Piper Boles drew deep on his cigarette. He was hungry. One-eleven pounds to make tomorrow, and only a five-ounce steak in his belly. He resented fat people, particularly rich fat people. He was putting away his own small store of fat in real estate and growth bonds, but at thirty-eight the physical struggle was near to defeating him. He couldn't face many more years of starvation, finding it worse as his body aged. A sense of urgency had lately led him to consider ways of making a quick fifty thousand that once he would have sneered at.

He said, 'He's straight. It'll have to be him.'

Marius thought it over, not liking it, but finally nodded.

'All right, then. Amberezzio.'

Piper Boles nodded, and prepared to move away. It didn't do for a jockey to be seen too long with Marius Tollman, not if he wanted to go on riding second string for the prestigious Somerset Farms, which he most assuredly did.

Marius saw the impulse and said smoothly, 'Did you give any thought to a diversion on Crinkle Cut?'

Piper Boles hesitated.

'It'll cost you,' he said.

'Sure,' Marius agreed easily. 'How about another ten thousand, on top?'

'Used bills. Half before.'

'Sure.'

Piper Boles shrugged off his conscience, tossed out the last of his integrity.

'OK,' he said, and sauntered away to his car as if all his nerves weren't stretched and screaming.

Fred Collyer had heard every word, and he knew, without having to look, that one of the voices was Marius Tollman's. Impossible for anyone long in the racing game not to recognize that wheezy Boston accent. He understood that Marius had been fixing up a swindle, and also that a good little swindle would fill his column nicely. He thought fuzzily that it was necessary to know who Marius had been talking to, and that as the voices had been behind him he had better turn round and find out.

Time however was disjointed for him, and when he pushed himself off the wall and made an effort to focus in the right direction, both men had gone.

'Bastards,' he said aloud to the empty night, and another late homegoer, leaving the hotel, took him compassionately by the elbow and led him to a taxi. He made it safely back to his own room before he passed out.

Since leaving LaGuardia that morning he had drunk six beers, four brandies, one double Scotch (by mistake), and nearly three litres of bourbon.

He woke at eleven the next morning, and couldn't believe it. He stared at the bedside clock.

Eleven.

He had missed the barns and the whole morning merry-go-round on the track. A shiver chilled him at that first realization, but there was worse to come. When he tried to sit up, the room whirled and his head thumped like a pile-driver. When he stripped back the sheet he found he had been sleeping in bed fully clothed with his shoes on. When he tried to remember how he had returned the previous evening, he could not do so.

He tottered into the bathroom. His face looked back at him like a nightmare from the mirror, wrinkled and red-eyed, ten years older overnight. Hung-over he had been any number of times, but this felt like no ordinary morning-after. A sense of irretrievable disaster hovered somewhere behind the acute physical misery of his head and stomach, but it was not until he had taken off his coat and shirt and pants, and scraped off his shoes, and lain down again weakly on the crumpled bed, that he discovered its nature.

Then he realized with a jolt that not only had he no recollection of the journey back to his motel, he could recall practically nothing of the entire evening. Snatches of conversation from the first hour came back to him, and he remembered sitting at table between a cross old writer from the *Baltimore Sun* and an earnest woman breeder from Lexington, neither of whom he liked; but an uninterrupted blank started from halfway through the fried chicken.

He had heard of alcoholic blackouts, but supposed they only happened to alcoholics; and he, Fred Collyer, was not one of those. Of course, he would concede that he did drink a little. Well, a lot, then. But he could stop any time he liked. Naturally he could.

He lay on the bed and sweated, facing the stark thought that one blackout might lead to another, until blackouts gave way to pink panthers climbing the walls. The Sports Editor's warning came back with a bang, and for the first time, uncomfortably remembering that twice he had missed his column, he felt a shade of anxiety about his job. Within five minutes he had reassured himself that they would never fire Fred Collyer, but all the same he would for the paper's sake lay off the drink until after he had written his piece on the Derby. This resolve gave him a glowing feeling of selfless virtue, which at least helped him through the shivering fits and pulsating headaches of an extremely wretched day.

Out at Churchill Downs three other men were just as worried. Piper Boles kicked his horse forward into the starting stalls and worried about what George Highbury, the Somerset Farms trainer, had said when he went to scale at two pounds overweight. George Highbury thought himself superior to all jocks and spoke to them curtly, win or lose.

'Don't give me that crap,' he said to Boles' excuses.

'You went to the Turfwriters' dinner last night, what do you expect?'

Piper Boles looked bleakly back over his hungry evening with its single martini and said he'd had a session in the sweat-box that morning.

Highbury scowled. 'You keep your fat ass away from the table tonight and tomorrow if you want to make Crinkle Cut in the Derby.'

Piper Boles badly needed to ride Crinkle Cut in the Derby. He nodded meekly to Highbury with downcast eyes, and swung unhappily into the saddle.

Instead of bracing him, the threat of losing the ride on Crinkle Cut took the edge off his concentration, so that he came out of the stalls slowly, streaked the first quarter too fast to reach third place, swung wide at the bend and lost his stride straightening out. He finished sixth. He was a totally experienced jockey of above average ability. It was not one of his days.

On the grandstand, Marius Tollman put down his race glasses shaking his head and clicking his tongue. If Piper Boles couldn't ride a better race than that when he was supposed to be trying to win, what sort of a goddam hash would he make of losing on Crinkle Cut?

Marius thought about the very many thousands he was staking on Saturday's little caper. He had not yet decided whether to tip off certain guys in organized crime, in which case they would cover the stake at no risk to himself, or to gamble on the bigger profit of going it alone. He lowered his wheezy bulk onto his seat and worried about the ease with which a fixed race could unfix itself.

Blisters Schultz worried about the state of his trade, which was suffering a severe recession.

Blisters Schultz picked pockets for a living, and was fed up with credit cards. In the old days, when he'd learned the skill at his grandfather's knee, men carried their billfolds in their rear pants' pockets, neatly outlined for all the world to see. Nowadays all these smash-and-grab muggers had ruined the market: few people carried more than a handful of dollars around with them, and those who did tended to divide it into two portions, with the heavy dough hidden away beneath zips.

Fifty-three years Blisters had survived: forty-five of them by stealing. Several shortish sessions behind bars had been regarded as bad luck, but not as a good reason for not nicking the first wallet he saw when he got out. He had tried to go straight once, but he hadn't liked it: couldn't face the regular hours and the awful feeling of working. After six weeks he had left his well-paid job and gone back thankfully to insecurity. He felt happier stealing ten dollars than earning fifty.

For the best haul at racemeets, you either had to spot the big wads before they were gambled away, or follow a big winner away from the pay-out window. In either case, it meant hanging around the pari-mutuel with your eyes open. The trouble was, too many racecourse cops had cottoned to his modus op, and were apt to stand around looking at people who were just standing there looking.

Blisters had had a bad week. The most promisingly fat wallet had proved, after half an hour's careful stalking, to contain little in money but a lot in pornography. Blisters, having a weak sex drive, was disgusted on both counts.

For his first two days' labour he had only fifty-three dollars to show, and five of these he had found on a stairway. His meagre back-street room in Louisville was costing him forty a night, and with transport and eating to take into account, he reckoned he'd have to clear eight hundred to make the trip worthwhile.

Always an optimist, he brightened at the thought of Derby day. The pickings would certainly be easier once the real crowd arrived.

Fred Collyer's private Prohibition lasted intact through Friday. Feeling better when he woke, he cabbed out to Churchill Downs at seven-thirty, writing his expenses on the way. They included many mythical items for the previous day, on the basis that it was better for the office not to know he had been paralytic on Wednesday night. He upped the inflated total a bunch more: after all, bourbon was expensive, and he would be off the wagon by Sunday.

The initial shock of the blackout had worn off, because during his day in bed he had remembered bits and pieces which he was certain were later in time than the fried chicken. The journey from dinner to bed was still a blank, but the blank had stopped frightening him. At times he felt there was something vital about it he ought to remember, but he persuaded himself that if it had been really important, he wouldn't have forgotten.

Out by the barns the groups of pressmen had already formed round the trainers of the most fancied Derby runners. Fred Collyer sauntered to the outskirts of Harbourne Cressie, and his colleagues made room for him with no reference to his previous day's absence. It reassured him: whatever he had done on Wednesday night, it couldn't have been scandalous.

The notebooks were out. Harbourne Cressie, long practised and fond of publicity, paused between every sentence to give time for all to be written down.

'Pincer Movement ate well last evening and is calm and cool this a.m. On the book we should hold Salad Bowl, unless the track is sloppy by Saturday.'

Smiles all round. The sky blue, the forecast fair.

Fred Collyer listened without attention. He'd heard it all before. They'd all heard it all before. And who the hell cared?

In a rival group two barns away the trainer of Salad Bowl was saying his colt had the beating of Pincer

Movement on the Hialeah form, and could run on any going, sloppy or not.

George Highbury attracted fewer newsmen, as he hadn't much to say about Crinkle Cut. The three-year-old had been beaten by both Pincer Movement and Salad Bowl on separate occasions, and was not expected to reverse things.

On Friday afternoon Fred Collyer spent his time up in the press room and manfully refused a couple of free beers. (*Entertaining various owners at track, $52.*)

Piper Boles rode a hard finish in the sixth race, lost by a short head, and almost passed out from hunger-induced weakness in the jocks' room afterwards. George Highbury, unaware of this, merely noted sourly that Boles had made the weight, and confirmed that he would ride Crinkle Cut on the morrow.

Various friends of Piper Boles, supporting him towards a daybed, asked anxiously in his ear whether tomorrow's scheme was still on. Piper Boles nodded. 'Sure,' he said faintly. 'All the way.'

Marius Tollman was relieved to see Boles riding better, but decided anyway to hedge his bet by letting the syndicate in on the action.

Blisters Schultz lifted two billfolds, containing respectively fourteen and twenty-two dollars. He lost ten of them backing a certainty in the last race.

Pincer Movement, Salad Bowl and Crinkle Cut,

guarded by uniformed men with guns at their waists, looked over the stable doors and with small quivers in their tuned-up muscles watched other horses go out to the track. All three would have chosen to go, too. All three knew well enough what the trumpet was sounding for, on the other side.

Saturday morning, fine and clear.

Crowds in their thousands converged on Churchill Downs. Eager, expectant, chattering, dressed in bright colours and buying mint juleps in takeaway souvenir glasses, they poured through the gates and over the infield, reading the latest sports columns on Pincer Movement versus Salad Bowl, and dreaming of picking outsiders that came up at fifty to one.

Blisters Schultz had scraped together just enough to pay his motel bill, but self-esteem depended on better luck with the hoists. His small lined face with its busy eyes wore a look near to desperation, and the long predatory fingers clenched and unclenched convulsively in his pockets.

Piper Boles, with one-twenty-six to do on Crinkle Cut, allowed himself an egg for breakfast and decided what to buy with the bundle of used notes which had been delivered by hand the previous evening, and with the gains (both legal and illegal) he should add to them that day. If he cleaned up safely that afternoon, he thought, there was no obvious reason why he shouldn't set up the same scheme again, even after he had retired from riding. He hardly noticed the shift in his mind from reluctant dishonesty to habitual fraud.

Marius Tollman spent the morning telephoning to various acquaintances, offering profit. His offers were accepted. Marius Tollman felt a load lift from his spirits and with a spring in his step took his two-sixty pounds downtown a few blocks, where a careful gentleman counted out one hundred thousand dollars in untraceable notes. Marius Tollman gave him a receipt, properly signed. Business was business.

Fred Collyer wanted a drink. One, he thought, wouldn't hurt. It would pep him up a bit, put him on his toes. One little drink in the morning would certainly not stop him writing a punchy piece that evening. The *Star* couldn't possibly frown on just *one* drink before he went to the races, especially not as he had managed to keep clear of the bar the previous evening by going to bed at nine. His abstinence had involved a great effort of will: it would be right to reward such virtue with just one drink.

He had, however, finished on Wednesday night the bottle he had brought with him to Louisville. He fished out his wallet to check how much he had in it: eighty-three dollars, plenty after expenses to cover a fresh bottle for later as well as a quick one in the bar before he left.

He went downstairs. In the lobby, however, his colleague Clay Petrovitch again offered a free ride in his Hertz car to Churchill Downs, so he decided he could postpone his one drink for half an hour. He gave himself little mental pats on the back all the way to the racecourse.

Blisters Schultz, circulating among the clusters of people at the rear of the grandstand, saw Marius Tollman going by in the sunshine, leaning backwards to support the weight in front and wheezing audibly in the growing heat.

Blisters Schultz licked his lips. He knew the fat man by sight: knew that somewhere around that gross body might be stacked enough lolly to see him through the summer. Marius Tollman would never come to the Derby with empty pockets.

Two thoughts made Blisters hesitate as he slid like an eel in the fat man's wake. The first was that Tollman was too old a hand to let himself be robbed. The second, that he was known to have friends in organized places, and if Tollman was carrying organization money Blisters wasn't going to burn his fingers stealing it, which was how he got his nickname in the first place.

Regretfully Blisters peeled off from the quarry, and returned to the throng in the comforting shadows under the grandstand.

At twelve-seventeen he infiltrated a close-packed bunch of people waiting for an elevator.

At twelve-eighteen he stole Fred Collyer's wallet.

*

Marius Tollman carried his money in cunning underarm pockets which he clamped to his sides in a crowd, for fear of pickpockets. When the time was due, he would visit as many different selling windows as possible, inconspicuously distributing the stake. He would give Piper Boles almost half the tickets (along with the second bunch of used notes), and keep the other half for himself.

A nice tidy little killing, he thought complacently. And no reason why he shouldn't set it up sometime again.

He bought a mint julep and smiled kindly at a girl showing more bosom than bashfulness.

The sun stoked up the day. The preliminary contests rolled over one by one with waves of cheering, each hard-ridden finish merely a sideshow attending on the big one, the Derby, the climax, the ninth race, the one they called the Roses, because of the blanket of red flowers that would be draped in triumph over the withers of the winner.

In the jocks' room, Piper Boles changed into the silks for Crinkle Cut and began to sweat. The nearer he came to the race the more he wished it was an ordinary Derby day like any other. He steadied his nerves by reading the *Financial Times*.

Fred Collyer discovered the loss of his wallet upstairs in the press room when he tried to pay for a beer. He cursed, searched all his pockets, turned the press room upside down, got the keys of the Hertz car from Clay Petrovitch and trailed all the way back to the car park. After a fruitless search there he strode furiously back to the grandstands, violently throttling in his mind the lousy stinking son of a bitch who had stolen his money. He guessed it had been an old hand; an old man, even. The new vicious young lot relied on muscle, not skill.

His practical problems were not too great. He needed little cash. Clay Petrovitch was taking him back to town, the motel bill was going direct to the *Manhattan Star*, and his plane ticket was safely lying on the chest of drawers in his bedroom. He could borrow fifty bucks or so, maybe, from Clay or others in the press room, to cover essentials.

Going up in the elevator he thought that the loss of his money was like a sign from heaven; no money, no drink.

Blisters Schultz kept Fred Collyer sober the whole afternoon.

Pincer Movement, Salad Bowl and Crinkle Cut were led from their barns, into the tunnel under the cars and crowds, and out again onto the track in front of the grandstands. They walked loosely, casually, used to the limelight but knowing from experience that this was only a foretaste. The first sight of the day's princes galvanized the crowds towards the pari-mutuel window like shoals of multicoloured fish.

Piper Boles walked out with the other jockeys towards the wire-meshed enclosure where horses, trainers and owners stood in a group in each stall. He had begun to suffer from a feeling of detachment and unreality: he could not believe that he, a basically honest jockey, was about to make a hash of the Kentucky Derby.

George Highbury repeated for about the fortieth time the tactics they had agreed on. Piper Boles nodded seriously, as if he had every intention of carrying them out. He actually heard scarcely a word; and he was deaf also to the massed bands and the singing when the Derby runners were led out to the track. 'My Old Kentucky Home' swelled the emotions of a multitude and brought out a flutter of eye-wiping handkerchiefs, but in Piper Boles it raised not a blink.

Through the parade, the canter down, the circling round, and even into the starting stalls, the detachment persisted. Only then, with the tension showing plain on the faces of the other riders, did he click back to realization. His heart-rate nearly doubled and energy flooded into his brain.

Now, he thought. It is now, in the next half-minute, that I earn myself an extra ten thousand dollars; and after that, the rest.

He pulled down his goggles and gathered his reins and his whip. He had Pincer Movement on his right and Salad Bowl on his left, and when the stalls sprang open he went out between them in a rush, tipping his weight instantly forward over the withers and standing in the stirrups with his head almost as far forward as Crinkle Cut's.

All along past the stands the first time he concentrated on staying in the centre of the main bunch, as unnoticeable as possible, and round the top bend he was still there, sitting quiet and doing nothing very much. But down the backstretch, lying about tenth in a field of twenty-six, he earned his mini-fortune.

No one except Piper Boles ever knew what really happened; only he knew that he'd shortened his left rein with a sharp turn of his wrist and squeezed Crinkle Cut's ribs with his right foot. The fast galloping horse obeyed these directions, veered abruptly left, and crashed into the horse beside him.

The horse beside him was still Salad Bowl. Under the impact Salad Bowl cannoned into the horse on his own left, rocked back, stumbled, lost his footing entirely, and fell. The two horses on his tail fell over him.

Piper Boles didn't look back. The swerve and collision had lost him several places which Crinkle Cut at the best of times would have been unable to make up. He rode the rest of the race strictly according to his instructions, finishing flat out in twelfth place.

Of the 140,000 spectators at Churchill Downs, only a handful had had a clear view of the disaster on the far side of the track. The buildings in the in-field, and the milling crowds filling all its furthest areas, had hidden the crash from nearly all standing at ground level and from most on the grandstands. Only the press, high up, had seen. They sent out urgent fact-finders and buzzed like a stirred-up beehive.

Fred Collyer, out on the balcony, watched the photographers running to immortalize the winner, Pincer Movement, and reflected sourly that none of them would have taken close-up pictures of the second favourite, Salad Bowl, down on the dirt. He watched the blanket of dark red roses being draped over the victor and the triumphal presentation of the trophies, and then went inside for the rerun of the race on television. They showed the Salad Bowl incident forwards, backwards and sideways, and then jerked it through slowly in a series of stills.

'See that,' said Clay Petrovitch, pointing at the screen over Fred Collyer's shoulder, 'it was Crinkle Cut caused it. You can see him crash into Salad Bowl . . . there! . . . Crinkle Cut, that's the joker in the pack.'

Fred Collyer strolled over to his place, sat down, and stared at his keyboard. Crinkle Cut. He knew something about Crinkle Cut. He thought intensely for five minutes, but he couldn't remember what he knew.

Details and quotes came up to the press room. All fallen jockeys shaken but unhurt, all horses ditto; stewards in a tizzy, making instant enquiries and rerunning the patrol-camera film over and over. Suspension for Piper Boles considered unlikely, as blind eye usually turned to rough riding in the Derby. Piper Boles had gone on record as saying, 'Crinkle Cut just suddenly swerved. I didn't expect it, and couldn't prevent him bumping Salad Bowl.' Large numbers of people believed him.

Fred Collyer thought he might as well get a few paras down on paper: it would bring the first drink nearer, and boy how he needed that drink. With an ear open for fresher information he tapped out a blow-by-blow I-was-there account of an incident he had hardly seen. When he began to read it through, he saw that the first words he had written were 'The diversion on Crinkle Cut stole the post-race scene . . .'

*Diversion* on Crinkle Cut? He hadn't meant to write that . . . Or not exactly. He frowned. And there were other words in his mind, just as stupid. He put his hands back on the keyboard and typed them out.

'It'll cost you . . . ten thousand in used notes . . . half before.'

He stared at what he had written. He had made it up, he must have. Or dreamed it. One or the other.

A dream. That was it. He remembered. He had had a dream about two men planning a fixed race, and one of them had been Marius Tollman, wheezing away about a diversion on Crinkle Cut.

Fred Collyer relaxed and smiled at the thought, but the next minute knew quite suddenly that it hadn't been a dream at all. He had heard Marius Tollman and Piper Boles planning a diversion on Crinkle Cut, and he had forgotten because he'd been drunk. Well, he reassured himself uneasily, no harm done, he had remembered now, hadn't he?

No, he hadn't. If Crinkle Cut was a diversion, what was he a diversion *from*? Perhaps if he waited a bit, he would find he knew that, too.

Blisters Schultz spent Fred Collyer's money on two hot dogs, one mint julep, and five losing bets. On the winning side, he had harvested three more billfolds and a woman's purse: total haul, a hundred and ninety-four bucks. Gloomily he decided to call it a day and not come back next year.

Marius Tollman lumbered busily from window to window of the pari-mutuel and the stewards asked to see the jockeys involved in the Salad Bowl pile-up.

The crowds, hot, tired and frayed at the edges, began to leave in the yellowing sunshine. The bands marched away. The stalls which sold souvenirs packed up their wares. Pincer Movement had his picture taken for the thousandth time and the runners for the tenth, last, and least interesting race of the day walked over from the barns.

Piper Boles was waiting outside the stewards' room for a summons inside, but Marius Tollman used the highest-class messengers, and the package he entrusted was safely delivered. Piper Boles, nodded, slipped it into his pocket, and gave the stewards a performance worthy of Hollywood.

*

Fred Collyer put his head in his hands, trying to remember. A drink, he thought, might help. Diversion. Crinkle Cut. Amberezzio.

He sat up sharply. *Amberezzio*. And what the hell did that mean? *It has to be Amberezzio.*

'Clay,' he said, leaning back over his chair, 'do you know of a horse called Amberezzio?'

Clay Petrovitch shook his bald head. 'Never heard of it.'

Fred Collyer called to several others through the hubbub, 'Know of a horse called Amberezzio?' And finally he got an answer. 'Amberezzio isn't a horse, he's an apprentice.'

'*It has to be Amberezzio. He's straight.*'

Fred Collyer knocked his chair over as he stood up. They had already called one minute to post time on the last race.

'Lend me a hundred bucks, there's a pal,' he said to Clay.

Clay, knowing about the lost wallet, amiably agreed and slowly began to bring out his money.

'Hurry, for Chrissake,' Fred Collyer said urgently.

'OK, OK.' He handed over the hundred dollars and turned back to his own work.

Fred Collyer grabbed his racecard and pushed through the post-Derby chatter to the pari-mutuel window further along the press floor. He flipped the pages . . . tenth race, Homeward Bound, claiming race, eight runners. His eye skimmed down the list, and found what he sought.

Phillip Amberezzio, riding a horse Fred Collyer had never heard of.

'A hundred on the nose, number six,' he said quickly, and received his ticket seconds before the window shut. Trembling slightly, he pushed back through the crowd, and out onto the balcony. He was the only pressman watching the race.

Those jocks did it beautifully, he thought in admiration. Artistic. You wouldn't have known if you hadn't known. They bunched him in and shepherded him along, and then at the perfect moment gave him a suddenly clear opening. Amberezzio won by half a length, with all the others waving their whips as if beating the last inch out of their mounts.

Fred Collyer laughed. That poor little so-and-so probably thought he was a hell of a fellow, bringing home a complete outsider with all the big boys baying at his heels.

He went back inside the press room and found everyone's attention directed towards Harbourne Cressie, who had brought with him the owner and jockey of Pincer Movement. Fred Collyer dutifully took down enough quotes to cover the subject, but his mind was on the other story, the big one, the gift.

It would need careful handling, he thought. It would need the very best he could do, as he would have to be careful not to make direct accusations while leaving it perfectly clear that an investigation was necessary. His old instincts partially reawoke. He was even excited. He would write his piece in the quiet and privacy of his own room in the motel. Couldn't do it here on the racecourse, with every turfwriter in the world looking over his shoulder.

Down in the jockeys' changing-room, Piper Boles quietly distributed the pari-mutuel tickets which Marius Tollman had delivered: three thousand dollars' worth to each of the seven 'unsuccessful' riders in the tenth race, and ten thousand dollars' worth to himself. Each jockey subsequently asked a wife or girlfriend to collect the winnings and several of these would have made easy prey to Blisters Schultz, had he not already started home.

Marius Tollman's money had shortened the odds on Amberezzio, but he was still returned at twelve to one. Marius Tollman wheezed and puffed from pay-out window to pay-out window, collecting his winnings bit by bit. He hadn't room for all the cash in the underarm pockets and finally stowed some casually in more accessible spots. Too bad about Blisters Schultz.

Fred Collyer collected a fistful of winnings and repaid the hundred to Clay Petrovitch.

'If you had a hot tip, you might have passed it on,' grumbled Petrovitch, thinking of all the expenses old

Fred would undoubtedly claim for his free rides to the racecourse.

'It wasn't a tip, just a hunch.' He couldn't tell Clay what the hunch was, as he wrote for a rival paper. 'I'll buy you a drink on the way home.'

'I should damn well think so.'

Fred Collyer immediately regretted his offer, which had been instinctive. He remembered that he had not intended to drink until after he had written. Still, perhaps one ... And he did need a drink very badly. It seemed a century since his last, on Wednesday night.

They left together, walking out with the remains of the crowd. The racecourse looked battered and bedraggled at the end of the day: the scarlet petals of the tulips lay on the ground, leaving rows of naked pistils sticking forlornly up, and the bright rugs of grass were dusty grey and covered with litter. Fred Collyer thought only of the dough in his pocket and the story in his head, and both of them gave him a nice warm glow.

A drink to celebrate, he thought. Buy Clay a thank-you drink, and maybe perhaps just one more to celebrate. It wasn't often, after all, that things fell his way so miraculously.

They stopped for the drink. The first double swept through Fred Collyer's veins like fire through a parched forest. The second made him feel great.

'Time to go,' he said to Clay. 'I've got my piece to write.'

'Just one more,' Clay said. 'This one's on me.'

'Better not.' He felt virtuous.

'Oh, come on,' Clay said, and ordered. With the faintest of misgivings Fred Collyer sank his third: but couldn't he still out-write every racing man in the business? Of course he could.

They left after the third. Fred Collyer bought a litre of bourbon for later, when he had finished his story. Back in his own room he took just the merest swig from it before he sat down to write.

The words wouldn't come. He deleted six attempts and poured some bourbon into a tooth glass.

Marius Tollman, Crinkle Cut, Piper Boles, Amberezzio . . . It wasn't all that simple.

He took a drink. He didn't seem to be able to help it.

The Sports Editor would give him a raise for a story like this, or at least there would be no more quibbling about expenses.

He took a drink.

Piper Boles had earned himself ten thousand bucks for crashing into Salad Bowl. Now how the hell did you write that without being sued for libel?

He took a drink.

The jockeys in the tenth race had conspired together to let the only straight one among them win. How in hell could you say that?

He took a drink.

The stewards and the press had had all their attention channelled towards the crash in the Derby and had virtually ignored the tenth race. The tenth race had been fixed. The stewards wouldn't thank him for pointing it out.

He took another drink. And another. And more.

His deadline for telephoning his story to the office was ten o'clock the following morning. When that hour struck he was asleep and snoring, fully dressed, on his bed. The empty bourbon bottle lay on the floor beside him, and his winnings, which he had tried to count, lay scattered over his chest.

# SPRING FEVER

Woman's Own *magazine unexpectedly asked me for a suitable story. (Five thousand words, please.)*

*They would leave the actual content to me, they said, but they would prefer a story geared to their women readers.*

Spring Fever, *which I very much enjoyed writing, was the result.*

Looking back, Mrs Angela Hart could identify the exact instant in which she fell irrationally in love with her jockey.

Angela Hart, plump, motherly, and fifty-two, watched the twenty-four-year-old man walk into the parade ring at Cheltenham races in her gleaming pink and white colours, and she thought: 'How young he is, how fit, how lean . . . how *brave*.'

He crossed the bright turf to join her for the usual few minutes of chit-chat before taking her horse away to its two-mile scurry over hurdles, and she looked at the way the weather-tanned flesh lay taut over the cheekbones and agreed automatically that yes, the spring sunshine was lovely, and that yes, the drier going should suit her Billyboy better than the rain of the past few weeks.

It was a day like many another. Two racehorses having satisfactorily replaced the late and moderately lamented Edward Hart in Angela's affections, she contentedly spent her time in going to jump meetings to see her darlings run, in clipping out mentions of them from the racing pages of newspapers and in telephoning her trainer, Clement Scott, to enquire after their health.

She was a woman of kindness and good humour, but suffered from a dangerous belief that everyone was basically as well-intentioned as herself. Like children who pat tigers, she expected a purr of appreciation in return for her offered friendship, not to have her arm bitten off.

Derek Roberts, jockey, saw Mrs Angela Hart prosaically as the middle-aged owner of Billyboy and Hamlet, a woman to whom he spoke habitually with a politeness borne from needing the fees he was paid for riding her horses. His job, he reckoned, involved pleasing the customers before and after each race as much as doing his best for them in the event, and as he had long years ago discovered that most owners were pathetically pleased when a jockey praised their horses, he had slid almost without cynicism into a way of conveying optimism even when not believing a word of it.

When he walked into the parade ring at Cheltenham, looking for Mrs Hart and spotting her across the grass in her green tweed coat and brown fur hat, he was thinking that as Billyboy hadn't much chance in today's company he'd better prepare the old duck for the coming disappointment and at the same time insure himself against being blamed for it.

'Lovely day,' he said, shaking her hand. 'Real spring sunshine.'

'Lovely.' After a short silence, when she said nothing more, he tried again.

'Much better for Billyboy, now all that rain's drying out.'

'Yes, I'm sure you're right.'

She wasn't as talkative as usual, he thought. Not the normal excited chatter. He watched Billyboy plod round the ring and said encouragingly, 'He should run well today . . . though the opposition's pretty hot, of course.'

Mrs Hart, looking slightly vague, merely nodded. Derek Roberts, shrugging his mental shoulders, gave her a practised, half-genuine smile and reckoned (mistakenly) that if she had something on her mind, and didn't want to talk, it was nothing to do with him.

A step away from them, also with his eyes on the horse, stood Billyboy's trainer, Clement Scott. Strong, approaching sixty, a charmer all his life, he had achieved success more through personality than any deep skill with horses. He wore good clothes. He could talk.

Underneath the attractive skin there was a coldness which was apparent to his self-effacing wife, and to his grown and married children, and eventually to anyone who knew him well. He was good company, but lacked compassion. All *bonhomie* on top: ruthlessly self-seeking below.

Clement Scott was old in the ways of jockeys and owners, and professionally he thought highly of the pair before him: of Derek, because he kept the owners happy and rode well enough besides, and of Angela because her first interest was in the horses themselves and not in the prize money they might fail to win.

Motherly sentimental ladies, in his opinion, were the least critical and most forgiving of owners, and he put up gladly with their gushing telephone calls because they also tended to pay his bills on receipt. Towards Angela, nicely endowed with a house on the edge of Wentworth golf course, he behaved with the avuncular roguishness that had kept many a widow faithful to his stable in spite of persistent rumours that he would probably cheat them if given half a chance.

Angela, like many another lady, didn't believe the rumours. Clement, dear naughty Clement, who made owning a racehorse such satisfying fun, would never in any case cheat *her*.

Angela stood beside Clement on the stands to watch the race, and felt an extra dimension of anxiety; not simply, as always, for the safe return of darling Billyboy, but also, acutely, for the man on his back. Such risks he takes, she thought, watching him through her binoculars. Before that day she had thought only of whether he'd judged the pace right, or taken an available opening, or ridden a vigorous finish. During that race her response to him crossed conclusively from objectivity to emotion, a change which at the time she only dimly perceived.

Derek Roberts, by dint of not resting the horse when it was beaten, urged Billyboy forwards into fourth place close to the winning post, knowing that Angela would like fourth better than fifth or sixth or seventh. Clement Scott smiled to himself as he watched. Fourth or seventh, the horse had won no prize money, but that lad Derek, with his good looks and his crafty ways, he certainly knew how to keep the owners sweet.

Her race glasses clutched tightly to her chest, Angela Hart breathed from the relief of pulse-raising tensions. She thought gratefully that fourth place wasn't bad in view of the hot opposition, and Billyboy had been running on at the end, which was a good sign . . . and Derek Roberts had come back safely.

With her trainer she hastened down to meet the returning pair, and watched Billyboy blow through his nostrils in his usual post-race sweating state, and listened to Derek talking over his shoulder to her while he undid the girth buckles on the saddle.

'. . . Made a bit of a mistake landing over the third last, but it didn't stop him . . . He should win a race pretty soon, I'd say.'

He gave her the special smile and a sketchy salute and hurried away to weigh-in and change for the next race, looping the girths round the saddle as he went. Angela watched until he was out of sight and asked Clement when her horses were running next.

'Hamlet had a bit of heat in one leg this morning,' he said, 'and Billyboy needs two weeks at least between races.' He screwed up his eyes at her, teasing. 'If you can't wait that long to see them again, why don't you come over one morning and watch their training gallops?'

She was pleased. 'Does Derek ride the gallops?'

'Sometimes,' he said.

It was on the following day that Angela, dreamily drifting around her house, thought of buying another horse.

She looked up Derek Roberts' number, and telephoned.

'Find you another horse?' he said. 'Yeah . . . sure . . . I think another horse is a grand idea, but you should ask Mr Scott . . .'

'If Clement finds me a horse,' Angela said, 'will you come with me to see it? I'd really like your opinion before I buy.'

'Well . . .' He hesitated, not relishing such a use of his spare time but realizing that another horse for Angela meant more fees for himself. 'All right, certainly I'll come, Mrs Hart.'

'That's fine,' she said. 'I'll ring Clement straight away.'

'Another horse?' Clement said, surprised. 'Yes, if you like, though it's a bit late in the season. Why not wait—?'

'No,' Angela interrupted. 'Dear Clement, I want him now.'

Clement Scott heard but couldn't understand the urgency in her voice. Four days later, however, when she came to see her existing two horses work – having made sure beforehand that Derek would be there to ride them – he understood completely.

Fiftyish, matronly Angela couldn't keep her eyes off Derek Roberts. She intently watched him come and go on horse and on foot, and scanned his face uninterruptedly while he spoke. She asked him questions to keep him near, and lost a good deal of animation when he went home.

Clement Scott, who had seen that sort of thing often enough before, behaved to her more flirtatiously than ever and kept his sardonic smile to himself. He had luckily heard of a third horse for her, he said, and would take her to see it.

'Actually,' Angela said diffidently, 'I've already asked Derek to come with me . . . and he said he would.'

Clement, that evening, telephoned Derek.

'Besotted with me?' said Derek. 'That's bloody nonsense. I've been riding for her for more than a year. You can't tell me I wouldn't have noticed.'

'Keep your eyes open, lad,' Clement said. 'I reckon she wants this other horse just to give her an excuse to see you more often; and that being so, lad, I've a little proposition for you.'

He outlined the little proposition at some length, and Derek discovered that his consideration of Mrs Hart's best interests came a poor second to the prospects of a tax-free instant gain.

He drove to her house at Wentworth a few days later, and they went on together in her car, a Rover, with Derek driving. The horse belonged to a man in Yorkshire, which meant, Angela thought contentedly, that the trip would take all day.

She had rationalized her desire to own another horse as just an increase in her interest in racing, and also she had rationalized her eagerness for the Yorkshire journey as merely impatience to see what Clement had described as 'an exciting bargain at twenty thousand, one to do you justice, my dear Angela'.

She could just afford it, she thought, if she didn't go on a cruise this summer, and if she spent less on clothes. She did not at any point admit to herself that what she was buying at such cost was a few scattered hours out of Derek Roberts' life.

Going north from Watford, he said: 'Mrs Hart, did Mr Scott tell you much about this horse?'

'He said you'd tell me. And call me Angela.'

'Er . . .' He cleared his throat. 'Angela . . .' He glanced at her as she sat beside him, plump and relaxed and happy. It couldn't be true, he thought. People like Mrs Hart didn't suffer from infatuations. She was far too old: fifty . . . an unimaginable age to him at twenty-four. He shifted uncomfortably in his seat and felt ashamed (but only slightly) of what he was about to do.

'Mr Scott thinks the horse has terrific potential. Only six years old. Won a hurdle race last year . . .' He went on with the sales talk, skilfully weaving in the few actual facts which she could verify from form books if she wanted to, and putting a delicately rosy slant on everything else. 'Of course, the frost and snow has kept him off the racecourse during the winter, but I'll tell you, just between ourselves . . . er, Angela . . . that Mr Scott thinks he might even enter him for the Whitbread. He might even be in that class.'

Angela listened entranced. The Whitbread Gold Cup, scheduled for six weeks ahead, was the last big race of the jumping season. To have a horse fit to run in it, and to have Derek Roberts ride it, seemed to her a pinnacle in her racing life that she had never envisaged. Her horizons, her joy, expanded like flowers.

'Oh, how lovely,' she said ecstatically; and Derek Roberts (almost) winced.

'Mr Scott wondered if you'd like me to do a bit of bargaining for you,' he said. 'To get the price down a bit.'

'Dear Clement is so thoughtful.' She gave Derek a slightly anxious smile. 'Don't bargain so hard I lose the horse, though, will you?'

He promised not to.

'What is it called?' she asked and he told her: 'Magic.'

Magic was stabled in the sort of yard which should have warned Angela to beware, but she'd heard often enough that in Ireland champions had been bought out of pigsties, and caution was nowhere in her mind. Dear Clement would naturally not buy her a bad horse, and with Derek himself with her to advise . . . She looked trustingly at the nondescript bay gelding produced for her inspection and saw only her dreams – not the mud underfoot, not the rotten wood round the stable doors, not the cracked leather of the horse's tack.

She saw Magic being walked up and down the weedy stable-yard and she saw him being trotted a bit on a leading rein in a small dock-ridden paddock; and she didn't see the dismay Derek couldn't keep out of his face.

'What do you think?' she asked, her eyes still shining in spite of all.

'Good strong shoulder,' he said judiciously. 'Needs a bit of feeding to improve his condition, perhaps.'

'But do you like him?'

He nodded decisively. 'Just the job.'

'I'll have him, then.' She said it without the slightest hesitation and he stamped on the qualms which pricked like teeth.

She waited in the car while Derek bargained with Magic's owner, watching the two men as they stood together in the stable-yard, shaking their heads, spreading their arms, shrugging, and starting again. Finally, to her relief, they touched hands on it, and Derek came to tell her that she could have the horse for nineteen thousand if she liked.

'Think it over,' he said, making it sound as if she needn't.

She shook her head. 'I've decided. I really have. Shall I give the man a cheque?'

'No,' he said. 'Mr Scott has to get a vet's report, and fix up transport and insurance and so on. He'll do all the paperwork and settle for the horse, and you can pay him for everything all at once. Much simpler.'

'Darling Clement,' she said warmly. 'Always so sweet and thoughtful.'

Darling Clement entered Magic for the Whitbread Gold Cup at Sandown Park, and also for what he called a 'warm-up' race three weeks before the big event.

'That will be at Stratford-upon-Avon,' he told Angela. 'In the Pragnell Cup, first week of April.'

'How marvellous,' Angela said enthusiastically.

She telephoned several times to Derek for long, cosy consultations about Magic's prospects, and drank in his easy optimism like the word of God. Derek filled her thoughts from dawn to dusk: dear Derek, who was so brave and charming and kind.

Clement and Derek took Magic out on to the gallops at home and found the 'exciting bargain' unwilling to keep up with any other horse in the stable. Magic waved his tail about and kicked up his heels and gave every sign of extreme bad temper. Both Clement and Derek, however, reported to a delighted Angela that Magic was a perfect gentleman and going well.

When Angela turned up by arrangement at ten one morning to watch Magic work, he had been sent out by mistake with the first lot at seven, and was consequently resting. Her disappointment was mild, though, because Derek was there, not riding but accompanying her on foot, full of smiles and gaiety and friendship. She loved it. She trusted him absolutely, and she showed it.

'Well done, lad,' Clement said gratefully, as she drove away later. 'With you around, our Angela wouldn't notice an earthquake.'

Derek, watching her go, felt remorse and regret. It was hardly fair, he thought. She was a nice old duck really. She'd done no one any harm. He belatedly began not to like himself.

They went to Stratford races all hoping for different things: Derek that Magic would at least get round, Angela that her horse would win, and Clement that he wouldn't stop dead in the first furlong.

Three miles. Fast track. Firm ground. Eighteen fences.

Angela's heart was beating with a throb she could feel as Magic, to the relief of both men, deigned to set off in the normal way from the start, and consented thereafter to gallop along steadily among the rear half of the field. After nearly two miles of this mediocrity both men relaxed and knew that when Magic ran out of puff and pulled up, as he was bound to do soon, they could explain to Angela that 'he had needed the race', and 'he'll be tuned up nicely for the Whitbread', and she would believe it.

A mile from home, from unconscious habit, Derek gave Magic the speeding-up signs of squeezing with his legs and clicking his tongue and flicking the reins. Magic unexpectedly plunged towards the next fence, misjudged his distance, took off too soon, hit the birch hard, and landed in a heap on the ground.

The horse got to his feet and nonchalantly cantered away. The jockey lay still and flat.

'Derek!' cried Angela, agonized.

'Bloody fool,' Clement said furiously, bustling down from the stands. 'Got him unbalanced.'

In a turmoil of anxiety, Angela watched through her binoculars as the motionless Derek was loaded slowly onto a stretcher and carried to an ambulance; and then she walked jerkily round to the first-aid room to await his return.

I should never have bought the horse, she thought in anguish. If I hadn't bought the horse, Derek wouldn't be . . . might not be . . .'

He was alive. She saw his hands move as soon as the blue-uniformed men opened the ambulance doors. Her relief was almost as shattering as her fear. She felt faint.

Derek Roberts had broken his leg and was in no mood to worry about Angela's feelings. He knew she was there because she made little fluttery efforts to reach his side – efforts constantly thwarted by the stretcher-bearers easing him out – saying to him over and over, 'Derek, oh, Derek are you all right?'

Derek didn't answer. His attention was on his leg, which hurt, and on getting into the first-aid room without being bumped. There was always a ghoulish crowd round the door pressing forward to look. He stared up at the faces peering down and hated their probing interest. It was a relief to him, as always on those occasions, when they carried him through the door and shut out the ranks of eyes.

Inside, waiting for the doctor and lying on a bed, he reflected gloomily that his present spot of trouble served him right.

Outside, Angela wandered aimlessly about. She thought that she ought to worry about the horse, but she couldn't; she had room in her mind only for Derek.

'Never mind, missus,' a voice said cheerfully. 'Yon Magic is all right. Cantering round the middle there and giving them the devil's own job of catching him. Don't you fret none.'

Startled, she looked at the sturdy man with the broad Yorkshire accent who stood confidently in her way.

'Came from my brother, did that horse,' he said. 'I'm down here special, like, to see him run.'

'Oh,' said Angela vaguely.

'Is the lad all right? The one who rode him?'

'I think he's broken his leg.'

'Dear, oh dear. Bit of hard luck, that. He drove a hard bargain with my brother, did that lad.'

'Did he?'

'Aye. My brother said Magic was a flier, but your

lad, he wouldn't have it, said the horse hadn't any form to speak of, and looked proper useless to him. My brother was asking seven thousand for it, but your lad beat him down to five. I came here, see, to learn which was right.' He beamed with goodwill. 'Tell you the truth, the horse didn't run up to much, did it? Reckon your lad was right. But don't you fret, missus, there'll be another day.'

He gave her a nod and a final beam, and moved away. Angela felt breathless, as if he had punched her.

Already near the exit gate, she turned blindly and walked out through it, her legs taking her automatically towards her car. Shaking, she sat in the driving seat, and with a feeling of unreality drove all of the hundred miles home. 'The man must have got it wrong,' she thought. 'Not seven and five thousand, but twenty and nineteen.' When she reached her house she looked up the address of Magic's previous owner and telephoned.

'Aye,' he said. 'Five thousand, that's right.' The broad Yorkshire voice floated cheerfully across the counties. 'Charged you a bit more, did they?' He chuckled. 'Couple of hundred, maybe? You can't grudge them that, missus. Got to have their commission, like. It's the way of the world.'

She put down the receiver, and sat on her lonely sofa, and stared into space. She understood for the first time that what she had felt for Derek was love. She understood that Clement and Derek must have seen it in her weeks ago, and because of it had exploited and manipulated her in a way that was almost as callous as rape.

All the affection she had poured out towards them, all the joy and fond thoughts and happiness . . . they had taken them and used them and hadn't cared for her a bit. 'They don't even like me,' she thought. 'Derek doesn't even like me.'

The pain of his rejection filled her with a depth of misery she had never felt before. How could she, she wondered wretchedly, have been so stupid, so blind, so pathetically immature.

She walked after a while through the big house, which was so quiet now that Edward wasn't there to fuss, and went into the kitchen. She started to make herself a cup of tea, and wept.

Within a week she visited Derek in hospital. He lay halfway down a long ward with his leg in traction, and for an instant he looked like a stranger: a thin young man with his head back on the pillows and his eyes closed. A strong young man no longer, she thought. More like a sick child.

That, too, was an illusion.

He heard her arrive at his bedside and opened his eyes, and because he was totally unprepared to find her there she saw quite clearly the embarrassment which flooded through him. He swallowed, and bit his lip; and then he smiled. It was the same smile as before, the outward face of treason. Angela felt slightly sick.

She drew up a chair and sat by his bed. 'Derek,' she said, 'I've come to congratulate you.'

He was bewildered. 'Whatever for?'

'On your capital gain: the difference between five thousand and nineteen.'

His smile vanished and he looked away from her. He felt trapped and angry and ashamed, and he wished above all things that she would go away.

'How much of it,' Angela said slowly, 'was your share, and how much was Clement's?'

There was a stretching silence of more than a minute. Then he said, 'Half and half.'

'Thank you,' Angela said. She got to her feet, pushing back the chair. 'That's all, then. I just wanted to hear you admit it.'

And to find out for sure, she thought, that she was cured; that the fever no longer ran in her blood; that she could look at him and not care any more – and she could.

'All?' he said.

She nodded. 'What you did wasn't illegal, just . . . well, horrid. I should have been more businesslike.' She took a step away. 'Goodbye, Derek.'

She'd gone several more steps before he called after her, suddenly, 'Angela . . . Mrs Hart.'

She paused and came halfway back.

'Please,' he said. 'Please listen. Just for a moment.'

Angela returned slowly to his bedside.

'I don't suppose you'll believe me,' he said, 'but I've been thinking about that race at Stratford . . . and I've a feeling Magic may not be so useless after all.'

'No,' Angela said. 'No more lies. I've had enough.'

'I'm not . . . This isn't a lie. Not this.'

She shook her head.

'Listen,' he said. 'Magic made no show at Stratford because nobody asked him to – except right at the end, when I shook him up. And then he fell because I'd done it so close to the fence, and because when I gave him the signal he just shot forward as if he'd been galvanized.'

Angela listened, disbelieving.

'Some horses,' he said, 'won't gallop at home. Magic won't and so we thought . . . I thought . . . that he couldn't race either. But I'm not so sure now.'

Angela shrugged. 'It doesn't change anything. But I'll find out when he runs in the Whitbread.'

'No.' He squirmed. 'We never meant to run him in the Whitbread.'

'But he's entered,' she said.

'Yes, but . . . well, Mr Scott will tell you, a day or two before the race, that Magic has a temperature, or has bruised his foot, or something, and can't run. He . . . we . . . planned it. We reckoned you wouldn't quibble about the price if you thought Magic was Whitbread class . . .'

Angela let out an 'Oh' like a deep sigh. She looked down at the young man who was pleating his sheets aimlessly in his fingers and not meeting her eyes. She saw the shame and the tiredness and the echo of pain from his leg, and she thought that what she had felt for him had been as destructive to him as to herself.

At home, Angela phoned Clement. 'Dear Clement, how is Magic?'

'None the worse, Angela, I'm glad to say.'

'How splendid,' she said warmly. 'And now there's the Whitbread to look forward to, isn't there?'

'Yes, indeed.' He chuckled. 'Better buy a new hat, my dear.'

'Clement,' Angela said sweetly, 'I am counting on you to keep Magic fit and well fed and uninjured in every way. I'm counting on his turning up to start in the Whitbread, and on his showing us just exactly how bad he is.'

'*What?*'

'Because if he doesn't, Clement dear, I might just find myself chattering to one or two people . . . you know, press men and even the tax man, and people like that . . . about your buying Magic for five thousand one day and selling him to me for nineteen thousand the next.'

Angela listened to the silence travelling thunderously down the wire, and she smiled with healthy mischief. 'And Clement dear, we'll both give his new jockey instructions to win if he can, won't we? Because it's got to be a fair test, don't you think? And just to encourage you, I'll promise you that if I'm satisfied that Magic has done his very best, win or lose, I won't mention to anyone what I paid for him. And that's a bargain, Clement dear, that you can trust.'

Clement put the receiver down with a crash and swore aloud. 'Bloody old bag. She must have checked up.' He telephoned to Yorkshire and found that indeed she had. Damn and blast her, he thought. He was going to look a proper fool in the eyes of the racing world, running rubbish like Magic in one of the top races. It would do his reputation no damn good at all.

Clement Scott felt not the slightest twinge of guilt. He had, after all, cheated a whole succession of foolish ladies in the same way. But if Angela talked – and she could talk for hours when she liked – he would find that the gullible widowed darlings were all suddenly suspicious and buying their horses from someone else. Magic, he saw furiously, would have to be trained as thoroughly as possible, and ridden by the best jockey free.

In the parade ring before the Whitbread, Angela was entirely her old self again: kind and gushing and bright-eyed.

She spoke to her new jockey, who was unlike Derek Roberts to a comfortable degree. 'I expect you've talked it over with darling Clement,' she said gaily, 'but I think it would be best, don't you, if you keep Magic back a bit among all the other runners for most of the way, and then about a mile from the winning post tell him to start winning, if you see what I mean, and, of course, after that it's up to both of you just to do what you can. I have my money on you, you know.'

The jockey glanced uncertainly at the stony face of Clement Scott. 'Do what the lady wants,' Clement said.

The jockey, who knew his business, carried out the instructions to the letter. A mile from home he dug Magic sharply in the ribs and was astonished at the response. Magic – young, lightly raced, and carrying bottom weight – surged past several older, tireder contenders, and came towards the last fence lying fifth.

Clement could hardly believe his eyes. Angela could hardly breathe. Magic floated over the last fence and charged up the straight and finished third.

'There,' she said, 'isn't that *lovely*.'

Since almost no one else had backed her horse, Angela collected a fortune in place money from the Tote; and a few days later, for exactly what she'd paid, she sold Magic to a scrap-metal merchant from Kent.

Angela sent Derek Roberts a get-well card. A week later she sent him an impersonal case of champagne and a simple message: 'Thanks.'

'I've learned a lot,' she thought, 'because of him. A lot about greed and gullibility, about façades and consequences and the transience of love. And about racing . . . too much.'

She sold Billyboy and Hamlet and went on her cruise.

# BLIND CHANCE

*In 1979 Julian Symons, Eminence of The Detection Club, hit on a wheeze to earn money to swell the Club's depleted coffers. As Editor, he invited a fistful of crime writers to contribute a short story towards a volume whose title was to be* Verdict of Thirteen: a Detection Club Anthology.

*Not being skilled at court scenes, I wrote a race-course tale called* Twenty-one Good Men and True, *and under that banner it was published by Faber in Britain and Harper in the US, both in 1979. In England the story was also run by the weekly magazine,* Woman's Own, *who gave it the title adopted here,* Blind Chance.

Arnold Roper whistled breathily while he boiled his kettle and spooned instant own-brand economy-pack coffee into the old blue souvenir from Brixham. Unmelodic and without rhythm, the whistling was none the less an expression of content – both with things in general and the immediate prospect ahead. Arnold Roper, as usual, was going to the races: and, as usual, if he had a bet, he would win. Neat, methodical, professional, he would operate his unbeatable system and grow richer, the one following the other as surely as chickens and eggs.

Arnold Roper at forty-five was one of nature's bachelors, a lean-bodied man accustomed to looking after himself, a man who found the chatter of companionship a nuisance. Like a sailor – though he had never been to sea – he kept his surroundings polished and shipshape, ordering his life in plastic dustbin-liners and reheated takeaway food.

The one mild problem on Arnold Roper's horizon was his wealth. The getting of the money was his most intense enjoyment. The spending of it was something he postponed to a remote and dreamlike future, when he would exchange his sterile flat for a warm unending idyll under tropical palms. It was the interim storage of the money which was currently causing him, if not positive worry, at least occasional frowns of doubt. He might, he thought, as he stirred dried milk grains into a brownish brew, have to find space for yet another wardrobe in his already crowded bedroom.

If anyone had told Arnold Roper he was a miser, he would have denied it indignantly. True, he lived frugally, but by habit rather than obsession: and he never took out his wealth just to look at it, and count, and gloat. He would not have admitted as miserliness the warm feeling that stole over him every night as he lay down to sleep, smiling from the knowledge that all round him, filling two oak-veneered sale-bargain bedroom suites, was a ton or two of negotiable paper.

It was not that Arnold Roper distrusted banks. He knew, too, that money won by betting could not be lost by tax. He would not have kept his growing gains physically around him were it not that his unbeatable system was also a splendid fraud.

The best frauds are only ever discovered by accident, and Arnold could not envisage any such accident happening to *him*.

Jamie Finland woke to his usual darkness and thought three disconnected thoughts within seconds of consciousness. 'The sun is shining. It is Wednesday. They are racing today here at Ascot.' He stretched out a hand and put his fingers delicately down on the top of his bedside tape-recorder. There was a cassette lying there. Jamie smiled, slid the cassette into the recorder, and switched on.

His mother's voice spoke to him. 'Jamie, don't forget the man is coming to mend the television at ten-thirty and please put the washing into the machine, there's a dear, as I am so pushed this morning, and would you mind having yesterday's soup again for lunch. I've left it in a saucepan ready. Don't lose all that money this afternoon or I'll cut the plug off your stereo. Home soon after eight, love.'

Jamie Finland's thirty-eight-year-old mother supported them both on her earnings as an agency nurse, and she had made a fair job, her son considered, of bringing up a child who could not see. He was fifteen. He studied in Braille at home and passed exams with credit.

He rose gracefully from bed and put on his clothes: blue shirt, blue jeans. 'Blue is Jamie's favourite colour,' his mother would say, and her friends would say, 'Oh yes?' and she could see them thinking: how could he possibly know? But Jamie could identify blue as surely as his mother's voice, and red, and yellow and every colour in the spectrum, as long as it was daylight.

'I can't see in the dark,' he had said when he was six, and only his mother, from watching his sureness by day and his stumbling by night, had understood what he meant. Walking radar, she called him. Like many young blind people he could sense easily the wavelength of light, and distinguish the infinitesimal changes of frequency reflected from coloured things close to him. Strangers thought him uncanny. Jamie believed everyone could see that way if they wanted to, and could not clearly understand what was meant by sight.

He made and ate some toast and thankfully opened

the door to the television-fixer. 'In my room,' he said, leading the way. 'We've got sound but no picture.'

The television-fixer looked at the blind eyes and shrugged. If the boy wanted a picture he was entitled to it, same as everyone else who paid their rental. 'Have to take it back to the workshop,' he said, judicially pressing buttons.

'The races are on,' Jamie said. 'Can you fix it by then?'

'Races? Oh yeah. Well, tell you what, I'll lend you another set. Got one in the van . . .' He staggered off with the invalid set and returned with the replacement. 'Not short of radios, are you?' he said, looking around. 'What do you want six for?'

'I leave them tuned to different things,' Jamie said. 'That one' – he pointed accurately – 'listens to aircraft, that one to the police, those three over there are on ordinary radio stations, and this one . . . local broadcasts.'

'What you need is a transmitter. Put you in touch with all the world.'

'I'm working on it,' Jamie said. 'Starting today.'

He closed the door after the man and wondered whether betting on a certainty was in itself a crime.

Greg Simpson had no such qualms. He paid his way into the Ascot paddock, and ambled off to add a beer and sandwich to a comfortable paunch. Two years now, he thought, munching, since he had first set foot on the Turf: two years since he had exchanged his principles for prosperity and been released from paralysing depression.

They seemed a distant memory, now, those fifteen months in the wilderness; the awful humiliating collapse of his seemingly secure and pensionable world. There was no comfort in knowing that mergers and cutbacks had thrown countless near-top managers like himself straight on to the redundancy heap.

At fifty-two, with long success-strewn experience and genuine administrative skill, he had expected that he at least would find another suitable post easily, but door after closed door, and a regretful chorus of 'Sorry, Greg', 'Sorry, old chap', 'Sorry, Mr Simpson, we need someone younger', had finally thrust him into agonized despair. And it was just when, in spite of all their anxious economies, his wife had had to deny their two children even the money to go swimming, that he had seen the curious advertisement:

'*Jobs offered to mature respectable persons who must have been unwillingly unemployed for at least twelve months.*'

Part of his mind told him he was being invited to commit a crime, but he had gone none the less to the subsequently arranged interview in a London pub, and he had been relieved, after all, to meet the very ordinary man holding out salvation – a man like himself, middle-aged, middle-educated, wearing a suit and tie and indoor skin.

'Do you go to the races?' Arnold Roper asked him bluntly, fixing a penetrating gaze on him. 'Do you gamble on anything at all? Do you follow the horses? Play to win?'

'No,' Greg Simpson said, prudishly, seeing the job prospect disappear but feeling all the same superior. 'I'm afraid not.'

'Do you bet on dogs? Go to bingo? Do the pools? Play bridge? Feel attracted by roulette?' the man persisted.

Greg Simpson silently but emphatically shook his head and prepared to leave.

'Good,' said Arnold Roper, cheerfully. 'Gamblers are no good to me, not for this job.'

Greg Simpson relaxed into a glow of self-congratulation on his own virtue. 'What job, then?' he asked.

Arnold Roper wiped out Simpson's complacent smugness. 'Going to the races,' he said bluntly. 'Betting when I say bet, and never at any other time. You would have to go to race meetings most days, like any other job. You would be betting on certainties, and after every win I would expect you to send me my reward.' He named a very reasonable sum. 'Anything you made above that would be yours. It is foolproof, and safe. If you go about it in a businesslike way, and don't get tempted into the mug's game of backing your own fancy, you'll do very well. Think it over. If you're interested, meet me here again tomorrow.'

Betting on certainties . . . every one a winner: Arnold Roper had been as good as his word, and Greg Simpson's lifestyle had returned to normal. His qualms had evaporated once he learned that even if the fraud were discovered, he himself would not be involved. He did not know how his employer acquired his infallible information and, if he speculated, he didn't ask.

He knew him only as Bob Smith, and had never met him since those first two days; but he heeded his warning that if he failed to attend the specified race meetings or failed to send his agreed payment, the bounty would stop dead.

He finished his sandwich and went down to mingle with the bookmakers as the horses cantered down to the post for the start of the first race.

From high on the stands Arnold Roper looked down through powerful binoculars, spotting his men one by one. The perfect workforce he thought: no absenteeism, no union troubles, no complaints.

There were twenty-one of them at present on his register, all contentedly receiving his information, all dutifully returning their moderate levies, and none of them knowing of the existence of the others. In an average week, after expenses, he easily added a thousand or more in readies to his bedroom hoard.

In the five years since he had begun in a small way to put his scheme into operation, he had never picked a defaulter. The thinking-it-over time gave the timid and the honest an easy way out; and if Arnold himself had doubts, he simply failed to return on day two.

The rest, added gradually one by one to the fold, lived comfortably with quiet minds and prayed that their benefactor would never be rumbled.

Arnold himself couldn't see why he ever should be. He put down the binoculars and began in his methodical fashion to get on with his day's work. There was always a good deal to see to in the way of filling in forms, testing equipment, and checking that the nearby telephone was working. Arnold never left anything to chance.

Down at the starting gate, sixteen two-year-olds bucked and skittered as they were fed by the handlers into the stalls. Two-year-old colts, thought the starter resignedly, looking at his watch, could behave like a pack of prima donnas in a heatwave in Milan. If they didn't hurry with that chestnut at present squealing and backing away, he would let the other runners off without him.

He was all too aware of the television cameras pointing his way, mercilessly awaiting his smallest error. Starters who got the races off minutes late were unpopular. Starters who got the races off early were asking for official reprimands and universal curses, because of the fiddles that had been worked in the past on premature departures.

The starter ruled the chestnut out of the race and pulled his lever at time plus three minutes twenty seconds, entering the figure meticulously in his records. The gates crashed open, the fifteen remaining colts roared out of the stalls, and along on the stands the serried ranks of race glasses followed their progress over the five furlongs.

Alone in his special box, the judge watched intently. A big pack of two-year-olds over five furlongs was a problem, presenting occasionally even to his practised eyes a multiple dead heat.

He had learned all the horses by name and all the colours by heart, a chore he shared every day with the race-reading commentators, and from long acquaintance he could recognize most of the jockeys by their riding style alone, but still the ignominy of making a mistake flitted uneasily through his dreams.

Up in his eyrie the television commentator looked through his high-magnification binoculars, which were mounted rock-steady like a telescope, and spoke unhurriedly into his microphone.

'Among the early leaders are Breakaway and Middle Park, followed closely by Pickup, Jetset, Darling Boy and Gumshoe . . . Coming to the furlong marker the leaders are bunched, with Jetset, Darling Boy, Breakaway all showing . . . One furlong out, there is nothing to choose between Darling Boy, Jetset, Gumshoe, Pickup . . . In the last hundred yards . . . Jetset, Darling Boy . . .'

The colts stretched their necks, the jockeys swung their whips, the crowd rose on tiptoes and yelled in a roar which drowned the commentary, and in his box the judge's eyes ached with effort. Darling Boy, Jetset, Gumshoe and Pickup swept past the winning post in line abreast, and an impersonal voice over the widespread loudspeakers announced: 'Photograph. Photograph.'

Half a mile away in his own room, Jamie Finland listened to the race on television and tried to imagine the pictures on the screen. Racing was misty to him. He knew the shape of horses from handling toys and riding a rocker, but their size and speed were mysterious; he had no conception at all of a broad sweep of a railed racecourse, or of the size or appearance of trees.

As he grew older, Jamie was increasingly aware that he had drawn lucky in the maternal stakes and he had become in his teens protective rather than rebellious, which sometimes touched his hard-pressed mother to tears. It was for her sake that he had welcomed the television-fixer, knowing that, for her, sound without pictures was almost as bad as pictures without sound were for himself.

Despite a lot of trying, he could pick up little from the screen through his ultra-sensitive fingertips. Electronically produced colours gave him none of the vibrations of natural light.

He sat hunched with tension at his table, the telephone beside his right hand and one of his radios at his left. There was no telling, he thought, whether the bizarre thing would happen again; but if it did, he would be ready.

'One furlong out, nothing to choose . . .' said the television commentator, his voice rising in excitement-inducing crescendo. 'In the last hundred yards, Jetset, Darling Boy, Pickup and Gumshoe . . . At the post, all in a line . . . perhaps Pickup got there in the last stride but we'll have to wait for the photograph. Meanwhile, let's see the closing stages of the race again . . .'

The television went back on its tracks, and Jamie waited intently with his fingers over the quick easy numbers of the push-button telephone.

Down the road at the racecourse the crowds buzzed like agitated bees round the bookmakers, who were transacting deals as fast as they could. Photo-finishes were always popular with serious gamblers, who bet with fervour on the outcome.

Some punters really believed in the evidence of their own quick eyes; others found it a chance to hedge their main bet or even recoup a positive loss. A photo was the second chance, the lifebelt to the drowning, the temporary reprieve from torn-up tickets and anti-climax.

'Six-to-four on Pickup,' shouted young Billy Hitchins hoarsely, from his prime bookmaking pitch in the front row facing the stands. 'Six-to-four on Pickup.' A rush of customers descending from the crowded steps enveloped him.

'A tenner, Pickup, right, sir. Five on Gumshoe, right, sir. Twenty, Pickup, you're on, sir. A hundred? Yeah, if you like. A hundred at evens, Jetset, why not . . .' Billy Hitchins, in whose opinion Darling Boy had taken the race by a nostril, was happy to take the money.

Greg Simpson accepted Billy Hitchins' ticket for an even hundred on Jetset and hurried to repeat his bet with as many bookmakers as he could reach. There was never much time between the arrival of the knowledge and the announcement of the winner. Never much, but always enough. Two minutes at least. Sometimes as much as five. A determined punter could strike five or six bets in that time, given a thick skin and a ruthless use of the elbows.

Greg reckoned he could burrow to the front of the closest throng after all those years of rush-hour commuting on the Underground, and he managed, that day at Ascot, to lay out all the cash he had brought with him; all at evens, all on Jetset.

Neither Billy Hitchins nor any of his colleagues felt the slightest twinge of suspicion. Sure, there was a lot of support for Jetset; but so there was for the three other horses, and in a multiple finish like this one a good deal of money always changed hands. Billy Hitchins welcomed it himself, because it gave him, too, a chance of making a second profit on the race.

Greg noticed one or two others scurrying with wads to Jetset and wondered, not for the first time, if they, too, were working for Mr Smith. He was sure he'd seen them often at other meetings, but he felt no inclination at all to accost one of them and ask. Safety lay in anonymity – for him, for them and, of course, for Bob Smith himself.

The judge in his box pored earnestly over the black-and-white print, sorting out which nose belonged to Darling Boy, and which to Pickup. He could discern the winner easily enough, and had murmured its number aloud as he wrote it on the pad lying beside him.

The microphone linked to the public announcement system waited mutely at his elbow for him to make his decision on second and third places, a task seemingly increasingly difficult. Number two, or number eight. But which was which? The seconds ticked by.

It was quiet in his box, the scurrying and shouting among the bookmakers' stands below hardly reaching him through the thick window-glass.

At his shoulder a racecourse official waited patiently, his job only to make the actual announcement, once the decision was made. With a bright light and a magnifying glass the judge studied the noses. If he got them wrong, a thousand knowledgeable photo-readers would let him know it.

He wondered if he should see about a new prescription for his glasses. Photographs never seemed so sharp in outline to him these days.

*

Greg Simpson thought regretfully that the judge was overdoing the delay. If he had known he would have had so much time, he would have brought with him more cash. Still, the clear profit he would shortly make was a fine afternoon's work, and he would send Mr Smith his meagre share with a grateful heart.

Greg Simpson smiled contentedly, and briefly, as if touching a lucky talisman, he fingered the tiny transistorized hearing aid he wore unobtrusively under hair and trilby behind his left ear.

Jamic Finland listened intently, head bent, his curling dark hair falling onto the radio with which he eavesdropped on aircraft. The faint hiss of the carrier wave reached him unchanged, but he waited with quickening pulse and a fluttering feeling of excitement. If it didn't happen, he thought briefly, it would be very boring indeed.

Although he was nerve-strainingly prepared, he almost missed it. The radio spoke one single word, distantly, faintly, without emphasis: 'Eleven.' The carrier wave hissed on, as if never disturbed, and it took Jamie's brain two whole seconds to light up with a laugh of joy.

He pressed the telephone buttons and connected himself to the local bookmaking firm. 'Hello? This is Jamie Finland. I have some credit arranged with you for this afternoon. Well, please will you put it all on the photo-finish of this race they've just run at Ascot? On number eleven, please.'

'Eleven?' echoed a matter-of-fact voice at the other end. 'Jetset?'

'That's right,' Jamie said patiently.

'Eleven. Jetset. All at evens, right?'

'Right,' Jamie said. 'I was watching it on the box.'

'Don't we all, chum,' said the voice in farewell, clicking off.

Jamie sat back with a tingling feeling of mischief. If eleven really had won, he was surely plain robbing the bookie. But who could know? How could anyone ever know? He wouldn't tell his mother, because she would disapprove and might make him give the winnings back.

He imagined her voice if she came home and found he had doubled her money. He also imagined it if she found he had lost it all on the first race, betting on the result of a photo-finish that he couldn't even see.

He hadn't told her that it was because of the numbers on the radio he had wanted to bet at all. He'd said that he knew people often bet from home while they were watching racing on television. He'd said it would give him a marvellous new interest, if he could do that while she was at work.

He had persuaded her without much trouble to lend him a stake and arrange things with the bookmaker's, and he wouldn't have done it at all if the certainty factor had been missing.

When he'd first been given the radio which received aircraft frequencies, he had spent hours and days listening to the calls of the jetliners overhead on their way in and out of Heathrow; but the fascination had worn off, and gradually he tuned in less and less.

By accident one day, having twiddled the tuning knob aimlessly without finding an interesting channel, he forgot to switch the set off. In the afternoon, while he was listening to the Ascot televised races, the radio suddenly emitted a number: 'Twenty-three.'

Jamie switched the set off but took little real notice until the television commentator, announcing the result of the photo-finish, spoke almost as if in echo. 'Twenty-three ... Swan Lake, number twenty-three, is the winner.'

'How odd,' Jamie thought. He left the tuning knob undisturbed, and switched the aircraft radio on again the following Saturday, along with Kempton Park races on television. There were two photo-finishes, but no voice-of-God on the ether. Ditto nil results from Doncaster, Chepstow and Epsom persuaded him, shrugging, to put it down to coincidence but, two weeks later with the rearrival of a meeting at Ascot, he decided to give it one more try.

'Five,' said the radio quietly; and later 'Ten.' And, duly, numbers five and ten were given the verdict by the judge.

*

The judge, now shaking his head over Darling Boy and Pickup and deciding he could put off the moment no longer, handed his written-down result to the waiting official, who leaned forward and drew the microphone to his mouth.

'First, number eleven,' he said. 'A dead heat for second place between numbers two and eight. First Jetset. Dead heat for second, Darling Boy and Pickup. The distance between first and second a short head. The fourth horse was number twelve.'

The judge leaned back in his chair and wiped the sweat from his forehead. Another photo-finish safely past . . . but there was no doubt they were testing to his nerves.

Arnold Roper picked up his binoculars the better to see the winning punters collect from the bookmakers. His twenty-one trusty men had certainly had time today for a thorough killing. Greg Simpson, in particular, was sucking honey all along the line; but then Greg Simpson, with his outstanding managerial skills, was always, in Arnold's view, the one most likely to do best. Greg's success was as pleasing to Arnold as his own.

Billy Hitchins handed Greg his winnings without a second glance, and paid out, too, to five others whose transistor hearing aids were safely hidden by hair. He reckoned he had lost, altogether, on the photo betting; but his book for the race itself had been robustly healthy. Billy Hitchins, not displeased, switched his mind to the next event.

Jamie Finland laughed aloud and banged his table with an ecstatic fist. Someone, somewhere, was talking through an open microphone, and if Jamie had had the luck to pick up the transmission, why shouldn't he? Why shouldn't he? He thought of the information as an accident, not a fraud, and he waited with uncomplicated pleasure for another bunch of horses to finish nose to nose.

Betting on certainties, he decided, quietening his voice of conscience, was not a crime if you came by the information innocently.

After the fourth race he telephoned to bet on number fifteen, increasing his winnings geometrically.

Greg Simpson went home at the end of the afternoon with a personal storage problem almost as pressing as Arnold's. There was a limit, he discovered, to the amount of ready cash one could stow away in an ordinary suit, and he finally had to wrap the stuff in a newspaper and carry it home under his arm, like fish and chips.

'Two in one day,' he thought warmly. 'A real clean-up. A day to remember.' And there was always tomorrow, back here at Ascot, and Saturday at Sandown, and next week, according to the list which had arrived anonymously on the usual postcard, Newbury and Windsor. With a bit of luck he could soon afford a new car, and Joan could book up for the skiing holiday with the children.

Billy Hitchins packed away his stand and equipment, and with the help of his clerk carried them the half-mile along the road to his betting shop in Ascot High Street. Billy at eighteen had horrified his teachers by ducking university and apprenticing his bright mathematical brain to his local bookie. Billy at twenty-four had taken over the business, and now, three years later, was poised for expansion.

He had had a good day on the whole and, after totting up the total and locking the safe, he took his betting-shop manager along to the pub.

'Funny thing,' said the manager over the second beer. 'That new account – you know, the one you fixed up yesterday, with that nurse.'

'Oh yes . . . the nurse. Gave me money in advance. They don't often do that.' He drank his Scotch and water.

'Yeah . . . Well, this Finland, while he was watching the telly, he phoned in two bets, both on the results of the photos, and he got it right both times.'

'Can't have that,' said Billy, with mock severity.

'He didn't place other bets, see? Unusual, that.'

'What did you say his name was?' Billy asked.

'Jamie Finland.'

The barmaid leaned towards them over the bar, her friendly face smiling and the pink sweater leaving little to the imagination. 'Jamie Finland?' she said. 'Ever such a nice boy, isn't he? Shame about him being blind.'

'What?' said Billy.

The barmaid nodded. 'Him and his mother, they live just down the road in those new flats, next door to my sister. He stays home most of the time, studying and listening to his radios. And you'd never believe it, but he can tell colours; he can really. My sister says it's really weird, but he told her she was wearing a green coat and she was.'

'I don't believe it.'

'It's true as God's my judge,' said the barmaid, offended.

'No,' Billy said. 'I don't believe that even if he can tell a green coat from a red that he could distinguish colours on a television screen with three or four horses crossing the line abreast. You can't do it often even if you can see.' He sat and thought. 'On the other hand, I lost a lot today on those photos.'

He thought longer. 'We all took a caning over those photos. I heard several of the other bookies complaining about the run on Jetset.' He frowned. 'I don't see how it could be rigged, though.'

Billy put down his glass with a crash which startled the whole bar. 'Did you say Jamie Finland listens to radios? What radios?'

'How should I know?' said the barmaid, bridling.

'He lives near the course,' Billy said, thinking feverishly. 'So just suppose he somehow overheard the photo result before it was given on the loudspeakers. But that doesn't explain the delay . . . how there was time for him, and probably quite a lot of others who heard the same thing, to get their money on.'

'I don't know what you're on about,' said the barmaid.

'I think I'll pop along and see Jamie Finland,' said Billy Hitchins. 'And ask who or what he heard . . . if he heard anything at all.'

'Bit far-fetched,' said the manager judiciously. 'The only person who could delay things long enough would be the judge.'

'Oh my God,' said Billy, awe-struck by the thought. 'What about the judge?'

Arnold Roper did not know about the long fuse being lit in the pub. To Arnold, Billy Hitchins was a name on a bookmaker's stand. He could not suppose that brainy Billy Hitchins would drink in a pub where the barmaid had a sister who lived next door to a blind boy who had picked up his discreet transmission on a carelessly left-on radio which was capable of receiving one-ten to one-forty megahertz on VHF.

Arnold Roper travelled serenely homeward with his walkie-talkie-type transmitter hidden as usual inside his inner jacket pocket, its short aerial retracted now safely out of sight.

The line-of-sight low-powered frequency he used was in his opinion completely safe, as only a passing aircraft was likely to receive it, and no pilot on earth would connect a simple number spoken on the air with the winner of the photo-finish down at Ascot, or Epsom, or Newmarket, or York.

Back on the racecourse Arnold had carefully packed away and securely locked up the extremely delicate and expensive apparatus which belonged to the firm which employed him. Arnold Roper was not the judge. Arnold Roper's job lay in operating the photo-finish camera. It was he who watched the print develop; he who could take his time delivering it to the judge; he who always knew the winner first.

# CORKSCREW

*The road to justice is winding, long, expensive and slow, and sometimes never arrives.* Corkscrew *gets there, more or less, scattering lessons on the way.*

*First lesson: if you aim to be kind, be careful.*

Sandy Nutbridge leaned on the white-painted rails of a private training circuit in the American state of South Carolina and tried to size up the undemonstrative man beside him.

Both were English. Sandy Nutbridge was trying to sell to the other (Jules Reginald Harlow) the two-year-old South Carolina-bred filly presently being fast-cantered round the track by the top-ranking exercise groom employed by Sandy Nutbridge whenever he wanted to make a multi-nought sale.

His spiel and patter about the filly's breeding and early showing of speed were for once truthful. The fervour he put into his admiration of the fine-boned skull, the kindly slanted eye and the deep-capacity chest was in fact justified. The filly at that moment was earning every compliment paid her – it was only the future, as in all of life, that couldn't be foretold.

Jules Reginald Harlow watched the filly's smooth action and listened to the genuine enthusiasm in the salesman's voice. He thought Sandy Nutbridge good at his job, but beyond that paid more attention to the scudding two-year-old that seemed to be all he needed.

The exercise groom finished two circuits – one walking and trotting, one a fast canter – and, pulling up, trotted to the two watchers on the rails.

'Thanks, Pete.' Nutbridge nodded.

'And thanks,' Jules Harlow added. He turned to the salesman. 'Subject to a vet passing the filly sound, I'll have her at the price we agreed.'

The two men shook hands on the deal and Jules Harlow without excitement climbed into the dark green Lincoln Town Car waiting near by and drove away.

Sandy Nutbridge telephoned the bloodstock agency for whom he acted and reported the successful sale. His principal, Ray Wichelsea, who owned the agency, greatly esteemed Sandy Nutbridge, chiefly as a salesman but partly as a man. Ray Wichelsea saw Sandy's thickset body, wiry greying hair and sensible English voice as reassuring assets encouraging customers to put their faith in the agency and their money on the line.

'Our Mr Harlow,' Sandy Nutbridge reported, 'is one of your silent types. I wouldn't say he knows a whole lot about horses. He shook hands on the deal for the filly but, like you told me not to, I didn't ask him for an up-front deposit.'

'No. What did he look like?'

Puzzled, Sandy Nutbridge did his best. 'Well . . . he was shortish. I suppose about fifty. Ordinary. Sort of posh English accent, though. Wore a grey suit, and a tie. He wouldn't stand out in a crowd.

'Our Mr Harlow,' Ray Wichelsea said with peaceful emphasis, 'the Mr Harlow you've just described, is, I am almost certain, a computer originator. An inventor. An entrepreneur.'

'How does that affect us?' Nutbridge asked.

'He can afford a whole bunch of fillies.'

The quiet Mr Harlow was buying the splendid two-year-old as an engagement gift for the lively widow who had decided he should be her husband number three. Numbers one and two had bossed her around and then died and left her huge fortunes: Jules Harlow, richer yet, found pleasure in letting her run the show. The widow adored him.

She knew all about horses and spent days of delight at the racetrack. Before he met her, Jules had been barely aware of the Kentucky Derby. He spent his days inventing and developing microchip circuits and was quiet because of the depth of his thoughts.

When these two had first dined and slept together, their different interests and personalities had surprisingly meshed. Time had thoroughly cemented their coalition.

In England, Sandy Nutbridge's mother packed her own suitcase with excitement and tried unsuccessfully to damp down the high spirits of her two grandchildren, Bob and Miranda (ten and eight), who were to accompany her to South Carolina to spend two weeks of the Easter school holidays with their father.

Sandy Nutbridge, divorced, seldom saw his children. The forthcoming visit, and that of his mother, filled him with genuine joy. Two whole weeks! He had told Ray Wichelsea not to line him up for any work during that time.

He had sent the money for all his family's fares: his widowed mother lived on a meagre pension, and his ex-wife, remarried, had said if he wanted to have the children to stay, he could pay for them. He went to meet them at the airport and in hugs and kisses considered every dollar well spent. His mother, in new clothes, wiped tears from her eyes, and the children, who had never left England before, stared at the surprising spaciousness of America and were open-mouthed with ingenuous awe.

Sandy Nutbridge lived in a rented fourth-floor two-bedroomed lakeside condominium apartment with entrancing views of sailboats, forests, blue-grey water and the setting sun. An hour's drive over easy rolling roads took him to the centre of horse country where, in Ray Wichelsea's office, he regularly put his feet up on a desk and drank coffee from disposable cups. Ray Wichelsea paid him by commission, not salary, and he collected his commissions in cash.

The Nutbridge life, on the day the children arrived, was coasting along comfortably at a fair standard of prosperity: the life of a reasonably honest operator with no political ambitions.

The children – and his mother – although tired from the transatlantic flight, were ecstatic over a real American fast-food chain supper of burgers and fries, learning the idiom 'Hold the mayo' with innocent glee.

That was Tuesday. At breakfast-time on Wednesday morning, Sandy Nutbridge put on a thin dressing-gown over his pyjamas and, leaving his family exploring unfamiliar breeds of cereal, went down in slippers to the condominium lobby, as he always did, to buy a daily paper from the vending machine there.

Behind a desk in the lobby sat the blue-uniformed condominium many-job factotum, who acted as security guard, receptionist, lister of callers and message taker. Sandy Nutbridge casually said, 'Hi, Bill,' as he always did and turned to go back to the elevator, paying no attention to the two armed policemen leaning on Bill's desk.

Bill, however, said, 'That's him,' to the policemen who, as if galvanized by puppet strings, straightened up fast and pounced on Sandy Nutbridge, slamming him face first against the green-patterned wallpaper and shouting at him to raise his hands and spread his legs apart.

Sandy Nutbridge had lived long enough in the United States to know that protest was futile. The policemen out of fear needed to know there were no handguns concealed in the sleeping pyjamas. Sandy might think it ludicrous that with maximum roughness they handcuffed his wrists behind his back and 'read him his rights', which mostly appeared to consist of a threat that if he said anything it would be held against him in court, but that seemed to be the American way of the world.

'What am I supposed to have done?' he asked.

The policemen didn't know. They had been dispatched merely to 'bring Nutbridge in for questioning'.

Sandy Nutbridge asked if they would accompany him upstairs so that he could dress and also tell his kids he would be gone for a couple of hours. The policemen didn't bother to answer but shoved him towards the outside doors.

'Tell my mother, Bill,' Sandy called over his shoulder, but wasn't sure his request would be granted. Bill couldn't be relied on for the slightest favour.

Sandy Nutbridge still didn't take the farcical arrest seriously and laughed a good deal to himself when the policemen drove in circles because they'd lost the way back to the main road into town. But stupidly hilarious or not, the situation hardened into seriously worrying when, at police headquarters, he was unceremoniously pushed into a barred cell and locked there.

Vigorously protesting, he was finally allowed one phone call, which he spent on alerting a friend who was also a lawyer to come at once to his aid after reassuring his no doubt frightened family.

Sandy Nutbridge had never before needed the services of a lawyer in criminal proceedings (had never in fact been arrested before) and wasn't aware that his friend was a better drinking companion than advocate. Wasn't aware either that his friend had got him arrested in the first place by sounding off within range of the wrong ears.

Patrick Green, the lawyer friend, saying he was trying to find out on what charge Sandy was being held, came no nearer pin-pointery than, 'The IRS wants you on a three-year-old tax matter involving drug money deposits in your bank.'

Baffled and by then deeply alarmed, Sandy Nutbridge found himself in court on Thursday morning (after a wretched night in the cells) before a judge who seemed equally unsure of the evidence for his presence there but who had a solution for everything. To Patrick Green's plea that Sandy be released at once, the public prosecutor responded that as Nutbridge was a British citizen with a resident alien 'green card' (which was in fact white) he might slip out of the country before the IRS completed its investigation. The public prosecutor, therefore, opposed setting Nutbridge free on bail.

The judge, with years of weary cases behind him, banged his gavel and set bail at one hundred thousand dollars.

Patrick Green had expected it, but to Sandy Nutbridge such a sum was a disaster. He didn't have a hundred thousand dollars, nor would his bank lend it to him without collateral. Unless he raised the money, however, he would stay behind bars until he came up for trial, and as no one seemed to be able to say accurately what he was being accused of, no trial date could be set.

Patrick Green reassured his friend Sandy that the bail money could quickly be raised: it would, after all, be repaid to the people lending it as soon as a trial date was set and Sandy appeared in court.

Between them, they did sums: so much from Sandy himself, so much from his mother, who telephoned and borrowed from neighbours and against her pension from her sympathetic bank in England; and so much from Ray Wichelsea, who lent his own money, not his firm's, because of his faith in Sandy's strong declaration of his innocence of any crime he could think of.

When all was added up, by Thursday late afternoon, they were still ten thousand dollars short. The money so far on its way by wire from England and the amounts already collected in cashier's cheques in South

Carolina were considered by nightfall to be in the hands of the US District Clerk, who would authorize the setting free from custody of Sandy Nutbridge but only when he physically held the complete one hundred thousand. If, he added not unkindly, *if* the missing ten thousand dollars were in his hands by noon on Friday, he would alert the facility holding Sandy Nutbridge behind bars, and if they received the instruction by two o'clock they would do the necessary paperwork and free Nutbridge that afternoon so that he could spend the weekend and the rest of their intended stay with his mother and children.

Mrs Nutbridge, in tears, telephoned Ray Wichelsea, whom she had never actually met, and begged him to get Sandy out of jail. Ray Wichelsea could afford no more than the substantial sum he had already sent. 'But . . .' he said slowly, 'if it's a last resort, you might try a man to whom Sandy sold a horse a couple of weeks ago. He's rich and he's British. He might listen to you, you never know.'

So Mrs Nutbridge telephoned Jules Reginald Harlow and poured her sensible heart out in sob-laden local-accent English.

'Sandy said I wasn't to bother you,' she finished despairingly. 'He was *adamant*, when I talked to him on the telephone. He says Mr Wichelsea should never have suggested I ask you, but the children have come such a long way from home, and they are *frightened* . . . and *I don't know what to do* . . .' Bewilderment and overwhelming distress closed her throat, and it was for her, the beleaguered grandmother, that Jules Harlow felt sympathy, not for her salesman son, who was probably guilty (he thought) of whatever he'd been hauled in for. Jules Harlow still had faith that justice ruled.

He said 'No promises' to Mrs Nutbridge, but wrote down the address and phone number of Sandy's condominium and said he would ring her back.

Harlow sat for a while with the receiver in his hand rehearing the desperation that he could alleviate. Then he phoned Ray Wichelsea and asked for his opinion.

'If Sandy says he'll surrender to his bail when the time comes,' Wichelsea said, 'then he will. I totally trust him. What's more, his mother has borrowed money all over the place in England towards that iniquitous hundred thousand dollars, and there's no way he's going to default and leave her in bankruptcy and disgrace. If you put up money for his bail, you'll definitely get it back. I wouldn't have put up my own personal savings if I hadn't been certain of it.'

'But,' Jules Harlow responded, 'what has he *done*?'

'He says he hasn't done anything wrong. He says he thinks the tax people believe he's been laundering drug money, but he hasn't.'

'Well . . .' Jules Harlow hesitated, 'has he?'

'If he says not, then he hasn't.'

Ray Wichelsea's certainty didn't altogether convince Jules Harlow, but as the computer genius realized that the essential question wasn't guilt or innocence but whether or not Sandy Nutbridge would surrender to his bail, he telephoned his accountant and asked him what he thought.

'If you want to do it, then do it,' the accountant said. 'There's no reason why you shouldn't.'

It was by then well after going-home time in the city's Thursday afternoon offices: Jules Harlow's day-to-day jobbing attorney had left and would be out of town until Monday, unavailable for advice. Jules Reginald Harlow drummed his fingers and looked out of the window and thought of poor Mrs Nutbridge, and finally dialled her number and put her miseries to rest.

'Oh!' she exclaimed, bereft of breath. 'Oh! Do you mean it? Do you really?'

'You'll have to tell me what to do.'

'Oh. Oh . . .' She slowly recovered. 'Sandy's lawyer,' she said. 'His name is Patrick Green. Well, he's gone to Texas.'

'He's done *what*?'

'He had another case there. He said he had to go tonight. But he's told a sort of colleague of his . . . well, at any rate, someone who shares office space with him . . . to deal with Sandy's bail.' Her voice wavered with uncertainty and doubt, a mirror reflection of Jules Harlow's own feelings. He wished bleakly that he'd never bought the filly from Sandy Nutbridge: that he'd never in the first place thought of giving his fiancée a horse.

Mrs Nutbridge said hastily, 'It's all right, I'm sure it is. Sandy's friend says if you get to his office with a cashier's cheque in time for him to courier it round to the District Clerk by twelve o'clock tomorrow morning Sandy will be freed in the afternoon.'

'Well, who is this friend?'

'He's a lawyer, too. His name is Carl Corunna. He said I should give you his phone number, and ask you to ring him just before nine tomorrow morning when he will be in his office.'

Jules Harlow, frowning, wrote down the number, and felt he couldn't honourably retreat, much as he would have liked.

'I'll see to it, Mrs Nutbridge,' he assured her. 'Do you have any money for food?'

'Mr Wichelsea gave us some. Ever so kind, he's been.'

On Friday morning before nine, Jules Reginald Harlow telephoned the lawyer who shared office space with Patrick Green and asked him how to proceed.

The colleague, Carl Corunna, gave simple instructions without emotion: Jules Harlow should go to his bank and withdraw ten thousand dollars on a cashier's cheque. Mr Harlow should then motor to his – Carl Corunna's – office on the outskirts of the financial centre. He, Carl Corunna, would receive the cheque, give Mr Harlow a receipt for it, and courier it round immediately to the courthouse.

Corunna the colleague gave detailed directions to his office and said he was sure all would go well. The collection of bail money was so common as to be routine.

'Um,' Jules Harlow said, 'do I make the cashier's cheque payable to you?'

'No, no. I'm only acting for Patrick Green as he's away. Get your bank to make it out to him. Come as soon as you can. My office is a good hour's drive from where you are, and time is of the essence, as you know.'

With a sigh of mild reluctance Jules Harlow followed all the instructions and reached a thoroughly conventional suite of attorneys' offices in a building a mile or so from the city centre. He parked outside at eleven-twenty-five.

A bustling receptionist showed him into the book-lined domain of Carl Corunna, who proved to be bulky, bearded and approximately his own age, fifty.

Jules Harlow, reassured, shook his hand. Carl Corunna saw a smallish, slight, unimpressive-looking man whose somewhat fluffy hair was turning grey; and as usual he had no trouble in dominating and conducting the meeting.

'You brought the cheque?' he asked, waving Harlow to a chair, and when he held the expensive piece of paper in his big hands he examined it line by line, nodding his assent.

He pushed buttons on his telephone and told Jules Harlow that he was without delay talking to the US District Clerk's office in the Federal courthouse.

'Yes,' he said into the mouthpiece, 'the last ten thousand for Nutbridge is here. Cashier's cheque, yes. I'll courier it round to you at once. And you do confirm that Nutbridge will be freed this afternoon? Great. Thanks very much.'

He put down the receiver, called for his secretary to make a photocopy of the cheque, and wrote and signed a receipt, giving it to Harlow.

'What's next?' Harlow asked.

'Nothing,' Corunna told him. 'When Sandy Nutbridge gives himself up for trial, you'll get your money back. Until then, you just wait.'

With a sense of anti-climax after the rush, Jules Harlow drove uneventfully home. Sandy Nutbridge was released at three o'clock from the cells. Mrs Nutbridge wept with relief when he walked in through his front door, and the children demanded and ate endless comfort burgers and fries.

Mrs Nutbridge telephoned Jules Harlow to thank him, and after joyful boat trips on the lake for the rest of their holiday, Sandy's family flew safely home to England. Sandy sold more horses. The court moved on to other cases, the Nutbridge urgency quietly receding. Jules Harlow, entranced with his fiancée, only thought about his bail adventure when the filly Sandy had sold him kicked up her tough little heels and won repeatedly.

Three months passed.

Towards the end of that time Jules Reginald Harlow married his delicious horse-racing lady and took her on a wedding trip to Paris. While they were away Sandy Nutbridge was summoned for trial.

Sandy Nutbridge, supported by his lawyer friend Patrick Green (long ago returned from Texas), successfully proved in court that the IRS (Internal Revenue Service – the tax people) had done its sums wrong and was prosecuting him in error. The judge agreed and dismissed the case. As Nutbridge had surrendered to his bail, the District Clerk duly dug out and distributed the one hundred thousand dollars in his care.

And that should have been the end of a fairly unremarkable no-crime event – except that it was only the beginning.

When Jules Harlow in good spirits returned from France he telephoned Ray Wichelsea, engaging him to find him another good young thoroughbred as a wedding gift for his new wife.

'And by the way,' Jules Harlow added, 'any news of Sandy Nutbridge? Is his trial date set yet?'

Ray Wichelsea related the dismissal of the charges and said that all was well. The US District Clerk had returned his – Ray Wichelsea's – money, and Jules

Harlow would no doubt receive his own in a few days' time, now that he was home again.

The few days passed and became three weeks. Jules Harlow wrote to Patrick Green, Sandy's lawyer, and explained that as he was in residence again, he was ready to receive his ten thousand dollars.

A week later he received not ten thousand dollars but a short sharp letter:

Dear Mr Harlow,

I am not forwarding the $10,000 received from the US District Clerk but made payable to me, as Sandy Nutbridge has told me you wish me to apply that sum to my fees incurred on his behalf.

Faithfully yours,
Patrick Green.

Mild Jules Harlow positively gasped. Very seldom did he lose his temper, but when he did it was in a cold sweat of fury, not a red-roaring rampage. He walked tautly into Ray Wichelsea's office and laid the letter on his desk.

Ray Wichelsea, not wanting to lose a top customer, but alarmed by his manner, read the page apprehensively and went pale in his turn. Sandy Nutbridge, summoned urgently by mobile phone, found himself facing two tight-faced hostile men.

He gave the letter on the desk barely a glance and

he shook with his own rage as he forestalled accusation.

'It's not true,' he declared intensely. 'I never said that. What's more, he sent a letter like that to my mother, and I've had her on the phone . . . she's *frantic*. She *borrowed* that money. She borrowed fifty-seven thousand dollars . . . and however will she pay it back if Patrick Green keeps the money? She borrowed against her pension left by my dad. She borrowed from her neighbours and friends and on the security of her sister's house . . . and I've yelled in Green's face but all he does is give me a sappy grin, and says he'll have me back in court if I make a fuss . . .'

'Could he?' Jules Harlow interrupted. 'Could he have you back in court? And on what charge?'

'Laundering drug money and selling drugs,' Sandy Nutbridge said fiercely. 'Which I didn't do. But when he tells lies, people believe him.'

Patrick Green felt secure in embezzling fifty-seven thousand dollars from Mrs Nutbridge and ten thousand dollars from Jules Harlow because he believed both of them to be weak foreigners who wouldn't do much beyond the first agitated squawking. He could make them believe that he wouldn't be able to disprove further IRS allegations of money-laundering and drug-dealing against Sandy Nutbridge if his fees weren't paid for the first case. The IRS had believed and acted on his allegations the first time and, because of its habitually suspicious outlook, he had faith it would do it again.

Patrick Green, well pleased with his clever scheme, used the Nutbridge bail money to pay off his own personally threatening debts. He had borrowed too much at exorbitant interest rates from dangerous people, and had come frighteningly close to their debt-collection methods, but no longer now need he fear being punched to pulp in a dark alley. Not a violent man himself, he shrank from even the thought of the crunch of fists. He felt very relieved indeed to have been able to steal the feeble old British people's money to get himself out of the certainty of pain, and no flutter of remorse troubled his self-satisfaction.

Patrick Green had reckoned correctly that Sandy Nutbridge would month by month send to his mother instalments to pay off what she'd borrowed on his behalf. Green knew it would cost Sandy Nutbridge far more then he could afford to pay lawyers to try to recover his mother's money through the courts. What Patrick Green had totally overlooked was the nature of the small quiet man whose ten thousand dollars he had pocketed with the help of his colleague Carl Corunna.

Carl Corunna, big and bearded, had reported Jules Harlow, after their meeting, to be an ineffectual mouse, ignorant and easily defeated. Carl Corunna had then insisted that he had earned half the embezzled ten thousand dollars for instructing Harlow to make the cashier's cheque payable to Patrick Green himself, and not more safely directly to the US District Clerk. Patrick Green, bitterly arguing, finally offered one thousand: they settled on two.

Jules Reginald Harlow, though he might be unworldly in matters of bail bonds, still had an implacable belief that justice should be done. He set about finding himself an attorney of sufficient brain to out-think frauds, and via businessmen with inside understanding came finally to a meeting with a young good-looking electric coil of energy called David T. Vynn.

'Mr Harlow,' Vynn said, 'even if you get your money back, which I have to tell you is doubtful, it will cost you maybe double in lawyers' fees.'

'Your fees, do you mean?'

'Yes, my fees. My advice to you is to write off the loss and put it down to experience. It will cost you less in the end.'

Jules Harlow spent a long minute looking at the boyish outcome of his attorney search. He had expected David T. Vynn to be more substantial, both in body and years: someone more like big, bearded Carl Corunna, he realized. He also remembered, however, that physicists, mathematicians, poets, painters, composers and nearly all innovators (including himself) had been struck by divine revelation in their twenties. He had asked for the best: he must trust that in David T. Vynn he had got it.

David T. Vynn (twenty-nine) spent the same minute remembering what he'd been told about Jules Harlow (fifty-one): that a chamois on a mountainside couldn't leap as fast or as far as this grey man's intellect. He had taken this – to him – minor case out of interest in the computer-genius mind.

'Mr Vynn,' the grey man said, 'it isn't a matter of money.'

'Of pride?' The question was nearly an insult, but the attorney wanted to know the strength and origin of his client's motivation.

Jules Harlow smiled. 'Perhaps of pride. But of principle, certainly.' He paused, then said, 'I don't know my way around the corkscrews of the American law. I need a champion who does. I want Patrick Green to curse the day he thought of robbing me, and I won't give up on you unless you yourself admit defeat.'

David T. Vynn thought drily, with inner delight, that Patrick Green had robbed the wrong man.

Client and attorney met again a week later.

David T. Vynn reported, 'To prevent the movement of large amounts of drug money, there is a law in America that says banks and other financial institutions must inform the IRS, the tax people, whenever ten thousand dollars or more in cash is either deposited or withdrawn from a private account in any one day.'

'Yes,' Jules Harlow nodded, 'I know.'

'Sandy Nutbridge was arrested because nearly three

years ago he had paid into his account three large sums of cash within two days. The payments aggregated twenty-two thousand dollars. The case against him was dismissed not because there was no evidence but because of affidavits from Ray Wichelsea and others that various legitimate commissions on horse sales had by coincidence been paid to him in cash in that time. He had declared the cash as income and paid tax on it. Case *then* dismissed.'

'End of story.'

'Not quite.' David Vynn smiled thinly. 'The IRS had had Sandy Nutbridge arrested in the first place because of information laid against him by a so-called friend in whom he had unwisely confided. A lawyer friend who saw all sorts of ways to profit.'

Jules Harlow said, 'Dear God.'

'Quite.' His attorney nodded. 'Patrick Green got Sandy Nutbridge first jailed and then bailed and is, I'm told, now stoking things up to have Nutbridge back behind bars on a charge of selling cocaine, that is if he doesn't pay Green something near another thirty thousand dollars for a fee. I have to say that in Green's leech-like machinations, your ten thousand is chicken feed.'

Jules Harlow said blankly, 'What can we do?'

'There are two roads to go.' David T. Vynn was cheerful: he liked a good fight. 'You can sue him for the money in court, and you can complain to the South

Carolina Bar Association in an effort to get him disqualified from practising law.'

'Which do you suggest?'

'Both.'

Hearing nothing from Jules Reginald Harlow for quite some time, Patrick Green told himself complacently that he'd been absolutely right, the pathetic little guy from England had discovered it would cost him too much to kick up a storm and had caved in without making trouble.

Patrick Green, approaching forty, had for many years scavenged on the fringes of the law, never achieving the recognition he thought his due. He dreamed of brilliantly defending successfully in major murder trials but more typically lost misdemeanour cases in county courts. Most of his work, by this stage in his unsatisfactory career, consisted of carrying out dishonest tasks for other dishonest lawyers. 'Gifts' like Sandy Nutbridge came along rarely.

It was a nasty shock for him when he received notice that Jules Harlow was suing him for conversion, civil theft and breach of constructive trust in the matter of his ten thousand dollars. He didn't like it that an attorney, David T. Vynn, was requesting a deposition. The grey little Englishman, Green frowned, should have learned his lesson and cut his losses. He, Green, would make sure that the little man not only lost his case, but would be much the poorer for having brought it.

Patrick Green didn't much fear the deposition itself: he would swear on oath to tell the truth and then lie from start to finish. He had done it many times. People tended to believe what was said in a deposition (a sworn statement of fact) because lying under oath constituted perjury punishable by imprisonment.

Patrick Green, skilful at misrepresentation and evasion, told believable lies for nearly two hours at his deposition, with an appearance throughout of sincerity and conviction.

Jules Reginald Harlow met his attorney David T. Vynn for breakfast in a hotel. David T. Vynn preferred dining-rooms to offices, first because no 'bugs' could be listening and second because he was permanently hungry.

Over cereal, eggs Benedict and bacon on the side he described Patrick Green at his deposition as ingratiating, smooth-eyed and plausible, and over strawberries, waffles and maple syrup he outlined Green's reply to Harlow's charges, which was that Jules Harlow on the telephone had told him – Green – to apply the ten thousand dollars to his – Green's – fees. He – Green – couldn't understand why Harlow should want to go back on the deal.

'Green was attended at his deposition by the attorney acting in his defence,' David Vynn said. 'He gave his name as Carl Corunna. Is he the person who told you to make your cashier's cheque payable to Green? Is he the one who received the cheque and gave you a receipt for it, and couriered it round to the court?'

'Yes.'

'Good.'

'How is it good?' Harlow asked.

'Because I can get him disqualified as defendant's counsel. Er . . .' he explained, seeing Harlow's mystification, 'Carl Corunna is also a witness, right? If we go before a judge in his chambers – that's just a room smaller than the whole court – I would hope to persuade him to make Green get himself a different attorney to defend him in court, and *that* will cost Mr Patrick Green a whole bucketful of his own cash, which I'm told he can't afford, as he has already spent the thousands he stole.'

'It seemed such a simple matter,' Jules Harlow sighed, 'to put up a bit of money towards a bail bond.'

'Don't despair.'

David Vynn ate warm English muffins spread with apple jelly and watched the slightly gloomy expression of his client change to radiant pleasure as they were joined by a vibrant woman who wore couture clothes as casually as overalls.

'My wife,' Harlow said, introducing her with pride. 'She thinks I was crazy to listen to poor Mrs Nutbridge, and she's fascinated by Patrick Green.'

'It was for your wife,' David Vynn asked, 'that you bought the filly and met Sandy Nutbridge?'

Jules Harlow nodded. David Vynn looked from one to the other and thought Patrick Green hadn't a hope of pinning drug-dealing sleaze on to people like this.

Even though the judge in chambers did agree with David Vynn that Patrick Green should engage a different counsel to defend him at trial, it was still Carl Corunna who acted for him when he demanded a deposition in his turn from Jules Reginald Harlow.

'I'll be sitting beside you,' young David Vynn told his client, 'but I'm not allowed to answer the questions. It will be you who does that. Remember that you'll have sworn on oath to speak the truth. Think before you answer. They'll be trying to trap you. Tricky questions. If they succeed in muddling you up, we'll lose in court.'

So reassuring, Jules Harlow thought. He and David Vynn went to the office suite of Carl Corunna and in a boardroom there Jules Reginald Harlow came face to face with Patrick Green for the first time. He had expected perhaps to see deviousness, but Green's success in the world was based on a plausibly persuasive exterior.

Green looked at Harlow as a fool throwing good money down the drain and didn't in the least understand the mind of the man he was facing. In the context of the war-torn famine-racked world, Jules Harlow considered the disputed ownership of ten thousand dollars to be an irrelevance. Yet he still believed that justice mattered, whether on a huge or a tiny scale, and he would try to the end to prove it existed.

Apart from the four men sitting opposite each other in side-by-side pairs at one end of a long polished table – Corunna and Green opposite Harlow and Vynn – there was a woman court reporter who, on her swift typing machine, wrote down every word verbatim. There was also a video camera recording the proceedings, so that if necessary the spoken words could be synchronized with the video tape, to prove there had been no illegal editing.

Jules Harlow swore on oath to tell the truth, and did so. Carl Corunna tried to get him to admit he had agreed that, when the District Clerk returned the bail money, Green should keep it as part of his fee.

'Absolutely not,' Jules Harlow said.

'You made the cashier's cheque out personally to Mr Green, did you not?'

'Yes, you told me to.'

'Did you stipulate on the cheque that it was to be used for any particular purpose?'

'You yourself knew that its purpose was to complete the bail bond so that Sandy Nutbridge could be freed to enjoy his family's visit.'

'Answer the question,' Corunna instructed. 'Did you stipulate on the cheque for what purpose it was to be used?'

'Well . . . no.'

'Did you stipulate on the cheque that you expected it to be returned to you?'

'No,' Harrow said. 'And why,' he added bitterly, 'why didn't you as a lawyer advise me to make out the cheque directly to the District Clerk? Ray Wichelsea did that, and had his money returned without trouble. You yourself told me to have the cheque made out to Patrick Green personally. If you knew that what I was doing on your instruction was inadvisable, why did you so instruct me?'

Carl Corunna refused to answer. It was *he*, he said, who was asking the questions.

The session lasted forty-five minutes.

'They won't want to use that deposition in court,' David T. Vynn said with satisfaction afterwards. 'You sounded much too genuine.'

'I spoke the truth.'

'It's not always the truth that's believed.'

The wheels of the justice system revolved with the speed of tortoises. It was well over two years from the day that Jules Harlow had bought the filly that he received a phone call from David T. Vynn saying that the grievance committee of the South Carolina Bar was ready to hear his plea for probable cause.

'My what?' Jules Harlow asked blankly. His mind at the time resonated with visions of storing personality and memory on microchips that could be implanted to restore order in confused brains. His loving wife, happy with her horses, held his elbow on kerbsides so that he wouldn't absent-mindedly step off in front of buses.

David Vynn said, 'Three weeks next Tuesday, in the evening, eight o'clock, in the hotel where we meet for breakfast.'

'I thought we were going to court.'

'No, no,' his attorney told him patiently. 'If you remember, I told you at the beginning there were two ways to go. One is to file suit and make the depositions and wind the way slowly into court, and the other is to file a grievance with the South Carolina Bar Association. That grievance – your grievance against Patrick Green – has now reached the top of the pile.'

'Double helix,' Jules Harlow murmured.

'What? Yes, I suppose so. You will turn up for the Bar hearing, won't you?'

Sandy Nutbridge, during the same two years, had been in and out of jail. Patrick Green, his one-time friend, had again invented information against him and delivered him to arrest with an approximation of a Judas kiss, but this time Sandy, with his family safe in England, had made no attempt to raise bail money, choosing instead to wait resignedly behind bars for the date of his trial.

He chose also to be defended not by Green but by an attorney appointed *pro bono* by the court, and although he lost his case and was found guilty of minor money irregularities through horse sales, the worse charge of selling cocaine didn't stick. He was sentenced only to time served, which meant he was freed immediately. Ray Wichelsea gladly put sales his way as before – but paid him commission with regular cheques, not cash.

As Sandy Nutbridge, on behalf of his mother, had also made a complaint to the South Carolina Bar along the same lines as David T. Vynn, the committee had decided to hear both complaints together. Mrs Nutbridge, as sturdily determined in her way as Jules Harlow in his, emptied the last few pounds from her piggy bank back home and on coupons for free-flier miles from her local supermarket made her way again across the Atlantic.

She met Jules Harlow for the first time in the waiting-room of the extensive business suite in the hotel chosen by the South Carolina Bar Association for their inquiry. No one formally introduced them, but tentatively they approached each other until Jules Harlow (as ever in a grey suit) said to the grey-haired grandmother in her best print wool dress, 'Are you . . . er . . .?' and she replied self-consciously 'Mr Harlow, is it?'

Without heat, they exchanged sorrows. Sandy Nutbridge was faithfully sending small amounts to help repay her borrowings, though to do it he had had to abandon his expensive lakeside home. She thought Patrick Green an unspeakable villain. Jules Reginald

Harlow looked back to the day when he'd succumbed to her sobs and supposed he would do it again if he had to.

Jules Harlow's vivacious wife, who said she wouldn't have missed the Bar Association gathering for all the thoroughbreds in Kentucky, immediately offered sympathy and light-hearted jokes to Mrs Nutbridge, the two women surprising and dissipating the general run of long faces. Mrs Nutbridge visibly strengthened from jitters to determination. Jules Harlow's wife said, 'Attagirl!'

Jules Harlow gradually understood that the grievance committee was already in session in the large boardroom across the suite's lobby and, when David T. Vynn arrived, he confirmed it. The fourteen lawyers at present forming the grievance committee had been listening to Patrick Green's lies and twisted version of things for almost an hour.

'They'll believe him!' Jules Harlow exclaimed, depressed.

David T. Vynn looked from him to Mrs Nutbridge. 'It's up to you two to convince them there's probable cause.'

Jules Harlow asked again, 'What is probable cause?'

'Basically if the committee finds there is probable cause, they may try a colleague among themselves at a later date and disbar him or her from practising as a lawyer if he or she has, say, disgraced his or her profession.'

'Like doctors?' Mrs Nutbridge asked.

David Vynn nodded. 'Like that.'

The committee called Mrs Nutbridge first, alone. Jules Harlow's summons came half an hour later. Each of them in turn walked into a big brightly lit room where the fourteen unsmiling lawyers sat round a long boardroom-like table. The committee chairman, at one end of the table, invited Mrs Nutbridge and later Jules Harlow to sit on one of the few empty chairs and answer questions.

Mrs Nutbridge was seated halfway down the table, but the chairman waved Jules Harlow to the only remaining empty seat at the far end which, to his alarm, was next to Patrick Green. Beyond Green sat Carl Corunna. Worse and worse. Expressionlessly, Jules Harlow took his allotted place and, rather woodenly, because of Green's physical nearness, began to answer the chairman's questions, most of which assumed Green's lies to be the facts.

Jules Harlow knew he was doing badly. The assembled lawyers looked disbelieving at his answers and Green, beside him, relaxed. Carl Corunna sniffed.

Jules Harlow, in his memory, heard David Vynn's voice. 'It's not always the truth that's believed.' If I'm not believed, he thought, it's my own fault.

The chairman, consulting notes spread on the table in front of him, asked Jules Harlow on which day he had promised Patrick Green, on the telephone, that he could keep the ten thousand dollars on its return from the court.

The chairman, overweight and suffering from chronic indigestion, was finding the proceedings tedious. Half of the rest of the committee were fighting cat-naps. Patrick Green was smiling.

Jules Harlow took a deep breath and said loudly, 'I would never have agreed to pay any fees whatsoever for Sandy Nutbridge.'

One of the dozing lawyers opened his eyes wide and said, 'Why not?'

'Because I didn't know him.'

'But—'

'When I advanced the money for his bail, I had met him only once. That was on the day I bought a horse from him. Quite a good horse, as it turned out. A mare. You might like a bet on her tomorrow in the fourth race.'

A ripple of amusement finished off the cat-naps.

'If you didn't know Nutbridge . . .' the chairman frowned, '. . . why did you put up money for his bail?'

'Because of his mother's distress. I did it for her.' Jules gestured towards her. 'I did it because she was crying. I did it because she's English, and so am I. You yourselves might have come to the aid of a fellow American if one begged you for help in a foreign country. I did it simply because I wanted to.'

There was a short moment of open-mouthed silence, then a lady among the committee cleared her throat and said with humour, 'If you don't mind me asking you, Mr Harlow, is ten thousand dollars a great deal of money to you?'

Jules Harlow smiled. 'Not really. It is not because I need the money that I ask you to make Patrick Green give back what he owes me. It's because of the principle involved. It's because he is letting you all down.'

Harlow took another deep breath and into a continuing silence said, 'If I hadn't been able to afford to lose ten thousand dollars, I wouldn't have gone to Mrs Nutbridge's aid. But I would absolutely never have agreed to pay her son's legal fees. Why should I? I did not at any time discuss fees with anyone, not Patrick Green nor Carl Corunna nor Sandy Nutbridge. I trusted Sandy Nutbridge to surrender to his bail, which he did. I trusted a lawyer to return the money he knew I'd put up in good faith for a bail bond, and he has kept it. I trusted a horse salesman and I trusted a lawyer. Which would you have put *your* money on, out of those two?'

The grievance committee debated among themselves and the following day announced that they found no 'probable cause' and that the subject was closed.

'I blew it,' Jules Harlow said gloomily at breakfast later in the week.

'You certainly did *not*,' David Vynn assured him.

'I've been told the committee nearly all believed *you*, not Patrick Green.'

'But . . . then why?'

'They almost never disbar a fellow lawyer. They may know Green is as guilty as hell, but if there's the slightest possibility of inserting any doubt into their deliberations, they'll let him off. All doubt is reasonable, didn't you know?'

Jules Harlow watched David T. Vynn begin to demolish a pile of buckwheat pancakes with bananas.

'All the same,' Jules Harlow said, 'Patrick Green has got away with it.'

David Vynn spooned whipped butter on to his pancakes and, enjoying a dramatic moment, extravagantly flourished his fork. 'Patrick Green,' he said, 'has done nothing of the sort.'

'He still has my money.'

'I did warn you at the beginning that you were unlikely to get it back.'

'Then how can you say he hasn't got away with it?'

David Vynn attended thoughtfully to his pancakes. 'I have incredibly knowledgeable sources. I'm told things, you know. I'm told you stunned the grievance committee. They say you are a transparently honest witness.' He paused. 'They all know it is you who will be believed if Patrick Green is tried in court.'

'*If!*'

'That's what I want to talk to you about. The path

to court leads from accusation to deposition, and after that point there's an offer of mediation to settle out of court. Only if that fails does the case come to trial. Well, Patrick Green has agreed to mediation.'

'I don't understand why you're so upbeat,' Harlow said.

'You will.'

The tortoise wheels rotated slowly along the road to mediation but eventually David Vynn took his client to a meeting with a mediator who proved to be a sophisticated version of grandmotherly Mrs Nutbridge.

'Our aim,' she said, 'is to agree the terms of settlement between Mr Green and Mr Harlow without the time or expense of a trial in court.' She paused. 'I've spoken to Mr Green.'

Silence.

'He is willing to negotiate,' she said.

David Vynn with irony commented, 'I suppose that means he's willing to avoid the loss of his house and car and his office equipment and all that he owns. He's willing to avoid triple penalties, in fines. He's willing not to have to pay punitive damages. How generous of him!'

'What can he offer that you will accept?'

*Dear Heaven*, Jules Harlow thought in a burst of understanding, *Patrick Green is admitting his guilt*.

Patrick Green, indeed, brought face to face with a stark choice between a sentence for conversion, civil theft and breach of constructive trust, followed by the automatic revocation of his licence to practise law – between that and the repaying of some at least of what he'd embezzled from Jules Harlow and Mrs Nutbridge – had discovered all of a sudden that there were dollars to be earned in the outside world, even if it meant stocking supermarket shelves.

The mediator said, 'Mr Green offers you five thousand dollars: half of the sum you put up for the bail bond.'

'Mr Green,' David Vynn said pleasantly, 'can multiply that by two. If my client was vengeful, he could multiply by four.'

'Mr Green spent the bond money paying off debtors who would otherwise have beaten him up.'

'Let's all weep,' David Vynn told her. 'Mr Green stole Mrs Nutbridge's pension fund.'

Jules Harlow listened in fascination.

'Sandy Nutbridge,' the mediator riposted, 'is paying to her what she advanced to free him. Mrs Nutbridge's debts are her son's affair.'

'Patrick Green twice betrayed Sandy Nutbridge to the IRS,' David Vynn drily pointed out. 'His purpose from the beginning was to steal a fortune in unnecessary legal fees from his so-called friend. Mr Harlow's ten thousand-dollar bond money came along as an unplanned bonus.'

'Mr Green will repay half of Mr Harlow's involvement.'

'No,' David Vynn said calmly. 'All of it.'

'He has no money.'

'Mr Harlow will wait.'

From old experienced eyes she looked with amusement at bright David T. Vynn; young enough to be her son, too young to feel pity for a crook. She set a future date for a final settlement.

Jules Harlow's devoted wife decided that as Jules was offering her a new horse for their third wedding anniversary she would go to Ray Wichelsea himself, to the head of the agency, for advice.

Ray Wichelsea, valuing her custom above all others, found her a two-year-old of starry promise for the following year's Triple Crown.

Mrs Harlow asked if there were any news of Mrs Nutbridge, whom she had immediately liked at the grievance committee meeting. Sandy Nutbridge had eventually saved enough to ask advice from David Vynn, Ray Wichelsea told her, and now Patrick Green had furiously agreed to mediation in her case, too.

Mrs Harlow said to Jules at bedtime, 'Even if she gets most of her money back, I don't suppose Mrs Nutbridge will put up bail for anyone ever again.'

Her husband thought of what he'd learned, and of the thousands he had quite gladly paid in attorneys' fees to defeat Patrick Green. 'I'm told,' he said, 'that there's a way to bail people out by merely *pledging* the bail money and paying up in full only if the accused absconds, but it's expensive. It might be better, might be worse. I'll have to ask our young marvel, David Vynn.'

They met quietly across yet another boardroom table, paired as before: Patrick Green and Carl Corunna opposite Jules Reginald Harlow and David T. Vynn.

The grandmotherly mediator, dressed in a grey business suit as formal as Jules Harlow's, as anonymous as the lawyers', shook hands briefly all round and, sitting at the table's head, distributed simple documents, asking them all to sign.

Jules Harlow, despite his losses, felt himself strongly filled by a sense of justice. Here they all were, he thought as he signed, fighting a battle to the death with pens, not guns. Patrick Green might rob people, but he didn't shoot.

Glumly Patrick Green admitted to himself that he'd underestimated both Jules Harlow's persistence and David Vynn's skill with the law. The chairman of the grievance committee, furthermore, had uttered fearsome threats: the slightest whisper of misdoing would find the Green licence in the bin. But in time, Patrick Green thought, in time he would rake up another sting; would find another mug . . .

He irritably signed the paper that committed him to repaying his debt to Jules Harlow in four chunks of twenty-five hundred bucks each.

*

The paper was in effect a full confession.

The law turned its back on Patrick Green and put no more work his way.

For a year he laboured in low-paid jobs, resentfully repaying Jules Harlow on time rather than finding himself in court.

For four more years, he sweated to repay Mrs Nutbridge. Punitive damages though, he knew, would have been much worse.

Freed at last from debt, but still dishonest at heart, he moved to another state and sold small-print insurance.

A man he swindled there took a more direct route to justice than Jules Reginald Harlow, and in a dark alley beat Patrick Green to pulp.

# THE DAY OF THE LOSERS

*People go to the Grand National to win: jockeys, gamblers and, in this case, the police.*

*In any day of good luck for the losers, those who believe they have lost may have won, and those who win may have lost.*

*It depends on the stake.*

Austin Dartmouth Glenn set off to the Grand National with a thick packet of new banknotes in his pocket and a mixture of guilt and bravado in his mind.

Austin Dartmouth Glenn knew he had promised not to put this particular clutch of banknotes into premature circulation. Not for five years, he had been sternly warned. Five years would see the heat off and the multi-million robbery would be ancient history.

The police would be chasing more recent villains and the hot serial numbers would have faded into fly-blown obscurity on out-of-date lists. In five years it would be safe to spend the small fortune he had been paid for his part in springing the bank-robbery boss out of unwelcome jail.

That was all very well, Austin told himself aggrievedly, looking out of the train window. What about inflation? In five years' time the small fortune might not be worth the paper it was printed on. Or the colour and size of the banknotes might be changed. He'd heard of a frantic safe-blower long ago who'd done twelve years and gone home to a cache full of the old thin white stuff. All that time served for a load of out-of-date, uncashable rubbish. Austin Glenn's mouth twisted in sympathy at the thought. It wasn't going to happen to him, not ruddy well likely.

Austin had paid for his train ticket with ordinary currency, and ditto for the cans of beer, packages of Cellophaned sandwiches, and copy of a racing newspaper. The hot new money was stowed safely in an inner pocket, not to be risked before he reached the bustling anonymity of the huge crowd converging on Aintree racecourse. He was no fool, of course, he thought complacently. A neat pack of banknotes, crisp, new and consecutive, might catch the most incurious eye. But no one would look twice now that he had shuffled them and crinkled them with hands dirtied for the purpose.

He wiped beer off his mouth with the back of his hand: a scrawny, fortyish man with neat, thin, grey-black hair, restless eyes and an overall air of self-importance. A life spent on the fringes of crime had given him hundreds of dubious acquaintances, an intricate memory-bank of information and a sound knowledge of how to solicit bribes without actually cupping the palm. No one liked him very much, but Austin was not sensitive enough to notice.

Nearer the front of the same train Jerry Springwood sat and sweated on three counts. For one thing, he was an outdoor man and found the heat excessive, and for another, owing to alcohol and sex, he had no time to spare and would very likely lose his job if he arrived late; but, above all, he sweated from fear.

Jerry Springwood at thirty-two had lost his nerve and was trying to carry on the trade of steeplechase jockey without anyone finding out. The old days when he used to ride with a cool brain and discount intermittent bangs as merely a nuisance were long gone. For months now he had travelled with dread to the meetings, imagining sharp ends of bone protruding from his skin, imagining a smashed face or a severed spine . . . imagining pain. For months he had been unable to take risks he would once not have seen as risks at all. For months he had been unable to urge his mounts forward into gaps, when only such urging would win; and unable to stop himself steadying his mounts to jump, when only kicking them on would do.

The skill which had taken him to the top was now used to cover the cracks, and the soundness of his longtime reputation bolstered the explanations for defeats which he gave to owners and trainers. Only the most discerning saw the disguised signs of disintegration, and fewer still had put private doubts into private words. The great British public, searching the list of Grand National runners for inspiration, held good old Jerry Springwood to be a plus factor in favour of the third favourite, Haunted House.

A year ago, he reflected drearily, as he stared out at the passing fields, he would have known better than to go to a party in London on the night before the big race. A year ago he had stayed near the course, swallowed maybe a couple of beers, gone to bed early, slept alone. He wouldn't have dreamed of making a four-hour dash south after Friday's racing, or getting drunk, or going to bed at two with a girl he'd known three hours.

He hadn't needed to blot out the thought of Saturday afternoon's marathon, but had looked forward to it with zest, excitement and unquenchable hope. Oh, God, he thought despairingly, what has happened to me? He was small and strong with soft mid-brown hair, deep-set eyes and a nose flattened by too much fast contact with the ground. A farmer's son, natural with animals, and with social manners sophisticated by success. People usually liked Jerry Springwood but he was too unassuming to notice.

The crowd poured cheerfully into Aintree racecourse primed with hope, faith and cash. Austin peeled off the first of the hot notes at the turnstiles, and contentedly watched it being sucked into the anonymity of the gate receipt. He safely got change for another in a crowded bar and for a third from a stall selling form sheets. Money for old rope, he thought sardonically. It didn't make sense, holding on to the stuff for five years.

The Tote, as usual, had opened its windows early to take bets on the Grand National because there was not time just before the race to sell tickets to all who wanted to buy. There were long queues already when Austin went along to back his fancy, for like him they knew from experience that it was best to bet early if one wanted a good vantage point in the stands.

He waited in the queue for the Tote window, writing his proposal on his racecard. When his turn came, he said, 'A hundred to win, number twelve – in the National,' and counted off the shuffled notes without a qualm. The busy woman behind the window gave him his ticket with a fast but sharp glance. 'Next?' she said, looking over his shoulder to the man behind. Dead easy, thought Austin smugly, stuffing his ticket into his jacket pocket. One hundred on number twelve to win. No point in messing about with place money, he always said. Mind you, he was a pretty good judge of form.

He always prided himself on that. Nothing in the race had a better chance than the third favourite, Haunted House, and you couldn't want a better jockey than Springwood, now could you? He strolled with satisfaction back to the bar and bought another beer.

In the changing-room, Jerry Springwood had no difficulty in disguising either his hangover or his fear. The other jockeys were gripped with the usual pre-National tension, finding their mouths a little dry, their thoughts a little abstracted, their flow of ribald jokes silenced to a trickle.

Twice over Becher's, Jerry thought, hopelessly; the Canal Turn, the Chair, how in God's name am I going to face it?

While Jerry sweated, Chief Superintendent Crispin, head of the local police, breathlessly considered an item of information just passed into his hands. He needed, he decided, to go to the very top man on the racecourse, if the most satisfactory results were to be achieved.

The top man on any racecourse, the Senior Steward of the Jockey Club, was lunching a party of eminent overseas visitors in a private dining-room when Chief Superintendent Crispin interrupted the roast saddle of lamb.

'I want to speak to you urgently, sir,' the policeman said, bending down to the Turf's top ear.

Sir William Westerland rested his bland gaze briefly on the amount of brass on the navy-blue uniform.

'You're in charge here?'

'Yes, sir. Can we talk privately?'

'I suppose so, if it's important.'

Sir William rose, glanced regretfully at his half-eaten lunch, and led the policeman to the outdoor section of his private box high in the grandstand. The two men stood hunched in the chilly air, and spoke against the background noise of the swelling crowd and the shouts of the bookmakers offering odds on the approaching first race.

Crispin said, 'It's about the Birmingham bank robbery, sir.'

'But that happened more than a year ago,' Westerland protested.

'Some of the stolen notes have turned up here, today, on the racecourse.'

Westerland frowned, not needing to be told details. The blasting open of the supposedly impregnable vault, the theft of more than three and a half million, the violent getaway of the thieves, all had been given wider coverage than the death of Nelson.

Four men and a small boy had been killed by the explosion outwards of the bank wall, and two housewives and two young policemen had been gunned down later. The thieves had arrived in a fire engine. Before the crashing echoes died, they had dived into the ruins to carry out the vault's contents for 'safekeeping' and driven clear away with the loot. They were suspected only at the very last moment by a puzzled constable, whose order to halt had been answered by a spray of machine-gun bullets. Only one of the gang had been recognized, caught, tried and sentenced to thirty years; and of that he had served precisely thirty days before making a spectacular escape. Recapturing him, and catching his confederates, was a number one police priority.

'It's the first lead we've had for months,' Crispin said earnestly. 'If we can catch whoever came here with the hot money . . .'

Westerland looked down at the scurrying thousands.

'Pretty hopeless, I'd have thought,' he said.

'No, sir.' Crispin shook his neat greying head. 'A sharp-eyed checker in the Tote spotted one of the notes, and now they've found nine more. One of the sellers remembers selling a ticket for a hundred early on to a man who paid in notes which *felt* new, although they had been roughly creased and wrinkled.'

'But even so—'

'She remembers what he looks like, and says he backed only one horse to win, which is unusual on Grand National day.'

'Which horse?'

'Haunted House, sir. And so, sir, if Haunted House wins, our fellow will bring his ticket with its single big bet to the pay-out, and we will have him.'

'But,' Westerland objected, 'what if Haunted House *doesn't* win?'

Crispin gazed at him steadily. 'We want you to arrange that Haunted House *does* win. We want you to fix the Grand National.'

Down in Tattersall's enclosure, Austin Dartmouth Glenn passed two hot banknotes to a bookmaker who stuffed them busily into his satchel without looking and issued a ticket to win on Spotted Tulip at eight to one in the first. In the noise, haste and flurry of the last five minutes before the first race, Austin elbowed his way up the stands to find the best view of his money on the hoof, only to see it finish lame and last. Austin tore up his ticket in disgust and threw the pieces to the wind.

In the changing-room, Jerry Springwood reluctantly climbed into his thin white breeches and fumbled with the buttons on his shiny red-and-white striped colours. His mind was filling like a well with panic, the terrible desire to cut and run growing deeper and deadlier with every passing minute. He had difficulty in concentrating and virtually did not hear when anyone spoke to him. His hands trembled. He felt cold. There was another hour to live through before he would have to force himself out to the parade ring, onto the horse, down to the start and right round those demanding four and a half miles with their thirty huge fences.

I can't do it, he thought numbly. I can't face it. Where can I hide?

The four stewards in charge of the meeting sat gloomily round their large table, reacting with varying degrees of incredulity and uneasiness to the urgings of Chief Superintendent Crispin.

'There's no precedent,' said one.

'It's out of the question. There isn't time,' said another.

A third said, 'You'd never get the trainers to agree.'

'And what about the owners?' asked a fourth.

Crispin held racing in as little esteem as crooked politicians and considered that catching the Birmingham mob was of far greater social importance than any horse finishing first. His inner outrage at the obstructive reaction of the stewards seeped unmistakably into his voice.

'The Birmingham robbers murdered *nine* people,' he said forcefully. 'Everyone has a public duty to help the police catch them.'

Surely not to the extent of ruining the Grand National, insisted the stewards.

'I understand,' Crispin said, 'that in steeplechasing in general, few stud values are involved, and in this year's National the horses are all geldings. It is not as if we were asking you to spoil the Stud Book by fixing the Derby.'

'All the same, it would be unfair on the betting public,' said the stewards.

'The people who died were part of the betting public. The next people to die, in the next violent bank raid, will also be the betting public.'

Sir William Westerland listened to the arguments with his bland expression unimpaired. He had gone far in life by not declaring his views before everyone else had bared their breasts, their opinions and their weaknesses. His mild subsequent observations had a way of being received as revealed truth, when they were basically only unemotional common sense. He watched Crispin and his fellow stewards heat up into emphasis and hubbub, and begin to slide towards prejudice and hostility. He sighed internally, looked at his watch and noisily cleared his throat.

'Gentlemen,' he said calmly and distinctly, 'before we reach a decision, I think we should consider the following points. First, possibility. Second, secrecy. Third, consequences.'

Stewards and policeman looked at him with united relief.

'Jump jockeys,' Westerland said, 'are individuals. Who do you think is going to persuade them to fix the race?'

No answer.

'Who can say that Haunted House will not fall?'

No answer.

'How long do you suppose it would be before someone told the press? Do we want the uproar which would follow?'

No answer, but a great shaking of stewardly heads.

'But if we refuse Chief Superintendent Crispin's request, how would we feel if another bank were blown apart and more innocent people killed, knowing we took no action to prevent it?'

The meeting looked at him in silence, awaiting his lead.

Jerry Springwood's head felt like a balloon floating somewhere above his uncoordinated body. The call of 'Jockeys out, please' had found him still unable to think of a way of escape. Too many people knew him. How could I run? he thought. How can I scramble to the gate and find a taxi when everyone knows I should be walking out to ride Haunted House? Can I faint? he thought. Can I say I'm ill? He found himself going out with the others, his leaden legs trudging automatically while his spirit wilted. He stood in the parade ring with his mouth dry and his eyes feeling like gritty holes in his skull, not hearing the nervously hearty pre-race chit-chat of owner and trainer. I can't, he thought. I can't.

The Senior Steward of the Jockey Club, Sir William Westerland, walked up to him as he stood rigidly in his hopeless hell.

'A word in your ear, Jerry,' he said.

Jerry Springwood looked at him blankly, with eyes like smooth grey pebbles. Westerland, who had seen that look on other faces and knew what it foreboded, suffered severe feelings of misgiving. In spite of Chief Superintendent Crispin's opposition, he had secured the stewards' wholehearted agreement. The National could not be fixed – even to catch murderers. He came to the conclusion that both practically and morally, it was impossible. The police would just have to keep a sharper check on future meetings, and one day soon, perhaps, they would catch their fish as he swam again to the Tote.

All the same, Westerland had seen no harm in wishing Jerry Springwood success, but he perceived now that Crispin had no chance of catching his man today. No jockey in this state of frozen fear could win the National. The backers of Haunted House would be fortunate if their fancy lasted half a mile before he pulled up or ran out or refused to jump because of the stranglehold on his reins.

'Good luck,' said Westerland lamely, with regret.

Jerry made no answer, even ordinary politeness being beyond him.

Up on his vantage point in the stands, Austin Glenn watched the long line of runners walk down the course. Ten minutes to race time, with half the bookies suffering from sore throats and the massed crowds buzzing with rising excitement. Austin, who had lost his money on Spotted Tulip in the first, and a good deal more to bookmakers on the second, was biting his knuckles over Haunted House.

Jerry Springwood sat like a sack in the saddle, shoulders hunched. The horse, receptive to his rider's mood, plodded along in confusion, not able to sort out whether or not he should respond to the crowd instead. To Austin and many others, horse and rider looked like a grade one losing combination. William Westerland shook his head ruefully and Crispin wondered irritably why that one horse, out of all of them, looked half asleep.

Jerry Springwood got himself lined up for the start by blotting out every thought. The well of panic was full and trying to flood over. Jerry, white and clammily sweating, knew that in a few more minutes he would have to dismount and run. Have to.

When the starter let them go, Haunted House was standing flat-footed. Getting no signal from the saddle, he started hesitantly after the departing field. The horse knew his job – he was there to run and jump and get his head in front of the rest. But he was feeling rudderless, without the help and direction he was used to. His jockey stayed on board by instinct, the long years of skill coming to his aid, the schooled muscles acting in a pattern that needed no conscious thought.

Haunted House jumped last over the first fence and was still last five fences later approaching Becher's Brook. Jerry Springwood saw the horse directly in front of him fall and knew remotely that if he went straight on he would land on top of him. Almost without thinking, he twitched his right hand on the rein and Haunted House, taking fire from this tiniest sign of life, swerved a yard, bunched his quarters and put his great equine soul into clearing the danger. Haunted House knew the course, had won there with Jerry Springwood up, in shorter races. His sudden surge over Becher's melted his jockey's defensive blankness and thrust him into freshly vivid fear.

Oh God! Jerry thought, as Haunted House took him inexorably towards the Canal Turn, how can I? How can I? He sat there, fighting his panic while Haunted House carried him sure-footedly round the Turn and over Valentine's and all the way to The Chair. Jerry thought forever after that he'd shut his eyes as his mount took the last few strides towards the most testing steeplechase fence in the world, but Haunted House met it perfectly and cleared the huge spread without the slightest stumble. Over the water jump in front of the stands and out again towards Becher's with the whole course to jump again. Jerry thought, if I pull up now, I'll have done enough. Horses beside him tired and stopped or slid and fell but Haunted House galloped at a steady thirty miles an hour with scant regard for his fate.

Austin Glenn on the stands and William Westerland in his private box and Chief Superintendent Crispin tense in front of a television set all watched with faster pulses as Haunted House made progress through the field. By the time he reached Becher's Brook on the second circuit he lay tenth, and seventh at the Canal Turn, and fifth after the third-last fence, three-quarters of a mile from home.

Jerry Springwood saw a gap on the rails and didn't take it. He checked his mount before the second-last fence so they jumped it safely but lost two lengths. On the stands William Westerland groaned aloud but on Haunted House Jerry Springwood just shrivelled inside at his own fearful cowardice. It's useless, he thought. I'd be better off dead.

The leader of the field had sprinted a long way ahead and Jerry saw him ride over the last fence while Haunted House was a good forty lengths in the rear. One more, Jerry thought. Only one more fence. I'll never ride another race. Never. He locked his jaw as Haunted House gathered his muscles and launched his half-ton weight at the green-faced birch. If he rolls on me, Jerry thought . . . if I fall and he crashes on top of me . . . Oh God, he thought, take me safely over this fence.

Haunted House landed surefootedly, his jockey steady and balanced by God-given instinct. The last fence was behind them, all jumping done.

The horse far in front, well backed and high in the handicap, was already taking the last flat half-mile at a spanking gallop. Jerry Springwood and Haunted House had left it too late to make a serious bid to catch them, but with a surge of what Jerry knew to be release from purgatory, they raced past everything else in a flat-out dash to the post.

Austin Glenn watched Haunted House finish second by twenty lengths. Cursing himself a little for not bothering about place money, he took out his ticket, tore it philosophically across, and again let the pieces flutter away to the four winds. William Westerland rubbed his chin and wondered whether Jerry Springwood could have won if he'd tried sooner. Chief Superintendent Crispin bitterly cursed the twenty lengths by which his quarry would escape.

Sir William took his eminent foreign visitors down to watch the scenes of jubilation round the winner in the unsaddling enclosure, and was met by flurried officials with horrified faces.

'The winner can't pass the scales,' they said.

'What do you mean?' Westerland demanded.

'The winner didn't carry the right weight! The trainer left the weight-cloth hanging in the saddling box when he put the saddle on the horse. The winner ran all the way with ten pounds less than he should have done . . . and we'll have to disqualify him.'

Forgetting the weight-cloth was done often enough – but in the National!

William Westerland took a deep breath and told the aghast officials to relay the facts to the public over the Tannoy system. Jerry Springwood heard the news while he was sitting on the scales and watching the pointer swing round to the right mark. He understood that he'd *won* the Grand National, and he felt not joyful but overwhelmingly ashamed, as if he'd taken the prize by cheating.

Crispin stationed his men strategically and alerted all the Tote pay-out windows. Up on the stands, Austin Glenn searched for the pieces of his ticket in a fury, picking up every torn and trampled scrap and peering at it anxiously.

The ground was littered with torn-up paper by the truckful. The brilliant colours of the bookmakers' tickets overshadowed the buff cards from the Tote, and made the search a haystack; and there was the detritus too not only of the Grand National's 'also-rans' but also those of the earlier races. Somewhere there was his torn ticket from Spotted Tulip, for instance. Tearing up losing tickets and entrusting them to the wind was a gambler's defiance of fate.

Austin Glenn searched and cursed until his back ached from bending down. He was not alone in having disregarded the punters' rule of not throwing tickets away until after the all-clear from the weigh-in, but to see others searching as hard as he was gave him no pleasure. What if someone else picked up his pieces of ticket and claimed his winnings? The idea enraged him: and what was more, he couldn't stay on the course indefinitely because he had to catch his return train. He couldn't afford to be late; he had to work that night.

Crispin's men shifted from foot to foot as time went by and they were left there growing more and more conspicuous while the crowd thinned and trooped out through the gates. When the Tote closed for the day, the Chief Superintendent called them off in frustrated rage and conceded that they would have to wait for another opportunity after all, and never would such a good one come that way again.

In the weighing-room, Jerry Springwood bore the congratulations as best he could and announced to surprised television millions that he would be hanging up his boots immediately, after this peak to his career.

He didn't realize he had ridden the bravest race of his life. When the plaudits were over he locked himself in the washroom and wept for his lost courage.

Austin Dartmouth Glenn travelled home empty-handed and in a vile mood, not knowing that his lost ticket had saved him from arrest. He cursed his wife and kicked the cat, and after a hasty supper, he put on his neat navy-blue uniform. Then he went scowling to work his usual night shift in the nearby high-security jail.

# HAIG'S DEATH

*What if? is the beginning of fiction. What if Haig died when he shouldn't?*

*There could be a hundred intertwined ripples but, anyway, here there are three.*

Unaware that it was for the last time, Christopher Haig steered his buzzing electric razor over the contours of his chin and watched its progress impersonally in the bathroom mirror.

Christopher Haig's beard grew strong and black; unfairly virile, he considered, when his crown was mercilessly thinning. Sighing, he straightened the transition line between beard and hair beside each ear, and blew the shaved-off ends of whiskers carefully into a plastic bag always ready for the purpose.

As middle-age and a gentle paunch had crept up and overtaken him, Christopher Haig had begun at forty-two to wish that he had dared more, had crazily set off to fly round the world in a hot-air balloon or spent a summer photographing penguins in Antarctica or had canoed up the Orinoco river to the Angel Falls. Instead, he had worked reliably day by day as an animal-feed consultant and, as the pinnacle of his suppressed urge to adventure, acted as the judge at race meetings.

He looked forward, on that particular Friday morning, to the bustle of the first half of the two-day Winchester Spring Meeting. He savoured his drive to Winchester racecourse from his home (an empty-feeling home now that his wife had run off with a raggle-taggle TV repair man), taking pleasure in the sunshine sparkling on the fresh green buds of regenerate trees. Happy enough without his wife (relieved, if the truth were told), he wondered how one actually set about dog-sledding in Alaska or driving across the vast red-dust wastes of Australia: could one's every-day travel agent arrange it?

Meticulous by nature, he packed imaginary suitcases for his fantasy journeys, wondering if snowshoes would glide over both powdery surfaces, and choosing audio books for the long nights. Dreams and daydreams plugged the empty spaces of a worthy working life.

He was one of the fifteen judges regularly called to

decide the winner and placed horses of the races. As there were fifteen judges but not fifteen race meetings every day (there were seldom more than four except on public holidays), acting as judge was to Chris Haig a sporadic and unpredictable pleasure more than an occupation. He never knew long in advance to which meeting he might be sent: none of the judges officiated always on the same course.

Christopher Haig regretted the passing of the old days when the word of the judge was law: if the judge said ‘So and so’ had won the race, then he darned well *had* won it, even if half the racegoers put ‘What d’ya macall’ in front. Nowadays the photo-finish camera gave unarguable short-head verdicts, which the judge did little more than announce. Fairer, Chris Haig acknowledged, but not much fun.

The photo-finish camera at Winchester races had been on the blink last time out, though the trouble (more pompously classified as a malfunction) had happened to another judge, not Christopher Haig. It had now not only reportedly been fixed but exhaustively tested. A pity, Haig reprehensibly thought.

Chris Haig parked his car (for the last time) in the ‘Officials only’ car park and made his way jauntily towards the weighing-room (the centre of officialdom), scattering ‘good mornings’ to gatemen and arriving jockeys as he passed.

The judge was feeling particularly well that day. He recognized in himself the awakening of nature’s year and, as often before, but more strongly this time, decided that as he could realistically look forward to thirty more years of life, he should change direction pretty soon. The urge was clear; the destination, still a mist. He would have been astounded to learn that it was already too late.

Christopher Haig was greeted as always with a smile by the stewards, the clerk of the course, the starter, the clerk of the scales and all the passing crowd of race organizers in the weighing-room. The judge was popular, not only because he did his job without mistakes, but for his effortless generosity, his good nature, and his calmness in a crisis. Those that thought him dull had no insight into the furnace of his private landscape. What if, he thought, I joined an oil-fire-fighting unit?

Before each race the judge sat at a table near the scales and learned the colours worn by each jockey as he or she weighed out. He learned also the name of each horse and made sure the jockeys carried on their number cloths the corresponding numbers on the race-card. Chris Haig, after years of practice, was good and quick.

The first three races gave him no problems. There were no finishes close enough to need to be settled by photo, and he'd been able to pronounce the winners and placed horses firmly and with confidence. He was enjoying himself.

The fourth race, the Cloister Handicap Hurdle, was the big event of the day. Chris Haig carefully made sure he could identify each of the eleven runners at a glance: it was always a shocking disgrace for a judge to hesitate.

Number 1, he noted: Lilyglit, top weight.

Number 2, Fable.

Number 3, Storm Cone.

He continued down the list. The runners' names were all familiar to him from other days, but the first three on the card for the Cloister Handicap were woven into his short future in ways he couldn't have imagined.

*Number 1. Lilyglit*

At about the time earlier on that Friday morning when Christopher Haig shaved with the help of a bathroom mirror and dreamed his dreams, Wendy Billington Innes sat on her low comfortable dressing stool and stared at her reflection in her dressing-table's triple-section looking-glass. She saw not the pale clear skin, the straight mid-brown hair nor the darkening shadows below her grey-blue eyes; she saw only worry and a disaster she didn't understand and couldn't deal with. An hour ago, she thought, life had seemed simple and secure.

There were four children upstairs with a resident nanny: three daughters and a yearling son. Downstairs there was a cook, a housekeeper, a manservant and, in the gatehouse of the estate, a chauffeur-gardener with his housemaid wife and daughter. Wendy Billington

Innes managed her large staff with friendly appreciation so that they all lived together without friction. Raised in similar cosseted ease, she knew to a fraction the effort one could expect from each employee and, most importantly, what request would be considered a breathtaking insult.

The house itself was a grand relic of grander times: it allowed everyone comfortable room but was terminally afflicted with dry rot. One day soon, she had thought peacefully, she would move everyone to a new home.

She had brought to her marriage a heavy portfolio of stocks and bonds and, like her mother before her, had thankfully handed it to her husband for management.

At thirty-seven she had reached serenity, if not overwhelming happiness. She could admit to herself (but to no one else) that Jasper, her husband, had been sporadically unfaithful ever since their wedding but, depending on him for friendship, she chose to ignore the true reason for the occasional one-night absences from which he always returned in great good spirits, making her laugh as he loaded her with flowers and little presents. When he came home at dawn empty-handed, as he more often did, it meant only that he'd been gambling all night in his favourite gaming club. He was a good-natured useless man, almost universally liked.

At seven-forty-five in the morning on the Friday of

Winchester races, as she lay cosily awake, planning her day ahead, Wendy Billington Innes answered her bedside telephone and listened to the voice of the family's accountant asking urgently to speak to Jasper.

Jasper's side of the big four-poster bed was uninhabited but, as he often slept in his dressing-room next door when he came home late, his wife went unworriedly to wake him.

Flat sheets; no Jasper.

'He isn't here,' his wife reported, returning to the phone. 'He didn't come home last night. You know what he's like when he's playing backgammon or blackjack. He'll play all night.' She excused his absence lightly, as she always did. 'When he gets home, do you want me to give him a message?'

The accountant asked weakly, knowing the reply in advance, if Wendy – Mrs Innes – had read today's financial columns in the newspapers. No, Mrs Innes had not.

Alarmed by then, Wendy Billington Innes demanded to know what was the matter and wished, when she heard the answer, that she hadn't.

'Basically,' the accountant said with regret, 'the firm of Stemmer Peabody has gone into receivership, which means . . . I find it difficult to tell you . . . but it means that Jasper's fortune – and that of several other people – is, shall we say, severely compromised.'

Wendy said numbly, 'What does "severely compromised" mean, exactly?'

'It means that the financial manager to whom Jasper and others entrusted their affairs has pledged all their money as security for an enterprise and ... er ... has lost it.'

'That can't happen!' Wendy protested.

'I did warn him,' the accountant said sadly, 'but Jasper trusted the manager and signed papers giving him too much power.'

'But there's *my* money,' Wendy exclaimed. 'Even if Jasper has lost some of his, we can live on *my* money perfectly well.'

After an appalling pause, the bad news paralysed her.

'Mrs Innes ... Wendy ... you gave Jasper total control of your affairs. You too, perhaps, signed away too much power. Your money has gone with his. I do hope we may be able to salvage enough so that you can live fairly comfortably, though not, of course, as you do now. There are the children's trusts, things like that. I need to talk to him about his plans.'

When she could get her tongue to speak, Wendy asked, 'Does Jasper know about this?'

'He found out yesterday, when the news broke in the City. He is an honourable man. I'm told he's been trying to raise money ever since, to pay off gambling debts. I know, for example, that he's trying to sell his racehorse, Lilyglit.'

'Lilyglit! He'd never do that! He worships that horse. He's running today at Winchester.'

'I'm afraid . . . in the future, Jasper won't be able to afford to keep racehorses in training.'

Wendy Billington Innes couldn't bear to ask what else he wouldn't be able to afford.

Jasper Billington Innes had already been told. Like many in the past who had been dreadfully impoverished by their blameless involvement in the collapse of insurance syndicates at Lloyd's of London, he was unable at first to understand the reason for, or the extent of, his losses.

He wasn't stupid, though not very bright either. He had inherited significant wealth, but no brain for business. He had left 'all that' to the trusted fellow at Stemmer Peabody, a course of action that had led, the evening before, to an emergency meeting of others facing the same depth of Stemmer Peabody ruin. Women had been furious and weeping; men shouting or pale. Jasper Billington Innes had felt sick.

Honourable in most things, even in the avalanche of calamity, he saw it as an obligation to pay his private debts at once. He wrote cheques to his tailor and his wine-merchant, and to his plumber – not quite enough to clear the whole outstanding sum in each case, but more than enough to prove intent. He could afford his usual household expenses for one more month if he gave all the domestic staff notice at once. That left his heavy debts to his bookmaker and his gaming club proprietors, whose present relaxed behaviour patterns would fly out of the window on hearing the bad news.

All that remained to him of real value, he thought miserably, was his splendid fast hurdler, Lilyglit. His other three jumpers were old now, and worth little.

By midnight on Thursday, he had lost another mini-fortune at the tables, trying lucklessly to play his way out of catastrophe. At four o'clock in the morning, having won back some of his losses, he struck Lilyglit bargains with his gaming creditors that even they recognized as unwise panic measures. They had learned by then of his extreme adversity. They accepted his signature gravely though, and, as they liked him, sincerely wished him well.

*Number 2. Fable*

While Christopher Haig was shaving on Friday morning, the brothers Arkwright were out in their stable-yard, seventy miles to the north, working on Fable, their runner in the Cloister Handicap Hurdle.

In the strengthening light of dawn they tidily plaited the horse's mane and brushed out his tail, wrapping it tightly in a bandage so that it would look neat and tidy when let free. They painted his hooves with oil (cosmetically pleasing) and fed him a bowl of oats to give him stamina and warmth on the horsebox journey south.

Vernon Arkwright, jockey, and his ten-year-older

brother, Villiers, trainer, welcomed the farrier who came to change Fable's all-purpose horseshoes to thin fast racing plates. The farrier took care that his nails didn't prick the hooves: the Arkwrights had a known talent for retaliating with practical jokes.

The Arkwright brothers, Vernon and Villiers, were as bent as right angles: everyone knew it, but proof proved a vanishing commodity. Fable had reached number 2 in the handicap for the Cloister Hurdle by a zigzag path of winning and losing as suspect as a ghost's footprints. Both brothers had been hauled before the stewards to explain 'discrepancies in running'. Both, with angelic hands on hearts, had declared horses not to be machines. On suspicion rather than evidence Villiers had been fined and Vernon given a short compulsory holiday. Both had publicly protested injured innocence and privately jumped with gleeful relief. The stewards longed to catch them properly and warn them off.

The horse's owner, an Arkwright cousin, had confused the inquiry by backing his horse every time – win or lose – with the same amount of money. The horse's owner had asked his jockey and trainer not to tell him what outcome to expect so that his joy or disappointment would be – and look – genuine.

Over the years, mostly with lesser horses than Fable, the conspiring trio of owner, trainer and jockey had salted away substantial tax-free harvests.

On the Friday of the Winchester Spring Meeting

they were as a team still open to suggestions. They hadn't decided whether Fable was out to win or lose. They doubted he was fast enough ever to beat Lilyglit, but, annoyingly, no one had so far bribed them to let him prove it. It looked disappointingly to the Arkwrights as if Fable would have to perform to the best of his ability and try for second or third place money.

Such honesty ran against all the Arkwright instincts.

*Number 3. Storm Cone*

On the Friday morning of the Winchester Spring Meeting, two hours at least before Christopher Haig began shaving with concentration and dreaming his dreams in his bathroom, Moggie Reilly slid away from the sweat-slippery nakedness of the young woman in his embrace and put a hand palm downwards on his alarm clock to cut off its clamour.

Moggie Reilly's head throbbed with hangover, his mouth dry and sticky in the aftermath of too carefree a mixture of drinks. Moggie Reilly, jump jockey, was due to perform at his athletic peak that afternoon at Winchester racecourse in two hurdle races and one three-mile steeplechase but, meanwhile, the trainer he rode for – John Chester – was expecting him to turn out for morning exercise at least sober enough to sit upright in his saddle.

Friday morning was work day, meaning that horses strengthened their muscles at a full training gallop. Old hands like Moggie Reilly – as lithe as a cat and all of twenty-four – could ride work half asleep. That Friday he squinted into his own bathroom mirror as he sought to revive his gums with a toothbrush and summoned up at least an echo of the light-hearted grin that had enticed a young woman between his sheets when she should have been safe in her own bed on the other side of the racing town of Lambourn.

Sarah Driffield: now *there* was a girl. There was Sarah Driffield, undeniably in his bed. Undeniably, also, he hadn't spent the few horizontal hours of his night in total inactivity. What a waste, he thought regretfully, that he could remember so little of it clearly.

When he'd pulled on his riding clothes and made a pot of strong coffee, Sarah Driffield was on her feet, dressed and saying, 'Tell me I didn't do this. My father will kill me. How the hell do I get home unseen?'

The inquisitive eyes of Lambourn awoke with the dawn. The tongues wagged universally by evening. Sarah Driffield, daughter of the reigning champion trainer, did not seek publicity concerning her unplanned escapade with the wickedly persuasive jockey who rode for John Chester, her father's most threatening rival.

Grinning but awake to the problem, Moggie Reilly handed her the keys to his car with instructions not to move out until the horse population had trotted off to the training grounds. He told her where to leave the car and where to hide its key, and he himself jogged on foot through the town to John Chester's stable, which did his hovering hangover minor good.

Sarah Driffield! His whole mind laughed.

It had all been due to a birthday party they had both attended the evening before in The Stag, one of the Lambourn area's best pubs. It had been due basically to the happy-go-lucky atmosphere throughout and specifically to the last round of drinks ordered by the host, that had mixed disastrously with earlier lager and whisky.

*Tequila Slammers.*

Never again, Moggie Reilly vowed. He seldom got drunk and hated hangovers. He remembered offering Sarah Driffield a lift home, but wasn't clear how they had ended at *his* home, three and a half miles from The Stag, and not hers, barely one. In view of his alcoholic intake, Sarah Driffield had been driving.

Moggie Reilly, though within the top ten of jump jockeys, wouldn't normally have looked on Sarah Driffield as possible kiss-and-cuddle material, admittedly on account of her father's power, status and legendary fists. Percy Driffield's well-known views on suitable company for his carefully educated nineteen-year-old only child excluded anybody who might hope to inherit his stable by marrying her. He was reported to have already frightened off shoals of minnows, and his daughter, no fool, used his universal disapproval as her umbrella against unwelcome advances. Which being so, jogged Moggie incredulously, *which being* so, how come the gorgeous Miss Driffield, the unofficial tiara-chosen Miss Lambourn, had climbed the Reilly stairs without protest?

John Chester observed the wince behind each step of his jockey's arrival but did no more than shrug. The fast gallops got done to his satisfaction (all that mattered) and he offered a tactics-planning breakfast on his Winchester runners.

At shortly after eight-thirty, while Wendy Billington Innes, twenty miles away, still sat in frozen and helpless disbelief on her dressing stool, John Chester, bulky and aggressive, told his jockey that Storm Cone was to win the fourth race, the Cloister Hurdle, at all costs. Moggie must somehow achieve it.

John Chester had been doing his sums, and the prize money of the Cloister Hurdle would put him into leading position on the stakes-won trainers' list. The big prizes were sparse at that time of year, as the main part of the jumping season was over: the very last was on the following day, Saturday, but Percy Driffield had no suitable runners. With luck John Chester could win the Cloister and stay ahead of Percy Driffield for the few weeks that were left.

John Chester *ached* to be leading trainer, and to humble Percy Driffield.

'Find a way,' he told his jockey, 'of beating that bugger Lilyglit. He must have a weak spot somewhere.'

Moggie Reilly knew all about Lilyglit, having followed the bright chestnut twice past the winning post on other occasions. He doubted that Storm Cone would ever beat Lilyglit, but had more tact than to say so. He ate dry toast to keep his weight down and let John Chester's wishful thinking roll over his head.

Sarah Driffield drove Moggie Reilly's car back to park it outside The Stag, as he'd asked, and hid its key out of sight in a magnetic box.

As it was daylight she took the shorter path home across fields that she had shunned the previous midnight, and was sitting in the kitchen, showered, changed and eating breakfast when her father returned from seeing his horses gallop.

Percy Driffield, shedding jacket and helmet, merely asked if she'd had a good time at the birthday party.

'Yes, thank you,' she answered. 'Moggie Reilly very kindly drove me home.'

Her father frowned. 'Don't encourage him.'

'No.'

*Tequila Slammer*, she thought. A pinch of salt on the tongue, toss back a jigger of neat tequila, suck a slice of lime. She had felt liberated. Sleeping with Moggie Reilly had become a fun and 'why not?' thing to do. She searched her conscience for guilt and came up with only a smile.

Percy Driffield talked compulsively about Lilyglit. 'Damn fool owner wants to sell him. I've told him he needs to insure him, but he keeps putting it off. Why don't very rich people insure things? Valuations invite crooks, he says. Jasper Billington Innes, nice enough, but daft. You've met him often, of course. I told him Lilyglit is a Champion Hurdle prospect, given another year. I can't think what's got into the man. He sounded panic-stricken on the phone yesterday evening, telling me to find a buyer at once. At least wait until after he wins the Cloister Hurdle, I said, but he's afraid of Storm Cone, at better weights in the handicap. He seemed to think I could make some sort of suggestion to Storm Cone's jockey. Not a chance. I told him to try it himself.'

His daughter raised her eyebrows over her cornflakes. If Moggie took a bribe she had finished with him, she thought.

Moggie 'the cat' Reilly, like many other jockeys, kept fit by regular running, and many, also, left their cars outside the pubs at night rather than be done for drink-driving, so no one paid any attention when Moggie jogged to The Stag, plucked his keys from their magnetic box and drove himself home.

When he walked through his door, the telephone began ringing: he picked up the receiver hoping the call would be short. He felt chilled, the warm jog ebbing. He wanted a hot shower and to sit in a warm woollen lumberjack sweater while he drank more coffee and read the newspapers.

A high nervous hurried voice in his ear said, 'I want

to speak to Reilly. It's Billington Innes here. Jasper . . . er . . . Billington Innes. I own Lilyglit . . . er . . . do you know who I mean?'

Moggie Reilly knew well. He said he was Reilly.

'Yes. Well . . . er . . . I'm selling my horse.' Billington Innes took a slow deep breath and tried to speak more slowly. 'I've arranged a sale . . . top price of course . . . really an excellent sale . . .'

Moggie Reilly said briefly, 'Congratulations.'

'Yes, but, well, do you see, it's a *conditional* sale.'

'Mm?' Moggie Reilly murmured, 'Conditional on *what*?'

'Well . . . actually, conditional on his winning this afternoon. Winning the Cloister Hurdle, to be precise . . .'

'I see,' Moggie said with calm, and indeed he did see.

'Yes . . . well, Percy Driffield refused to approach you with this proposition, but . . .' he spoke faster, 'this is not a bribe I'm offering you, not at all. I wouldn't do that, absolutely not.'

'No,' Moggie said.

'What I'm offering, do you see,' Jasper Billington Innes continued, coming awkwardly to the point, 'is in the nature of *commission*. If my horse Lilyglit wins the Cloister Hurdle, I can finalize the sale on better terms, and . . . er, well, if you and Storm Cone could have assisted the result in any way, then you would have earned a commission, don't you see?'

What I see, Moggie Reilly thought to himself, is a quick way to lose my licence. To Jasper Billington Innes he replied reassuringly, 'Your horse Lilyglit is good enough to win without help.'

'But think of the handicap. It alters everything. And last time out Lilyglit at level weights beat Storm Cone by only two lengths . . .' The voice rose in worry.

'Mr Billington Innes,' Moggie Reilly said patiently, near to shivering, 'there are eleven runners in the Cloister. Theoretically it's anybody's race because of the handicap, and if Storm Cone makes his way to the front, I shan't stop him.'

'Are you saying you won't help me?'

'I'm saying good luck.'

The phone went dead abruptly. Jasper Billington Innes, thought Moggie Reilly, as he headed, undressing, for the shower, was one of the last people he'd have expected to aim to win by flim-flam.

Moggie didn't know, of course, about the manager at Stemmer Peabody.

Jasper Billington Innes sat beside the telephone, staring unseeingly at the carpet of a small hotel bedroom next door to his gaming club. The deal he had made with his bookmaker and the club proprietors no longer seemed so brilliant as at four in the morning, but he had to admit that they'd been fair and even kind. He'd realized too late, though, that Lilyglit *had* to win the Cloister Hurdle for him to be left with enough to hold up his head around town. In effect, if Lilyglit won, the prize money would go a long way towards paying his gambling debts. Lilyglit's value would have risen and his sale would leave a useful surplus. If Lilyglit lost, his sale proceeds would be swallowed by debt. If he lost the race he would be worth less than he would fetch at that moment. His hard-pressed owner had agreed that the horse's value should decline slightly with every length he was beaten.

Jasper saw betting on Lilyglit to win as a way out, but his bookmaker had shaken his head and refused to increase his debt.

Jasper Innes made a hopeless list of his other saleable assets, none of which were unentailed antiques or portraits. He and Wendy had both from childhood lived among precious objects that belonged for ever to the next generation. Even his old house, dying of rot, belonged to his son and *his* son and *his* son, for ever.

Jasper Billington Innes, until that morning, would never have tried to bribe a jockey. He was only vaguely aware of the graceful manner of Moggie's refusal, and he could think of nothing except his own desolation.

He read again the newspaper assessment of the Cloister Hurdle that lay before him on his room-service breakfast tray.

*No. 1 Lilyglit. Worthy favourite, needing to fight all the way with top weight.*

*No. 2 Fable. In the good strong hands of Arkwright, will he or won't he be able to come and join the dance?*

*No. 3 Storm Cone. Jockey, 'Nine lives' M. Reilly. They'll try forever, and the weights favour them, but have they the finishing speed?*

Jasper swallowed hard and telephoned a friend who would know how to get in touch with the Arkwrights. He then reached and talked to Vernon Arkwright, who listened without excitement.

Jasper found it easier, the second time, to offer a 'commission'. He almost believed in it himself.

'What you want me to do,' Vernon said, clarifying things baldly, 'is to prevent Storm Cone from beating Lilyglit.'

'Er . . .'

'And I don't get paid unless Lilyglit wins and I've in some way helped to bring that about. Is that right?'

'Er . . . yes.'

Vernon Arkwright sighed. It wasn't much of a proposition, but the only one they'd been offered.

'OK,' he said, 'I'll do it. But if you default on the agreement, I'll report your offer to the stewards.'

Jasper wasn't used to threats. Vernon Arkwright's bluntness forced him to understand how far he'd travelled towards plain dishonesty. He felt humiliated and wretched. He wavered. He didn't turn back.

He telephoned Percy Driffield and asked him to place a big bet for him on Lilyglit to win. Driffield, who had done this before, agreed without protest and telephoned his own bookmaker, who accepted the wager.

*

Christopher Haig, sitting at his table in the weighing-room, smiled at each jockey as he checked colours and number cloth.

Lilyglit, the favourite, was to be ridden as usual by the long-time champion steeplechase jockey: married, three children, a face well known to the public. Trainer Percy Driffield stood by, alert in case of trouble.

Next on the judge's list came Vernon Arkwright, partner of Fable. Vernon Arkwright, though a villain from eyeballs to spleen, nevertheless amused Christopher Haig who fought to keep his grin within officially suitable limits. The stewards in Christopher Haig's hearing had sworn to follow Fable every step of the way in the Cloister Hurdle with sword-sharp patrol-camera lenses, trying to catch him in crime. Chris Haig thought of warning the jockey but, looking at Arkwright's cheeky confidence, thought he probably knew.

Storm Cone's jockey next. Moggie the cat, second-generation Irish, agile in body, clever in mind, a honey trap for good-looking women and quite likely a future ambassador for the sport.

When he'd learned and checked off all the runners, Christopher Haig stood in the parade ring for a final familiarization and watched the jockeys go out to race; watched them – young, thin and careless of danger – and envied them sorely. What if, he thought, what if I'd gone to a racing stable at sixteen, instead of school and university? What if it's still not too late to learn stunt flying? To try wing-walking?

But it was already too late for both.

The judge's box at Winchester races was situated in the main part of the grandstand, a storey above the stewards' room and (of course) directly in line with the winning post.

On some tracks, particularly minor country ones, the judge's box was down on the grass, itself marking the finishing line, but Christopher Haig preferred the height of places like Winchester, where one could look down on the course and distinguish more easily one speeding horse from another.

He climbed to his vantage point for the Cloister Hurdle and laid out his notes on the shelf thoughtfully provided by the window for the purpose. He had binoculars for watching the more distant parts of the mile-and-a-half circuit and an assistant whose job it was to announce 'Photograph, photograph' over the loudspeaker if the judge told him to: and the judge told him to whenever the leading horses finished within half a length of each other. The photo-finish camera at Winchester was operated by technicians in a room above the judge's box.

Christopher Haig counted the horses as they cantered to the start: eleven, all correct. Through his binoculars he watched the horses circle and line up for the start. Lilyglit lined up on the inside rail and, when the starting tapes flew up, was effortlessly first and fast away.

Percy Driffield with Sarah beside him watched Lilyglit from the stands. Neither Jasper Billington Innes nor Wendy had found enough courage to appear on the racecourse. Driffield hoped Moggie Reilly would prove as honest as his reputation: his daughter pledged her life on it.

Wendy sat at home in front of the television set in her small private sitting-room with her fists clenched, her hair unbrushed and tear stains on her cheeks. Jasper hadn't telephoned her and she didn't know where he was. She had tried the bookmakers, the gaming club and the hotel. She had tried the telephone in his car. Jasper had left no messages anywhere and his wife was becoming afraid.

Lilyglit, always a front runner, sped over the first few flights of hurdles defying gravity like an impala fleeing a lion. Storm Cone lay fifth, with Fable behind him.

On the stands the Arkwrights – trainer and owner-cousin – cheerfully watched young Vernon set off in Moggie Reilly's shadow with the secretly stated purpose of ending Storm Cone's chances by flipping his jockey over the rails. With Storm Cone out of the way, Lilyglit had the best chance to win. Vernon Arkwright had no intention of letting anything else interfere with Lilyglit's progress – except that if Fable himself should take unexpected wings . . . well then . . . allegiance to the prize money began at home.

Storm Cone's owner with John Chester, his trainer, stood on the balcony of the owner's private box up on the same level as the stewards' eyrie, with no one to interfere with their view. The owner, almost as rich as Jasper had been a few days earlier, had been trying for several years to buy himself into leading-owner status, but he, as so many before him, had found that if money can't buy love, neither can it lead in the winner of the Grand National.

John Chester had put all his skill into sending Storm Cone to this test with every piston smoothly firing. If Moggie Reilly gave away an unnecessary inch, and he, John Chester, lost his best and perhaps only chance of heading the trainers' list, he thought he would probably kill him.

Down on the turf emotions were simpler. To the champion jockey, comfortable on his regular partner, Lilyglit, it was just another race, which he would win if all went well. He liked front-runners. Lilyglit jumped the hurdles cleanly.

To Moggie Reilly also, it was just another race, though he would strain to give John Chester his championship if Lilyglit blinked. Storm Cone telegraphed vigour and good feeling through the reins, the best of signs for his rider.

The eleven runners stretched out past the stands first time round, and swung round the top bend to set out on the last mile. Christopher Haig watched them, counted them, checked that Lilyglit still led on the inside.

It was on the curve at the top of the long bend, where the horses were backside-on to the stewards and half hidden by white rails, that Vernon Arkwright put his hand under Moggie Reilly's boot and heaved upwards with all his strength.

Moggie Reilly, fiercely unbalanced, felt his foot fly out of the stirrup as his head swung inexorably over the horse's withers and down towards the thundering shoulder and the ground below. Moggie's fingers locked in the horse's mane. His weight was all on one side of the great creature surging beneath him. He had dropped his whip. *There was a flight of hurdles ahead, as soon as one got round the bend.*

Vernon Arkwright couldn't believe that Moggie Reilly was still technically in the saddle, even though clinging there with his fingernails and with his centre of gravity a yard off sideways. Moggie the cat let Storm Cone put himself as right as possible to jump the hurdle ahead, and fatalistically accepted that he would probably be thrown off into the path of the other half-ton runners, all striving to hold their positions at thirty miles an hour.

He said afterwards that it was an acute fear of falling among hooves that kept him bumping along round Storm Cone's neck, hanging on literally for life, forcing every muscle he could command to avoid being trampled. Ten strides, not more, before he reached the lethal row of wood-and-birch lattice jumps ahead, a hand stretched down, grasped the bright nylon cloth of his scarlet-and-orange striped shirt, and hauled him upwards.

Moggie Reilly's heroic saviour, partnering one of the eventual also-rans, shrugged off his action later with, 'You'd have done it for me, mate.' What he did at the time was to give Moggie Reilly precious seconds in which to grasp the saddle-tree, throw his legs astride Storm Cone and lurch into some sort of equilibrium before his mount bunched his quarters and shot over the hazardous hurdles as if powered by rockets.

Moggie Reilly had no hands on the reins nor feet in the stirrups, but his will to win persisted. Storm Cone had lost maybe ten lengths behind Lilyglit, but both the horse and his rider, not ready for defeat, flattened their aerodynamic profile and accelerated determinedly down the far side. Moggie collected and shortened the reins, the horse grateful for the control. Round the final bend they raced resolutely into clear second place, with only Lilyglit still there to beat.

Vernon Arkwright cursed hugely, seeing no hope of catching Storm Cone again for another attack. Up in the stewards' box, the three eminent gentlemen there were clapping each other on the shoulder and almost hopping around with joy. They had all plainly seen Vernon Arkwright's attack on Moggie Reilly, bottom-end on or not. The patrol camera would have filmed it, and wouldn't lie. This time, *this time*, they had caught out Vernon Arkwright in a thoroughly visible misdemeanour, and they would hold another inquiry, and this time shunt the villain *off*.

Christopher Haig, one storey above them, marvelled that Moggie Reilly, without his feet in the stirrups, was still on board at all, even though, with Lilyglit well ahead coming to the final hurdle, he had no hope of winning. Tiring, indeed, Storm Cone would find it difficult, Chris Haig thought from his long judging experience, to hang on to finish second. Two horses he had passed were closing on him again.

That clear assessment was Christopher Haig's last coherent thought.

He saw Lilyglit approach the final flight of hurdles. He saw the horse make a rare mistake in taking off too soon to reach the far side without stumbling. He saw Lilyglit's nose go down in the classic pattern of fallers . . . and before Lilyglit had crashed to the ground at high speed, his own heart had stopped.

The judge's assistant had no medical knowledge and was hardly a fast thinker on his feet. When Christopher Haig collapsed beside him into a graceless sprawled-leg heap on the floor, the assistant bent over him in horror and didn't know what to do.

He'd heard Chris Haig's head crunch onto the floor-boards of the judge's box, and he heard also the brief rattle of the last lungful of air escaping. He saw Chris Haig's face flush suddenly to a greyish dark blue. He saw the dark colour vanish and the skin fade to white.

He loosened Christopher Haig's adventurous tie in shaking shock and several times called his name.

Christopher Haig's eyelids were partly open, but neither he nor his devastated assistant witnessed the close finish of the Cloister Hurdle. No one called 'Photograph, photograph' over the loudspeaker. No one announced the winner.

One of the stewards with presence of mind ran up the stairs to the judge's box to complain crossly about the silence. The sight of Chris Haig's immobile body temporarily clogged his own tongue instead. A man of experience, he knew irreversible death when he saw it and, having conclusively checked on the absence of pulse in the Haig neck, he sent the assistant to fetch the doctor and hurried downstairs again with the unthinkable news.

'We, as stewards,' he told his fellows, 'will have to determine the winner from the photo-finish recording. As you know, it's in the basic rules.' He called on the intercom for the technicians to furnish a print of the moment when the leading horses crossed the line, saying he needed it quickly.

A technician appeared fast, but red faced and empty handed. In deep embarrassment he explained that the former trouble had resurfaced, and the photo system had scrambled itself just when Lilyglit lay in front, before the last hurdle, two furlongs from home.

The stewards, dumbfounded, were advised by the Stipendiary Steward – the official interpreter at the meeting of all Rules of Racing – that in the absence of the judge (and Christopher Haig, being dead, could be classed as absent) and in the absence of photo-finish evidence (the equipment having malfunctioned) the stewards themselves could announce who had won.

The stewards looked at each other. One of them was certain Storm Cone had won by a nose. One thought Moggie Reilly had tired and had let Storm Cone fall back in the last two strides. One of them had been looking down the course to see if the motionless Lilyglit had broken his neck.

In confusion they announced over the broadcasting system that there would be a stewards' inquiry.

The Tote, in the absence of an announced winner, had refused to pay out at all. Bookmakers were shouting odds on every outcome but the right one. Media people scurried round with microphones at the ready.

Television cameras, perched near the roof of the stands, favoured a slightly blurred dead-heat.

The two other jockeys involved in the close finish believed that Storm Cone had beaten them by an inch, but their opinion wasn't required.

Moggie had ridden most of the race without his feet in the stirrups (as Tim Brookshaw once did in the Grand National). He'd knelt on Storm Cone's withers and squeezed with the calves of his legs and kept his balance precariously over the hurdles. It had been a great feat of riding and he deserved the cheers that greeted his return. He was sure he had won despite everything, and he would personally get even one day, he thought, with that crazy dangerous Arkwright.

John Chester, Storm Cone's trainer, who couldn't imagine why the judge hadn't called for a photograph, had no doubt at all that his horse had won. The owner, with pride, led his excited winner and his exhausted jockey into the enclosure allocated to the victor and received provisional compliments. John Chester savoured the exquisite joy of for once, and at last, dislodging Percy Driffield from his arrogant pinnacle as top trainer. John Chester *preened.*

Percy Driffield himself cared not a peanut at that moment for John Chester or the trainers' championship. His dazed jockey had been collected uninjured by ambulance, but Lilyglit still lay ominously flat on the landing side of the last flight of hurdles, and as he ran down the course towards him the trainer's mind was filled only with grief. Lilyglit, fast and handsome, was the horse he loved most in his stable.

On the stands, his daughter Sarah stood watching her father's terrible urgency and was torn between pity for him and admiration for Moggie's skill. Along with all the knowledgeable race crowd, she'd seen the empty stirrups swinging wildly as Storm Cone had jumped the hurdles and sped to the finish.

Percy Driffield reached the prostrate Lilyglit and went down on his knees beside him. His own breath shortened and practically deserted him when he found the brilliant chestnut still alive, and realized that the crash to the ground had been so fast and hard that it had literally knocked all the air out of the horse's lungs. The term 'winded' sounded relatively minor: the reality could be frightening. Lilyglit needed time for his shocked chest muscles to regain a breathing rhythm and, while Percy Driffield stroked his neck, the horse suddenly heaved in a gust of air, and in a moment more had staggered to his feet, unharmed.

There was a cheer from the distant stands. Lilyglit was near to an idol.

Wendy Billington Innes, clutching a wet handkerchief in her sitting-room, had believed Lilyglit had died, even though the television race commentator, still stalwartly filling up air-time for viewers, had discussed 'winded' as a cause for hope. When Lilyglit stood up, Wendy Billington Innes wept again, this time with relief. Jasper, wherever he was – and she still hadn't reached him – would rejoice that the hurdler he worshipped had survived.

Back on the racecourse Vernon Arkwright, disgruntled, reckoned the whole Cloister enterprise had been a waste of time. True, he had stopped Storm Cone from beating Lilyglit, but Lilyglit hadn't won anyway. Vernon thought his chances of being paid his 'commission' by Jasper Billington Innes were slim to nowhere, which was unfair when one took into account the risk involved.

Vernon had chosen the top bend on the course for his attack because the curve of the rail and the horses bunched end-on behind him there would hide his swift move on Moggie. He didn't know and couldn't expect that the runners to his rear would unexpectedly part like curtains, revealing him nakedly to the patrol camera's busy lens.

The racing authorities had for several years yearned for damningly clear evidence of Arkwright skulduggery. Now they had almost enough for attempted manslaughter. They couldn't believe their luck.

In the stewards' room, film from various other patrol cameras flickered on the screen. Hurriedly the officials viewed the head-on pictures that would reveal bumping incidents during the finishing furlong. In this case there weren't any, but neither was there any firm indication as to which horse had crossed the line first.

The side-on patrol camera nearest to the winning post showed Storm Cone probably a short head in front, but that particular camera was positioned a few yards short of the finishing line and couldn't be relied on for last-second decisions.

It seemed there was nothing in the rule book giving the incident-gathering patrol cameras ultimate authority in proclaiming the winner.

The doctor, summoned to the stewards' anxious inquiry, confirmed that Christopher Haig was dead and had died, according to the judge's assistant, well before Storm Cone or any other horse had reached the finishing line. The actual cause of death would depend on post-mortem findings.

The Stipendiary Steward, having consulted the Jockey Club big-wigs in London as well as his own soul, told the three officiating stewards that they would have to declare the race void.

*Void.*

It was announced that the race had been declared void primarily because of the death of the judge. All bets were off. Money staked would be repaid.

The word 'void' reverberated round the racecourse, and John Chester in a fury barged into the weighing-room like a tank, insisting his horse had won, demanding to be credited with Storm Cone's prize money, dogmatically asserting that he had dislodged Driffield at the top of the trainers' list.

Sorry, sorry, he was told. Void meant void. Void meant that the race was judged not to have taken place. No one had won any prize money, which meant that Percy Driffield was still ahead on the list.

John Chester lost control and yelled with rage.

Moggie Reilly, who believed that he and Storm Cone had certainly won on the line, shrugged philosophically over the loss of his percentage of the winner's prize. Poor old Christopher Haig, he thought; and couldn't know on that Friday that his own exalted riding and his trustworthiness had won him both huge upward moves in his career and also the lasting devotion of the divine Sarah Driffield, the toast of all Lambourn; his future wife.

The worst gnashing of teeth came from the stewards themselves. They could hardly believe it! They had in their hands and before their mesmerized eyes a clear sharp film showing Vernon Arkwright stretching his hand out under the heel of Moggie Reilly's boot and jerking upwards with all his strength. They could see the force. They could see Moggie Reilly rise in the air and then plunge down over his horse's shoulder, clinging on for life with only taut-pulled tendons to save himself.

They could see it all ... and now the Stipendiary Steward – the uncontestable interpreter of the Rules of Racing – now he was telling these three in-charge stewards that they couldn't use either the patrol-camera film or the evidence of their own eyes. They couldn't accuse Vernon Arkwright of any sort of misdeed, because the Cloister Handicap Hurdle was deemed never to have taken place. If the race was void, so were its sins.

Void meant void in all respects.

Too bad. Couldn't be helped. Rules were rules.

'Dear God, Christopher,' the competent steward thought, calling on his friend the judge, 'why didn't your heart beat just five minutes longer?'

Haig's death prevented John Chester from becoming top trainer (ever).

Haig's death saved Vernon Arkwright (that spring) from being warned-off. Amazed by his luck he prudently 'forgot' the reason for his (now voided) assault on Moggie. It was definitely not the moment to say he'd agreed to be bribed.

Christopher Haig's death, in keeping Vernon Arkwright quiet, saved Jasper Billington Innes his untainted reputation.

Jasper himself, grindingly unhappy, watched Winchester's fourth race on banks of rectangular screens in a shop selling television sets. Large and small, the sets showed identical action, but all were silent. The shop favoured pop music to bring in trade: loud music, throbbing with a heavy bass beat, wholly at odds with the cool pictures of horses and riders moving round the parade ring, anonymous in their absence of commentary.

Jasper asked a shop helper for sound with the races. Sure, he was told, but the music continued unabated.

With a feeling of unreality, Jasper watched the runners go down to the start for the Cloister Handicap Hurdle. His own beautiful Lilyglit moved fluidly, packed with power. Jasper's jumbled feelings tore him apart. However could he have doubted his horse would win? *However* could he have been ready to let him win dishonestly? Jasper wanted to believe that his telephone call to Vernon Arkwright hadn't happened. He tried to convince himself that Arkwright wouldn't be able to do anything anyway to impede Storm Cone. Not Storm Cone or any other horse. Lilyglit would win without help . . . he *had* to win to pay the debts . . . but the weights favoured Storm Cone . . . and if Moggie Reilly couldn't be bought, he had to be stopped . . .

Jasper's thoughts pendulumed from self-loathing to self-justification, from belief in Lilyglit to a vision of poverty. He'd never in his life earned even a bus fare – he rarely went on a bus – and he'd had no training in anything. How could he provide for a wife and four children? And how deep ran his belief in his own honour when at the first test it had crumbled? When his first solution to financial heartbreak had been to bribe a jockey?

On the multiple silent screens the Cloister runners lined up and set off, with Lilyglit fast away and setting the pace as usual.

Nothing bad would happen, Jasper told himself. Lilyglit would stay in front all the way. He watched the close-up of his favourite crossing the winning line first time round, and saw him set off round the top bend, only his rump-end clearly showing.

The television camera operator, focusing on Lilyglit, missed Vernon Arkwright's swerve towards Storm Cone but, with a wild swing of his lens, caught the moment when Moggie Reilly, unbalanced, flew out of his saddle. Mostly hidden though he was by white rails, by Storm Cone himself, and by other horses, Moggie Reilly, in his scarlet-and-orange silks, could be glimpsed struggling, and finally, with help, winning his fight against gravity. The banks of screens showed him jumping the next flight of hurdles without control of reins or stirrups and then, immediate story over, swung back to the leader, to Lilyglit, now far and by many lengths established in the lead.

Jasper's whole body went cold with sweat. His mind refused to accept what his eyes had seen. He couldn't ... he *couldn't* have offered to pay to have Moggie Reilly put in danger of hideous injury ... it was impossible.

And Moggie Reilly was still there, on his horse, without his feet in the stirrups, but still trying to make up lost ground, still trying to catch the five or six runners ahead, but with no hope of winning.

Vernon Arkwright had dropped back out of television sight, his task accomplished. The screens all switched to Lilyglit galloping alone, uncatchable now and stretching with long sweeping strides towards the last hurdle.

I've won, Jasper thought, and felt little joy in it.

Lilyglit fell.

Lilyglit lay inert on the green turf.

The television picture switched to the finish. Storm Cone's violent colours flashed there inconclusively, and after a moment the focus was back on Lilyglit, still unmoving, looking dead.

Jasper Billington Innes all but fainted in the shop.

Somewhere in the depth of the store a control

button, pressed, changed the racing programme to a children's teatime frolic. Three walls full of identical cartoon characters wobbled about simultaneously, uttering unheard squeaks and platitudes. They drew in a laughing audience (which the racing had not) but the thump-thump deafening background music drummed on and on.

Jasper walked dizzily out of the store and on jerky uncoordinated legs made his way back towards the multi-storey park where he'd left his car when he'd decided where to go to watch the Cloister.

He unlocked the car door and in mental agony sat in the driver's seat listing again his dreadful woes.

Lilyglit – he couldn't bear it – was dead. Dead, uninsured, worth nothing: and he was now heavily in debt to Percy Driffield for his last desperate bet.

Vernon Arkwright, hauled before the stewards, would testify that Jasper had bribed him to put Moggie Reilly's life in danger.

Jasper realized that he might himself be warned-off. Might suffer that ultimate disgrace. He was drowning in unpayable debt, and he had lost his wife's fortune. But it was his inner awareness of dishonour that had most shattered his self-respect.

Not for the first time, he thought of killing himself.

Wendy Billington Innes had dried her tears and stiffened her backbone at the sight of Lilyglit walking safely back unhurt, and a short time later she listened half in relief and half in horror to a trainer-to-owner telephone call from Percy Driffield.

'You do understand, don't you?' he asked, as she fell silent.

'I'm not sure,' she said.

'Tell Jasper that everything about that race is void. *Everything*. Including his bet.'

'All right.'

'A void race shouldn't detract very much from Lilyglit's value . . . and tell Jasper I've a buyer for him in my own yard. I frankly don't want to lose that horse.'

'I'll tell him,' Wendy said, disconnecting, and started again for the third time trying everywhere she could think of to find her husband.

No one had seen him since breakfast. The fear she'd been smothering all day rose sharply and prodded her towards panic.

She knew that Jasper had unbending pride. Below the sweet-natured exterior lived a man of serious honour, and it was this uprightness that had attracted her years ago.

Stemmer Peabody had smashed Jasper's pride. He would hate ruin as if it were despicable. He might find it too much to bear.

She had twice phoned Jasper's car, but he hadn't answered. The car phone service was rigged to speak messages aloud when the ignition was switched on, but her pleas to Jasper to phone her back had gone unanswered. That didn't mean he hadn't heard them. She feared he'd ignored them and wiped them off.

With nowhere else offering the slightest hope she tried his car again.

'Leave a message . . .'

She cursed the disembodied voice and spoke from her heart.

'Jasper, if you can hear me, listen . . . *Listen.* Lilyglit is alive, he fell, but he was only winded. He's unharmed . . . *listen* . . . and Percy Driffield has a buyer. And that whole race was declared void because the judge died before the finish. Nothing that happened in the race counts. *Nothing*, do you understand? Percy Driffield told me to tell you particularly. All bets are void. So Jasper . . . my dear, my dear, come home . . . We'll get by . . . I quite like cooking and looking after the children . . . but we all need you . . . Come home . . . please come home . . .' She stopped abruptly, feeling that she'd been talking to the empty air, pointlessly.

Jasper, indeed, didn't hear her. With the car's ignition still turned off, the message machine remained silent.

Jasper in black humour couldn't decide *how* to kill himself. He had no piece of tubing for carbon monoxide. He knew of no cliffs to jump over. He had no knife for his wrists. Dying didn't seem easy. Never a handyman, he sat uselessly trying to work it out. Meanwhile, he found an old envelope in a door pocket and in total despair but no haste wrote a farewell note.

*I am ashamed.*

*Forgive me.*

After that he decided to find a good solid tree somewhere and accelerate head-on into a killing crash.

He slotted the car key into the ignition to start the engine . . . and the car phone message service spoke Wendy's words aloud, as if she were there by his side.

Utterly stunned, Jasper Billington Innes played his wife's message three times.

Gradually he understood that Lilyglit lived, that his bet with Percy Driffield was void, and that neither he nor Vernon Arkwright would be charged with breaking racing law.

He trembled for long unwinding minutes.

He realized he was undeservedly being given a second chance and would never get a third.

He tore up the envelope, and drove slowly home.

Officially, nothing that had happened in the Cloister Handicap Hurdle was deemed to have happened.

Nothing . . . except the death of Christopher Haig.

# SHATTERED

To
Her Majesty Queen Elizabeth, The Queen Mother
in celebration of her 100th birthday
With endless gratitude, love and every good wish,
from Dick Francis

My thanks also to
Stephen Zawistowski, glass-blower
Stephen Spiro, Professor of Respiratory Medicine
Tanya Williams, West Mercia Police

to Matthew Francis, my grandson, for the title

and to my son, Felix, for everything

# CHAPTER ONE

Four of us drove together to Cheltenham races on the day that Martin Stukely died there from a fall in a steeple-chase.

It was 31 December, the eve of the year two thousand. A cold midwinter morning. The world approaching the threshold of the future.

Martin himself, taking his place behind the steering wheel of his BMW, set off before noon without premonition, collecting his three passengers from their Cotswold hills bases on his way to his afternoon's work. A jockey of renown, he had confidence and a steady heart.

By the time he reached my sprawling house on the hillside above the elongated tourist-attracting village of Broadway, the air in his spacious car swirled richly full of smoke from his favourite cigar, the Montecristo No 2, his substitute for eating. At thirty-four he was spending longer and longer in a sauna each day, but was all the same gradually losing the metabolic battle against weight.

Genes had given him a well-balanced frame in general,

and an Italian mother in particular had passed on a love of cooking, and vivacity.

He quarrelled incessantly with Bon-Bon, his rich, plump and talkative wife, and on the whole ignored his four small children, often frowning as he looked at them as if not sure exactly who they were. Nevertheless his skill and courage and rapport with horses took him as often as always into the winner's enclosure, and he drove to Cheltenham calmly discussing his mounts' chances that afternoon in two fast hurdle races and one longer 'chase. Three miles of jumping fences brought out the controlled recklessness that made him great.

He picked me up last on that fateful Friday morning, as I lived nearest to Cheltenham's racecourse.

Already on board, and by his side, sat Priam Jones, the trainer whose horses he regularly rode. Priam was expert at self-aggrandisement but not quite as good as he believed at knowing when a horse in his care had come to a performance peak. That day's steeplechaser, Tallahassee, was, according to my friend Martin on the telephone, as ready as he would ever be to carry off the day's gold trophy, but Priam Jones, smoothing his white late-middle-age thinning hair, told the horse's owner in a blasé voice that Tallahassee might still do better on softer ground.

Lounging back beside me on the rear seat, with the tip of one of Martin's cigars glowing symmetrically to ash, Tallahassee's owner, Lloyd Baxter, listened without noticeable pleasure, and I thought Priam Jones would have done better to keep his premature apologies in reserve.

It was unusual for Martin to be the one who drove Tallahassee's owner and trainer anywhere. Normally he took other jockeys, or me alone, but Priam Jones from arrogance had just wrecked his own car in a stupid rash of flat tyres, thanks to his having tried to ignore head-on a newly installed deterrent no-parking set of rising teeth. It was the council's fault, he insisted. He would sue.

Priam had taken it for granted, Martin had told me crossly, that he – Martin – would do the driving, and would take not only Priam himself but would also chauffeur the horse's owner, who was staying overnight with Priam for the Cheltenham meeting, having flown down from the north of England to the local Staverton airfield in a small rented air taxi.

I disliked Lloyd Baxter as thoroughly as he disliked me. Martin had warned me of the Priam tyre situation ('keep your sarcastic tongue behind your splendid teeth') and had begged me also to swamp the grumpy, dumpy millionaire owner with anaesthetizing charm in advance, in case Priam Jones's fears materialized and the horse drew a blank.

I saw Martin's face grinning at me in the driving mirror as he listened to me sympathize with the flat tyres. He more than paid any debt he owed me by ferrying me about when he could, as I'd lost my licence for a year through scorching at ninety-five miles an hour round the Oxford ring road (fourth ticket for speeding) to take him and his broken leg to see his point-of-death old retired gardener. The gardener's heart had then thumped away insecurely for six further weeks – one of life's little ironies. My loss of licence now had three months to run.

The friendship between Martin and myself, unlikely at first sight, had sprung fully grown in an instant four or more years ago, the result of a smile crinkling round his eyes, echo, I gathered, of my own.

We had met in the jury room of the local crown court, chosen for jury duty to hear a fairly simple case of domestic murder. The trial lasted two and a half days. Over mineral water afterwards, I'd learned about the tyranny of weight. Though my life had nothing to do with horses, or his with the heat and chemistry of my own days, we shared, perhaps, the awareness of the physical ability that we each needed for success in our trade.

In the jury room Martin had asked with merely polite curiosity, 'What do you do for a living?'

'I blow glass.'

'You do *what*?'

'I make things of glass. Vases, ornaments, goblets. That sort of thing.'

'Good grief.'

I smiled at his astonishment. 'People do, you know. People have made things of glass for thousands of years.'

'Yes, but . . .' he considered, 'you don't look like someone who makes ornaments. You look . . . well . . . tough.'

I was four years younger than he and three inches taller, and probably equal in muscles.

'I've made horses,' I said mildly. 'Herds of them.'

'The Crystal Stud Cup,' he said, identifying one of Flat racing's more elaborate prizes. 'Did you make that?'

'Not that one, no.'

'Well . . . Do you have a *name*? Like, say, Baccarat?'

I smiled lopsidedly. 'Not so glamorous. It's Logan, Gerard Logan.'

'Logan Glass.' He nodded, no longer surprised. 'You have a place on the High Street in Broadway, side by side with all those antique shops. I've seen it.'

I nodded. 'Sales and workshop.'

He hadn't seemed to take any special notice, but a week later he'd walked into my display gallery, spent an intense and silent hour there, asked if I'd personally made all the exhibits (mostly) and offered me a lift to the races. As time went by we had become comfortably accustomed to each other's traits and faults. Bon-Bon used me as a shield in battle and the children thought me a bore because I wouldn't let them near my furnace.

For half the races that day at Cheltenham things went as normal. Martin won the two-mile hurdle race by six lengths and Priam Jones complained that six lengths was too far. It would ruin the horse's position in the handicap.

Martin shrugged, gave an amused twist to his eyebrows and went into the changing room to put on Lloyd Baxter's colours of black and white chevrons, pink sleeves and cap. I watched the three men in the parade ring, owner, trainer and jockey, as they took stock of Tallahassee walking purposefully round in the hands of his stable lad. Tallahassee stood at odds of six to four with the bookmakers for the Coffee Forever Gold Trophy: clear favourite.

Lloyd Baxter (ignoring his trainer's misgivings) had put his money on, and so had I.

It was at the last fence of all that Tallahassee uncharacteristically tangled his feet. Easily ahead by seven lengths he lost his concentration, hit the roots of the unyielding birch and turned a somersault over his rider, landing his whole half-ton mass upside down with the saddle-tree and his withers crushing the rib cage of the man beneath.

The horse fell at the peak of his forward-to-win acceleration and crashed down at thirty or more miles an hour. Winded, he lay across the jockey for inert moments, then rocked back and forwards vigorously in his struggle to rise again to his feet.

The fall and its aftermath looked truly terrible from where I watched on the stands. The roar of welcome for a favourite racing home to a popular win was hushed to a gasp, to cries, to an endless anxious murmur. The actual winner passed the post without his due cheers, and a thousand pairs of binoculars focused on the unmoving black and white chevrons flat on the green December grass.

The racecourse doctor, though instantly attending him from his following car, couldn't prevent the fast gathering group of paramedics and media people from realizing that Martin Stukely, though still semi-conscious, was dying before their eyes. They glimpsed the blood sliding frothily out of the jockey's mouth, choking him as the sharp ends of broken ribs tore his lungs apart. They described it, cough by groan, in their news reports.

The doctor and paramedics loaded Martin, just alive, into the waiting ambulance and as they set off to the hospital they worked desperately with transfusions and oxygen, but quietly, before the journey ended, the jockey lost his race.

Priam, not normally a man of emotion, wept without shame as later he collected Martin's belongings, including his car keys, from the changing rooms. Sniffing, blowing his nose, and accompanied by Lloyd Baxter who looked annoyed rather than grief-stricken, Priam Jones offered to return me to my place of business in Broadway, though not to my home in the hills, as he intended to go in the opposite direction from there, to see Bon-Bon; to give her comfort.

I asked if he would take me on with him to see Bon-Bon. He refused. Bon-Bon wanted Priam alone, he said. She had said so, devastated, on the telephone.

Lloyd Baxter, Priam added, would now also be off-loaded at Broadway. Priam had got him the last available room in the hotel there, the Wychwood Dragon. It was all arranged.

Lloyd Baxter glowered at the world, at his trainer, at me, at fate. He should, he thought, have won the gold trophy. He had been robbed. Though his horse was unharmed, his feelings for his dead jockey seemed to be resentment, not regret.

As Priam, shoulders drooping, and Baxter, frowning heavily, set off ahead of us towards the car park, Martin's changing-room valet hurried after me, calling my name. I stopped, and turned towards him, and into my hands he thrust the lightweight racing saddle that, strapped firmly to Tallahassee's back, had helped to deal out damage and death.

The stirrups, with the leathers, were folded over the saddle plate, and were kept in place by the long girth wound round and round. The sight of the girth-wrapped piece of professional equipment, like my newly dead mother's Hasselblad camera, bleakly rammed into one's consciousness the gritty message that their owners would never come back. It was Martin's empty saddle that set me missing him painfully.

Eddie, the valet, was elderly, bald and, in Martin's estimation, hardworking and unable to do wrong. He turned to go back to the changing room but then stopped, fumbled in the deep front pocket of the apron of his trade and, producing a brown-paper-wrapped package, called after me to wait.

'Someone gave this to Martin to give to you,' he shouted, coming back and holding it out for me to take. 'Martin asked me to give it back to him when he was leaving to go home, so he could pass it on to you . . . but of course . . .' he swallowed, his voice breaking . . . 'he's gone.'

I asked. 'Who gave it to *him*?'

The valet didn't know. He was sure, though, that Martin himself had known, because he had been joking about it being worth a million, and Eddie was clear that the ultimate destination of the parcel had been Gerard Logan, Martin's friend.

I took the package and, thanking him, put it into my raincoat pocket, and we spent a mutual moment of sharp sadness for the gap we already felt in our lives. I supposed, as Eddie turned to hurry back to his chores in the changing room, and I continued into the car park, that I might have gone to the races for the last time, that without Martin's input the fun might have flown.

Priam's tears welled up again at the significance of the empty saddle, and Lloyd Baxter shook his head with disapproval. Priam recovered enough however to start Martin's car and drive it to Broadway where, as he'd intended, he off-loaded both me and Lloyd Baxter outside the Wychwood Dragon and then departed in speechless gloom towards Bon-Bon and her fatherless brood.

Lloyd Baxter paid me no attention but strode without pleasure into the hotel. During the journey from the racecourse he'd complained to Priam that his overnight bag was in Priam's house. He'd gone by hired car from Staverton airfield, intending to spend the evening at Priam's now-cancelled New Year's Eve party, celebrating a win in the Gold Coffee Cup before flying away the following morning to his thousand-acre estate in Northumberland. Priam's assertion that, after seeing Martin's family, he would himself ferry the bag to the hotel, left Tallahassee's owner unmollified. The whole afternoon had been a disaster, he grumbled, and in his voice one could hear undertones of an intention to change to a different trainer.

My own glass business lay a few yards away from the Wychwood Dragon on the opposite side of the road. If one looked across from outside the hotel, the gallery's windows seemed to glitter with ultra-bright light, which they did from breakfast to midnight every day of the year.

I walked across the road wishing that time could be reversed to yesterday: wishing that bright-eyed Martin would march through my door suggesting improbable glass sculptures that in fact, when I made them, won both commissions and kudos. He had become fascinated by the actual composition of glass and never seemed to tire of watching whenever I mixed the basic ingredients myself, instead of always buying it the easy way – off the shelf.

The ready-made stuff, which came in 200-kilo drums, looked like small opaque marbles, or large grey peas, half the size of the polished clear-glass toys. I used the simple option regularly, as it came pure and clean and melted without flaws.

When Martin first watched me load the tank of the furnace with a week's supply of the round grey pebbles, he repeated aloud the listed ingredients. 'Eighty per cent of the mix is white silica sand from the Dead Sea. Ten per cent is soda ash. Then add small specific amounts of antimony, barium, calcium and arsenic per fifty pounds of weight. If you want to colour the glass blue, use ground lapis lazuli or cobalt. If you want yellow, use cadmium, which changes with heat to orange and red and I don't believe it.'

'That's soda crystal glass,' I nodded, smiling. 'I use it all the time as it's safe in every way for eating or drinking from. Babies can lick it.'

He gazed at me in surprise. 'Isn't all glass safe to suck?'

'Well . . . no. You have to be exceedingly careful making things with lead. Lead crystal. Lovely stuff. But lead is mega mega poisonous. Lead silicate, that is, that's used for glass. It's a rusty red powder and in its raw state you have to keep it strictly separate from everything else and be terribly meticulous about locking it up.'

'What about cut lead-crystal wine glasses?' he asked. 'I mean, Bon-Bon's mother gave us some.'

'Don't worry,' I told him with humour. 'If they haven't made you ill yet, they probably won't.'

'Thanks a bunch.'

I went in through my heavy gallery door of bevelled glass panes already feeling an emptiness where Martin had been. And it wasn't as if I had no other friends. I had a pack of beer and wine cronies for whom fizzy water and sauna sweats were on their anathema lists. Two of those, Hickory and Irish, worked for me as assistants and apprentices, although Hickory was approximately my own age and Irish a good deal older. The desire to work with glass quite often struck late in life, as with Irish, who was forty, but sometimes, as with me, the fascination arrived like talking, too early to remember.

I had an uncle, eminent in the glass-blowing trade, who was also a brilliant flameworker. He could heat solid glass rods in the flame of a gas burner until, among other things, he could twiddle them into a semblance of lace, and make angels and crinolines and steady flat round bases for almost anything needing precision in a science laboratory.

He was amused at first that an inquisitive kid should shadow him, but was then interested, and finally took it seriously. He taught me whenever I could dodge school, and he died about the time that my inventiveness grew to match his. I was sixteen. In his will he left me plans and instructions for the building of a basic workshop, and also, much more valuably, his priceless notebooks into which he'd detailed years of unique skill. I'd built a locked safe-like bookcase to keep them in, and ever since had added my own notes on method and materials needed when I designed anything special. It stood always at the far end of the workshop between the stock shelves and a bank of four tall grey lockers, where my assistants and I kept our personal stuff.

It was he, my Uncle Ron, who named his enterprise Logan Glass, and he who drilled into me an embryonic business sense and an awareness that anything made by one glass-blower could in general be copied by another, and that this drastically lowered the asking price. During his last few years he sought and succeeded in making pieces of uncopyable originality, working out of my sight and then challenging me to detect and repeat his methods. Whenever I couldn't, he generously showed me how; and he laughed when I grew in ability until I could beat him at his own game.

In the late afternoon of Martin's death both the gallery and showroom were crowded with people looking for ways of remembering the advent of the historic millennium day. I'd designed and made a whole multitude and variety of small good-looking calendar-bearing dishes in every colour combination that I knew from experience attracted most tourist dollars, and we had sold literally hundreds of them. I'd scratched my signature on the lot. Not yet, I thought, but by the year 2020, if I could achieve it, a signed Gerard Logan calendar dish of 31 December 1999 might be worth collecting.

The long gallery displayed the larger, unusual, one-off and more expensive pieces, each spot-lit and available: the showroom was lined by many shelves holding smaller, colourful, attractive and less expensive ornaments, which could reasonably be packed into a tourist suitcase.

One side wall of the showroom rose only to waist height, so that over it one could see into the workshop beyond, where the furnace burned day and night and the little grey pebbles melted into soda crystal at a raised heat of 2,400 degrees Fahrenheit.

Hickory or Irish, or their colleague Pamela Jane, took turns to work as my assistant in the workshop. One of the other two gave a running commentary of the proceedings to the customers and the third packed parcels and worked the till. Ideally the four of us took the jobs in turn, but experienced glass-blowers were scarce, and my three enthusiastic assistants were still at the paperweight and penguin stage.

Christmas sales had been great but nothing like the New Year Two Thousand. As everything sold in my place was guaranteed hand-made (and mostly by me), the day I'd spent at the races had been my first respite away from the furnace for a month. I'd worked sometimes into the night, and always from eight onwards in the morning, with one of my three helpers assisting. The resulting exhaustion hadn't mattered. I was physically fit, and as Martin had said, who needed a sauna with 2,400 degrees in one's face?

Hickory, twirling colour into a glowing paperweight on the end of a slender five-foot-long steel rod called a punty iron, looked extremely relieved at my return from the races. Pamela Jane, smiling, earnest, thin and anxious, lost her place in her commentary and repeated instead, 'He's here. He's here . . .' and Irish stopped packing a cobalt-blue dolphin in bright white wrapping paper and sighed, 'Thank God' very heavily. They relied on me too much, I thought.

I said, 'Hi, guys,' as usual and, walking round into the workshop and stripping off jacket, tie and shirt, gave the millennium-crazy shoppers a view of a designer-label white string singlet, my working clothes. Hickory finished his paperweight, spinning the punty iron down by his feet to cool the glass, being careful not to scorch his new bright trainers. I made, as a frivolity, a striped hollow blue, green and purple fish with fins, a geodetic-type of ornament that looked impressively difficult and had defeated me altogether at fourteen. Light shone through it in rainbows.

The customers, though, wanted proof of that day's origin. Staying open much later than usual, I made endless dated bowls, plates and vases to please them, while Pamela Jane explained that they couldn't be collected until the next morning, New Year's Day, as they had to cool slowly overnight. No one seemed deterred. Irish wrote their names and told them jokes. There were hours of good nature and celebration.

Priam Jones called in fleetingly at one point. When he had been at Martin and Bon-Bon's house, he'd found my raincoat lying on the back seat in the car. I was most grateful, and thanked him with New Year fervour. He nodded, even smiled. His tears had dried.

When he'd gone I went to hang up my raincoat in my locker. Something hard banged against my knee and I remembered the package given to me by Eddie, the valet. I put it on a stock shelf out of the way at the rear of the workshop and went back to satisfy the customers.

Shop closing time was elastic but I finally locked the door behind the last customer in time for Hickory, Irish and Pamela Jane to go to parties, and for me to realize I hadn't yet opened the parcel that Priam Jones had returned in my raincoat. The parcel that had come from Martin . . . he'd sat heavily on my shoulder all evening, a laughing lost spirit, urging me on.

Full of regrets I locked the furnace against vandals and checked the heat of the annealing ovens, which were full of the newly made objects slowly cooling. The furnace, that I'd built to my uncle's design, was constructed of fire-bricks and fuelled by propane gas under pressure from a fan. It burned day and night at never less than 1,800 degrees Fahrenheit, hot enough to melt most metals, let alone burn paper. We were often asked if a memento like a wedding ring could be enclosed in a glass paper-weight, but the answer was sorry, no. Liquid glass would melt gold – and human flesh – immediately. Molten glass, in fact, was pretty dangerous stuff.

I slowly tidied the workshop, counted and recounted and then enclosed the day's takings in their canvas bag ready to entrust to the night safe of the bank. Then I put on my discarded clothes and eventually took a closer look at my neglected parcel. The contents proved to be exactly what they felt like, an ordinary-looking videotape, a bit disappointing. The tape was wound fully back to the beginning, and the black casing bore no label of any sort. There was no protective sleeve. I stacked it casually beside the money, and the sight of it reminded me that my videotape player was at my home, that I'd sold my car, and that rising midnight on a thousand years' eve wasn't the best time to phone for a taxi.

Plans for my own midnight, with a neighbourhood dance next door to my house, had disintegrated on Cheltenham racecourse. Maybe the Wychwood Dragon, I thought, not caring much, still had a broom cupboard to rent. I would beg a sandwich and a rug and sleep across the dark night into the new century, and early in the morning I would make an obituary for a jockey.

Just as I was about to cross to the Wychwood Dragon someone tapped heavily on the glass-paned door, and I went to open it, intending to say it was far too late, the year two thousand lay fifteen minutes ahead in Broadway, even if it had been tomorrow for hours in Australia. I unlocked the door and, prompted by inexorable courtesy, faced politely an unexpected and unwanted visitor in Lloyd Baxter, telling him with a half-smothered yawn that I simply hadn't enough energy to discuss the disaster at Cheltenham or anything else to do with horses.

He advanced into the brightest area on the threshold and I saw he was carrying a bottle of Dom Pérignon and two of the Wychwood Dragon's best champagne glasses. The heavily disapproving expression, despite these pipes of peace, was still in place.

'Mr Logan,' he said formally, 'I know no one at all in this place except yourself, and don't say this isn't a time for rejoicing, as I agree with you in many ways . . . not only because Martin Stukely is dead but because the next century is likely to be even more bloody than the last and I see no reason to celebrate just a change of date, particularly as there's no doubt the date is incorrect to begin with.' He took a breath. 'I therefore decided to spend the evening in my room—' He stopped abruptly, and I would have finished the tale for him, but instead I merely jerked my head for him to come right in, and closed the heavy door behind him.

'I'll drink to Martin,' I said.

He looked relieved at my acquiescence, even though he thought little of me and was old enough to be my father. Loneliness, though, still propelling him, he set the glasses on the table beside the till, ceremoniously popped the expensive cork and unleashed the bubbles.

'Drink to whatever you like,' he said in depression. 'I suppose it was a bad idea, coming here.'

'No,' I said.

'I could hear the music, you see . . .'

Music in the distance had forced him out of his lonely room. Music powerfully attracted the gregarious human race. No one welcomed two thousand years in silence.

I looked at my watch. Only nine minutes to ring-the-bells time.

Regardless of cynical withdrawals from organized enjoyment, regardless even of thrusts of raw unprocessed grief, I found there was inescapable excitement after all in the sense of a new chance offered, a fresh beginning possible. One could forgive one's own faults.

New numbers themselves vibrated with promise.

Five minutes to ring-the-bells . . . and fireworks. I drank Lloyd Baxter's champagne and still didn't like him.

Tallahassee's owner had changed, thanks to his transferred bag, into formal clothes, complete with black tie. His almost Edwardian type of grooming seemed to intensify rather than lighten his thunderous personality.

Even though I'd been introduced to him at least two years earlier, and had drunk his fizz on happier occasions, I'd never before bothered to read his face feature by feature. Rectifying that, I remembered that he'd earlier had thick strong dark hair, but as his age had advanced from fifty there were grey streaks that to my eyes had multiplied quite fast. His facial bone structure was thick and almost Cro-Magnon, with a powerful-looking brow and a similar no-nonsense jaw.

Perhaps in the past he had been lean and hungry, but as the twentieth century rolled away he had thickened round the neck and stomach and taken on the authoritative weight of chairman. If he looked more like an industrialist than a landowner, it was because he'd sold his majority share in a shipping line to buy his racehorses and his acres.

He disapproved, he'd told me severely, of young men like myself who could take days off work whenever they cared to. I knew he considered me a hanger-on who sponged off Martin, regardless of Martin's insisting it was more likely the other way round. It seemed that when Lloyd Baxter formed a set of opinions he was slow to re-arrange them.

Distantly, out in the cold night, bells in England pealed the passing of the all-important moment, celebrating the artificial date change and affirming that humankind could impose its own mathematics on the unresponsive planet. Lloyd Baxter raised his glass to drink to some private goal, and I, following his gesture, hoped merely that I would see in January 2001 in safety. I added in fact with banal courtesy, that I would drink to his health outside, if he'd forgive me my absence.

'Of course,' he said, his voice a mumble.

Pulling open the gallery door I walked out into the street still holding my golden drink, and found that dozens of people had felt impelled in the same way. A host, myself included, had been moved by an almost supernatural instinct to breathe free new air under the stars.

The man who sold antique books in the shop next to my gallery shook my hand vigorously, and with warm goodwill wished me a happy new year. I smiled and thanked him. Smiling was easy. The village, a fairly friendly place at any time, greeted the new year and the neighbours with uncomplicated affection. Feuds could wait.

Nearby, a large group of people had linked arms and were swaying across the road singing 'Auld Lang Syne' with half the words missing, and one or two cars crept along slowly, headlights full on, horns blaring, with enthusiastic youths yelling from open windows. Up and down the High Street local sophistication found its own level, but everywhere with a benign slant of mind.

Perhaps because of that, it was longer than I'd intended before I reluctantly decided I should return to my shop, my ready-for-the-bank takings and my unwelcome visitor, whose temper wouldn't have been improved by my absence.

Declining with regret a tot of single malt from the bookseller, I ambled along to Logan Glass feeling the first twitch of resignation for the lack of Martin. He had known always that his job might kill him, but he hadn't expected it. Falls were inevitable but they would happen 'some other time'. Injuries had been counted a nuisance that interfered with winning. He would 'hang up his boots', he'd told me lightheartedly, the minute he was afraid to put them on.

It was the *thought* of fear that bothered him, he'd once said.

I pushed open the heavy door preparing my apologies and found that an entirely different sort of action was essential.

Lloyd Baxter lay face down, unmoving and unconscious, on my showroom floor.

Dumping my empty glass rapidly on the table that held the till I knelt anxiously beside him and felt for a pulse in his neck. Even though his lips were bluish he hadn't somehow the look of someone dead, and there was to my great relief a slow perceptible thud-thud under my fingers. A stroke, perhaps? A heart attack? I knew very little medicine.

What an appallingly awkward night, I thought, sitting back on my heels, for anyone to need to call out the medics. I stood up and took a few paces to the table which held the till and all the business machines, including the telephone. I dialled the come-at-once number without much expectation, but even on such a New Year's Eve, it seemed, the emergency services would respond, and it wasn't until I'd put down the receiver on their promise of an instant stretcher that I noticed the absence beside the till of the ready-for-the-bank canvas bag. It had gone. I searched for it everywhere, but in my heart I knew where I'd left it.

I swore. I'd worked hard for every cent. I'd sweated. My arms still ached. I was depressed at that point as well as furious. I began to wonder if Lloyd Baxter had done his best; if he'd been knocked out trying to defend my property against a thief.

The black unidentified videotape had gone as well. The wave of outrage common to anyone robbed of even minor objects shook me into a deeper anger. The tape's loss was a severe aggravation, even if not on the same level as the money.

I telephoned the police without exciting them in the least. They were psyched up for bombs, not paltry theft. They said they would send someone in the morning.

Lloyd Baxter stirred, moaned and lay still again. I knelt beside him, removed his tie, unfastened his belt and in general rolled him slightly onto his side so that he wasn't in danger of choking. There were flecks of blood, though, around his mouth.

The chill of the deep night seeped into my own body, let alone Baxter's. The flames of the furnace roared captive behind the trapdoor which rose and fell to make the heat available, and finally, uncomfortably cold, I went and stood on the treadle that raised the trap, and let the heat flood into the workshop to reach the showroom beyond.

Normally, even in icy winter, the furnace in constant use gave warmth enough, supplemented by an electric convector heater in the gallery, but by the time help arrived for Baxter I had wrapped him in my jacket and everything else handy, and he was still growing cold to the touch.

The ultra-efficient men who arrived in the prompt ambulance took over expertly, examining their patient, searching and emptying his pockets, making a preliminary diagnosis and wrapping him in a red warming blanket ready for transport. Baxter partially awoke during this process but couldn't swim altogether to the surface of consciousness. His gaze flickered woozily once across my face before his eyes closed again into a heavier sleep.

The paramedics did some paperwork and had me provide them with Baxter's name, address, and as much as I knew (practically nothing) of his medical history. One of them was writing a list of all the things they had taken from him, starting with a Piaget gold watch and ending with the contents of a pocket of his trousers – a handkerchief, a bottle of pills, and a businesslike hotel-room key in the shape of a ball-and-chain deterrent to forgetfulness.

I didn't even have to suggest that I should return the key myself to the hotel, the paramedics suggested it themselves. I rattled it into my own trousers without delay, thinking vaguely of packing Lloyd Baxter's things into his much-travelled case and more positively of sleeping in his bed, since the paramedics were adamant that he would have to stay in hospital all night.

'What's wrong with him?' I asked. 'Has he had a heart attack? Or a stroke? Has he been . . . well, attacked and knocked out?'

I told them about the money and the tape.

They shook their heads. The most senior of them discounted my guesses. He said that to his experienced eyes Lloyd Baxter wasn't having a non-fatal heart attack (he would be awake, if so) nor a stroke, nor were there any lumpy bruises on his head. In his opinion, he announced authoritatively, Lloyd Baxter had had an epileptic fit.

'A *fit*?' I asked blankly. 'He's seemed perfectly well all day.'

The medics nodded knowledgeably. One of them picked up the pill bottle whose contents were listed as phenytoin and said he was certain that this was the preventative for epilepsy.

'Epilepsy,' the chief medic nodded, 'and who'll bet that he was overdue with a dose? We have all the other symptoms here. Alcohol.' He gestured to the depleted bottle of Dom. 'Late night without sleep. Stress . . . isn't he the one whose jockey was done for at the races today? Then there's the slow pulse and bluish lips, the blood flecks from where he's bitten his tongue . . . and did you notice that his trousers are wet? They urinate, you know.'

# CHAPTER TWO

The resident Dragon of the Wychwood Dragon Hotel being its fierce lady manager, I could ooze in and out of the halls unseen (as it were) owing both to the collection of small coloured glass animals marching round her dressing table, and to her occasional invitations to bed. The glass animals weren't so much trophies as apologies, however, as she was fortunately resigned to accepting that a thirty-year difference in age was a fair enough reason for me to say no. Her habit of calling me 'Lover' in public was embarrassment enough, though, and I knew that most of Broadway believed she ate me with eggs for breakfast.

Anyway, no one questioned my takeover of Lloyd Baxter's room. In the morning I packed his belongings and, explaining all to the Dragon, arranged for the hotel to send them to the hospital. Then I walked down and across to the workshop, where Martin, though vivid in my mind, refused to fly as a statement in glass. Inspiration operated at its own good speed, and many a time I'd found that trying to force it didn't work.

The furnace roared in its firebox. I sat beside the stainless-steel table (called a marver) on which I should have been rolling eternity into basic balls of liquid glass, and thought only of Martin alive in the body, Martin laughing and winning races, and Martin's lost message on videotape. Where was that tape, what did it contain and who thought it worth stealing?

These profitless thoughts were interrupted by the door-bell ringing early at nine o'clock, when we'd said we'd open at ten.

On the doorstep stood no recognizable customer but a young woman in a vast sloppy sweater hanging round her knees, topped by a baseball cap over a shock of brassily dyed streaky hair. We stared at each other with interest, her brown eyes alive and curious, her jaw rhythmic with chewing gum.

I said politely, 'Good morning.'

'Yeah. Yeah.' She laughed. 'Happy New Century and all that rubbish. Are you Gerard Logan?'

Her accent was Estuary, Essex or Thames: take your pick.

'Logan.' I nodded. 'And you?'

'Detective Constable Dodd.'

I blinked. 'Plain clothes?'

'You may laugh,' she said, chewing away. 'You reported a theft at twelve thirty-two this a.m. Can I come in?'

'Be my guest.'

She stepped into the gallery spotlights and glowed.

From habit I dramatized her in glass in my mind, an abstract essence as a conduit of feeling and light, exactly the instinctive process I'd tried in vain to summon up for Martin.

Oblivious, Detective Constable Dodd produced a down-to-earth warrant card, identifying her in uniform and adding a first name, Catherine. I handed the warrant card back and answered her questions, but the police opinion was already firm. Too bad I'd left a bagful of money lying around, she said. What did I expect? And videotapes came by the dozen. No one would think twice about snapping one up.

'What was on it?' she asked, pencil poised over a notepad.

'I've no idea.' I explained how it had come to me originally in a brown-paper parcel.

'Pornography. Bound to be.' Her pronouncement was brisk, world-weary and convinced. 'Unidentified.' She shrugged. 'Would you know it from any other tape if you saw it again?'

'It hadn't any labels.'

I dug the wrapping out of the rubbish bin and gave her the wrinkled and torn paper. 'This came to me by hand,' I said. 'There's no postmark.'

She took the paper dubiously, enclosed it in a plastic bag, got me to sign across the join and tucked it away somewhere under the extra-loose sweater.

My answers to her questions about the stolen money caused her eyebrows to rise over the amount, but she obviously thought I'd never again see the canvas bag or the mini bonanza inside. I still had cheques and credit card slips, of course, but most of my tourist customers paid in cash.

I told her then about Lloyd Baxter and his epileptic fit. 'Maybe he saw the thief,' I said.

She frowned. 'Maybe he *was* the thief. Could he have faked the fit?'

'The paramedics didn't seem to think so.'

She sighed. 'How long were you out in the street?'

'Bells. "Auld Lang Syne", fireworks, happy new thousand years . . .'

'Getting on for half an hour?' She consulted her notebook. 'You phoned the ambulance service at twelve twenty-seven.'

She wandered through the showroom looking at the small colourful vases, the clowns, sailing boats, fishes and horses. She picked up a haloed angel and disapproved of the price sticker under the feet. Her swathe of hair fell forward, framing her intent face, and I again clearly saw the bright analytical intelligence inside the sloppy hippie-type disguise. She was through and through a police officer, not primarily a come-hither female.

Replacing the angel with decision on the shelf, she folded her notebook, stored it out of sight and with body language announced that the investigation, despite its lack of results, was over. It was the go-to-work version of Constable Dodd that prepared to step into the street.

'Why?' I asked.

'Why what?' She concentrated on her change of character.

'Why the too big sweater and the baseball cap?'

She flashed me an aware, amused glance and turned back to the world outside. 'You happened to have been robbed on my allotted beat. My assignment in Broadway is to spot the gang stealing cars on bank holidays in this area. Thanks for your time.'

She grinned with cheerfulness and shuffled off down the hill, pausing to talk to a homeless-looking layabout sitting in a shop doorway, huddling against the chill of morning.

A pity the hippie and the hobo hadn't been car-thief spotting at midnight, I thought vaguely, and telephoned the hospital to enquire about Baxter.

Awake and grumbling, I gathered. I left a message of goodwill.

Bon-Bon next.

She wailed miserably into my ear. 'But, darling Gerard, *of course* I didn't tell Priam not to bring you with him. How could you believe it? You are the *first* person Martin would want to come here. Please, please come as soon as you can, the children are crying and everything's dreadful.' She drew a shaky breath, the tears distorting her voice. 'We were going to a midnight party . . . and the baby-sitter came and said she wanted her full money anyway, even if Martin was dead, can you believe it? And Priam talked about the inconvenience of finding another jockey halfway through the season. He's an old fool and he kept patting me . . .'

'He was seriously upset,' I assured her. 'A matter of tears.'

'*Priam?*'

I frowned at the memory, but the tears had looked real.

'How long did he stay with you?' I asked.

'Stay? He didn't stay long. Ten to fifteen minutes, maybe. My mother descended on us while he was here and, you've met her, you know what she's like. Priam was mostly in Martin's den, I think. He kept saying he had to be back for evening stables, he couldn't sit still.' Bon-Bon's despair overflowed. 'Can't you *come*? Please, please come. I can't deal with my mother by myself.'

'As soon as I've done one job, and found some transport. Say . . . about noon.'

'Oh yes, I forgot your bloody car. Where are you? Did you get home?'

'I'm in my workshop.'

'I'll come and fetch you . . .'

'No. First, fill your mama with gin and let the children loose on her, then shut yourself in Martin's den and watch the tapes of him winning his three Grand Nationals but don't drive anywhere while you're so upset. I'll find transport, but at the worst we could persuade your remarkable parent to lend me Worthington and the Rolls.'

Bon-Bon's mother's versatile chauffeur raised his eyebrows to heaven frequently at Marigold's odd requirements, but had been known to drive a roofless Land Rover at breakneck speed at night across stubble fields, headlights blazing in the dark, while his employer stood balancing behind him with a double-barrelled shotgun loosing off at mesmerized rabbits over his head. Martin said he'd been afraid to watch, but Worthington and Marigold had achieved a bag of forty and freed her land of a voracious pest.

Worthington, bald and fifty, was more an adventure than a last resort.

On New Year's Day 2000 in England the world in general came to a stop. Saturday's running of one of the best steeplechasing afternoon programmes of the whole midwinter season was stuck in a silly halt because the people who worked the Tote betting machines wanted to stay at home. There was no racing – and no football – to entertain the non-workers on or off the television.

Logan Glass astounded the other residents of Broadway by opening its doors to the day-before's customers, who arrived to collect their overnight-cooled souvenirs. To my own astonishment two of my assistants turned up, even though bleary-eyed, saying they couldn't leave me to pack the whole delivery job alone, so it was with speed and good humour that my new century began. I looked back later at the peace of that brief morning with a feeling of unreality that life could ever have been so safe and simple.

Pamela Jane, twittery, anxious, stick-thin and wanly pretty, insisted on driving me to Bon-Bon's place herself, leaving me in the driveway and departing with a wave, hurrying back to the shop as she'd left Irish alone there.

Martin and Bon-Bon had agreed at least on their house, an eighteenth-century gem that Marigold had helped them buy. I admired it every time I went there.

A small van stood on the gravel, dark-blue with a commercial name painted on it in yellow: '*Thompson Electronics*'. I suppose it was because I'd been working myself that I didn't immediately remember that that day was a national holiday; definitely a moratorium for television-repair vans.

Chaos was too weak a word to describe what I found inside Martin's house. For a start, the front door was visibly ajar and, when I touched it, it swung wide. It was normally the kitchen door the family left hospitably unlocked, both for friends and visiting tradesmen.

Beginning to feel slight unease, I stepped through the heavily carved front doorway and shouted, but there was no response, and a pace or two later I learned why I had misgivings.

Bon-Bon's mother Marigold, frothy grey hair and floaty purple dress in disarray as usual, lay unconscious on the stairs. Worthington, her eccentric chauffeur, sprawled like a drugged medieval guard dog at her feet.

The four children, out of sight, were uncannily quiet, and the door to Martin's room, his den, was closed on silence.

I opened this door immediately and found Bon-Bon there, lying full-length on the wood-block floor. Again, as with Lloyd Baxter, I knelt to feel for a pulse in the neck, but this time with sharp anxiety; and I felt the living ga-bump ga-bump with a deeper relief. Concentrating on Bon-Bon I saw too late in peripheral sight a movement behind my right shoulder . . . a dark figure speeding from where he'd been hiding behind the door.

I jerked halfway to standing but wasn't quick enough on my feet. There was a short second in which I glimpsed a small metal gas cylinder – more or less like a quarter-sized fire extinguisher. But this cylinder wasn't red. It was orange. It hit my head. Martin's den turned grey, dark grey, and black. A deep well of nothing.

I returned slowly to a gallery of watchers. To a row of eyes dizzily in front of my own. I couldn't think where I was or what was happening. It had to be bad, though, because the children's eyes looked huge with fright.

I was lying on my back. Into the blank spaces of memory slowly crept the picture of an orange gas cylinder in the hands of a figure in a black head-mask with holes cut out for eyes.

As a return to awareness grew clearer I focused on Bon-Bon's face and tried to stand up. Bon-Bon, seeing this minor revival, said with great relief, 'Thank God you're all right. We've all been gassed and we've all been sick since we woke up. Totter to the loo next door, there's a chum. Don't be sick in here.'

I had a headache, not nausea. My head had collided with the outside of a metal gas cylinder, not with the contents. I felt too lethargic to explain the difference.

Worthington, notwithstanding the muscular physique he painstakingly developed by regular visits to a punch-bag gym, looked pale and shaky and far from well. He held each of the two youngest children by the hand, though, giving them what comfort and confidence he could. In their eyes he could do everything, and they were nearly right.

Bon-Bon had once mentioned that Worthington's top value to her mother was his understanding of book-makers' methods, because, as Marigold herself disliked walking along between the rows of men shouting the odds, Worthington got her the best prices. A versatile and compulsive good guy, Worthington, though he didn't always look it.

Only Marigold herself was now missing from the sick parade. I asked about her, and the eldest of the children, a boy called Daniel, said she was drunk. She was snoring on the stairs, the elder girl said. So pragmatic, 2000-year children.

While I peeled myself slowly off the wood blocks,

Bon-Bon, with annoyance, remarked that her doctor had announced he no longer made house calls, even for those recovering from bereavement. He said all would be well with rest and fluid. 'Water,' he'd said.

'Gin,' corrected one of the children dryly.

I thought it scandalous that Bon-Bon's doctor should have refused to tend her and had a go at him myself. Capitulating with apologetic grace he promised he would 'look in', New Year's Day holiday notwithstanding. He hadn't understood Mrs Stukely, he excused himself. He didn't realize she'd been attacked. She'd been partly incoherent. Had we informed the police?

It did seem obvious that robbery had been the purpose of the mass anaesthesia. Three television sets with integral tape players were missing. Bon-Bon had been angry enough to count things.

Also gone was a separate video player on which she'd been watching Martin, together with dozens of tapes. Two lap-top computers, with printers and racks of filing disks were missing too, but Worthington prophesied that the police would offer little hope of recovering these things, as Martin had apparently not recorded any identifying numbers anywhere.

Bon-Bon began crying quietly from the strain of it all and it was Worthington, recovering and worth his weight in videotapes, who talked to the overburdened local nick. My Constable Catherine Dodd, he found, was attached to a different branch. Detectives, however, would arrive on the Stukely doorstep soon.

Not surprisingly, the '*Thompson Electronics*' van had gone.

Marigold went on snoring on the stairs.

Worthington made calming sandwiches of banana and honey for the children.

Feeling queasy, I sat in Martin's black leather chair in his den, while Bon-Bon, on an opposite sofa, dried her complicated grief on tissues and finally gave no complete answer to my repeated question, which was, 'What was on the tape that Martin meant to give me after the races, and where did it come from? That's to say, who gave it to Martin himself at Cheltenham?'

Bon-Bon studied me with wet eyes and blew her nose. 'I know Martin wanted to tell you something yesterday, but he had those other men in the car, and I know he wanted to talk to you without Priam listening so he planned to take you home last, after the others, even though you live nearest to the racecourse.'

Even in distress she looked porcelain pretty, the plumpness an asset in a curvy black wool suit cut to please a living husband rather than a mourning neighbourhood.

'He trusted you,' she said finally.

'Mm.' I'd have been surprised if he hadn't.

'No, you don't understand.' Bon-Bon hesitated and went on slowly. 'He knew a secret. He wouldn't tell me what it was. He said I would fret. But he wanted to tell *someone*. We did discuss *that*, and I agreed it should be you. *You* should be his back-up. Just in case. Oh dear . . .

He had what he wanted you to know put onto a plain old-fashioned recording tape, not onto a CD or a computer disk, and he did that, I think, because whoever was giving him information preferred it that way. I'm not sure. And also it was easier to play, he said. Better on video than computer because, darling Gerard, you know I never get things right when it comes to computers. The children laugh at me. I can play a videotape easily. Martin wanted me to be able to do that if he died, but of course . . . of *course* . . . he didn't think he'd die, not really.'

I asked, 'Could you yourself make a home movie on a videotape?'

She nodded. 'Martin gave me a video camera for Christmas. It makes your own home films but I've hardly had time to learn how to use it.'

'And he didn't say *anything* about what was on that tape he meant for me?'

'He was awfully careful not to.'

I shook my head in frustration. The tape stolen from the glass showroom was surely the one with the secret on it. The one passed to Martin, then to Eddie the valet, and then to me. Yet if the Broadway thieves, or thief, had viewed it – and they'd had all night to do so – why were they needing to rob Martin's house ten hours later?

Did the tape taken from the showroom actually contain Martin's secret?

Perhaps not.

Was the second robbery carried out by a *different* thief, who didn't know about the first one?

I had no answers, only guesses.

Marigold at that point tottered into the den as if coming to pieces in all directions. I had been used to Marigold for the four years since Martin had straight-facedly presented me to his buxom mother-in-law, a magnified version of his pretty wife. Marigold could be endlessly witty or tiresomely belligerent according to the gin level, but this time the effect of gas on alcohol seemed to have resulted in pity-me pathos, a state that aroused genuine sympathy, not serve-you-right.

In Bon-Bon's house it was the police that turned up first, and Bon-Bon's children who described down to the laces on his shoes the clothes worn by their attacker. He had stared with wide eyes through his black head-mask while he'd pointed the orange cylinder at them and squirted a nearly invisible but fierce mist, sweeping from face to face and knocking them out before they'd realized what was happening. Asked about it, Daniel, the eldest child, described the black-masked man having something white tied over his face underneath. An elementary gas mask, I surmised. Something to prevent the robber from inhaling his own gas.

Worthington had been attacked most strongly and had fallen unconscious first, and Bon-Bon – in the den – last. The gas had perhaps been exhausted by the time I arrived; a direct bang on the head had sufficed.

Worthington had been right in guessing the police would offer no hope of Bon-Bon ever again seeing the missing goods. She felt less pain than I would have expected over the loss of tapes showing Martin winning the Grand National because, as she explained, she could get duplicates.

Scarcely had the police notebooks been folded away than Bon-Bon's doctor hurried in without apology, giving the impression he was making an exception, out of the goodness of his heart.

It was the colour orange that slowed him into frowns and more thorough care. He and the police all listened to Daniel, brought out paper, and took notes. The doctor told the departing detectives to look for villains with access to the anaesthetic gas cyclopropane, which came in orange cylinders, and wasn't much used because of being highly flammable and explosive.

Slowly, after decently thorough peerings into eyes and throats and careful stethoscope chest checks, each of the family was judged fit to go on living. Sweet Bon-Bon, when her house was finally free of official attention, sat sprawling on the office sofa telling me she was utterly exhausted and needed help. Specifically she needed *my* help and Martin would have asked for it.

So I stayed and looked after things, and because of that I saved myself at least another sore head, as thieves broke into my house on the hill that night and stole everything that could remotely be called a videotape.

On the Monday, after an early morning session in the workshop making new little items for stock, I went to

Cheltenham races again (by taxi) to talk to Martin's valet, Eddie Payne.

Ed or Eddie (he answered to both) was ready to help, he said, but he couldn't. He'd spent all weekend thinking it over and he said, his gaze darting over my shoulder and back again to my face, he couldn't – however hard he tried – remember any more than he'd told me on Friday. I thought back to the moment of empathy between us, when we had each realized what we'd lost. That moment of genuine emptiness had gone.

The difference between Friday and Monday was a fierce-eyed woman of approaching forty, now standing a pace or two behind me, a woman Ed referred to as his daughter. He slid a second glance at her expressionlessly and like a ventriloquist not moving his lips, said to me almost too quietly for me to hear, '*She* knows the man who gave Martin the tape.'

The woman said sharply, 'What did you say, Dad? Do speak up.'

'I said we'd miss Martin badly,' Eddie said, 'and I'm due back in the changing room. Tell Gerard – Mr Logan – what he wants to know, why don't you?'

He walked away with a worried shuffle, apologetically saying to me as he went, 'Her name's Rose. She's a good girl really.'

Rose, the good girl, gave me such a bitter flash of hate that I wondered what I'd ever done to annoy her, as I hadn't known of her existence until moments earlier. She was angularly bony and had mid-brown hair with frizzy sticking-out curls. Her skin was dry and freckled, and although her clothes looked too big for the thin body inside, there was about her an extraordinary air of magnetism.

'Er . . . Rose—' I started.

'Mrs Robins,' she interrupted abruptly.

I cleared my throat and tried again.

'Mrs Robins, then, could I buy you some coffee, or a drink in the bar?'

She said, 'No, you could *not*.' She bit the words off with emphasis. She said, 'You'd do better to mind your own business.'

'Mrs Robins, did you see who gave a brown-paper parcel to Martin Stukely at Cheltenham races last Friday?'

Such a simple question. She primped her lips together tightly, swivelled on her heel, and walked away with an air of not intending to come back.

After a short pause, I followed her. Looking down from time to time at my racecard as any prospective punter would, I trickled along in her wake as she made for the ranks of bookmakers' pitches in front of the open-to-the-public Tattersalls stands. She stopped at a board announcing *Arthur Robins, Prestwick, Established 1894*, and talked to an Elvis Presley lookalike with heavy black side-whiskers who was standing on a box, leaning down to take money from the public and dictating his transactions to a clerk, who was punching the bets into a computer.

Rose Robins, established long after 1894, had a fair

amount to say. The Elvis lookalike frowned, listening, and I retreated: I might have strength and reasonable agility but Rose's contact made my muscle-power look the stuff of kindergartens. Whichever Robins filled the shoes of Arthur nowadays, if he were the Elvis lookalike, he weighed in with grandfather-gorilla shoulders.

Patiently I climbed the stands and waited while the *Arthur Robins, Est. 1894* bookmakers – three of them – took bets on the final two races of the afternoon, and then I watched their chief, the Elvis lookalike, pack up the board and take charge of the money bag and walk towards the exit with Rose and his two helpers beside him. I watched them go out of sight. As far as I could tell, they all left the racecourse. As a group, they equalled an armoured tank.

From experience with Martin, I knew that jockeys' valets finished their work after most of the crowds had gone home. A valet was a man who helped the jockeys change rapidly between races. He also looked after and cleaned their gear, saddles, breeches, boots and so on, so it was all ready for next time they raced. Martin had told me that a single valet would look after a whole bunch of jockeys, and the valets would work as a team to cover all the race meetings. While Eddie packed up his hampers of saddles, kit and clothes for laundering, I waited with hope for him to reappear out of the changing room at the end of his day.

When he came out and saw me, he was at first alarmed, and then resigned.

'I suppose,' he said, 'Rose wouldn't tell you.'

'No,' I agreed. 'So would you ask her something, for Martin's sake?'

'Well . . .' he hesitated. 'It depends.'

I said, 'Ask her if the tape Martin gave you was the one she thought it was.'

He took a few seconds to work it out.

'Do you mean,' he asked doubtfully, 'that my Rose thinks Martin had the wrong tape?'

'I think,' I confessed, 'that if Martin's tape ever surfaces after all the muddle and thieving, it'll be a matter of luck.'

He protested self-righteously that he'd given me Martin's tape in good faith. I insisted that I believed him. No more was said about Rose.

Eddie knew, as did the whole racing world after that day's newspapers, that Martin's funeral was planned for Thursday, providing no jinx upset Wednesday's inquest. Eddie, eyes down, mumbled a few words about seeing me there, he supposed, and in discomfort hurried away to the inner realms of the changing rooms, from where the public with awkward questions were banned.

Rose Robins and her enmity added complexity to an already tangled situation.

I caught a bus from the racecourse which wound its way from village to village and, in the end, to Broadway. In spite of my having spent all the time tossing around in my mind the unexpected involvement of Eddie's scratchy daughter I came to a no more satisfactory or original conclusion than that someone had given some tape or other to Martin who had given it to Eddie who had given it to me who had carelessly lost it to a thief.

Still drifting in outer space was whatever confidential data Martin had meant to entrust to me. In some respects that didn't matter, and never would, just as long as the hidden nugget of information didn't heat up or collide with an inconvenient truth. Additionally, as I had no road map to the ingredients of the nugget, I had no way either of foreseeing or preventing trouble.

Unrealistically, I simply hoped that Martin's secret would remain forever hidden in uncharted orbit, and all of us could return to normal.

It was after five-thirty by the time I reached the doors of Logan Glass, and again my assistants were there, two of them making paperweights with enthusiasm and the third keeping shop. Bon-Bon had telephoned, they told me, saying she was begging me to go on organizing her household in return for transport; at least until after the funeral, and, much to the amusement of my assistants, the transport she sent that afternoon wasn't her own runabout, but was Marigold's Rolls.

Whenever we were alone together, I sat beside Worthington as he drove. He had offered me the comfort and prestige of the rear seat usually taken by his employer, but I felt wrong there. Moreover, on the showing of the last few days, if I sat at the back he tended both to call me 'sir' and to favour respectful silence instead of pithy and irreverent observation. When I sat in the front, Marigold was 'Marigold': when in the back, 'Mrs Knight'. When I sat beside her chauffeur, he showed his inner self.

In addition to being bald, fifty and kind to children, Worthington disliked the police force as a matter of principle, referred to marriage as bondage and believed in the usefulness of being able to out-kick any other muscle-man in sight. It wasn't so much as a chauffeur that I now valued Worthington at my elbow, but as a prospective bodyguard. The Elvis lookalike had radiated latent menace at an intensity that I hadn't met before and didn't like; and for detonator there was fierce thorny Rose, and it was with her in mind that I casually asked Worthington if he'd ever placed a bet at the races with *Arthur Robins, Est. 1894*.

'For a start,' he said with sarcasm, fastening his seat belt as if keeping to the law were routine, 'the Robins family don't exist. That bunch of swindlers known as Arthur Robins are mostly Veritys and Webbers, with a couple of Browns thrown in. There hasn't been a bona-fide Arthur Robins *ever*. It's just a pretty name.'

Eyebrows raised in surprise I asked, 'How do you know all that?'

'My old man ran a book,' he said. 'Fasten your seat-belt, Gerard. The cops in this town would put eagles out of business. Like I said, my old man was a bookmaker, he taught me the trade. You've got to be real sharp at figures, though, to make a profit, and I never got quick enough. But Arthur Robins, that's the front name for some whizzers of speed merchants. Don't bet with them, that's my advice.'

I said, 'Do you know that Eddie Payne, Martin's valet, has a daughter called Rose who says her last name is Robins and who's on cuddling terms with an Elvis Presley lookalike taking bets for Arthur Robins?'

Worthington, who had been about to start the car outside Logan Glass to drive us to Bon-Bon, sat back in his seat, letting his hands fall laxly on his thighs.

'No,' he said thoughtfully, 'I didn't know that.' He thought for a while, his forehead troubled. 'That Elvis fellow,' he said finally, 'that's Norman Osprey. You don't want to mix with *him.*'

'And Rose?'

Worthington shook his head. 'I don't know her. I'll ask around.' He roused himself and started the purring car.

By Thursday, the day of Martin's funeral, the police as predicted hadn't found one identifiable videotape in a country awash with them.

On the day before the funeral a young woman on a motor bike – huge helmet, black leather jacket, matching trousers, heavy boots – steered into one of the five parking spaces at the front of Logan Glass. Outside in the January chill she pulled off the helmet and shook free a cap of fair fine hair before walking without swagger into the gallery and showroom as if she knew the way well.

I was putting the pre-annealing final touches to a vase, with Pamela Jane telling a group of American tourists how it was done, but there was something attention-claiming about the motor cyclist, and as soon as I thought of her in terms of glass, I knew her infallibly.

'Catherine Dodd,' I said.

'Most people don't recognize me.' She was amused, not piqued.

With interest I watched the tourists pack somewhat closer together as if to elbow out the stranger in threatening clothes.

Pamela Jane finished her spiel and one of the American men said the vases were too expensive, even if they were hand-made and handsome. He collected nods and all-round agreement, and there was relief in the speed with which the tourists settled instead on simple dolphins and little dishes. While Hickory wrapped the parcels and wrote out bills I asked the motor cyclist if there were any news of my lost tape.

She watched me handle the vase in heat-proof fibre and put it to cool in the annealing oven.

'I'm afraid,' said Detective Constable Dodd in plain – well, plainer – clothes, 'your tape is gone for good.'

I told her it held a secret.

'What secret?'

'That's the point, I don't know. Martin Stukely told his wife he was giving me a secret on tape for safekeeping – that's a bit of a laugh – in case he was killed in a car crash, or something like that.'

'Like a steeplechase?'

'He didn't expect it.'

Catherine Dodd's detective mind trod the two paths I'd reluctantly followed myself since Normal Osprey and his Elvis sideburns had appeared on my horizon. First, *someone* knew Martin's secret, and second, *someone*, and maybe not the same someone, could infer, one way or another, that that secret was known to me. Someone might suppose I'd watched that tape during the evening of Martin's death, and for safety had wiped it off.

I hadn't had a tape player on the Logan Glass premises, but the Dragon over the road made one available generously to the paying guests, and she distributed brochures by the hundred advertising this.

'If I'd had a tape player handy,' I said, 'I probably *would* have run that tape through early in the evening, and if I thought it awful I *might* have wiped it off.'

'That's not what your friend Martin wanted.'

After a brief silence I said, 'If he'd been sure of what he wanted he wouldn't have fiddled about with tapes, he would just have *told* me this precious secret.' I stopped abruptly. 'There are too many ifs. How about you coming out for a drink?'

'Can't. Sorry. I'm on duty.' She gave me a brilliant smile. 'I'll call in another day. And oh! There's just one loose end.' She produced the ever-essential notebook from inside her jacket. 'What are your assistants' names?'

'Pamela Jane Evans and John Irish and John Hickory.

We leave off John for the men and use their last names, as it's easier.'

'Which is the elder?'

'Irish. He's about ten years older than both Hickory and Pamela Jane.'

'And how long have they all worked for you?'

'Pamela Jane about a year, Irish and Hickory two to three months longer. They're all good guys, believe me.'

'I do believe you. This is just for the records. This is actually . . . er . . . what I dropped in for.'

I looked at her directly. She all but blushed.

'I'd better go now,' she said.

With regret I walked with her as far as the door, where she paused to say goodbye as she didn't want to be seen with me too familiarly out in the street. She left, in fact, in the bunch of winter tourists, all of them overshadowed by the loud voice of a big man who judged the whole afternoon a waste of time and complained about it all the way back to the group's warm tour bus. His broad back obscured my view of the departure of Detective Constable Dodd, and I surprised myself by minding about that quite a lot.

On Bon-Bon's telephone, the night before Martin's funeral, I learned from the Dragon herself that Lloyd Baxter had deemed it correct to fly down for 'his jockey's last ride' (as he put it) but hadn't wanted to stay with Priam Jones, whom he was on the point of ditching as his trainer. The Dragon chuckled and went on mischievously, 'You didn't have to go all that way to stay with Bon-Bon Stukely, if you didn't fancy sleeping in your burgled house, lover boy. You could have stayed here with me.'

'News gets around,' I said dryly.

'You're always news in this town, lover, didn't you know?'

In truth I did know it, but I didn't feel it.

On that evening before Martin's funeral Priam Jones telephoned, meaning to talk to Bon-Bon but reaching me instead. I had been fielding commiserations for her whenever I was around. Marigold, Worthington and even the children had grown expert at thanks and tact. I thought how Martin would have grinned at the all-round grade A improvement in his family's social skills.

Priam blustered on a bit, but was, I gathered, offering himself as an usher in the matter of seating. Remembering his spontaneous tears I put him on the list and asked him if, before he'd picked me up from my home on Friday morning, Martin had by any chance mentioned that he was expecting delivery of a tape at the races.

'You asked me that the day after he died,' Priam said impatiently. 'The answer is still yes. He said we wouldn't leave the racecourse until he'd collected some package or other to give to you. And I did give it to you, don't you remember? I brought it back to Broadway after you'd left it in your raincoat in the car . . . Well, I'll see you tomorrow, Gerard. Give my regards to Bon-Bon.'

Also, on the evening before Martin's funeral, Eddie

Payne went to his local Catholic church and in the confessional recited his past and present sins, asking for pardon and absolution. He told me this with self-righteousness when I intercepted his condolences to Bon-Bon. He'd tried and tried to get someone else to do his racecourse work, he said, but such was life, he hadn't succeeded, and he was going to have to miss the funeral, and it grieved him sorely as he'd been Martin's racecourse valet for six or seven years. Eddie, to my disparaging ear, had plucked up half a bottle of Dutch courage before stretching out his hand to the phone, and wouldn't remain long in a state of grace owing to his distance from the fact that he could more easily have got stand-ins to free him to go to that particular funeral than if it was for his own grandmother.

On the same evening, before Martin's funeral (though I didn't learn of it until later), Ed Payne's daughter, Rose, described to a small group of fascinated and ruthless knaves how to force Gerard Logan to tell them the secret he'd been given at Cheltenham races.

# CHAPTER THREE

On the first Thursday of January, the sixth day of the next thousand years, I, with Priam Jones and four senior jump jockeys carried Martin into church in his coffin and later delivered him to his grave.

The sun shone on frosty trees. Bon-Bon looked ethereal, Marigold stayed fairly sober, Worthington took off his chauffeur's cap, baring his bald pate in respect, the four children knocked with their knuckles on the coffin as if they could wake their father inside, Lloyd Baxter read a short but decent eulogy and all the racing world, from the Stewards of the Jockey Club to the men who replaced the divots, everyone crowded into the pews in church and packed the wintry churchyard grass outside, standing on the moss-grown ancient slabs of stone. Martin had been respected, and respects were paid.

The new burial ground lay on a hillside a mile away by hearse and heavy limousines. Among banks of flowers Bon-Bon cried as the man who'd quarrelled with her daily sank into the quiet embracing earth and I, who'd stage-managed the second farewell party in a month (my mother the other), prosaically checked that the caterers had brought enough hot toddy and that the choristers were paid, along with other mundane greasings of the expensive wheels of death.

After the hundreds who had turned up for Martin had drunk and eaten and had kissed Bon-Bon and left, I sought her out to say my own goodbye. She was standing with Lloyd Baxter, asking about his health. '*Do* take the pills,' she was saying, and he with embarrassment promised he would. He nodded to me coldly as if he had never brought Dom Pérignon to me for company.

I congratulated Baxter on his eulogy. He received the praise as his due, and stiffly invited me to dine with him in the Wychwood Dragon.

'Don't go,' Bon-Bon exclaimed to me, alarmed. 'Stay here one more night. You and Worthington have tamed the children. Let's have this one more night of peace.'

Thinking of Martin, I excused myself to Baxter and stayed to help Bon-Bon, and after midnight, when only I was awake, I sat in Martin's squashy chair in his den and thought intently of him. Thought of his life and of what he'd achieved, and thought eventually about that last day at Cheltenham, and about the videotape and whatever he'd had recorded on it.

I had no minutest idea what he could have known that needed such complex safe-keeping. I did see that, much as I thought Bon-Bon a darling and as sweet as her name, she wasn't the most reticent person on earth. To Bon-Bon a secret would be safe until her next nice chat with her best friend. Many of her and Martin's shouting matches had been the result of Bon-Bon repeating publicly what she'd been privately told or overheard about some horse or other's prospects.

I slouched in Martin's chair, deep in regret. One had so few close friends in life. None to spare. His personality filled the room to the extent that it seemed that if I turned I would see him standing by his bookcase, looking up some race's result in the form book. The feeling of his presence was so intense that I actually swivelled his chair round to see, but of course there were only books, row on row, and no Martin.

It was time, I supposed, to make sure the outside doors were locked and to sleep away the last hours in Martin's house. I'd lent him a couple of books a few weeks earlier on ancient glass-making techniques, and as they were lying on the long table by the sofa, it seemed a good time to pick them up to take home without bothering Bon-Bon too much. One of the things I would most miss was, I thought nostalgically, Martin's constant interest in historic difficult-to-make goblets and bowls.

In the morning, saying goodbye, I mentioned I was taking the books. 'Fine, fine,' Bon-Bon said vaguely. 'I wish you weren't going.'

She was lending me Worthington to drive me in her white runabout to Broadway. 'If you weren't getting your butt out of that house pronto,' Worthington said bluntly as we drove away, 'Bon-Bon would catch you like a Venus fly-trap.'

'She's unhappy,' I protested.

'Sticky, attractive, and once caught, you can't escape.' Worthington grinned. 'Don't say I haven't warned you.'

'And Marigold?' I teased him. 'How's the Marigold fly-trap?'

'I can leave her any day I want,' he protested, and drove for miles smiling, as if he believed it.

Stopping to unload me at my gallery door in Broadway he said more seriously, 'I got a low-life investigator to ask about that woman, Rose.' He paused. 'He didn't get much further than you did. Eddie Payne thinks she saw who gave that damned tape to Martin, but I wouldn't rely on it. Eddie's afraid of his own daughter, if you ask me.'

I agreed with him on that, and we left it there. My three assistants welcomed me back to a regular work-day, and I taught Hickory – as I'd taught Pamela Jane before Christmas – how to collect a third gather of glass, so hot that it was red and semi-liquid, and fell in a heavy tear-drop shape that drooped towards the floor (and one's feet) if one didn't marver it fast enough on the steel table. He knew how to press its lengthened tip into long heaps of dust-like colours before returning the revolving head into the heat of the furnace to keep the now heavy chunk of glass at working temperature. I showed him how to gather glass neatly on the end of a blowing iron, before lifting it into the air ready to blow, and how to keep the resulting slightly ballooned shape constant while he continued to develop his ideas towards a final goal.

Hickory watched the continuous process with anxious

eyes and said that, like Pamela Jane when she'd tried it, he couldn't go the whole way.

'Of course not. Practise handling three gathers. You can do two now easily.'

A gather was the amount of molten glass that could be brought out of the tank at one time on the tip of the steel punty rod. A gather could be of any size, according to the skill and strength of the glass-blower. Glass in bulk, very heavy, demanded muscle.

Owing to the space limitation of tourist suitcases, few pieces of 'Logan Glass' sold in the shop were of more than three gathers. Pamela Jane, to her sorrow, had never quite mastered the swing upwards and blow technique. Irish, in spite of enthusiasm, would never be a top-rated glass-blower. Of Hickory, though, I had hopes. He had ease of movement and, most importantly, a lack of fear.

Glass-blowers were commonly arrogant people, chiefly because the skill was so difficult to learn. Hickory already showed signs of arrogance but if he became a notable expert he would have to be forgiven. As for myself, my uncle (as arrogant as they came) had insisted that I learn humility first, second and third, and had refused to let me near his furnace until I'd shed every sign of what he called 'cockiness'.

'Cockiness' had broken out regularly after his death, humbling me when I recognized it. It had taken perhaps ten years before I had it licked, but vigilance would be necessary for life.

Irish had grown accustomed to brewing the large jugs

of tea to replace the sweat lost to the furnace. I sat on a box and drank thirstily and all day watched my apprentice improve considerably, even though, with exhausted rests, there was generally a lot of swearing and a whole heap of shattered glass.

There were few customers to interrupt the lesson and by five o'clock on this bleakly cold January afternoon I sent my three helpers home and with gloom did some long overdue paperwork. The cash stolen on New Year's Eve left a depressing hole in what was otherwise a cheerful season. It wasn't difficult, after a while, to lay aside the minus figures and pick up the books I'd lent to Martin.

My favourite of all historic goblets was a glowing red cup, six and a half inches high, constructed around the year 300 and something AD (a fair time ago, when one looked back from 2000). It was made of lumps of glass, held fast in an intricate gold cage (a technique from before blowing was invented), and would appear green in different lights. Flicking through the early pages in one of the books I came across the goblet's picture with my usual pleasure and a few pages later smiled over the brilliant gold and blue glass Cretan Sunrise necklace that I'd once spent days copying. Sleepily, by accident, I let the book begin to slide off my knees towards the smooth brick floor and, by luck, caught it without damage to its glossy construction.

Relieved at the catch, and berating myself for such clumsiness in not holding on more tightly to a valued treasure, I didn't notice at first a thin buff envelope that lay at my feet. With a reaction accelerating from puzzlement to active curiosity I laid the old book down carefully and picked up the new-looking envelope, which I supposed had been held within the pages and had fallen out when I made my grab.

The envelope from inside my book was addressed by computer printer not to me but to Martin Stukely Esq., Jockey.

I had no qualms at all in taking out the single-page letter inside, and reading it.

> Dear Martin.
>
> You are right, it is the best way. I will take the tape, as you want, to Cheltenham races on New Year's Eve.
>
> This knowledge is dynamite.
>
> Take care of it.
>
> Victor Waltman Verity.

The letter too was typed on a computer, though the name given as signature had been printed in a different font. There was no address or telephone number on the letter itself, but faintly across the stamp on the envelope there was a round postmark. After long concentration with a magnifying glass, the point of origin seemed to me only 'xet' round the top and 'evo' round the bottom. The date alone was easily readable, though looking anaemic as to ink.

The letter had been sent on 17.XII.99.

17 December. Less than a month ago.

xet

evo

There weren't after all many places in Great Britain with an x in their name, and I could think of nowhere else that fitted the available letters other than Exeter, Devon.

When I reached Directory Enquiries I learned that there was indeed a Victor Verity in Exeter. A disembodied voice said, 'The number you require is . . .'. I wrote it down, but when I called Victor Verity I spoke not to him, but to his widow. Her dear Victor had passed away during the previous summer. Wrong Verity.

I tried Enquiries again.

'Very sorry,' said a prim voice, not sounding it. 'There is no other Victor or V. Verity in the Exeter telephone area which covers most of Devon.'

'How about an ex-directory number?'

'Sorry, I can't give you that information.'

Victor Waltman Verity was either ex-directory or had posted his letter far from home.

Cursing him lightly I glanced with reluctance at the money job half done on my computer . . . and there, of course, lay the answer. Computers. Internet.

The Internet, among other miracles, might put an address to a name anywhere. That's to say, it would if I could remember the open sesame code. I entered my Internet access number and typed in my password, and sat hopefully, flicking mentally through possibilities as the machine burped and whined until a connection was made.

After a while a web-site address drifted into my mind, but it was without certainty that I tried it: www.192.com.

192.com was right.

I started a search for Verity in Devon and, as if eager to be of service, the Internet, having surveyed every fact obtainable in the public domain (such as the electoral registers) came up with a total of twenty-two Devon-based Veritys, but none of them any longer was Victor.

Dead end.

I tried Verity in Cornwall: sixteen but still no Victor.

Try Somerset, I thought. Not a Victor Verity in sight.

Before reaching to switch off, I skimmed down the list and at the end of it noticed that at number 19 Lorna Terrace, Taunton, Somerset, there lived a *Mr Waltman* Verity. Good enough to try, I thought.

Armed with the address I tried Directory Enquiries again, but ran up against the same polite barrier of virtual non-existence. Ex-directory. Sorry. Too bad.

Although Saturday was a busier day in the showroom, my thoughts returned continuously to Taunton and Victor Waltman Verity.

Taunton . . . Having nothing much else urgently filling my Sunday, I caught a westbound train next morning, and in Taunton asked directions to Lorna Terrace.

Whatever I expected Victor Waltman Verity to look like, it was nothing near the living thing. Victor Waltman Verity must have been all of fifteen.

The door of number 19 was opened by a thin woman dressed in trousers, sweater and bedroom slippers, with a cigarette in one hand and big pink curlers in her hair. Thirty something, perhaps forty, I thought. Easy going, with a resigned attitude to strangers on her doorstep.

'Er . . . Mrs Verity?' I asked.

'Yeah. What is it?' She sucked smoke, unconcerned.

'Mrs Victor Waltman Verity?'

She laughed. 'I'm Mrs Waltman Verity, Victor's my son.' She shouted over her shoulder towards the inner depths of the narrow terraced house. 'Vic, someone to see you,' and while we waited for Victor Waltman Verity to answer the call, Mrs Verity looked me over thoroughly from hair to trainers and went on enjoying a private giggle.

Victor Waltman Verity appeared quietly from along the narrow hallway and regarded me with curiosity mixed, I thought, with the possibility of alarm. He himself was as tall as his mother, as tall as Martin. He had dark hair, pale-grey eyes and an air of knowing himself to be as intelligent as any adult. His voice, when he spoke, was at the cracked stage between boy and man, and his face had begun to grow from the soft lines of childhood into adult planes.

'What've you been up to, young Vic?' his mother asked, and to me she said, 'It's bloody cold out there. Want to come in?'

'Er,' I said. I was suffering more from the unexpected than the cold, but she waited for no answer and walked back past the boy until she was out of sight. I pulled the envelope sent to Martin out of a pocket and immediately set the alarm racing above the curiosity in young Victor.

'You weren't supposed to find me,' he exclaimed, 'and, in any case, you're dead.'

'I'm not Martin Stukely,' I said.

'Oh.' His face went blank. 'No, of course, you aren't.' Puzzlement set in. 'I mean, what do you want?'

'First of all,' I said plainly, 'I'd like to accept your mother's invitation.'

'Huh?'

'To be warm.'

'Oh! I get you. The kitchen is warmest.'

'Lead on, then.'

He shrugged and stretched to close the door behind me, and then led the way down beside the staircase to the heart of all such terrace houses, the space where life was lived. There was a central table covered with a patterned plastic cloth, four attendant unmatched upright chairs and a sideboard deep in clutter. A television set stood aslant on a draining-board otherwise stacked with unwashed dishes, and checked vinyl tiles covered the floor.

In spite of the disorganization, there was bright new paint and nothing disturbingly sordid. I had an overall impression of yellow.

Mrs Verity sat in one of the chairs, rocking on its back legs and gulping smoke as if she lived on it.

She said pleasantly enough, 'We get all sorts of people here, what with Vic and his wretched Internet. We'll get a full-sized genie one of these days, I shouldn't wonder.' She gestured vaguely to one of the chairs, and I sat on it.

'I was a friend of Martin Stukely,' I explained, and I asked Vic what was on the videotape that he had sent or given to Martin at Cheltenham.

'Yes, well, there wasn't a tape,' he said briefly. 'I didn't go to Cheltenham.'

I pulled his letter to Martin out of the envelope and gave it to him to read.

He shrugged again and handed it back when he'd reached the end.

'It was just a game. I made up the tape.' He was nervous, all the same.

'What knowledge was it that was dynamite?'

'Look, none.' He grew impatient. 'I told you. I made it up.'

'Why did you send it to Martin Stukely?'

I was careful not to let the questions sound too aggressive, but in some way that I didn't understand, they raised all his defences and coloured his cheeks red.

His mother said to me, 'What's all this about a tape? Do you mean a *video* tape? Vic hasn't got any videotapes. We're going to get a new video machine any day now, then it will be different.'

I explained apologetically. 'Someone did give to Martin a videotape at Cheltenham races. Martin gave it to Ed Payne, his valet, to keep safe, and Ed gave it to me, but it was stolen before I could see what was on it. Then all the videotapes in Martin's house and all the videotapes in my own house were stolen too.'

'I hope you're not suggesting that *Vic* stole anything, because I can promise you he wouldn't.' Mrs Verity had grasped one suggestion wrongly and hadn't listened clearly to the rest, so she too advanced to the edge of anger, and I did my best to retreat and placate, but her natural good humour had been dented, and her welcome had evaporated. She stubbed out a cigarette instead of lighting another from it, and stood up as a decisive signal that it was time I left.

I said amiably to young Victor, 'Call me,' and although he shook his head I wrote my mobile number on the margin of a Sunday newspaper.

Then I stepped out of number 19 Lorna Terrace and walked unhurriedly along the street pondering two odd unanswered questions.

First, how did Victor happen to come to Martin's attention?

Second, why had neither mother nor son asked my name?

Lorna Terrace curved sharply to the left, taking number 19 out of sight behind me.

I paused there, wondering whether or not to go back. I was conscious of not having done very well. I'd set off expecting to unearth the mysteries of the videotape, if not with ease, then actually without extreme trouble. Instead, I seemed to have screwed up even what I'd thought I'd understood.

Irresolutely I wasted time and missed the train I'd thought of catching. I might be OK at glass, but not excellent at Sherlock Holmes. Dim Dr Watson, that was me. It grew dark and took me a long time to reach Broadway, luckily finding a willing neighbour on the train to give me a lift from the station.

Without Martin, I reflected with depression, I was either going to spend a fortune on cabs or thumb a thousand lifts. There were still eighty-one days before I could apply to get my licence-to-speed out of the freezer.

I thanked my generous companion with a wave as he drove away and, fishing out a small bunch of keys I plodded towards the gallery door. Sunday evening. No one about. Brilliant lights shining from Logan Glass.

I hadn't learned yet to beware of shadows. Figures in black materialized from the deep entrance to the antique bookshop next door and from the dark line of the rubbish bins put out ready for collection on Monday morning.

I suppose there were four of them leaping about in the dark; an impression, not an accurate count. Four was profligate, anyway. Three, two, maybe only one could have done the job. I guessed they'd been waiting there for a long time and it hadn't improved their temper.

I hadn't expected another physical attack. The memory of the orange cylinder of cyclopropane had faded. The cylinder, I soon found, had delivered a less painful message than the one on my doorstep. This one consisted of multiple bashes and bangs and of being slammed two or three times against the lumpy bit of Cotswold stone wall that joined the bookshop to my own place.

Disorientated by the attack itself I heard demands as if from a distance that I should disclose information that I knew I didn't have. I tried to tell them. They didn't listen.

All that was annoying enough, but it was their additional aim that lit my own inner protection furnace and put power into half-forgotten techniques of kick-boxing left over from my teens.

It seemed that a straightforward pulping was only half their purpose, as a sharp excited voice specifically instructed over and over again, 'Break his wrists. Go on. *Break his wrists* . . .' And later, out of the dark, the same voice exulting, 'That got him.'

No, it bloody didn't. Pain screeched up my arm. My thoughts were blasphemy. Strong, whole and flexible wrists were as essential to a glass-blower as to a gymnast on the Olympic high rings.

Two of the black-clad agile figures waved baseball bats. One with heavily developed shoulders was recognizably Norman Osprey. Looking back later from a huddled sort of collapse on the pavement, I saw that only one of those two had the bright idea of holding my fingers tightly together in a bunch against the wall before getting his collcague to aim just below them with the bat.

I had too much to lose and I hadn't been aware of how desperately one could fight when it was the real thing.

My wrists didn't get broken but my watch stopped, in pieces from a direct hit. There were lumps and bruised areas all over everywhere. A few cuts. Torn skin. Enough. But my fingers worked, and that was all that mattered.

Maybe the fracas would have ended with my taking a fresh hole in the ground beside Martin, but Broadway wasn't a ghost town in a western desert; it was somewhere that people walked their dogs on a Sunday evening, and it was a dog-walker who yelled at my attackers, and with three toothy Dobermanns barking and pulling at their leashes, got the shadowy figures to change their minds smartly and vanish as fast as they'd come.

'Gerard *Logan*!' The tall dog-walker, astounded, bending to look at me, knew me by sight, as I did him. 'Are you all right?'

No, I wasn't. I said, 'Yes,' as one does.

He stretched down to help me to my feet, when all I really wanted to do was lie on a soft mattress.

'Shall I call the police?' he asked, though he wasn't a police lover; far from it.

'Tom . . . Thanks. But no police.'

'What was it all about?' He sounded relieved. 'Are you in trouble? That looked to me like pay-back business.'

'Muggers.'

Tom Pigeon, who knew a thing or two about the rocky sides of life, gave me a half-smile, half-disillusioned look, and shortened the leashes of his hungry life-preservers.

More bark than bite, he'd assured me once. I wasn't certain I believed it.

He himself looked as if he had no need to bark. Although not heavily built and without a wrestler's neck, he had unmistakable physical power, and, at about my own age, a close-cut dark pointed beard that added years of menace.

Tom Pigeon told me there was blood in my hair and said if I would give him my keys he would open the door for me.

'I dropped them,' I said and leaned gingerly against the lumpy bit of wall. The dizzy world revolved. I couldn't remember ever before feeling so pulverized or so sick, not even when I'd fallen bottom of the scrum in a viciously unfriendly school rugby match and had my shoulder blade broken.

Tom Pigeon persevered until he kicked against my keys and found them by their clinking. He unlocked and opened the gallery door and with his arm round my waist got me as far as the threshold. His dogs stayed watchfully by his legs.

'I better not bring the canines in amongst your glass, had I?' he said. 'You'll be all right now, OK?'

I nodded. He more or less propped me against the door frame and made sure I could stand up before he let go.

Tom Pigeon was known locally as 'The Backlash', chiefly on account of being as quick with his wits as his fists. He'd survived, unharmed, eighteen months inside for aggravated breaking and entering and had emerged as a toughened hotshot, to be spoken of with awe. Whatever his dusty reputation, he had definitely rescued me, and I felt in an extraordinary way honoured by the extent of his aid.

He waited until I could visibly control things and stared shrewdly into my eyes. It wasn't exactly friendship that I saw in his, but it was . . . in a way . . . recognition.

'Get a pit-bull,' he said.

I stepped into my bright lights and locked the door against the violence outside. Pity I couldn't as easily blot out the woes of battery. Pity I felt so stupid. So furious. So wobbly, so dangerously mystified.

In the back reaches of the workshop there was running water for rinsing one's face, and a relaxing chair for recovery of all kinds of balance. I sat and ached a lot, and then phoned the taxi firm, who apologized that this Saturday and Sunday had already overstretched their fleet, but they would put me on their priority list from now on . . . yeah . . . yeah . . . never mind . . . I could have done with a double cyclopropane, shaken, with ice. I thought of Worthington, tried for him on the phone, got Bon-Bon instead.

'Gerard, darling. I'm so *lonely.*' She sounded indeed in sorrowing mode, as her elder son would have put it. 'Can't you come over to cheer me up? Worthington will come to fetch you, and I'll drive you home myself. I promise.'

I said with regret that I didn't want to give her flu (which I hadn't got) and simply went on doing very little through a highly unsatisfactory evening. Worthington's fly-trap vision itched. I loved Bon-Bon as a friend, but not as wife.

At about ten-thirty I fell asleep in the soft chair and half an hour later was awakened again by the doorbell.

Disorientated as I woke, I felt stiff, miserable and totally unwilling to move.

The doorbell rang insistently. I went on feeling shivery and unwilling, but in the end I wavered upright and creaked out of the workshop to see who wanted what at such an hour. Even then, after the dire lessons I'd been given, I hadn't enough sense to carry with me a weapon of defence.

As it happened, my late-evening visitor looked pretty harmless. In addition, she was welcome. More than that, I thought that with a kiss or two and a hug she might prove therapeutic.

Detective Constable Catherine Dodd took her finger off the doorbell when she saw me, and smiled with relief when I let her in.

'We had reports from two separate Broadway residents,' she said first. 'They apparently saw you being attacked outside here. But we had no complaint from yourself, even though you were hardly walking, it seemed

. . . so anyway, I said I would check on you on my way home.'

She again wore motor-cycle leathers, and had parked her bike at the kerb. With deft speed, as before, she lifted off her helmet and shook her head to loosen her fair hair.

'One of the reports,' she added, 'said that your attacker had been Tom Pigeon, with his dogs. That man's a damned pest.'

'No, no! It was he who got rid of the pests. Really depressing pests.'

'Could you identify them?'

I made a non-committal gesture and meandered vaguely through the showroom to the workshop, pointing to the chair for her to sit down.

She looked at the chair and at the sweat I could feel on my forehead, and sat on the bench normally the domain of Irish, Hickory and Pamela Jane. Gratefully I sank into the soft armchair and half answered her who? and why? queries, not knowing whether they had a police basis or were ordinary curiosity.

She said, 'Gerard, I've seen other people in your state.'

'Poor them.'

'Don't laugh, it's hardly funny.'

'Not tragic, either.'

'Why haven't you asked my colleagues for more help?'

Well, I thought, why not?

'Because,' I said lightly, 'I don't know who or why,

and every time I think I've learned something, I find I haven't. Your colleagues don't like uncertainty.'

She thought that over with more weight than it deserved.

'Tell *me*, then,' she said.

'Someone wants something I haven't got. I don't know what it is. I don't know who wants it. How am I doing?'

'That makes nonsense.'

I winced and turned it into a smile. 'It makes nonsense, quite right.' And in addition, I thought to myself with acid humour, I have the Dragon and Bon-Bon on my watch-it list, and policewoman Dodd on my wanted-but-can-I-catch-her list, and Tom Pigeon and Worthington on my save-my-skin list, Rose Payne/Robins on my black-mask possible list and young Victor Waltman on my can't-or-won't-tell list.

As for Lloyd Baxter and his epilepsy, Eddie Payne keeping and delivering videotapes, Norman Osprey running a book with the massive shoulders of 1894, and dear scatty Marigold, often afloat before breakfast and regularly before lunch, all of them could have tapes on their mind and know every twist in the ball of string.

Constable Dodd frowned, faint lines crossing her smooth clear skin, and as it seemed to be question time I said abruptly, 'Are you married?'

After a few seconds, looking down at her ringless hands, she replied 'Why do you ask?'

'You have the air of it.'

'He's dead.'

She sat for a while without moving, and then asked, 'And you?' in calm return.

'Not yet,' I said.

Silence could sometimes shout. She listened to what I would probably ask quite soon, and seemed relaxed and content.

The workshop was warmed as always by the furnace, even though the roaring fire was held in control for nights and Sundays by a large screen of heat-resistant material.

Looking at Catherine Dodd's face above the dark close-fitting leather, I most clearly now saw her in terms of glass: saw her in fact so vividly that the urge and desire to work at once couldn't be stifled. I stood and unclipped the fireproof screen and put it to one side, and fixed instead the smaller flap which opened to allow access to the tankful of molten glass.

I pressed extra time into the light switch, overriding the midnight cut-off, and with boringly painful movements took off my jacket and shirt, leaving only normal working gear of bare arms and singlet.

'What are you doing?' She sounded alarmed but had no need to be.

'A portrait,' I said. 'Sit still.' I turned up the heat in the furnace and sorted out the punty blowing irons I would need, and fetched a workable amount of glass manganese powder which would give me black in colour eventually.

'But your bruises . . .' she protested. 'Those marks. They're terrible.'

'I can't feel them.'

I felt nothing indeed except the rare sort of excitement that came with revelation. I'd burned myself often enough on liquid glass and not felt it. That Sunday night the concept of one detective darkly achieving insight into the sins of others, and then the possibility that good could rise above sin and fly, these drifting thoughts set up in me in effect a mental anaesthesia, so that I could bleed and suffer on one level and feel it only later after the flame of imagination had done its stuff. Sometimes in the disengagement from this sort of thing, the vision had shrunk to disappointment and ash, and when that happened I would leave the no-good piece on the marver table and not handle it carefully into an annealing oven. After a while, its unresolved internal strains would cause it to self-destruct, to come to pieces dramatically with a cracking noise; to splinter, to fragment . . . to shatter.

It could be for onlookers an unnerving experience, to see an apparently solid object disintegrate for no visible reason. For me, the splitting apart symbolized merely the fading and insufficiency of the original thought. On that particular Sunday I had no doubts or hesitation, and I gathered glass in muscle-straining amounts that even on ordinary days would have taxed my ability.

That night I made Catherine Dodd in three pieces that later I would join together. I made not a literal lifelike sculpture of her head, but an abstract of her daily occupation. I made it basically as a soaring upward spread of wings, black and shining at the base, rising through a black, white and clear centre to a high rising pinion with streaks of gold shining to the top.

The gold fascinated my subject.

'Is it *real* gold?'

'Iron pyrites. But real gold would melt the same way . . . only I used all I had a week ago.'

I gently held the fragile top wing in layers of heat-proof fibre and laid it carefully in one of the six annealing ovens, and only then, with all three sections safely cooling, could I hardly bear the strains in my own limbs and felt too like cracking apart myself.

Catherine stood up and took a while to speak. Eventually she cleared her throat and asked what I would do with the finished flight of wings and I, coming down to earth from invention, tried prosaically (as on other such occasions) just to say that I would probably make a pedestal for it in the gallery and light it with a spotlight or two to emphasize its shape.

We both stood looking at each other as if not knowing what else to say. I leaned forward and kissed her cheek, which with mutual small movements became mouth to mouth, with passion in there somewhere, acknowledged but not yet overflowing.

Arms round motor-cycle leathers had practical drawbacks. My own physical aches put winces where they weren't wanted, and with rueful humour she disengaged herself and said, 'Maybe another time.'

'Delete the maybe,' I said.

# CHAPTER FOUR

All three of my assistants could let themselves in through the gallery with a personal key, and it was Pamela Jane alone whom I saw first with a slit of eyesight when I returned unwillingly to consciousness at about eight o'clock on Monday morning. I'd spent the first hour after Catherine had gone considering the comfort of a Wychwood Dragon bed (without the Dragon herself) but in the end from lack of energy had simply flopped back into the big chair in the workshop and closed my eyes on a shuddering and protesting nervous system.

Catherine herself, real and abstract, had kept me warm and mobile through the darkest hours of night, but she'd left long before dawn, and afterwards sleep, which practically never knitted up any ravelled sleave of care, had made things slightly worse.

Pamela Jane said, horrified, 'Honestly, you look as if you've been hit by a steamroller. Have you been here all night?'

The answer must have been obvious. I was unshaven, for a start, and any movement set up quite awful and stiffened reactions. One could almost hear the joints creak. Never again, I promised myself.

I hadn't considered how I was going to explain things to my little team. When I spoke to Pamela Jane, even my voice felt rough.

'Can you . . .' I paused, cleared my throat and tried again. 'Pam . . . mug of tea?'

She put her coat in her locker and scurried helpfully around, making the tea and unbolting the side door which we were obliged to have ready to use as a fire escape if necessary. By the advent of Irish I was ignoring the worst, and Hickory, arriving last, found me lifting the three wing sections of the night's work out of the ovens and carefully fitting them together before fusing them into place. All three of my helpers wished they'd seen the separate pieces made. One day, I agreed with them, I would make duplicates to show them.

They couldn't help but notice that I found too much movement a bad idea, but I could have done without Hickory's cheerful assumption it was the aftermath of booze.

The first customer came. Life more or less returned to normal. Irish began building a plinth in the gallery to hold the wings. If I concentrated on blowing glass I could forget four black jersey-wool masks with eyeholes.

Later in the morning Marigold's Rolls drew up outside and occupied two of the parking spaces, with Worthington at the wheel looking formal in his badge-of-office cap.

Marigold herself, he reported through his wound-down

window, had gone shopping with Bon-Bon in Bon-Bon's car. Both ladies had given him the day off and the use of the Rolls, and he appreciated their generosity, he said solemnly, as he was going to take me to the races.

I looked back at him in indecision.

'I'm not going,' I said. 'And where am I not going?'

'Leicester. Jump racing. Eddie Payne will be there. Rose will be there. Norman Osprey will be there with his book. I thought you wanted to find out who gave the videotape to Martin? Do you want to know what was on it, or who stole it, and do you want to know who gassed me with the kids and the ladies, or do you want to stay here quietly and make nice little pink vases to sell to the tourists?'

I didn't answer at once and he said judiciously, making allowances, 'Mind you, I don't suppose you want another beating like you got last night, so stay here if you like and I'll mooch around by myself.'

'Who told you about last night?'

He took off his cap and wiped his bald crown with a white handkerchief.

'A little bird told me. A not so little bird.'

'Not . . . a pigeon?'

'Quick, aren't you.' He grinned. 'Yeah, a Pigeon. It seems he thinks quite a bit of you. He phoned me specially at Bon-Bon's. He says to put it around that in future any hands laid on you are laid on him.'

I felt both grateful and surprised. I asked, 'How well do you know him?'

He answered obliquely. 'You know that gardener of

Martin's that was dying? That you lost your licence for, speeding to get him there in time?'

'Well, yes, I remember.'

'That gardener was Tom Pigeon's dad.'

'Ah. He didn't die, though. Not then, anyway.'

'It didn't matter. Are you coming to Leicester?'

'I guess so.'

I went back into the workshop, put on my outdoor clothes and told Irish, Hickory and Pamela Jane to keep on making paperweights while I went to the sports. They had all known Martin alive, as my friend, and all of them in brief snatches, and in turn, had been to his sending off. They wished me luck with many winners at the races.

I sat beside Worthington for the journey. We stopped to buy me a cheap watch, and to pick up a daily racing newspaper for the runners and riders. In a section titled 'News Today' on the front page I read, among a dozen little snippets, that the Leicester Stewards would be hosts that day to Lloyd Baxter (owner of star jumper Tallahassee) to honour the memory of jockey Martin Stukely.

Well, well.

After a while I told Worthington in detail about my visit to Lorna Terrace, Taunton. He frowned over the more obvious inconsistencies put forward by mother and son, but seemed struck to consternation when I said, 'Didn't you tell me that the bookmaking firm of Arthur Robins, established 1894, was now owned and run by people named Webber, Brown . . . and Verity?'

The consternation lasted ten seconds. 'And the mother

and son in Taunton were Verity!' A pause. 'It must be a coincidence,' he said.

'I don't believe in coincidences like that.'

Worthington slid a silent glance my way as he navigated a roundabout, and after a while said, 'Gerard, if you have any clear idea of what's going on . . . what is it? For instance, who were those attackers in black masks last night, and what did they want?'

I said, 'I'd think it was one of them who squirted you with cyclopropane and laid me out with the empty cylinder, and I don't know who that was. I'm sure, though, that one of the black-masks was the fragrant Rose.'

'I'm not staying she wasn't, but why?'

'Who else in the world would scream at Norman Osprey – or anyone else, but I'm pretty sure it was him – to break my wrists? Rose's voice is unmistakable. And there is the way she moves . . . and as for purpose . . . partly to put me out of business, wouldn't you say? And partly to make me give her what I haven't got. And also to stop me from doing what we're aiming to do today.'

Worthington said impulsively, 'Let's go home, then.'

'You just stay beside me, and we'll be fine.'

Worthington took me seriously and body-guarded like a professional. We confirmed one of the black-mask merchants for certain simply from his stunned reaction to my being there and on my feet when anyone with any sense would have been knocking back aspirins on a sofa with an ice-pack. Martin himself had showed me how jump jockeys walked around sometimes with broken ribs and arms and other injuries. Only broken legs, he'd said, postponed actual riding for a couple of months. Bruises, to him, were every-day normal, and he dealt with pain by putting it out of his mind and thinking about something else. 'Ignore it,' he'd said. I copied him at Leicester as best I could.

When he saw me, Norman Osprey had stopped dead in the middle of setting up his stand, his heavy shoulders bunching; and Rose herself made the mistake of striding up to him in a carefree bounce at that moment, only to follow his disbelieving gaze and lose a good deal of her self-satisfaction. What she said explosively was 'Bloody hell.'

If one imagined Norman Osprey's shoulders in a black jersey, he was recognizably the figure who'd smashed my watch with his baseball bat, while aiming at my wrist. I'd jerked at the vital moment and I'd kicked his shin very hard indeed. The sharp voice urging him to try again had, without doubt, been Rose's.

I said to them jointly, 'Tom Pigeon sends his regards.'

Neither of them looked overjoyed. Worthington murmured something to me urgently about it not being advisable to poke a wasps' nest with a stick. He also put distance between himself and Arthur Robins 1894 and, with unobvious speed, I followed.

'They don't know exactly what they're looking for,' I pointed out, slowing down. 'If they knew, they would have asked for it by name last night.'

'They might have done that anyway, if Tom Pigeon

hadn't been walking his dogs.' Worthington steered us still further away from Norman Osprey, looking back all the same to make certain we weren't being followed.

My impression of the events of barely fifteen hours earlier was that damage, as well as information, had been the purpose. But if Tom Pigeon hadn't arrived, and if it had been to save the multiple wrist bones that Martin had said never properly mended, and if I *could* have answered their questions, then would I . . .?

Sore as I already felt all over, I couldn't imagine any piece of knowledge that Martin might have had that he thought was worth my virtual destruction, and I didn't like the probability that they – the black-masks – wrongly believed that I did know what they wanted, and that I was being merely stubborn in not telling them.

Mordantly I admitted to myself that if I'd known for certain what they wanted and if Tom Pigeon hadn't arrived with his dogs, I wouldn't at that moment be strolling round any racecourse, but would quite likely have told them *anything* to stop them, and have been considering suicide from shame. And I was *not* going to confess that to anyone at all.

Only to Martin's hovering presence could I even admit it. Bugger you, pal, I thought. What the sod have you let me in for?

Lloyd Baxter lunched at Leicester with the Stewards. His self-regarding nature found this admirable invitation to be merely his due. He told me so, condescendingly, when our paths crossed between parade ring and stands.

To Lloyd Baxter the meeting was unexpected, but I'd spotted him early and waited through the Stewards' roast beef, cheese and coffee, talking to Worthington outside, and stiffening uncomfortably in the cold wind.

Cold weather emphasized the Paleolithic-like weight of Baxter's facial structure and upper body, and even after only one week (though a stressful one) his hair seemed definitely to have greyed a further notch.

He wasn't pleased to see me. I was sure he regretted the whole Broadway evening, but he concentrated hard on being civil, and it was churlish of me, I dare say, to suspect that it was because I knew of his epilepsy. Nowhere in print or chat had his condition been disclosed, but if he was afraid I would not only broadcast but snigger, he had made a judgement of my own character which hardly flattered.

Worthington melted temporarily from my side and I walked with Lloyd Baxter while he oozed compliments about the Stewards' lunch and discussed the worth of many trainers, excluding poor old Priam Jones.

I said mildly, 'It wasn't his fault that Tallahassee fell at Cheltenham.'

I got an acid reply. 'It was Martin's fault. He unbalanced him going into the fence. He was too confident.'

Martin had told me that *it* – whatever *it* might be – was, with a disgruntled owner, normally the jockey's fault. 'Pilot error.' He'd shrugged philosophically. 'And then you get the other sort of owner, the cream to ride for, the ones who understand that horses aren't infallible, who say, "That's racing," when something shattering happens, and who comfort the jockey who's just lost them the win of a lifetime. And believe me,' Martin had said, 'Lloyd Baxter isn't one of those. If I lose for him, it is, in his opinion, my fault.'

'But,' I said without heat to Lloyd Baxter during his trainer-spotting at Leicester, 'if a horse falls, it surely isn't the trainer's fault? It wasn't Priam Jones's fault that Tallahassee fell and lost the Coffee Cup.'

'He should have schooled him better.'

'Well,' I reasoned, 'that horse had proved he could jump. He'd already won several races.'

'I want a different trainer.' Lloyd Baxter spoke with obstinacy: a matter of instinct, I saw.

Along with lunch, the Stewards had given Tallahassee's owner an entry ticket to their guests' viewing box. Lloyd Baxter was already apologizing for shedding me at the entrance when one of the Stewards, following us, changed our course.

'Aren't you the glass man?' he boomed genially. 'My wife's your greatest fan. We have lumps of your stuff all over our house. That splendid horse you did for her, you came to rig its spotlights, didn't you?'

I remembered the horse and the house with enough detail to be invited into the Stewards' guests viewing balcony, not entirely to Lloyd Baxter's delight.

'This young man's a genius, according to my wife,'

the Steward said to Baxter, ushering us in. The genius merely wished he felt less weak.

Lloyd Baxter's poor opinion of the Steward's wife's judgement was written plain on his heavy features, but perhaps it did eventually influence him because, after the cheering for the next winner had faded, he surprised me very much by resting his hand lightly on my arm to indicate that I should stay and hear what he felt like telling me. He hesitated further, though, so I gave him every chance.

'I've often wondered,' I said mildly, 'if you saw who came into my showroom on New Year's Eve. I mean, I know you were ill . . . but before that . . . when I'd gone out into the street, did anyone come?'

After a long pause, he faintly nodded. 'Someone came into that long gallery you have there. I remember he asked for you and I said you were out in the street. But I couldn't see him properly as my eyes . . . my sight develops zigzags sometimes . . .' He stopped, but I continued for him.

'You surely have pills.'

'Of course I do!' He was irritated. 'But I'd forgotten to take them because of the terrible day it had been, and I hate those very small air taxis to begin with, and I do want a different trainer.' His voice died away, but his troubles had been laid out clearly enough for a chimpanzee to understand.

I asked if, in spite of the zigzag aura, he could describe my unknown visitor.

'No,' he said. 'I told him you were in the street and the next time I was properly awake I was in hospital.' He paused while I regretted the cut-short sequence, and then with diffidence he said slowly, 'I am aware that I should thank you for your reticence. You could still cause me much embarrassment.'

'There's no point in it,' I said.

He spent a while studying my face as in the past I'd learned his. The result surprised me. 'Are you ill?' he said.

'No. Tired. Didn't sleep well.'

'The man who came,' he said abruptly, making no other comment, 'was thin and had a white beard and was over fifty.'

The description sounded highly improbable as a thief, and he must have seen my doubt because he added to convince me, 'When I saw him, I immediately thought of Priam Jones, who's been saying for years he's going to grow a beard. I tell him he'd look weedy.'

I nearly laughed: the picture was true.

Baxter said the white-bearded man reminded him chiefly of a university professor. A lecturer.

I asked, 'Did he speak? Was he a normal customer? Did he mention glass?'

Lloyd Baxter couldn't remember. 'If he spoke at all, I heard him only as a jumble. Quite often things seem wrong to me. They're a sort of warning. Often I can control them a little, or at least prepare . . . but on that evening it was happening too fast.'

He was being extraordinarily frank, I thought. I wouldn't have expected so much trust.

'That man with the whisker job,' I said, 'he must have seen the beginning at least of your . . . er . . . seizure. So why didn't he help you? Do you think he simply didn't know what to do, so ran away from trouble, as people tend to, or was it he who made off with the loot . . . er . . . that money, in the canvas bag?'

'And the videotape,' Baxter said.

There was an abrupt breath-drawing silence. Then I asked, 'What videotape?'

Lloyd Baxter frowned. 'He asked for it.'

'So you gave it to him?'

'No. Yes. No. I don't know.'

It became clear that, in fact, Lloyd Baxter's memory of that evening in Broadway was a scrambled egg of order into chaos. It wasn't certain that any university lecturer in any white beard existed outside fiction.

While we occupied for another ten uninterrupted minutes the most private place on a racecourse – the Stewards' guests' viewing balcony in between races – I managed to persuade Lloyd Baxter to sit quietly and exchange detailed memories of the last few minutes of 1999, but try as he might, he still clung to the image of the scrawny man in the white beard who probably – or maybe it was some other man at some other time – asked for a videotape . . . perhaps.

He was trying his best. His manner to me had taken a

ninety-degree angle of change, so that he'd become more of an ally than a crosspatch.

One of the things he would never have said in the past was his reassessment of my and Martin's friendship. 'I see I was wrong about you,' he admitted, heavily frowning. 'Martin relied on you for strength, and I took it for granted that it was the other way round.'

'We learned from each other.'

After a pause he said, 'That fellow in the white beard, he was real, you know. He did want a videotape. If I knew more than that, I would tell you.'

I finally believed him. It was just unlucky that Baxter's fit had struck at the wrong random moment; unlucky from White-Beard's point of view that Baxter had been there at all; but it did now seem certain that during the time I was out in the street seeing the year 2000 arrive safely, a white-bearded thin middle-aged professor-type individual had come into my showroom and had said something about a videotape, and had left before I returned, taking the tape and, incidentally, the money with him.

I hadn't seen any white-bearded figure out in the street. It had been a week too late for the ho ho ho joker from the North Pole. Lloyd Baxter said he couldn't tell whether or not the beard was real or left over from Father Christmas.

When we parted we shook hands for the first time ever. I left him with the Stewards and fell into step with Worthington, who I found shivering outside and obviously hungry. Accordingly we smelled out some food which he galloped through with endless appetite.

'Why don't you eat?' he demanded, chomping.

'Habit,' I said. A habit caught from a scales-conscious jockey. Martin seemed to have influenced my life more than I'd realized.

I told Worthington while he saw off two full plates of steak and kidney pie (his and mine) that we were now looking for a thin man, in late middle age, white beard, who looked like a college lecturer.

Worthington gazed at me earnestly while loading his fork with pastry. 'That,' he pointed out, 'doesn't sound at all like someone who would steal a bagful of money.'

'I'm surprised at you, Worthington,' I teased him. 'I thought you, of all people, would know that beards aren't automatic badges of honesty! So how does this sit with you? Suppose Mr White-Beard gives a tape to Martin, which Martin gives to Eddie Payne, who hands it on to me. Then, when Martin died, Mr White-Beard decided to take his videotape back again, so he found out where the tape would be . . . that's to say, he turned up in Broadway. He found the tape and took it back, and on impulse he also whisked up the bag of money that I'd stupidly left lying around, and in consequence he cannot tell anyone that he has his tape back.'

'Because he would be confessing he'd stolen the cash?'

'Dead right.'

My bodyguard sighed and scraped his plate clean. 'So what next?' he said. 'What happened next?'

'I can only guess.'

'Go on, then. Guess. Because it wasn't some old guy that gassed us with that cyclopropane. Young Daniel described the trainers that the gas-man wore, and nobody but a teenager, I don't think, would be seen dead in them.'

I found I disagreed. Eccentric white-beards might wear anything. They might also make erotic tapes. They might also tell someone the tape was worth a fortune, and that it was in Gerard Logan's hands. A few little lies. Diversionary tactics. Beat up Logan, make him ready to cough up the tape or, failing that, whatever information had been on it.

*What* had Martin been going to give me for safekeeping?

Did I any longer really want to know?

If I didn't know, I couldn't tell. But if they believed I knew and I wouldn't tell . . . dammit, I thought, we've almost been through that already, and I couldn't expect Tom Pigeon and Dobermanns to rescue me every time.

Not knowing the secret on the tape was perhaps worse than knowing it. So somehow or other, I decided, it wasn't enough to discover who took it, it was essential after all to find out what they expected as well as what they'd actually got.

Once Worthington's hunger had retreated temporarily

and we had lost our money on a horse Martin should have ridden, we walked back to where the serried ranks of bookmakers were shouting their offers for the getting-out stakes, the last race.

With Worthington's well-known muscle as guarantee of immunity from onslaught, we arrived in the living-and-breathing space of the 1894 Arthur Robins' operation 2000. Norman Osprey's raucous voice soared unselfconsciously above his neighbours' until he realized we were listening, at which point a sudden silence gave everyone else a chance.

Close enough to see the scissor marks on the Elvis sideburns, I said, 'Tell Rose—'

'Tell her yourself,' he interrupted forcefully. 'She's just behind you.'

I turned without haste, leaving Worthington at my back. Rose glared, rigid with a hatred I didn't at that point understand. As before, the dryness of her skin echoed the lack of generosity in her nature, but earlier, at our first and last racecourse encounter, neither of us held the subsequent memory of fists, stone walls, baseball bats, a smashed watch and a whole bunch more of assaults-to-the-person, all orchestrated and encouraged as Sunday evening entertainment for the troops.

Being as close to her as a couple of yards gave my outraged skin goose pimples, but she seemed to think a black mask and leotard had made her invisible.

I asked again the question she had already refused to answer.

'Who gave a videotape to Martin Stukely at Cheltenham races?'

She answered this time that she didn't know.

I said, 'Do you mean you didn't see anyone give Martin a parcel, or that you saw the transfer but didn't know the person's name?'

'Dead clever, aren't you,' Rose said sarcastically. 'Take your pick.'

Rose, I thought, wasn't going to be trapped by words. At a guess she had both seen the transfer and knew the transferor, but even Torquemada would have had trouble with her, and I hadn't any thumbscrews handy in Logan Glass.

I said without much hope of being believed, 'I don't know where to look for the tape you want. I don't know who took it and I don't know why. But I haven't got it.'

Rose curled her lip.

As we walked away Worthington sighed deeply with frustration.

'You'd think Norman Osprey would be the "heavy" in that outfit. He has the voice and the build for it. Everyone thinks of him as the power behind Arthur Robins. But did you see him looking at Rose? She can make any blunder she likes, but I'm told she's still the brains. She's the boss. She calls the tune. My low-life investigator gave me a bell. He finds her very impressive, I'm afraid to say.'

I nodded.

Worthington, a practised world-traveller, said, 'She hates you. Have you noticed?'

I told him I had indeed noticed. 'But I don't know why.'

'You'd want a psychiatrist to explain it properly, but I'll tell you for zilch what I've learned. You're a man, you're strong, you look OK, you're successful at your job and you're not afraid of her. And I could go on, but that's for starters. Then she has you roughed up, doesn't she, and here you are looking as good as new, even if you aren't feeling it, and sticking two fingers up in her face, more or less and, believe me, I'd've chucked a rival down the stairs for less if they as much as yawned in my presence.'

I listened to Worthington's wisdom, but I said, 'I haven't done her any harm.'

'You threaten her. You're too much for her. You'll win the tennis match. So maybe she'll have you killed first. She won't kill you herself. And don't ignore what I'm telling you. There are people who really have killed for hate. People who've wanted to win.'

Not to mention murders because of racism or religious prejudice, I thought, but it was still hard to imagine it applying to oneself – until one had felt the watch smash, of course.

I expected that Rose would have told Eddie Payne, her father, that I was at the races, but she hadn't. Worthington and I lay in wait for him after the last race and easily ambushed him in a pincer movement when he came out of the changing room on his way to his car.

He wasn't happy. He looked from one to the other of us like a cornered horse, and it was as if to a fractious animal that I soothingly said, 'Hi, Ed. How's things?'

'I don't know anything I haven't told you,' he protested.

I thought if I cast him a few artificial flies, I might startle and hook an unexpected fish; a trout, so to speak, sheltering in the reeds.

So I said, 'Is Rose married to Norman Osprey?'

His face lightened to nearly a laugh. 'Rose is still Rose Payne but she calls herself Robins and sometimes *Mrs* Robins when it suits her, but she doesn't like men, my Rose. Pity, really, but there it is.'

'But she likes to rule them?'

'She's always made boys do what she wants.'

'Were you with her yesterday evening?' I asked him the question casually, but he knew instantly what I meant.

'I didn't lay a finger on you,' he said quickly. 'It wasn't me.' He looked from me to Worthington and back again, this time with puzzlement. 'Look,' he said wheedlingly, as if begging for forgiveness, 'they didn't give you a chance. I told Rose it wasn't fair . . .' He wavered to a stop.

With interest I asked, 'Do you mean that you yourself wore a black mask in Broadway yesterday evening?' and almost with incredulity saw in his face an expression of shame that he had.

'Rose said we would just frighten you.' He stared at me with unhappy eyes. 'I tried to stop her, honest. I never thought you'd be here today. So it can't have been as bad as it looked . . . but I know it was *awful*. I went to confession first to ask forgiveness . . .'

'So there was you and Rose,' I said it matter of factly, though stunned beneath. 'And Norman Osprey, and who else? One of Norman Osprey's bookmaking clerks, was it?'

'No. Not them.'

Horror suddenly closed his mouth. He had already admitted far too much from his daughter's point of view, and if the other so far unidentified black-mask shape were one of the other two clerks working with Norman Osprey as Arthur Robins Est. 1894, Eddie was no longer going to admit it easily.

I tried another fly.

'Do you know anyone who could lay their hands on anaesthetics?'

A blank.

Try again.

'Or anyone with a white beard, known to Martin?'

He hesitated over that, but in the end shook his head.

I said, 'Do you yourself know anyone with a white beard who looks like a university lecturer?'

'No.' His reply was positive, his manner shifty.

'Was the brown-paper parcel you gave me at Cheltenham the self-same one that Martin gave you earlier in the day?'

'Yes,' he nodded this time with no need for thought. 'It was the same one. Rose was furious. She said I should have stuck onto it when Martin died, and I shouldn't have mentioned it. We should have kept it ourselves and then there wouldn't have been all this fuss.'

'Did Rose know what was in it?'

'Only Martin knew for sure. I did more or less ask him what was in it but he just laughed and said the future of the world, but it was a joke, of course.'

Martin's joke sounded to me too real to be funny.

Ed hadn't finished. 'A couple of weeks before Christmas,' he said, still amused, 'Martin said that what he was giving Bon-Bon – a few of the jockeys were talking about presents for their wives and girlfriends while they were changing to go home . . . it wasn't a big deal – anyway, what he was giving Bon-Bon was a gold and glass antique necklace, but he was laughing and he said he would have to get you to make him a much cheaper and modern copy. He said you had a videotape to tell you how. But next minute he changed his mind because Bon-Bon wanted new fur-lined boots, and anyway he was mostly talking about the King George Chase at Kempton on Boxing Day and how much weight he'd have to take off by not eating turkey. I mean, he was always worried about his weight, like most of them are.'

'He talked to you a lot,' I commented. 'More than most.'

Ed didn't think so. He liked to chat with the boys, he said. He could tell us a thing or two about them. He winked on it, as if all jockeys were real sexual rogues, and with this confidence his manner more or less returned to the calm and efficient valet I'd met through Martin.

Worthington, driving us home, summed up the day's haul of information. 'I'd say Martin and the white-bearded guy were serious about this tape.'

'Yes,' I agreed.

'And somehow or other, through her father, Rose may have imagined that that tape showed how to make an antique necklace.'

I said doubtfully, 'It must be more than that.'

'Well . . . perhaps it actually says where the necklace can be found.'

'A treasure hunt?' I shook my head. 'There's only one valuable antique gold and glass necklace that I know of, and I do know a fair amount about antique glass, and it's in a museum. It's priceless. It was probably designed in Crete, or anyway somewhere round the Aegean Sea sometime about 3,500 years ago. It's called the Cretan Sunrise. I did make a copy of it, though, and I once lent it to Martin. I also made a videotape to explain the methods I used. I lent that to Martin too and he still has it – or rather, heaven knows where it is now.'

'What if there's another one?' Worthington asked.

'Are you talking about *two tapes* now? Or two necklaces?'

'Why not two tapes?' Worthington reasoned, as if it had suddenly become likely. 'Rose could have muddled them up.'

I thought it just as likely that it was Worthington and I who'd muddled everything up, but we arrived safely at Bon-Bon's house richer with at least two solid new facts: first, that Rose, Norman Osprey and Eddie Payne had spent their Sunday evening in Broadway; and, second, that an elderly, thin, white-bearded, university-lecturer-type man had walked into my shop as the new century came in with bells, and had not stayed to help Lloyd Baxter with his epileptic fit.

As we scrunched to a halt on Bon-Bon's gravel, Marigold came with wide-stretched arms out of the front door to greet us.

'Bon-Bon doesn't need me any more,' she announced dramatically. 'Get out the maps, Worthington. We're going skiing.'

'Er . . . when?' her chauffeur asked, unsurprised.

'Tomorrow morning, of course. Fill up the petrol tanks. We'll call at Paris on the way. I need new clothes.'

Worthington looked more resigned than I felt. He murmured to me that Marigold bought new clothes most days of the week and prophesied that the skiing trip would last less than ten days overall. She would tire of it quickly, and come home.

Bon-Bon was taking the news of her mother's departure with well-hidden relief, and asked me with hope whether 'the upsetting videotape business' was now concluded. She wanted calm in her life, but I had no idea if she would get it. I didn't tell her of Rose's existence or the distinct lack of calm she represented.

I asked Bon-Bon about White-Beard. She said she'd never seen or heard of him. When I explained who he was, she telephoned to Priam Jones who, though with his self-esteem badly hurt by Lloyd Baxter's ditching of him, regretted he couldn't help.

Bon-Bon tried several more trainers, but thin, elderly, white-bearded owners of racehorses seemed not to exist. After she'd tired of it she persuaded her mother to let Worthington continue our journey, to take me where I wanted. I kissed her gratefully and chose to go straight home to my hillside house and flop.

Worthington liked skiing, he said as we drove away. He liked Paris. He liked Marigold. He regularly admired her more bizarre clothes. Sorry, he said, about leaving me with the lioness, Rose. Good luck, he said cheerfully.

'I could throttle you,' I said.

While Worthington happily chuckled at the wheel, I switched on my mobile phone again to call Irish at his home to find out how the day had finally gone in the shop, but before I could dial the number the message-service called, and the disembodied voice of young Victor W. V. said briefly in my ear, 'Send your e-mail address to me at vic@freenet.com.'

Holy hell, I thought, Victor had things to say. Flopping could wait. The only computer I owned that handled e-mail was in Broadway. Worthington with resignation changed direction, at length stopping by my main glass door and insisting he came in with me, to check the place for black masks and other pests.

The place was empty. No Rose in wait. Worthington returned with me to the Rolls, shook my hand, told me to look after myself and left lightheartedly, again prophesying his swift return well within two weeks.

Almost at once I missed the muscle man, missed him as a safety umbrella and as a source of a realistic view of life. Paris and skiing attracted powerfully. I sighed over my inescapable bruises, roused my sleeping computer into action, connected it to the Internet, and sent an e-mail message to Victor, with my address.

I expected I'd have to wait a good long time to hear from Victor, but almost immediately – which meant he had been sitting at his computer, waiting – the screen of my lap-top demanded 'Who are you?'

I typed and sent, 'Martin Stukely's friend.'

He asked, 'Name?' and I told him, 'Gerard Logan.'

His reply was, 'What do you want?'

'How did you know Martin Stukely?'

'I've known him for ages, saw him often at the races with my grandad.'

I wrote, 'Why did you send that letter to Martin? How had you heard of any tape? Please tell me the truth.'

'I heard my aunt telling my mother.'

'How did your aunt know?'

'My aunt knows everything.'

I began to lose faith in his common sense, and I remembered his saying he was playing a game.

'What is your aunt's name?' I expected nothing much: certainly not the breath-taker that came back.

'My aunt's name is Rose. She keeps changing her last name. She's my mother's sister.' There was barely an interval before his next remark. 'I'd better log off now. She's just come!'

'Wait.' Stunned by the revelation I rapidly typed, 'Do you know of a thin old man with a white beard?'

A long time after I'd settled for no answer three words appeared.

'Doctor Force. Goodbye.'

# CHAPTER FIVE

To my considerable delight Catherine Dodd again stood her motor bike by my kerb and pulled off her helmet before walking across the pavement to the door I held open for her. It seemed natural to us both to kiss hello, and for her to stand in front of the soaring flight of wings that I had barely finished lighting.

'It's tremendous.' She meant it. 'It's too good for Broadway.'

'Flattery will get you an awfully long way,' I assured her, and took her into the workshop, where it was warmest.

The sheet printed of my e-mail conversation with Victor lay folded on the marver table and I passed it to her to read. 'What do you think?' I asked.

'I think you need better pain killers.'

'No. Think about Victor.'

She sat this time in the armchair on my promise that on the next day I would walk down the hill looking in second-hand and antique furniture shops to buy another one.

'If,' I amended the promise, 'if you will come and sit in it.'

She nodded as if it were an 'of course' decision and read Victor's e-mail. When she'd finished she laid the sheet on her black leather-clad knees and asked her own questions.

'OK,' she said. 'First of all, remind me, who is Victor?'

'The fifteen-year-old grandson of Ed Payne, Martin Stukely's racecourse valet. Ed gave me the videotape that was stolen from here, that you came to see about. Victor sent this letter to Martin.' I gave her the letter to read, which raised her eyebrows in doubt.

'Victor said he was playing games,' I acknowledged.

'You can't believe a word he says!' Catherine agreed.

'Well, yes, you can, actually. He's made a game of actual bits of fact. Or anyway, he's done what everyone does at some point – he's heard one thing and thought it meant another.'

'The wrong end of the stick?' Catherine suggested. 'How about the right end?'

'Well . . . the stick as I see it, then.' I stopped for a minute or two to make coffee which, in spite of her being off duty, she said she preferred to wine. No milk, no sugar, cool rather than hot.

'Have to begin with a "suppose",' I said.

'Suppose away.'

'Start with a white-bearded man who looks like a university lecturer and who might be called Dr Force.

Suppose that this Dr Force has somehow got to know Martin. Dr Force has some information he wants to put into safekeeping so he takes it to Cheltenham races and gives it to Martin.'

'Crazy,' Catherine sighed. 'Why didn't he put it in a bank?'

'We'll have to ask him.'

'And you are crazy, too. How do we find him?'

'It's you,' I pointed out, smiling, 'who is the police officer.'

'Well, I'll try.' She smiled back. 'And what then?'

'Then Dr Force went to the races as planned. He gave his tape to Martin. After Martin crashed, our Dr Force must have gone through a lot of doubt and worry, and I'd guess he stood around near the changing room wondering what to do. Then he saw Ed Payne give the tape in its brown-paper parcel to me, and he knew it was the right tape as he'd packed it himself.'

'You should join the police,' Catherine teased. 'So, OK, Dr Force finds out who you are and takes himself here to Broadway, and when you leave your door unlocked for a spell in the new-age air, he nips in and takes back his own tape.'

'Right.'

'And steals your cash on impulse.'

'Right. But up to that point he hasn't realized that there is someone else in the depths of the shop, and that's Lloyd Baxter, who proceeds to have an epileptic fit.'

'Upsetting for Dr White-Beard Force.' She spoke dryly.

I nodded. 'He did a bunk.'

Catherine said thoughtfully, 'One of our detective constables interviewed Lloyd Baxter in hospital. Mr Baxter said he didn't see anyone at all come into the showroom.'

'Lloyd Baxter didn't care about getting the tape back, nor the money either. He did care very much about keeping his illness as private as possible.'

Catherine showed irritation. 'However can we solve cases if people don't give us the facts?'

'You must be used to it.'

She said that being used to something wrong didn't make it right. The starchy disapproval common to her profession had surfaced briefly. Never forget, I told myself, that the inner crime fighter is always there, always on duty, and always part of her. She shook herself free of the moment and made a visible gear-change back to a lighter approach.

'OK,' she nodded, 'so Dr Force has his tape back. Fine. So who squirted anaesthetic at the Stukelys and took their TVs, and who ransacked your own house, and beat you up last night? And I don't really understand how this boy Victor got involved.'

'I can't answer everything, but think Rose.'

'Pink?'

'Rose. She is Ed Payne's daughter, and Victor's aunt. She's sharp featured, sharp tongued, and I think is on the edge of criminal. She jumps a bit to conclusions, and she's all the more dangerous for that.'

'For instance?'

'For instance . . . I'd guess it was she who stole all the videotapes in Bon-Bon's house and mine because they could possibly have been mixed up with the one I brought from the racecourse.'

'But heavens!' Catherine exclaimed. 'Tapes do so easily get mixed up.'

'Rose probably thought so, too. I would think it likely that Rose chatters to her sister – Victor's mother – quite a lot and I think it's fairly certain that Victor did overhear her when she said she knew of a tape worth a fortune.'

If only Martin had explained what he was doing! There was too much guesswork, and definitely too much Rose.

Sighing, Catherine gave me back Victor's print-out and stood up, saying with apparent reluctance, 'I have to go. I was so glad to find you here, but I've promised to be with my parents tonight. I was wondering, though, if you by any chance want to go to your house now, then – um – you don't need a licence to ride pillion.'

She necessarily shed the police half of herself. I clasped her close round her waist, having more or less strapped on her spare helmet, which was too small and inclined to wobble. We set off insecurely, but the bike had guts enough to take both of us up the hills without stuttering, and she was laughing when she stopped by the weedy entrance to my drive.

I thanked her for the ride. She roared off still laughing.

I was conscious of wishing that Worthington, or failing him, Tom Pigeon and his Dobermanns, were by my side, but there were no thorny briar Roses lying in wait this time. When I unlocked a side door and let myself in, it seemed that the house gave back in peace the years the Logan family had prospered there, father, mother and two sons, each in a different way. I was the only one left, and with its ten rooms still filled with sharp memories, I'd made no move to find a smaller or more suitable lair. One day, perhaps. Meanwhile the house felt like home in all senses: home to me, the home of all who'd lived there.

I walked deliberately through all the rooms thinking of Catherine, wondering both if she would like the place, and whether the house would accept her in return. Once in the past the house had delivered a definite thumbs down, and once I'd been given an ultimatum to smother the pale plain walls with brightly patterned paper as a condition of marriage, but to the horror of her family I'd backed out of the whole deal and, as a result, I now used the house as arbiter and had disentangled myself from a later young woman who'd begun to refer to her and me as 'an item' and to reply to questions as 'we'. *We* think.

No, we don't think.

I knew that several people considered me heartless. Also promiscuous, also fickle. Catherine would be advised not to get herself involved with that fellow whose reputation was as brittle as his glass. I knew quite well what the gossips said, but it wasn't going to be to please any gossip that the house and I one day would settle on a mate for life.

The burglars who'd taken all my videotapes hadn't made a lot of mess. There had been television sets with video recorders in three rooms: in the kitchen, and in each of the sitting rooms in which for nearly ten years my mother and I had lived our semi-separate lives.

As I hadn't yet done anything about the rooms since her death, it seemed as if she would soon come out of her bedroom, chiding me for having left my dirty clothes on the floor.

There wasn't a single tape left anywhere that I could find. My parent had had a radically different taste from me in films and recorded TV programmes, but it no longer mattered. Out of my own room I'd lost a rather precious bunch of glass-blowing instruction tapes that I might be able to replace if I could find copies. I'd been commissioned to make some of them myself for university courses. Those courses were basic and mostly dealt with how to make scientific equipment for laboratories. I couldn't imagine those teaching tapes being the special target of any thief.

In the kitchen there had been game shows, tennis, American football and cooking. All gone. The police had suggested I list them all. What a hope!

There wasn't much left to tidy, except for patches of dust and a couple of dead spiders here and there where once the televisions had stood.

With the Rose-induced bruises growing gradually less sore, I slept safely behind bolted doors, and in the morning walked (as usual while sans car) downhill to Logan Glass, getting there before Irish, Hickory and Pamela Jane. Relief was the emotion I chiefly felt about the soaring wings; relief that somehow someone hadn't managed to smash them overnight.

Irish's pedestal and my lighting system had combined to make accidental breakage very difficult, but one couldn't easily guard against hurricane or axe.

I made a fleet of little ornamental sailing ships all morning and bought a comfortable armchair at lunchtime which minimized every remaining wince. Followed by a brown-overalled chair pusher (with chair), I returned to Logan Glass and rearranged the furniture. My assistants grinned knowingly.

I straightened out the worst of Hickory's growing hubris by giving him a sailing boat as an exercise, which resulted in a heap of sad lumps of stunted mast and a mainsail that no breeze would ever fill.

Hickory's good looks and general air of virility would always secure him jobs he couldn't do. In less than the first week of his attractive company I'd learned more of his limitations than his skills, but every customer liked him and he was a great salesman.

'It's all right for *you*,' he now complained, looking from the little boat I'd made in demonstration to the heap of coloured rubble he'd painstakingly achieved, 'you know what a sailing boat *looks* like. When I make them they come out flat.'

Half the battle in all I did, as I tried to explain to him without any 'cockiness' creeping in, was the draughtsman's inner eye that saw an object in three-dimensional terms. I could draw and paint all right, but it was the three-dimensional imagination that I'd been blessed with from birth that made little sailboats a doddle.

As Hickory's third try bit the dust amid commiserating murmurs from the rest of us, the telephone interrupted the would-be star glass-blower's spurious explanation of how drops of water had unfairly fallen on his work at the crucial moment and splintered it, which was definitely not his fault . . .

I didn't listen. The voice on the line was Catherine's.

'I've been a police officer all morning,' she said. 'Did you really get another chair?'

'It's here waiting for you.'

'Great. And I've collected some news for you. I'll be along when I go off duty, at six o'clock.'

To fill in time I e-mailed Victor, expecting to have to wait for a reply as he should have been in school but, as before, he was ready.

He typed. 'Things have changed.'

'Tell me.'

There was a long gap of several minutes.

'Are you still there?' he asked.

'Yes.'

'My dad's in jail.'

E-mail messages cross the ether without inflection. Victor's typed words gave no clues to his feelings.

I sent back, 'Where? What for? How long? I'm very sorry.'

Victor's reply had nothing to do with the questions.

'I hate her.'

I asked flatly, 'Who?'

A pause, then, 'Auntie Rose, of course.'

I itched for faster answers but got only a feeling that if I pressed too hard I would lose him altogether.

Without the tearing emotion I could imagine him trying to deal with, he wrote, 'He's been there ten weeks. They sent me to stay with my Uncle Mac in Scotland when the trial was on, so I wouldn't know. They told me my dad had gone on an Antarctic expedition as a chef. He is a chef, you see. He got sent down for a year, but he'll be out before that. Will you go on talking to me?'

'Yes,' I sent back. 'Of course.'

A long pause again, then: 'Rose sneaked on Dad.' I waited, and more came. 'He hit Mum. He broke her nose and some ribs.' After an even longer pause, he sent, 'E-mail me tomorrow,' and I replied fast, while he might still be on line, 'Tell me about Dr Force.'

Either he'd disconnected his phone line or didn't want to reply, because Dr Force was a non-starter. Victor's silence lasted all day.

I went back to the teaching session. Hickory finally fashioned a boat that might have floated had it been full-size and made of fibreglass with a canvas sail. He allowed himself a smirk of satisfaction which none of us grudged him. Glass-blowing was a difficult discipline even for those like Hickory, who apparently had everything on their side – youth, agility, imagination. Hickory put the little boat carefully in the annealing oven, knowing I would give him the finished ornament to keep in the morning.

By six I'd managed to send them all home, and by six plus twenty-three Detective Constable Dodd was approving the new armchair and reading Victor Waltman Verity's troubles.

'Poor boy,' she said.

I said ruefully, 'As he hates his Aunt Rose for grassing on his Pa, he might not tell me anything else himself. Sneaking appears to be a mortal sin in his book.'

'Mm.' She read the printed pages again, then cheerfully said, 'Well, whether or not you have Victor's help, your Dr Force is definitely on the map.' It pleased her to have found him. 'I chased him through a few academic *Who's Who*s with no results. He's not a university lecturer, or not primarily, anyway. He is, believe it or not, a medical doctor. Licensed, and all that.' She handed me an envelope with a grin. 'One of my colleagues spends his time chasing struck-off practitioners. He looked for him, and in the end he did find him.'

'Is he struck off?' It would make sense, I thought, but Catherine shook her head.

'No, not only is he not struck off, he was working in

some research lab or other until recently. He took a lot of finding, because of that. It's all in this envelope.'

'And is he fiftyish with a white beard?'

She laughed. 'His date of birth will be in the envelope. A white beard's expecting too much.'

Both of us at that point found that there were more absorbing facets to life than chasing obscure medics.

I suggested food from the take-away; she offered another pillion ride up the hill: we saw to both. I'd left central heating on for comfort, and Catherine wandered all over the house, smiling.

'I've been warned that you'll dump me,' she said casually.

'Not in a hurry.'

I still held the envelope of Dr Force details, and I opened it then with hope, but it told me very few useful facts. His name was Adam Force, age fifty-six, and his qualifications came by the dozen.

I said blankly, 'Is that all?'

She nodded. 'That's all folks when it comes to facts. As to hearsay – well – according to a bunch of rumours he's a brilliant researcher who has published star-spangled work since his teens. No one could tell my colleague about a white beard. He didn't speak to anyone who'd actually met the subject.'

I asked, 'Does Dr Force have an address?'

'Not in these notes,' she answered. 'In the *Who's Who* we used, it gives only the information provided by the people themselves. Those reference books leave people out if they don't want to be in.'

'Utterly civilized.'

'No, very annoying.'

She didn't sound very annoyed, however, as she knew all about the Internet. The next morning, we decided, we would catch him on the Web.

We ate the take-away food, or a little of it, owing to a change of appetite, and I switched up the heating a little in my bedroom without any need for explanation.

She'd shed somewhere in her life whatever she had ever suffered in the way of overpowering shyness. The Catherine who came into my bed came with confidence along with modesty, an intoxicating combination as far as I was concerned. We both knew enough, anyway, to give to each other as much pleasure as we received, or at least enough to feel slumberous and fulfilled in consequence.

The speed of development of strong feeling for one another didn't seem to me to be shocking but natural, and if I thought about the future it unequivocally included Catherine Dodd. 'If you wanted to cover the pale plain walls with brightly patterned paper, go ahead,' I said.

She laughed. 'I like the peace of pale walls. Why should I want to change them?'

I said merely, 'I'm glad you don't,' and offered her thirst quenchers. Like Martin, it seemed she preferred fizzy water to alcohol, though in her case the cause wasn't weight but the combination of a police badge and a motor bike. She went soberly home before dawn, steady on two wheels. I watched her red rear light fade into what was left of the night and quite fiercely wanted her to stay with me instead.

I walked restlessly downhill through the slow January dawn, reaching the workshop well before the others. The Internet, though, when I'd accessed it, proved less obliging about Adam Force than the address of Waltman Verity in Taunton. There had been a whole clutch of Veritys. Adam Force wasn't anywhere in sight.

Hickory arrived at that point, early and eager to take his precious sailboat out of the Lehr annealing oven. He unbolted the oven door and lifted out his still warm treasure. Although he would get the transparent colours clearer with practice, it wasn't a bad effort and I told him so. He wasn't pleased, however. He wanted unqualified praise. I caught on his face a fleeting expression of contempt for my lack of proper appreciation of his ability. There would be trouble ahead if he tackled really difficult stuff, I thought: but, as I'd done once in the past with someone of equal talent, I would give him good references when he looked for a different teacher as, quite soon now, he would.

I would miss him most in the selling department for results and in the humour department for good company.

Irish, more humble about his skills, and Pamela Jane, twittery and positively self-deprecating, came sweeping in together in the cold morning and gave the sailboat the extravagant admiration Hickory thought it deserved. Harmony united the three of them as usual, but I hadn't much faith in its lasting much longer.

Watched and helped by all three of them I spent that day replacing the minaret-shaped scent bottles we'd sold at Christmas, working fast at eight pieces an hour, using blue, turquoise, pink, green, white and purple in turn and packing the finished articles in rows in the ovens to cool. Speed was a commercial asset as essential as a three-dimensional eye, and winter in the Cotswold hills was the time to stock up for the summer tourists. I consequently worked flat out from morning to six in the evening, progressing from sailboats via scent bottles to fishes, horses, bowls and vases.

At six in the evening when my semi-exhausted crew announced all six ovens to be packed, I sent them off home, tidied the workshop and put everything ready for the morrow. In the evening Catherine Dodd, straight off duty, rode her bike to Broadway, collected a pillion passenger and took him to his home. Every night possible that week Detective Constable Dodd slept in my arms in my bed but left before the general world awoke and, during that time, no one managed to stick an address on Adam Force.

Glass-blowing aside, by Friday afternoon, three days after Worthington and Marigold had joyfully left for Paris, the weekend held no enticements as Catherine had departed on Friday morning to a promised school-friends' reunion.

On the same Friday, aching, I dare say, from the

absence of their daily quarrel, Bon-Bon filled her need of Martin by driving his BMW, bursting at the seams with noisy children, to pick me up at close of day in Broadway.

'Actually,' Bon-Bon confessed as we detoured to my hill house for mundane clean shirts and socks, 'Worthington didn't like you being out here alone.'

'*Worthington* didn't?'

'No. He phoned from somewhere south of Paris and specially told me a whole gang of people jumped on you in Broadway last Sunday evening when there were dog-walkers about, and this place of yours out here is asking for trouble, he said. He also said Martin would have taken you home.'

'Worthington exaggerated,' I protested, but after we'd all unloaded at Bon-Bon's house, I used the evening there to invent a game for the children to compete in, a game called 'Hunt the orange cylinder and the shoelaces.'

Bon-Bon protested. 'But they told everything they know to the police! They won't find anything useful.'

'And after that game,' I said, gently ignoring her, 'we'll play "Hunt the letters sent to Daddy by somebody called Force", and there are prizes for every treasure found, of course.'

They played until bedtime with enthusiasm on account of the regular hand-outs of gold coin treasure (money), and when they'd noisily departed upstairs I laid out their final offerings all over Martin's desk in the den.

I had watched the children search uninhibitedly in places I might have left untouched so that their haul was in some ways spectacular. Perhaps most perplexing was the original of the letter Victor had sent a copy of to Martin.

Dear Martin, it said, and continued word for word as far as the signature, which didn't say Victor Waltman Verity in computer-print, but was scrawled in real live handwriting – Adam Force.

'The kids found that letter in a secret drawer in Martin's desk,' Bon-Bon said. 'I didn't even know there was a secret drawer, but the children did.'

'Um.' I pondered. 'Did any of these other things come out of the drawer?'

She said she would go and ask, and presently returned with Daniel, her eleven-year-old eldest, who opened a semi-hidden drawer in the desk for us with an easy twiddle, and asked if it were worth another hand-out. He hadn't emptied the drawer, he explained, as he'd found the letter straight away, the letter that was the point of the whole game, the letter sent to Daddy by someone called Force.

Of course, no one had found any trace of an orange cylinder or of recognizable laces for trainers.

I gladly handed over another instalment of treasure, as the hidden drawer proved to stretch across the whole width of the desk under the top surface, and to be about four inches deep. Daniel patiently showed me how it opened and closed. Observant and quick-witted, he offered other discoveries with glee, especially when I gave him a coin for every good hiding place with nothing in it. He found four. He jingled the coins.

Bon-Bon, searching the desk drawer, found with blushing astonishment a small bunch of love letters from her that Martin had saved. She took them over to the black leather sofa and wept big slow tears, while I told her that her son knew the so-called secret drawer wasn't a secret at all but was a built-in feature of the modern desk.

'It's designed to hold a lap-top computer,' I told Bon-Bon. 'Martin just didn't keep a lap-top in it, as he used that table-top one over there, the one with the full keyboard and the screen.'

'How do you know?'

'Daniel says so.'

Bon-Bon said through her tears, 'How disappointing it all is,' and picked up a tissue for mopping.

I however found the lap-top drawer seething with interest, if not with secrets as, apart from Adam Force's letter to Martin, there was a photocopy of Martin's letter to Force, a not much longer affair than the brief reply.

It ran:

Dear Adam Force,

I have now had time to consider the matter of your formulae and methods. Please will you go ahead and record these onto the videotape as you suggested and take it to Cheltenham races on New Year's Eve. Give it to me there, whenever you see me, except, obviously, not when I'm on my way out to race.

Yours ever,
Martin Stukely

I stared not just at the letter, but at its implications.

Daniel looked over my shoulder, and asked what formulae were. 'Are they secrets?' he said.

'Sometimes.'

When Bon-Bon had read the last loving letter and had dried her tears I asked her how well Martin had known Dr Adam Force.

With eyes darkened from crying she said she didn't know. She regretted desperately all the hours the two of them had spent in pointless arguing. 'We never discussed anything without quarrelling. You know what we were like. But I *loved* him . . . and he loved *me*, I know he did.'

They had quarrelled and loved, both intensely, throughout the four years I'd known them. It was too late to wish that Martin had confided more in her, even in spite of her chattering tongue, but together for once they had decided that it should be I and not Bon-Bon who held Martin's secret for safekeeping.

What secret? *What secret*, dear God.

Alone in the den since Bon-Bon and Daniel had gone upstairs to the other children, I sorted through everything in the drawer, putting the many loose letters in heaps according to subject. There were several used old cheque books with sums written on the stubs but quite often not dates or payees. Martin must have driven his accountant crazy. He seemed simply to have thrust tax papers, receipts, payments and earnings haphazardly into his out-of-sight drawer.

Semi-miracles occasionally happen, though, and on one stub, dated November 1999 (no actual day) I came across the plain name Force (No Dr, no Adam). On the line below there was the single word BELLOWS, and in the box for the amount of money being transferred out of the account there were three noughts, ooo, with no whole numbers and no decimal points.

Searches through three other sets of stubs brought to light a number of similar unfinished records: Martin deserved secrets, curse him, when he wrote so many himself.

The name Force appeared again on a memo pad, when a Martin handwritten scrawl said, 'Force, Bristol, Wednesday, if P doesn't declare Legup at Newton Abbot.'

Legup at Newton Abbot . . . Say Legup was a horse and Newton Abbot the racecourse where he was entered? I stood up from Martin's desk and started on the form books in his bookcase, but although Legup had run in about eight races in the autumn and spring over four or five years, and seldom, as it happened, on Wednesdays, there wasn't any mention of days he'd been entered but stayed at home.

I went back to the drawer.

A loose-leaf notebook, the most methodically kept of all his untidy paperwork, appeared as a gold-mine of order compared with all the rest. It listed, with dates, amounts given by Martin to Eddie Payne, his racecourse valet, since the previous June. It included even the day he died, when he'd left a record of his intentions.

As there was, to my understanding, a pretty rigid scale of pay from jockeys to valets, the notebook at first sight looked less important than half the neglected rest, but on the first page Martin had doodled the names of Ed Payne, Rose Payne, Gina Verity and Victor. In a box in a corner, behind straight heavy bars, he'd written Waltman. There were small sketches of Ed in his apron, Gina in her curlers, Victor with his computer and Rose . . . Rose had a halo of spikes.

Martin had known this family, I reflected, for almost as long as Ed had been his valet. When Martin had received the letter from Victor Waltman Verity, he would have known it was a fifteen-year-old's game. Looking back, I could see I hadn't asked the right questions, because I'd been starting from the wrong assumptions.

With a sigh I put down the notebook and read through the letters, most of which were from the owners of horses that Martin's skill had urged first past the post. All of the letters spoke of the esteem given to an honest jockey and none of them had the slightest relevance to secrets on videotapes.

A 1999 diary came next, though I found it not in the drawer but on top of the desk, put there by one of the children. It was a detailed jockey's diary, with all race meetings listed. Martin had circled everywhere he'd ridden, with the names of his mounts. He had filled in Tallahassee on the last day of the century, the last day of his life.

I lolled in Martin's chair, both mourning him and

wishing like hell that he could come back alive just for five minutes.

My mobile phone, lying on the desk, gave out its brisk summons and, hoping it was Catherine, I switched it on.

It wasn't Catherine.

Victor's cracked voice spoke hurriedly.

'Can you come to Taunton on Sunday? Please say you will catch the same train as before. I'm running out of money for this phone. Please say yes.'

I listened to the urgency, to the virtual panic.

I said, 'Yes, OK,' and the line went dead.

I would have gone blithely unwarned to Taunton on that Sunday if it hadn't been for Worthington shouting in alarm over crackling lines from a mountain top.

'Haven't you learned the first thing about not walking into an ambush?'

'Not Victor,' I protested. 'He wouldn't lure me into a trap.'

'Oh yeah? And does the sacrificial lamb understand he's for the chop?'

Lamb chop or not, I caught the train.

# CHAPTER SIX

Tom Pigeon, who lived within walking distance away with his three energetic Dobermanns, strolled to the gallery door of Logan Glass late on Saturday morning and invited me out for a beer in a local pub. Any bar, but not the Dragon's across the road, he said.

With the dogs quietly tied to a bench outside, Tom Pigeon drank deep of a pint in a crowded dark inn and told me that Worthington thought that I had more nerve than sense when it came to the Verity–Paynes.

'Mm. Something about a wasps' nest,' I agreed. 'When, exactly, did he talk to you?'

Tom Pigeon looked at me over the rim of his glass as he swallowed the dregs. 'He said you were no slouch in the brain box. He told me this morning.' He smiled. 'He phoned from Gstaad. Only the best for his lady employer, of course.'

He ordered a second pint while I still dawdled with my first. His slightly piratical dark little pointed beard and his obvious physical strength turned heads our way. I might be of his age and height, but no one sidled away at my approach, or found me an instinctive threat.

'It was only a week ago tomorrow,' he said, 'that they hammered you until you could hardly stand.'

I thanked him for my deliverance.

He said, 'Worthington wants you to stay away from any more trouble of that sort. Especially, he said, while he's in Switzerland.'

I listened, though, to the Tom Pigeon view of that course of inaction. He sounded as bored with the safe road to old age as Worthington himself had been the day he had goaded me to go to Leicester races.

'Worthington's coming across like a father,' Tom said.

'A bodyguard,' I commented wryly, 'and I miss him.'

Tom Pigeon said casually but with unmistakable sincerity, 'Take me on board instead.'

I reflected briefly that Tom's offer wasn't what Worthington had intended to spark off, and wondered what my dear Constable Dodd would think of my allying myself to an ex-jail occupant with a nickname like Backlash. I said regardless, 'Yes, if you'll do what I ask . . .'

'Maybe.'

I laughed and suggested how he might spend his Sunday. His eyes widened and came to vivid approving life. 'Just as long as it's legal,' he bargained. 'I'm not going back in the slammer.'

'It's legal,' I assured him, and when I caught the train the following morning I had a new rear defender in the guards' van, accompanied by three of the most dangerous-looking black dogs that ever licked one's fingers.

There was only one possible train combination to travel on which would achieve the same time of arrival at Lorna Terrace as I'd managed the previous Sunday. It would be the time that Victor meant. Tom had wanted to rethink the plan and go by car. He would drive, he said. I shook my head and changed his mind.

Suppose, I'd suggested, this is not the ambush that Worthington feared, but just the frantic need of a worried boy. Give him a chance, I'd said.

We would compromise, though, about the awkward return journey. We would hire a car with driver to follow us from Taunton station, to shadow us faithfully, to pick us up when we wanted and finally drive us to Broadway and home.

'Expensive,' Tom Pigeon complained.

'I'm paying,' I said.

Victor himself was waiting on the Taunton platform when the train wheels ran smoothly into the station. I'd travelled near the front of the train so as to be able to spot and to pass any little unwelcoming committee where I had plenty of space to assess them, but the boy seemed to be alone. Also, I thought, anxious. Also cold in the January wind. Beyond that, an enigma.

Tom's dogs, travelling at the rear of the train, slithered down onto the platform and caused a sharp local division between dog-lovers and those with anti-fang reservations.

I reckoned, or anyway hoped, that Victor himself

wouldn't know Tom or his dogs by sight, even though Rose and the rest of her family probably would, after the rout of the black-masks in Broadway.

I needed no black-mask to meet Victor but, learning from the plain-clothes police, I wore a baseball cap at the currently with-it angle above a navy-blue tracksuit topped with a paler-blue sleeveless padded jacket. Normal enough for many, but different from my usual grey trousers and white shirt.

Bon-Bon's children having sniggered behind their hands, and Tom having swept his gaze over me blankly as if I had been a stranger, I walked confidently and silently in my trainers to Victor's back and said quietly in his ear, 'Hello.'

He whirled round and took in my changed appearance with surprise, but chief of his emotions seemed to be straightforward relief that I was there at all.

'I was afraid you wouldn't come,' he said. 'Not when I heard them saying how they'd smashed you up proper. I don't know what to do. I want you to tell me what to do. They tell me lies.' He was shaking slightly, more with nervousness, I guessed, than with cold.

'First of all, we get off this windy platform,' I said, 'then you tell me where your mother thinks you are.'

Down in front of the station the driver I'd engaged was polishing a dark-blue estate car large enough for the occasion. Tom Pigeon came out of the station with his dogs, made contact with the driver and loaded the Dobermanns into the big rear space designed for them.

Victor, not yet realizing that the car and dogs had anything to do with him, answered my question and a dozen others. 'Mum thinks I'm at home. She's gone to see my dad in jail. It's visiting day. I listened to her and my Auntie Rose planning what they would say to me, and they made up some story about Mum going to see a woman with a disgusting illness that I wouldn't like. Every time she goes to see Dad they make up another reason why I stay at home. Then, when I listened some more, I heard them say they're going to try again, after Mum sees Dad, to make you tell them where the tape is you had from Grandad Payne. They say it's worth millions. My Auntie Rose says it's all nonsense for you to say you don't know. Please, please tell her where it is, or what's on it, because I can't bear her *making* people tell her things. I'd heard them twice up in our attic screaming and groaning and she just laughs and says they have toothache.'

I turned away from Victor so that he shouldn't see the absolute horror that flooded my mind and assuredly appeared on my face. Just the idea of Rose using teeth for torture melted at once any theoretical resistance I might have thought to be within my own capacity.

*Teeth.*

Teeth and wrists and hell knew what else . . .

The need intensified to a critical level to find out what secrets I was supposed to know, and then to decide what to do with the knowledge. Victor, I thought, might be able to dig from the semi-conscious depths of his memory the scraps I still needed if I were to glue together a credible whole. I had pieces. Not enough.

I asked with an inward shudder, 'Where is your Auntie Rose today? Did she visit your dad too?'

He shook his head. 'I don't know where she is. She doesn't usually go to the jail because Dad's not talking to her since she shopped him.' He paused, and then said passionately, 'I wish I belonged to an ordinary family. I wrote to Martin once and asked if I could stay with him for a while but he said they didn't have room. I begged him . . .' His voice cracked. 'What can I do?'

It seemed clear that Victor's need for someone to advise him stretched very far back. It wasn't odd that he was now close to breakdown.

'Come for a ride?' I suggested with friendliness, and held open for him the door behind the estate-car driver. 'I'll get you back home before you're missed, and before that we can talk about what you need.'

He hesitated only briefly. He had, after all, brought me there to help him, and it appeared he was reaching out to someone he trusted even though his family considered that person to be an enemy. Victor couldn't invent or act at this level of desperation.

If this were an ambush, then Victor was the lamb who didn't know it.

I asked him if he knew where I could find Adam Force. The question caused a much longer hesitation and then a shake of the head. He knew, I thought, but perhaps telling me came into the category of squealing.

Tom Pigeon sat beside the driver, making him nervous simply by being himself. Victor and I sat in the rear passenger seats with the dogs behind, separated from us by a netting divider. The driver, taciturn from first to last, set off as soon as we were all aboard and headed at first through winding Somerset country roads and finally out to the wide expanses of Exmoor. Even in the summer, I imagined, it would be a bare and daunting place, grim with sunny dreams unfulfilled and long skylines blurring into drizzly mist. On that Sunday in January the cloudless air was bright, cold and crisp and on the move. The driver pulled off the road onto an area consolidated for tourist parking, and with a few spare words pointed to a just perceptible path ahead, telling me it led onto trackless moorland if I went far enough.

He would wait for us, he said, and we could take our time. He had brought a packed picnic lunch for all of us, as I had arranged.

Tom Pigeon's dogs disembarked and bounded free ecstatically, sniffing with unimaginable joy round heather roots in rich dark red earth. Tom himself stepped out of the car and stretched his arms and chest wide, filling his lungs with deep breaths of clean air.

Victor's face, transformed by the exchange of terrace-house-Taunton for wide open sky, looked almost carefree, almost happy.

Tom and his black familiars set off fast along the track and were soon swallowed into the rolling scenery. Victor and I followed him but eventually more slowly, with

Victor pouring out his devastating home life and difficulties, as I guessed he'd never done before.

'Mum's all right,' he said. 'So's Dad really, except when he comes home from the pub. Then if Mum or I get too near him he belts us one.' He swallowed. 'No, I didn't mean to say that. But last time he broke her ribs and her nose and her face was black all down one side, and when Auntie Rose saw it she went to the cops, and it was funny, really, because other times I'd seen *her* hit my dad. She's got fists like a boxer when she gets going. She can deal it out until the poor buggers beg her to stop, and that's when she laughs at them, and often when she's clouted them once or twice more, she'll step back a bit and smile . . . And then sometimes she'll *kiss* them.' He glanced at me anxiously, sideways, to see what I made of his Aunt Rose's behaviour.

I thought that possibly I'd got off fairly lightly at the hands of the black-masks, thanks to Rose having met her equal in ferocity, my friend with his dogs ahead now on the moor.

I asked Victor, 'Has Rose ever attacked you, personally?'

He was astonished. 'No, of course not. She's my aunt.'

I'd give him perhaps another two years, I thought, before his aunt looked on him as a grown man, not a child.

We walked another length of track while I thought how little I understood of the psychology of women like Rose. Men who enjoyed being beaten by women weren't the sort that attracted Rose. For her to be fulfilled they had to hate it.

The track had narrowed until I was walking in front of Victor, which made talking difficult, but then suddenly the ground widened into a broader flat area from which one could see distant views in most directions. Tom Pigeon stood out below us, his Dobermanns zigzagging around him with unfettered joy.

After watching them for several moments I gave life to an ear-splitting whistle, a skill taught me by my father and brother who had both been able to accomplish the near-impossible of summoning taxis in London in the rain.

Tom stopped fast, turned towards me from lower down the rolling hills, waved acknowledgement, and began to return to where I stood. His dogs aimed towards me without a single degree of deviation.

'Wow,' Victor said, impressed. 'How do you do that?'

'Curl your tongue.' I showed him how, and I asked him again to tell me more about Dr Force. I needed to talk to him, I said.

'Who?'

'You know damn well who. Dr Adam Force. The man who wrote the letter you copied and sent to Martin.'

Victor, silenced, took a while to get going again.

In the end he said, 'Martin knew it was a game.'

'Yes, I'm sure he did,' I agreed. 'He knew you well, he knew Adam Force, and Adam Force knows you.' I watched Tom Pigeon trudge towards us up the hill. 'You may know their secret, that one that was on the tape everyone's talking about.'

'No,' Victor said, 'I don't.'

'Don't lie,' I told him. 'You don't like liars.'

He said indignantly, 'I'm not lying. Martin knew what was on the tape, and so did Dr Force, of course. When I sent that letter to Martin I was just pretending to be Dr Force. I often pretend to be other people, or sometimes animals. It's only a game. Sometimes I talk to people who don't really exist.'

Harvey the rabbit, I thought: and I'd been engine drivers and jockeys in my time. Victor would grow out of it soon, but not soon enough for now in January 2000.

I asked him how he had obtained a copy of Dr Force's letter, which he had sent to Martin with his own name attached in place of Force's.

He didn't reply but just shrugged his shoulders.

I asked him yet again if he knew where I could find his Dr Force, but he said dubiously that Martin had for sure written it down somewhere.

Probably he had. Victor knew where, but he still wasn't telling that either. There had to be some way of persuading him. Some way of bringing him to the point of wanting to tell.

Tom Pigeon and his three bouncing companions reached us at the flattened viewing area, all clearly enjoying the day.

'That's some whistle,' Tom commented admiringly, so I did it again at maximum loudness, which stunned the dogs into pointing their muzzles in my direction, their noses twitching, their eyes alert. Tom patted them, and their stumpy tails wagged excessively.

Walking back towards the car Victor did his breathy best at a whistle that would equally affect the dogs, but they were unimpressed. Water in dishes and handfuls of dog biscuits, brought from home by their owner, suited them better as a prelude to lying down for a doze.

Tom himself, the driver, Victor and I ate sandwiches inside the car, out of the wind, and afterwards sleep came easily to the other three. I left the car and walked back slowly along the track sorting out and simplifying Victor's muddling game of pretence and reducing the Verity–Payne videotape roundabout to probabilities. Still, the absolutely first thing to do next, I concluded, was to find Adam Force, and the path to him still lay with Victor.

What I needed was to get Victor to trust me so instinctively that his deepest secret thoughts would pop out of him without caution. Also I needed to get him to that state fast, and I didn't know if that sort of total brainwash were possible, let alone ethical.

When there was movement around the car I returned to tell the yawning passengers that, according to my new cheap watch, it was time to leave if we were to get back to Lorna Terrace in advance of the time that Victor was expecting his mum.

Tom walked off to find comfort behind bushes, and jerked his head for me to go with him.

Contingency planning was in his mind. The day had gone too smoothly. Had I considered a few 'what ifs'?

We considered them together and returned to the car, where the taciturn driver had taken a liking for Victor and was deep in esoteric chat about computers.

The contentment of the day high on the moor slowly sank and evaporated as the estate car inevitably drew nearer to Lorna Terrace. Victor's nervous tremor reasserted itself and he watched me anxiously for signs of thrusting him back into his unsatisfactory life. He knew pretty well that at fifteen he would be at the mercy of the courts, and that the courts' mercy would undoubtedly be to consign him to the care of his mother. Gina, his mother, even a Gina chain-smoking in large pink curlers, would quite likely be seen as the badly-done-by parent of a thankless child. Gina Verity, unlike her sister Rose who couldn't help radiating a faint air of menace, would be seen by any court in the way that I had seen her at first, as a relaxed, tolerant and fond mother doing her best in difficult circumstances.

The driver stopped the car where Tom Pigeon asked him, which was round the bend that kept him out of sight of number 19. Victor and I disembarked at that point, and I sympathized very much with the misery and hopelessness reappearing in the droop of his shoulders. I went with him to the front door of number 19 which, as in many terraced houses, opened from a concrete path across a small square front garden of dusty grass. Victor produced a key from a pocket and let us in, leading me as before down the passage to the bright little kitchen where life was lived, and where I had promised to stay as company until his mother came back, even though she might not like it.

The door from the kitchen brought Victor to a standstill of puzzlement and unease.

He said, 'I'm sure I bolted the door before I went out.' He shrugged. 'Anyway, I know I bolted that gate from the backyard into the lane. Mum gets furious if I forget it.'

He opened the unbolted kitchen door and stepped out into a small high-walled square of backyard. Across the weeds and dead-looking grass, a tall brown-painted door was set into the high brick wall, and it was this door that freshly upset Victor by again not having its bolts, top and bottom, firmly slid into place.

'Bolt them now,' I said urgently, but Victor stood still in front of me in puzzlement and dismay, and although understanding flashed like lightning through my mind, I couldn't get round him fast enough. The door from the lane opened the moment I stepped towards it across the grass from the kitchen.

Rose had come into the backyard from the lane. Gina and the quasi-gorilla Norman Osprey marched out triumphantly from the house behind us. Both Rose and Osprey were armed with a cut-off section of garden hose. Rose's piece had a tap on it.

Victor at my side stood like a rock, not wanting to

believe what he was seeing. When he spoke, the words addressed to his mother were a scramble of 'You've come back early.'

Rose prowled like a hunting lioness between me and the door to the lane, swinging the heavy brass tap on the supple green hose, and almost licking her lips.

Gina, for once without curlers and pretty as a result, tried to justify the prospect ahead by whining to Victor that his caged father had told her to eff off, he wasn't in the mood for her silly chatter. In her anger she told Victor for the first time that his father was 'inside', and deserved it.

'He can be a mean brute, your dad,' Gina said. 'And when we'd gone all that way! So Rose drove me home again, and that bitch next door told me you'd sneaked off craftily to the station. She followed as she was going that way anyhow, and you met that fellow, that one over there, that Rose says is stealing a million from us. How *can* you, young Vic? So Rose says this time she'll make him tell us what we want to know, but it's no thanks to you, Rose says.'

I heard only some of it. I watched Victor's face, and saw with relief his strong alienation from Gina's smug voice. The more she said, the more he didn't like it. Teenage rebellion visibly grew.

The present and future scene here hadn't been exactly one of the 'what ifs' that Tom and I had imagined in the bushes, but now what if . . . if I could think it out fast enough . . . if I could use Victor's horrified reaction to his mother's outpouring . . . if I could put up with a bit of Rose's persuasion . . . then perhaps – on top of the carefree day on the moor – perhaps Victor would indeed feel like telling me what I was sure he knew. Perhaps the sight of his Aunt Rose's cruelty in action would impel him to offer a gift in atonement . . . to offer me the one thing he knew I wanted. Maybe the prize was worth a bit of discomfort. So get on with it, I told myself. If you're going to do it, do it fast.

Last Sunday, I thought, the black-masks had jumped me unawares. It was different this Sunday. I could invite the assault head on and I did, at a run towards the door to the lane, straight towards Rose and her swinging tap.

She was fast and ruthless and managed to connect twice before I caught her right arm and bent it up behind her, her face close to mine, her dry skin and freckles in sharp focus, hate and sudden pain drawing her lips back from her teeth. Gina, yelling blasphemy, tore at my ear to free her sister.

I caught a glimpse of Victor's horror an instant before Norman Osprey lashed out at me from behind with his own length of hose. Rose wrenched herself out of my grip, pushed Gina out of her way and had another swing at me with her tap. I managed a circular kick-box which temporarily put the gorilla Norman face down on the grass, and in return got another fearful clout from Rose along the jaw that ripped open the skin.

Enough, I thought. Far and away too much. Blood trickled everywhere. I used my only real weapon, the piercing whistle for help, that Tom and I in the bushes had agreed meant 'come at once'.

What if I whistle and he doesn't come . . .?

I whistled again, louder, longer, calling not for a taxi in the rain in London, but quite likely for life without deformity and certainly for self-respect. I couldn't have told Rose from direct knowledge where to find that videotape, but if I'd needed to badly enough I would have invented something. Whether or not she would have believed me was another matter and one I hoped not to find out.

I fortunately also didn't find out what conclusion Rose intended for her Sunday afternoon sports. There was a vast crashing and tinkling noise and Tom's voice roaring at his dogs, and then three snarling Dobermann Pinschers poured like a torrent out of the house's wide open kitchen door into the confined space of the backyard.

Tom carried an iron bar he'd borrowed from local town railings. Norman Osprey backed away from him, his hose soft and useless in opposition, his Sunday pleasure no longer one long laugh.

Rose, the quarry of the dogs, turned tail and ignominiously left the scene through the gate into the lane, sliding through a small opening and pulling it shut behind her.

Trusting that the dogs knew me well enough to keep their fangs to themselves I walked among them and slid the bolts across on the wall-to-lane door, blocking Rose's immediate way back.

Gina screeched at Tom only once and without much

conviction, Tom's fierce physical closeness reducing her protests to nil. She was silent even when she discovered Tom's mode of entry had been to smash open her front door. She didn't try to stop her son when he ran past her along the passage from backyard to front, and called to me in the few steps before I reached the road.

Tom and the Dobermanns were already out on the pavement on their way back to the car.

I stopped at once when Victor called me, and waited until he came up. Either he would tell me or he wouldn't. Either the hose and tap had been worth it, or they hadn't. Pay-off time.

'Gerard . . .' He was out of breath, not from running but from what he'd seen in the yard. 'I can't bear all this. If you want to know . . . Dr Force lives in Lynton,' he said. 'Valley of the Rocks Road.'

'Thanks,' I said.

Victor unhappily watched me use tissues scrounged from his mother's kitchen to blot the oozing blood on my face. I said, 'There's always e-mail, don't forget.'

'How can you even speak to me?'

I grinned at him. 'I still have all my teeth.'

'Look out for Rose,' he warned me anxiously. 'She never gives up.'

'Try to arrange to live with your grandfather,' I suggested. 'It would be safer than here.'

Some of his misery abated. I touched his shoulder in parting and walked along Lorna Terrace to where Tom Pigeon waited.

Tom looked at my battered face and commented, 'You were a hell of a long time whistling.'

'Mm.' I smiled. 'Silly of me.'

'You delayed it on purpose!' he exclaimed in revelation. 'You let that harpy hit you.'

'You get what you pay for, on the whole,' I said.

Most bruises faded within a week, Martin had said; also, this time, I got a doctor on the Monday to stick together the worst of the cuts with small adhesive strips.

'I suppose you walked into another black-masked door,' guessed Constable Dodd, horrified. 'Rose may not frighten you but, from what I've heard, she'd terrify me.'

'Rose didn't bother about a mask,' I said, putting together a spicy rice supper on Monday evening in the kitchen of my house on the hill. 'Do you like garlic?'

'Not much. What are you planning to do about Rose Payne? You should go to the Taunton police and make a complaint against her for assault. That wound might even constitute GBH.'

Grievous Bodily Harm, I thought. Not half as grievous as she had intended.

'What would I tell them – a thin woman beat me up so a friend of mind with a criminal record smashed down her front door and set his dogs on her?'

She was not amused but simply repeated, 'So what are you going to do about her?'

I didn't answer directly. I said instead, 'Tomorrow I'm

going to Lynton in Devon and I'd rather she didn't know.' I frowned over a green pepper. 'It's a wise man as knows his enemies,' I asserted, 'and I do know our Rose.'

'In the biblical sense?'

'God forbid!'

'But Rose Payne is only one person,' Catherine said, drinking fizzy water routinely. 'There were four black-masks, you said.'

I nodded. 'Norman Osprey, bookmaker, he was Number Two, and Ed Payne, who was Martin Stukely's racecourse valet and is Rose's father, he was Number Three and he's sorry for it, and all those three know I recognized them. One other seemed familiar to me at the time but I can't have been right. He was a clutcher setting me up for the others and I think of him as Number Four. He was behind me most of the time.'

Catherine listened in silence and seemed to be waiting.

Skidding now and then across a half-formed recollection went the so far unidentified figure that I called simply Black-mask Four, and I remembered him most for the inhumanity he took to his task. It had been Norman Osprey who'd smashed my watch, but it had been Black-mask Four who'd bunched my fingers for him. For all Norman Osprey's awesome strength, in retrospect it was Black-mask Four who'd scared me most, and who now, nine days later, intruded fearsomely in my dreams, nightmares in which Black-mask Four intended to throw me into the 1,800 degrees Fahrenheit of the liquid glass in the tank in the furnace.

That night, while Constable Dodd slept peacefully in my arms, it was she whom Black-mask Four threw to a burning death.

I awoke sweating and cursing Rose Payne with words I'd rarely used before, and I felt more reluctant than ever to leave Catherine to the risks of her plain-clothes operation.

'Come back safe yourself this time,' she said worriedly, zooming off in the dawn, and I, with every intention of carrying out her instructions, walked down to my blameless furnace and did the day's work before my three helpers arrived.

The day before they had joked about my recurring Monday bruises, which Irish had sworn were the result of pub brawls. I hadn't disillusioned them, and on the Tuesday cheerfully left them practising dishes for the day while I walked out of the village for a mile to catch a bus.

Neither Rose nor Gina, nor anyone else I knew, came into sight, and I felt, when I disembarked outside a busy newsagents in the next town and climbed into another pre-arranged car with driver, that there could be no one on my tail. Tom Pigeon, who had designed 'the simple exit for glass-blowers', had begged me at least to take one of his dogs with me, if I wouldn't take *him*. Hadn't I been bashed enough? he asked. Hadn't I needed him to rescue me twice? Wasn't I now being insane to insist on travelling alone?

Yes, quite likely, I agreed. So give me advice.

Thanks to him, then, I went to Lynton on the north Devon coast unmolested, and in the electoral register found the full address of Dr Adam Force, in the Valley of the Rocks Road.

The chief disappointment to this successful piece of research was that there was no one in the house.

I knocked and rang and waited and tried again, but the tall grey old building had a dead air altogether and an empty-sounding reverberation when I tried the back door. The neighbours weren't helpful. One was out, and one was deeply deaf. A passing housewife said she thought Dr Force worked in Bristol during the week and only came to Lynton for the weekends. Not so, contradicted a shuffling old man angrily waving a walking stick, on Tuesdays Dr Force could be found up Hollerday Hill, at the nursing home.

The old man's anger, explained the housewife, was a form of madness. Dr Force went up to Hollerday Phoenix House every Tuesday, insisted the walking stick.

My driver – 'call me Jim' – long-sufferingly reversed and returned into the town's centre when the double bull's-eye more or less left us both laughing. Dr Force worked in Bristol half the time *and* opened up his Valley of the Rocks dreary house on Sundays and Mondays, *and* went up to Hollerday Phoenix House on Tuesdays. A small girl with plaited blonde hair pointed out the road to Hollerday Phoenix House, then told us not to go there because of the ghosts.

*Ghosts?*

The Phoenix House was haunted, didn't we know?

The town hall scoffed at the idea of ghosts, afraid of deterring holiday visitors in spring and summer.

That useful person 'A Spokesman' explained that the mansion, built by Sir George Newnes on Hollerday Hill, had been totally arsonized in 1913 by persons still unknown and later blown up as part of an army exercise. The Phoenix House recently built close to the grown-over ruins was a private nursing home. There were positively no ghosts. Dr Force had patients in the nursing home whom he visited on Tuesdays.

My driver, who believed in the supernatural, cravenly balked at driving up to the Hollerday Phoenix House, but swore he would wait for me to walk there and back, which I believed, as I hadn't yet paid him.

I thanked 'A Spokesman' for his help. And could he describe Dr Force, so I would know him if I saw him?

'Oh yes,' 'A Spokesman' said, 'you'd know him easily. He has very blue eyes, and a short white beard, and he'll be wearing orange socks.'

I blinked.

'He can't see red or green,' 'A Spokesman' said. 'He's colour blind.'

# CHAPTER SEVEN

I took the quiet old back way through the woods, climbing the overgrown, gently sloping carriage road that thoughtful Sir George Newnes had had blasted through rock to save his horses having to haul a coach up a heart-straining incline to his house.

On that January Tuesday I walked alone through the trees. Traffic motored sparsely along a modern road on the other side of the hill, raising not even a distant hum on its way to the new complex that had risen on the memory of the old.

There were no birds where I walked; no song. It was dark even in daylight, the close-growing evergreens crowding overhead. My feet trod noiselessly on fallen fir needles and in places there were still bare upright slabs of raw grey blasted rock. Atmospherically, the hundred-year-old path raised goosebumps. There were ruins of a tennis court where long ago people had laughed and played in another world. Eerie, I thought, was the word for it, but I saw no ghosts.

I came down to Hollerday Phoenix House from above,

as 'A Spokesman' had foretold, and saw that much of the roof was covered with large metal-framed panes of glass, which opened and closed like roofs of greenhouses. The glass, of course, interested me – it was thick float glass tinted to filter out ultra violet A and B rays of sunlight – and I thought of the departed days of sanatoria, where people with tuberculosis most unromantically coughed their lives away in the vain hope that airy sunshine would cure them.

Hollerday Phoenix House spread wide in one central block with two long wings. I walked round to the impressive front door and found that the building I entered at the conclusion of the spooky path was definitely of the twenty-first century, and in no way the haunt of apparitions.

The entrance hall looked like a hotel, but I saw no further into the nursing home's depths because of the two white-coated people leaning on the reception desk. One was female and the other grew a coat-coloured beard, and did indeed wear orange socks.

They glanced briefly my way as I arrived, then straightened with resigned professional interest when I presented with cuts and bruises that actually, until they peered at me, I had forgotten.

'Dr Force?' I tried, and White-Beard satisfactorily answered, 'Yes?'

His fifty-six years sat elegantly on his shoulders, and his well-brushed hair, along with the beard, gave him the sort of shape to his head that actors got paid for. Patients would trust him, I thought. I might have been pleased myself to have him on my case. His manner held authority in enough quantity to show me I was going to have difficulty jolting him the way I wanted.

Almost at once I saw, too, that the difficulty was not a matter of jolting him but of following the ins and outs of his mind. All through the time I was with him I felt him swing now and then from apparently genuine and friendly responses to evasion and stifled ill will. He was quick and he was clever, and although most of the time I felt a warm liking for him, occasionally there was a quick flash of antipathy. Powerfully attractive overall, the charm of Adam Force, it seemed to me, could flow in and out like a tide.

'Sir,' I said, giving seniority its due, 'I'm here on account of Martin Stukely.'

He put on a sorry-to-tell-you expression, and told me that Martin Stukely was dead. At the same time there was a rigidity of shock on his facial muscles: it wasn't a name he'd expected to hear up Hollerday Hill in Lynton. I said I knew Martin Stukely was dead.

He asked with suspicion, 'Are you a journalist?'

'No,' I said. 'A glass-blower.' I added my name, 'Gerard Logan.'

His whole body stiffened. He swallowed and absorbed the surprise and eventually asked pleasantly, 'What do you want?'

I said equally without threat, 'I'd quite like back the videotape you took from the Logan Glass showroom in Broadway on New Year's Eve.'

'You would, would you?' He smiled. He was ready for the question. He had no intention of complying, and was recovering his poise. 'I don't know what you are talking about.'

Dr Force made a slow survey from head to foot of my deliberately conservative suit and tie and I felt as positive as if he had said it aloud that he was wondering if I had enough clout to cause him trouble. Apparently he realistically gave himself an honest but unwelcome answer, as he suggested not that I buzz off straight away, but that we discuss the situation in the open air.

By open air, it transpired he meant the path I'd just ascended. He led that way and sneaked a sideways glance to measure my discomfort level, which was nil. I smiled and mentioned that I hadn't noticed any ghosts on the prowl on my way up.

Should he be aware of small damages to my face and so on, I said, it was as a result of Rose Payne being convinced that I either had his tape in my possession, or that I knew what was on it. 'She believes that if she's unpleasant enough, I'll give her the tape or the knowledge, neither of which I have.' I paused and said, 'What do you suggest?'

He said promptly, 'Give this person anything. All tapes are alike.'

'She thinks your tape is worth a million.'

Adam Force fell silent.

'Is it?' I asked.

Under his breath Force said what sounded like the truth, 'I don't know.'

'Martin Stukely,' I murmured without hostility, 'wrote a cheque for you with a lot of noughts on.'

Force, very upset, said sharply, 'He promised never to say – '

'He didn't say.'

'But – '

'He died,' I said. 'He left cheque stubs.'

I could almost feel him wondering '*What else* did Martin leave?' and I let him speculate. In the end, in genuine-looking worry, he said, 'How did you find me?'

'Didn't you think I would?'

He very briefly shook his head and faintly smiled. 'It didn't occur to me that you would bother to look. Most people would leave it to the police.'

He would have been easy to like all the time, I thought, if one could forget Lloyd Baxter's epileptic fit, and a missing bank bag full of money.

'Rose Payne,' I said distinctly again – and somewhere in Adam Force this time her name touched a sensitive reaction – 'Rose,' I repeated, 'is convinced I know where your videotape is and, as I said before, she is certain I know what's on it. Unless you find a way of rather literally getting her off my back I may find her attentions too much to tolerate and I'll tell her what she's anxious to know.'

He asked, as if he hadn't any real understanding of what I'd said, 'Are you implying that I know this person, Rose? And are you also implying that I am in some way responsible for your . . . er . . . injuries?'

I said cheerfully, 'Right both times.'

'That's nonsense.' His face was full of calculation as if he weren't sure how to deal with an awkward situation, but wouldn't rule out using his own name, Force.

On the brink of telling him why I reckoned I could answer my own questions I seemed to hear both Worthington and Tom Pigeon shrieking at me to be careful about sticks and wasps' nests. The silence of the dark fir wood shook with their urgent warnings. I glanced at the benevolent doctor's thoughtful face and changed my own expression to regret.

Shaking my head, I agreed with him that what I'd said was of course nonsense. 'All the same,' I added, after quizzically checking with my two absent bodyguards, 'you did take the tape from my shop, so please can you at least tell me where it is now?'

He relaxed inwardly a good deal at my change of tone. Worthington and Tom Pigeon went back to sleep. Dr Force consulted his own inner safeguards and answered the question unsatisfactorily.

'Just suppose you are right and I have the tape. As Martin could no longer keep the information safe, there was no longer any need for it. Perhaps, therefore, I ran it through to record a sports programme from first to last. That tape might now show horse racing and nothing else.'

He had written to Martin that the knowledge on the tape was dynamite. If he'd wiped the dynamite out with racing, boasting he'd poured millions down the drain (or past the recording head) he still surely had whatever he needed for a clone.

No one would casually wipe out a fortune if not sure he could bring it back. Nobody would do it *on purpose*, that was.

So I asked him, 'Did you obliterate it on purpose, or by mistake?'

He laughed inside the beard. He said, 'I don't make mistakes.'

The frisson I felt wasn't a winter shudder from a daunting fir wood but a much more prosaic recognition of a familiar and thoroughly human failing: for all his pleasant manner, the doctor thought he was God.

He stopped by a fallen fir trunk and briefly rested one foot on it, saying he would go back from there as he had patients to see. 'I find business is usually completed by this point,' he went on and his voice was dismissive, 'I'm sure you'll find your own way down to the gate.'

'There are just a couple of things,' I said. My voice sounded flat, the acoustics dead between the trees.

He took his foot off the log and started to go back up the hill. To his obvious irritation I went with him.

'I said,' he commented with a stab at finality, 'that we'd completed our conversation, Mr Logan.'

'Well . . .' I hesitated, but Worthington and Tom

Pigeon were quiet and there wasn't even a squeak from the dogs, 'how did you get to know Martin Stukely?'

He said calmly, 'That's none of your business.'

'You knew each other but you weren't close friends.'

'Didn't you hear me?' he protested. 'This is not your concern.'

He quickened his step a little, as if to escape.

I said, 'Martin gave you a large chunk of money in return for the knowledge that you referred to as dynamite.'

'No, you're wrong.' He walked faster, but I kept up easily with him stride for stride. 'You completely do not understand,' he said, 'and I want you to leave.'

I said I feared I had no intention of leaving any time soon, now that I saw beside me the likely answer to multiple riddles.

'Did you know,' I asked him, 'that Lloyd Baxter, the man you abandoned to his epileptic fit in my showroom, is the owner of Tallahassee, the horse that killed Martin Stukely?'

He walked faster up the slope. I stayed close, accelerating.

'Did you know,' I asked conversationally, 'that in spite of the onset of an epileptic seizure, Lloyd Baxter was able to describe you down to the socks?'

'Stop it.'

'And of course you know Norman Osprey and Rose and Gina are as violent as they come . . .'

'No.' His voice was loud, and he coughed.

'And as for my money that you whipped with that tape . . .'

Adam Force quite suddenly stopped walking altogether, and in the stillness I could clearly hear his breath wheezing in his chest.

It alarmed me. Instead of pretty well bullying him, I asked him anxiously if he were all right.

'No, thanks to you.' The wheezing continued until he pulled from a pocket in his white coat the sort of inhaler I'd often seen used for asthma. He took two long puffs, breathing deeply while staring at me with complete dislike.

I was tempted to say 'Sorry', but in spite of his charming ways and pleasant looks he'd been the cause of my being chucked to both the black-masks in Broadway and to a piece of hosepipe in a Taunton backyard, and if that were all, I'd count myself lucky. So I let him wheeze and puff his way up the rest of the incline. I went with him to make sure he didn't collapse on the way, and inside the reception area I checked him into a comfortable chair and went to find someone to pass him on to, for safe keeping.

I heard his wheezy voice behind me demanding my return, but by then I'd hurried halfway down one of the wings of the building and seen no human being at all, whether nurse, patient, doctor, cleaner, flower-arranger or woman pushing a trolley of books. It wasn't that there weren't any beds in the rooms that lined the wing. In all the rooms there were beds, tray tables, armchairs and bathrooms off, but no people. Each room had glass French doors opening to a well-swept area of paving stones. Parts of the glass roof above were as wide open as they would go.

I stopped briefly at a room marked 'Pharmacy' which had an open skylight and a locked door of openwork grating to the passage. There was a host of visibly named pharmacy items inside, but still no people.

There had to be someone *somewhere*, I thought, and through the only closed door, at the end of the wing, I found a comparative bee-hive coming and going.

Twenty or more elderly men and women in thick white towelling bathrobes appeared to be contentedly taking part in comprehensive medical assessments, each test being brightly presented in play-school lettering, like 'Your blood pressure measured here' and 'Where does your cholesterol stand today?' A very old lady walked fast on 'a jolly treadmill', and on the wall of a separate hard-sided booth was the notice 'X-rays here. Please keep out unless asked to step in.'

Results were carefully written onto clipboards and then filed into computers at a central desk. An air of optimism prevailed.

My entrance brought to my side a nurse who'd been drawing curtains round a cubicle simply called Urology. Squeaking across a polished floor on rubber soles she smilingly told me I was late, and said only 'Oh dear' when I mentioned that the good Dr Force might be gasping his last.

'He often does have attacks when he has visitors,' the motherly nurse confided. 'When you've gone I expect he'll lie down and have a sleep.'

The good Dr Force was planning nothing of the sort. Registering annoyance like a steaming boiler, he wheezed to my side and pointed to a door coyly labelled 'Here it is', then 'Way out, too.' I explained, as if harmlessly, that I'd only come to find help for his asthma and he replied crossly that he didn't need it. He walked towards me with a syringe in a metal dish, advancing until I could see it almost full of liquid. He picked up the highly threatening syringe and then jabbed it towards me and the exit; and this time I thanked him for his attention and left.

The door out of the medical examination hall led past lavish changing rooms to a generous lobby, and from there to a forecourt outside.

Unexpectedly I found the Rover waiting there, Jim my driver nervously pacing up and down beside it. He held the door open for me while explaining that his concern for my welfare had overcome his natural instincts. I thanked him with true feeling.

Dr Force followed me out and waited until I was in the car and went indoors only after I'd given him a cheerfully innocent farewell wave, which he did not return.

'Is that the guy you came to see?' asked Jim.

'Yes.'

'Not very friendly, is he?'

I couldn't identify exactly what was wrong with that

place, and was little further enlightened when a large coach turned smoothly through the entrance gate and came to a gentle halt. The name, *Avon Paradise Tours*, read black and white on lilac along the coach's sides, with smaller letters underneath giving an address in Clifton, Bristol.

Jim drove rapidly downhill until we had returned to, in his eyes, the unsupernatural safety of the town centre. He did agree, though, subject to no further mention of things that go bump in the night, to drive round Lynton simply to enjoy it as a visitor.

Truth to tell, I was dissatisfied with myself on many counts and I wanted time to think before we left. I badly missed having my own car and the freedom it allowed, but there it was. I had indeed broken the speed limit often and got away with it before I'd been caught on the way to the dying gardener, and I could see that if policewoman Catherine Dodd had a permanent toe in my future, I would have to ration my foot on the accelerator.

Meanwhile, I persuaded Jim to stop in a side road. From there, town-hall map in hand, I found my way to North Walk, a path round the seaward side of a grassy cliff, cold in the January wind and more or less deserted.

There were benches at intervals. I sat for a while on one and froze, and thought about the Adam Force who was colour blind, asthmatic, volatile and changeable in nature, and who visited an obscure nursing home only to do good. A minor practitioner, it seemed, though with a string of qualifications and a reputation for sparkling research. A man wasting his skills. A man who took a visitor outside to talk on a noticeably cold day and gave himself an asthmatic attack.

I trudged slowly round, soaking up the spectacular views of the North Walk, wishing for summer. I thought of inconsequential things like coincidence and endurance and videotapes that were worth a million and could save the world. I also thought of the jewel I had made of glass and gold that not only looked truly old, but couldn't be distinguished from a 3,500-year-old original. A necklace worth a million . . . but only one had that value, the genuine antiquity in a museum. The copy I had made once and could make again would be literally and only worth its weight in 18 carat gold, plus the cost of its coloured glass components, and as much again, perhaps, for the knowledge and ability it took to make it.

Like many an artist of any sort, it was to my own self alone that I could admit to the level I'd reached in my trade. It was also thanks to my Uncle Ron's embargo on arrogance that I let the things I made achieve birth without trumpets.

That the existence of the videotape explaining how to make the necklace was common knowledge among jockeys in the changing rooms didn't trouble me. I'd made it myself. It had my voice and hands on it, describing and demonstrating step by step what to do. I'd recorded it the way my Uncle Ron had taught me in my teens. The actual gold necklace I'd made was in my bank where I normally kept the tape as well. I'd better check on that,

I supposed. I'd lent the instruction tape to Martin, of course, and didn't care if he'd shown it to anyone else, although I dearly wished he had returned it before it disappeared, along with all the others from his den.

I made a fairly brisk return to the end of the Walk to find Jim striding up and down again and trying to warm his fingers. I thought perhaps he might not want to double the experience on the following day, but to my surprise, he agreed. 'Tom Pigeon'll set his dogs on me if I don't,' he said. 'He phoned me just now in the car to check on you.'

I swallowed a laugh. I prized those bodyguards, not resented them.

Jim apologized for not being in the same class as Worthington and Tom at kick-boxing.

'I can bash heads against walls,' he said.

I smiled and said that would do fine.

'I didn't know anything about you when I picked you up,' Jim confessed. 'I thought you were some useless sort of git. Then Tom tells me this and that on the phone and where Tom says he'll put his fists, you can count on mine.'

'Well, thanks,' I said weakly.

'So where do we go tomorrow?'

I said, 'How does Bristol grab you? A hospital area, best of all?'

He smiled broadly, transforming his face in one second from dour to delighted. He knew his way round Bristol. Up Horfield Road we would find a hospital, or on

Commercial Road down by the river. No problem at all. He'd driven an ambulance there one year, he said.

Jim said to count him out when it came to fists or feet, but no one could catch him in a car. We shook hands on it, and I acquired bodyguard number three, one who could slide round corners faster than Formula One.

Jim took me home and, apparently on Tom Pigeon's urging, came indoors with me and checked all ten rooms for uninvited occupants.

'You need a smaller pad,' he judged, finishing the inspection of the window locks. 'Or . . .' he looked sideways, 'a swarm of children.'

Catherine arrived at that moment on her motor bike. The driver gave her a leer, and I had to explain . . . a swarm of children. Constable Dodd seemed not to think it a bad idea.

Much amused, the driver left. Catherine fussed over my fresher crop of trouble and said she'd been bored by the class reunion from registration to wrap.

I said, 'Next time ditch the boredom and come home.'

The words slid out as if on their own. I hadn't intended to say 'home'. I'd been going simply to offer the house as a refuge. I explained. She nodded. It was later, holding her in bed, that I thought of Sigmund Freud and his tell-tale slip.

*

Bristol was wet with drizzle.

My driver – 'Call me Jim' – was short and stout and pronounced himself shocked that I preferred quiet in the car to perpetual radio.

Quite reasonably he asked where were we going exactly in the city. To find a phone book, I replied, and in the *Yellow Pages* singled out Avon Paradise Tours without trouble. They advertised that they operated adventures throughout Cornwall, Devon and Somerset and all points to London.

Jim, with his ambulance memory, more useful than any paper map, drove us unerringly to their lilac headquarters and with a flamboyant gesture drew the busy bus depot to my attention like a rabbit from an abracadabra top hat.

Once they understood what I was asking, the women in the Avon Paradise Tours office were moderately helpful but reluctant to say too much in case they broke house rules.

I did understand, didn't I?

I did.

They then opened the harmless floodgates and told me all.

On Tuesdays, members of a Bristol area Health Clubs Association went on a scenic coach tour to the Hollerday Phoenix House nursing home in Lynton for medical check-ups and advice on healthy living. Dr Force, who ran the clinic because he lived in Lynton, was paid jointly by the health clubs and Avon Paradise Tours for his one day's work per week. After extra consultation together, the office staff admitted they'd been told Dr Force had been *let* go (given the sack, did I understand?) by the research lab he used to work for.

Which research lab? They didn't know. They shook their heads in general, but one of them said she'd heard he'd been working on illnesses of the lungs.

Another phone book – listing all things medical – borrowed from the Avon Paradise ladies, had me trying all the remotely possible establishments, asking them via Paradise Tours phone if they knew a Dr Force. Dr Force? Unknown, unknown, unknown. The forever unknown Dr Force had me looking out of the window at the distant sheen of the River Avon at high tide and wondering what to try next.

Illnesses of the lungs.

Cheque stubs. A lot of zeros. The payee . . . Bellows. In Martin's handwriting, it had meant nothing to Bon-Bon and nothing to me.

There wasn't any listing for Bellows in the Bristol area phone book, nor had Directory Enquiries ever heard of it.

Martin, though, had written BELLOWS boldly in unmistakable capital letters.

Lungs were bellows, of course.

My mind drifted. Rain spattered on the window. The ladies began to fidget, implying I'd overstayed my time.

BELLOWS.

Well . . . maybe, why not?

Abruptly I asked if I might borrow their office telephone again and with their by now rather grudging permission I spelled out BELLOWS in phone dial numbers, which resulted in 235 5697. I punched them in carefully. There was nothing to lose.

After a long wait through maybe a dozen rings I was about to give up, when a brisk female voice hurriedly spoke, 'Yes? Who is that?'

'Could I speak to Dr Force, please,' I said.

A long silence ensued. I was about to disconnect and call it a waste of time when another voice, deep and male, enquired if I were the person asking for Dr Force.

'Yes,' I said. 'Is he there?'

'Very sorry. No. He left several weeks ago. Can I have your name?'

I wasn't sure how to answer. I was beginning to learn caution. I said I would phone back very soon, and clicked off. To the Paradise ladies' curiosity, I offered only profound thanks and left promptly, taking Jim in tow.

'Where to?' he asked.

'A pub for lunch.'

Jim's face lightened like a cloudless dawn. 'You're the sort of customer I can drive for all day.'

In the event he drank one half-pint of lemonade shandy, which was my idea of a good hired driver.

The pub had a pay phone. When we were on the point of leaving I dialled BELLOWS again and found the male voice answering me at once.

He said, 'I've been talking to Avon Paradise Tours.'

I said, smiling, 'I thought you might. You probably have this pub's public phone booth's number in front of your eyes at the moment. To save time, why don't we meet? You suggest somewhere and I'll turn up.'

I repeated to Jim the place suggested, and got a nod of recognition. 'Thirty minutes,' Jim said, and twenty-two minutes later he stopped the car in a no-waiting zone near the gate of a wintry public park. Against the united teaching of Worthington, Tom Pigeon and Jim not to go anywhere unknown without one of them close, I got out of the car, waved Jim to drive on, and walked into the park on my own.

The drizzly rain slowly stopped.

The instructions for the meeting had been 'Turn left, proceed to statue', and along the path, by a prancing copper horse, I met a tall, civilized, sensible-looking man who established to his own satisfaction that I was the person he expected.

# CHAPTER EIGHT

He spoke as if to himself. 'He's six feet tall, maybe an inch or two more. Brown hair. Dark eyes. Twenty-eight to thirty-four years, I'd say. Personable except for recent injury to right side of jaw which has been medically attended to and is healing.'

He was talking into a small microphone held in the palm of his hand. I let him see that I understood that he was describing me in case I attacked him in any fashion. The notion that I might do that would have made me laugh on any other day.

'He arrived in a grey Rover.' He repeated Jim's registration number and then described my clothes.

When he stopped I said, 'He's a glass-blower named Gerard Logan and can be found at Logan Glass, Broadway, Worcestershire. And who are you?'

He was the voice on the telephone. He laughed at my dry tone and stuffed the microphone away in a pocket. He gave himself a name, George Lawson-Young, and a title, Professor of Respiratory Medicine.

'And 235 5697?' I asked. 'Does it have an address?'

Even with modern technology he didn't know how I'd found him.

'Old-fashioned perseverance and guesswork,' I said. 'I'll tell you later in return for the gen on Adam Force.'

I liked the professor immediately, feeling none of the reservations that had troubled me with Force. Professor Lawson-Young had no ill will that I could see, but on the contrary let his initial wariness slip away. My first impression of good humour and solid sense progressively strengthened, so that when he asked what my interest was in Adam Force I told him straightforwardly about Martin's promise to keep safe Dr Force's tape.

'Martin wanted me to keep it for him instead,' I said, 'and when he died the tape came into my hands. Force followed me to Broadway and took his tape back again, and I don't know where it is.'

Out on the road, Jim in the grey Rover drove slowly by, his pale face through the window on watch on my behalf.

'I came with a bodyguard,' I said, waving reassurance to the road.

Professor Lawson-Young, amused, confessed he had only to yell down his microphone for assistance to arrive at once. He seemed as glad as I was that he would not have to use it. His tight muscles loosened. My own Worthington-Pigeon-driven alertness went to sleep.

The professor said, 'How did you cut your face so deeply?'

I hesitated. What I'd done in the backyard of 19 Lorna

Terrace sounded too foolish altogether. Because I didn't reply Lawson-Young asked again with sharper interest, pressing for the facts like any dedicated news man. I said undramatically that I'd been in a fight and come off worst.

He asked next what I'd been fighting about, and with whom, his voice full of the authority that he no doubt needed in his work.

Evading the whole truth I gave him at least a part of it. 'I wanted to find Dr Force, and in the course of doing that I collided with a water tap. Clumsy, I'm afraid.'

He looked at me intently with his head on one side. 'You're lying to me, I'm sorry to say.'

'Why do you think so?'

'It's unusual to fight a water tap.'

I gave him a half-strength grin. 'OK then, I got hit with one that was still on a hose-pipe. It's unimportant. I learned how to find Adam Force, and I talked to him yesterday in Lynton.'

'Where in Lynton? In that new nursing home?'

'Phoenix House.' I nodded. 'Dr Force's clinic looks designed for children.'

'Not for children. For mentally handicapped patients. He does good work there with the elderly, I'm told.'

'They seemed pretty happy, it's true.'

'So what's your take-away opinion?'

I gave it without much hesitation. 'Force is utterly charming when he wants to be, and he's also a bit of a crook.'

'Only a bit?' The professor sighed. 'Adam Force was in charge here of a project aimed at abolishing snoring by using fine optical fibres and microlasers . . .' He briefly stopped. 'I don't want to bore you . . .'

My own interest however had awoken sharply as in the past I'd designed and made glass equipment for that sort of enquiry. When I explained my involvement, the professor was in his turn astonished. He enlarged into detail the work that Force had been busy with and had stolen.

'We'd been experimenting with shining a microlaser down a fine optical fibre placed in the soft tissues of the throat. The microlaser gently warms the tissues, which stiffens them, and that stops a person from snoring. What Adam Force stole was our results of the trials to find the optimum laser light wavelength needed to penetrate the tissues and heat them to the precise temperature necessary . . . Do you follow?'

'More or less.'

He nodded. 'A reliable way of abolishing snoring would be invaluable for severe sufferers. Adam Force stole such data and sold it to a firm of marketers whose business it is to advertise and inform prospective buyers of goods available. Force sold our latest but incomplete data to people we had dealt with occasionally before and who had no reason to suspect anything was wrong. Adam produced the right paperwork. It was weeks before the theft was discovered and really no one could believe it when we went to the marketers and they told us they had already bought the material and paid Adam Force for what we were now trying to sell them.'

'So you sacked him,' I commented.

'Well, we should have. He must have thought we might, but he was crucial to our research programme.' The professor however looked regretful, not enraged.

I said, 'Let me guess, basically you let him off. You didn't prosecute him because you all liked him so much.'

Lawson-Young ruefully nodded. 'Adam apologized more or less on his knees and agreed to pay the money back in instalments, if we didn't take him to court.'

'And did he?'

In depression the professor said, 'He paid on the dot for two months, and then we found he was trying to sell some even more secret information . . . and I mean *priceless* information in world terms—' He stopped abruptly, apparently silenced by the enormity of Adam Force's disloyalty.

Eventually he went on, 'He repaid us for our generosity by stealing the most recent, the most dynamite-laden data in our whole laboratory, and we are certain that he is offering this work to the highest bid he can raise around the world. This is the information recorded on the tape Force took back from you, and it is this tape we have been praying you would find.'

I said with incredulity, 'But you didn't know that I existed.'

'We did know you existed, our investigators have been

very diligent. But we weren't sure you hadn't been indoctrinated by Adam, like your friend Stukely.'

'*Martin?*'

'Oh yes. Force can be utterly charming and persuasive, as you know. We think it likely he also swindled Stukely of a fairly large sum of money, saying it was to be applied to our research.'

'But,' I protested, 'Martin wasn't a fool.'

'It is quite likely that Stukely had no idea that the contents of the tape had been stolen. Believe me, you don't need to be a fool to be taken in by a con man. I wouldn't consider myself a fool, but he took *me* in. I treated him as a friend.'

I said, 'Where did Martin meet Dr Force? I don't suppose you know.'

'I actually do. They met at a fund-raising dinner for cancer research. Adam Force was there raising money on behalf of the charity, and Stukely was there as a guest of a man for whom he raced, who was also a patron of the charity. I too as it happens am a patron, and I also saw Martin Stukely briefly on that evening.'

I vaguely remembered Martin mentioning the dinner but hadn't paid much attention. It was typical of Martin, though, to make friends in unexpected places. I had myself, after all, met him in a jury room.

After a while Lawson-Young said, 'We searched absolutely everywhere for proof that Adam had in his possession material that belonged to the laboratory. We know . . . we're ninety per cent certain . . . that he recorded every relevant detail onto the videotape which he entrusted to the care of Martin Stukely.'

There was nothing, I heard with relief, about trying to make me reveal its whereabouts through the use of black-mask methods or threats of unmerciful dentistry. I was aware, though, that the former tension in the professor's muscles had returned, and I wondered if he thought I was fooling him, as Adam Force had done.

I said simply, 'Force has the tape. Ask him. But yesterday he told me he'd recorded a sports programme on top of your formulae and conclusions, and all that remained on the tape now was horse racing.'

'Oh God.'

I said, 'I don't know that I believe him.'

After a few moments the professor said, 'How often can you tell if someone's lying?'

'It depends who they are and what they're lying about.'

'Mm,' he said.

I glanced back in my mind to a long line of half-truths, my own included.

'Discard the lies,' George Lawson-Young said, smiling, 'and what you're left with is probably the truth.'

After a while he repeated, 'We've searched absolutely *everywhere* for proof that Adam had in his possession material that belongs to the laboratory. We believe that he recorded every relevant detail onto the videotape because one of our researchers thought he saw him doing it, but as he works in an altogether different field he believed Adam when he said he was making routine notes. Adam himself entrusted a tape into the care of Martin Stukely at Cheltenham races. When Stukely died, we learned from asking around that his changing-room valet had passed the tape on to Stukely's friend, as previously planned.' He paused. 'So as you are the friend, will you tell us where best to look for the missing tape? Better still, bring it to us yourself . . . as we believe you can.'

I said baldly, 'I can't. I think Force has it.'

Lawson-Young shivered suddenly in the cold damp wind, and my own thoughts had begun to congeal. I proposed that we found somewhere warmer if we had more to say and the professor, after cogitation and consultation with his microphone, offered me a visit to his laboratory, if I should care to go.

Not only would I like to go, I felt honoured to be asked, a reaction clearly visible on my face from the professor's own return expression. His trust, however, didn't reach as far as stepping into my car, so he went in one which arrived smoothly from nowhere, and I followed with Jim.

The professor's research laboratory occupied the ground floor of a fairly grand nineteenth-century town house with a pillared entrance porch. Antiquity stopped right there on the doorstep: everything behind the front door belonged to the future.

George Lawson-Young, very much the professor on his own turf, introduced me to his team of young research doctors whose chief if not only interest in my existence lay in my having long ago invented a way of making perfect glass joins between tiny tubes of differing diameters so that liquid or gases would move at a desired speed from one tube to the next.

They hadn't much else of my work there, but the words 'Logan Glass' etched on mini pipettes and a few specialized test tubes got me accepted as a sort of practitioner rather than simply a sightseer. Anyway, my ability to identify things like vacutaires, cell separators, tissue culture chambers and distillation flasks meant that when I asked what exactly had been stolen the second time by Adam Force, I got told.

'Actually, we now think there was a third thing,' a young woman in a white coat murmured sorrowfully. 'It seems likely that he also took out of here the formula of our new asthma drug aimed at preventing permanent scar tissue occurring on the airways of chronic asthmatics. Only recently did we realize what had happened, as, at the time, of course, we believed his assurances that he was borrowing some finished work from last year.'

The nods all round were indulgent. In spite of all, there were friendly faces for Adam Force. It was the professor himself, whose eyes had opened, who told me finally what I'd been in need of knowing all along.

'The videotape made and stolen by Adam Force showed the formation of a particular tissue culture and its ingredients. The tissue culture was of cancer cells of the commoner sorts of cancer like that of the lung and the breast. They were concerned with the development of genetic mutations that render the cancer cell lines more sensitive to common drugs. All common cancers may be curable once the mutated gene is implanted into people who already have the cancer. The tape probably also shows photographs of the chromatography of the different components of the cancer cell genetic constituents. It is very complicated. At first sight it looks like rubbish, except to the educated eye. It is, unfortunately, quite likely anyone might override the "don't record on top of this" tab.'

He lost me halfway through the technical details, but I at least understood that the tape that could save the world contained the cure for a host of cancers.

I asked the professor, 'Is this for real?'

'It's a significant step forward,' he said.

I pondered, 'But if Force is going around asking millions for it, is it worth millions?'

Sombrely, Lawson-Young said, 'We don't know.'

Adam Force had said the same thing, 'I don't know.' Not a lie, it seemed, but a statement that the process hadn't yet been extensively tested. The tape was a record of a possibility, or of an almost certainty whose worth was still a gamble.

I said, 'But you do have back-up copies of everything that's on that tape, don't you? Even if the tape itself should now show horse racing?'

Almost as if he were surrendering to an inevitable execution, the professor calmly stated the guillotine news.

'Before he left with the videotape, Adam destroyed all our at present irreplaceable records. We *need* that tape, and I hope to God you're right that he's lying. It's two years' work. Others are working along these lines, and we would be beaten to the breakthrough. We'd more likely *lose* the millions we might have earned.'

Into a short silence the telephone buzzed. George Lawson-Young picked up the receiver, listened, and mutely handed it to me. The caller was Jim in a high state of fuss.

He said with lively alarm, 'That medic you saw yesterday, the one with the white beard?'

'Yes?'

'He's here in the street.'

'Bugger . . . what's he doing?'

'Waiting. He's in a car parked fifty yards up the road, facing towards you, and there's a big bruiser sitting next to him. He's got another car waiting and facing towards you, but coming the other way. It's classic squeeze set-up, with you in the middle. So, what do you want me to do?'

'Where exactly are you?' I asked. 'To reach you, do I turn left or right?'

'Left. I'm four cars in front of White-Beard, pointing towards the door you went in at. I'm parked there, but there's a traffic warden creeping about. I'm on double yellow lines here, which White-Beard isn't, and I can't afford any more parking tickets, it's not good for my business.'

'Stay on the yellow lines,' I said. 'Move only if you have to, because of the warden. Dr Force saw you and your car yesterday. It can't be helped.'

Jim's voice rose, 'White-Beard's got out of his car. What shall I do? *He's coming this way . . .*'

'Jim,' I said flatly, 'don't panic. Also don't look at Dr Force if he comes near you, and don't open the window. Keep on talking to me, and if you have anything near you that you can read, read it aloud to me now.'

'Jeez.'

Lawson-Young's eyebrows were up by his hairline.

I said to him, 'Adam Force is in the road outside here, alarming my driver.' And I didn't say that on our last encounter the doctor had seen me off with a poisonous-looking syringe.

Jim's voice wobbled in my ear with the opening paragraphs of the Rover's instruction manual and then rose again an octave as he said, 'He's outside my window, he's rapping on it. Mr Logan, what shall I do?'

'Keep on reading.'

I gave the receiver to the professor and asked him to continue listening, and without wasting time I hurried from the part of the laboratory where we'd been standing, along the hallway and out into the street. Along to my left, Adam Force stood in the roadway tapping hard on the window of the grey Rover on the driver's side and clearly getting agitated at the lack of response from Jim.

I walked fast along the pavement, and then, strolling the last part, crossed the road and came up quietly behind

Dr White-Beard and, as I'd done to Victor on Taunton station, said, 'Hello,' at his shoulder.

Worthington and Tom Pigeon wouldn't have approved. Adam Force spun round in astonishment.

'Are you looking for me?' I asked.

Inside the car, Jim, in great agitation, was stabbing with his finger towards the lab's front door and the road beyond. Traffic in this secondary road was light, but one of the approaching cars, Jim was indicating to me, was ultra bad news.

'Adam Force,' I said loudly, 'is too well known in this street,' and with total lack of complicated advance planning, and with unadulterated instinct, I grabbed the charming doctor by the wrist, spun him round and ended with him standing facing the oncoming car with his arm twisted up behind him, held in the strongest grip resulting from years of manoeuvring heavy molten glass.

Adam Force yelled, at first with pain and then, also, with bargaining surrender. 'You're hurting me. Don't do it. I'll tell you everything. Don't do it . . . God . . . Let me go, *please*.'

In between the two phases, from defiance to entreaty, a small object fell from the hand I'd gripped. It lay in the gutter quite close to a storm-drain grating, and I'd have paid it no attention were it not for Force trying hard to kick it down through the grating into the sewer, to be forever lost.

I didn't know what he meant when he said 'everything',

but I didn't in the least mind learning. He screeched again under my jerking pressure and I wondered whatever Professor Lawson-Young was making of it, if he were still listening. The advancing car stopped at the sight of Adam Force's predicament and the four cars behind it exercised their horns, the drivers impatient, not knowing what was going on.

'Everything,' I prompted Force from behind his ear.

'Rose,' he began, and then thought better of it. Rose would frighten anyone.

I jerked his arm fiercely to encourage him and, with some dismay, I saw the big bruiser now lumbering out of his car to come to his aid, to be Norman Osprey, with his gorilla-type shoulder development. Over my shoulder I could see the second car of the classic squeeze moving towards me. In consequence of these unwelcome surprises I jerked my captive's arm yet again, then feared to break or dislocate his shoulder. There were tears of real pain in the doctor's eyes.

Imploring for release, he half said, half sobbed, desperately, 'I got the cyclopropane gas for Rose . . . I took it from the clinic's pharmacy . . . I can't see red from green, but I'm sure of orange . . . now let me go.'

It was hard to hear him distinctly because of the street noises and the blaring horns, and his 'everything' only confirmed what had already seemed likely, but I kept the pressure on just long enough for him to shriek out the answer I badly wanted to the question, 'How come you know Rose?'

To him it seemed unimportant. He answered impatiently, 'Her sister Gina came with her mother-in-law to my clinic. I met Rose at Gina's house.'

Satisfied, I was faced with a fast, unharmed disengagement. The cars had advanced until they were radiator to radiator and going nowhere and blocking the street. The driver of the second was hurriedly disembarking, and to my horror, I saw that it was Rose. Uninvolved cars made a constant cacophony. The busy traffic warden, notebook to the ready, spotted the fracas from a distance and veered back towards Jim and his yellow lines infringement.

Norman Osprey, a mountain on the move, charged towards Force and myself to release the doctor and maybe continue with the entertainment Tom Pigeon and his dogs had interrupted in Broadway.

Not seeing anything except straight ahead, the traffic warden and Norman the bookmaker bumped into each other violently which slowed their pace and purpose while they cursed their mutual carelessness.

Jim unhelpfully kept his eyes fixed faithfully down on his instruction manual, as I'd told him, and went on steadfastly reading.

I tried screaming at him to gain his attention, but uselessly, and in the end I let out the loudest possible London-rain taxi whistle, which pierced even Jim's concentration.

'Window,' I shouted.

He at last understood, but it took him aeons to switch on the ignition and press the window-lowering button.

Rose started running. The traffic warden unwound herself from Norman Osprey. Car horns deafened because of the blockage of the highway.

I shouted at my driver, 'Jim, get the car out of here. I'll phone you.'

Jim suddenly proved his stunt-driving skills weren't a rumour. With not much more than two hand spans' clearance, he locked the wheels of his Rover and circled like a circus horse, bumping over the pavement, brushing me and my captive strongly out of the way with the rear wing and leaving us standing where the car had been, with the white-bearded doctor no longer in agony but still not going anywhere while I held him gripped. Jim's tail-light flashed briefly at the first corner as he slid round it and left the scene.

Everyone else seemed to be running and shouting to no real purpose. I let go of Force's wrist while at the same time shoving him heavily into the joint arms of the warden and Osprey, with a bounce-off weight that unbalanced them all.

In that disorganized few seconds I bent down, scooped up the small object Force had dropped and *ran*, ran as if sprinting off the starting blocks on an athletics track. It was only the unexpectedness of my speed, I thought, that made the difference. I ran, dodging cars and irate drivers, swerving round Rose's grasp like a player evading tackles in a rugby match, and believing – making myself believe – that I was fit enough to out-run them all, so long as no busybody stranger tripped me up.

I didn't have to test fate too much. The front door of the laboratory house swung open ahead of me, with George Lawson-Young, still with the telephone clutched in his hand, coming out under the pillared porch, looking my way and beckoning me to safety. I fairly bolted through the heavy shining black-painted door, and ended breathless and laughing in his hall.

He closed the door. 'I can't see what there is to laugh about,' he said.

'Life's a toss-up.'

'And today it came up heads?'

I *liked* the professor. I grinned and held out to him the small object I'd salvaged from the gutter, asking him with moderate urgency, 'Can you find out what this contains?'

He looked with shock at what I'd brought him, and I nodded as if in confirmation that I'd got it right. He asked a shade austerely if I knew what he was with great care holding.

'Yes. It's a sort of syringe. You can put the needle into any liquid drug and suck it into the bubble,' I said. 'Then you push the needle into the patient and squeeze the bubble to deliver the drug. Vets sometimes use them on horses that are upset by the sight of an ordinary hypodermic syringe.'

He said, 'You're right. You seem to know a lot about it.'

'I was with Martin once . . .' I broke off. So much of my life seemed to have touched Martin's.

Lawson-Young made no comment about Martin but

said, 'These little syringes can be used too on manic patients, to make them manageable and calm them down.'

Phoenix House treated patients with mental illnesses. Adam Force had access to a well-stocked pharmacy.

George Lawson-Young turned away from me and, holding the tiny balloon with great care, led the way back to that part of the laboratory that held the gas chromatograph.

The thumb-nail sized balloon was still full of liquid, and was also wet outside from lying in the gutter. George Lawson-Young laid it carefully in a dish and asked one of his young doctors to identify the baby balloon's contents as soon as possible.

'Should it be one of several forms of poison,' he warned me, 'it might be impossible to find out what it is.'

'It surely had to be something already in the Phoenix House pharmacy,' I said. 'It was only yesterday afternoon that I met Force. He hadn't much time to mobilize anything too fancy.'

The balloon's contents raised little but smiles.

It took the young research doctor barely ten minutes to come back with an identification. 'It's insulin,' he said confidently. 'Plain ordinary insulin, as used by diabetics.'

'Insulin!' I exclaimed, disappointed. 'Is that all?'

Both the young research doctor and the professor smiled indulgently. The professor said, 'If you have diabetes, the amount of insulin in that syringe might send you into a permanent coma. If you *don't* have diabetes, there's enough to kill you.'

'To *kill*?'

'Yes, certainly,' Lawson-Young nodded. 'That amount is a lethal dose. It's reasonable to suppose it was intended for you, not your chauffeur; but I can hardly believe it of Adam.' He sounded shattered. 'We knew he'd steal, but to kill . . .' He shook his head. 'Are you *sure* that syringe came from him? You didn't just find it lying in the road?'

'I'm positive he was holding it in his hand and I dislodged it.'

The professor and I by that time were sitting on swivelling chairs in the professor's personal office-like room section of the laboratory.

'Actually,' I murmured, 'the big question is *why*?'

George Lawson-Young couldn't say.

'Do me a favour,' he finally begged. 'Start from the beginning.'

'I will phone my driver first.'

I used my mobile. When Jim answered his car-phone he sounded, first, relieved that I was free and talking to him, and second, anxious that he was going to be late home for his wife's risotto, and third, worried about where he was going to find me safe and on my own. I was glad enough that he proposed to wait for me. The professor, taking my mobile, gave Jim pin-pointing instructions for one hour's time, and suggested to me that I waste none of it.

'It's a tale of two tapes,' I tentatively began.

'Two?' said the professor.

'Yes, two,' I replied, but then hesitated.

'Do go on, then.' The professor was in a natural hurry.

'One was filmed here and stolen by Adam Force,' I said. 'He persuaded Martin Stukely to keep it safe for him, so that it couldn't be found.'

'We obtained a Search and Seizure Order from the Courts, and had already started searching everywhere for it,' said Lawson-Young, 'including in Adam's own home, but we didn't ever think of it being in the care of a jockey.'

'That must be why he did it,' I said. 'But as I understand it, Martin thought Force's tape would be safer still with me, a friend who hasn't four inquisitive children.' And no talkative or quarrelsome wife, I could have added. But, I thought, would Martin have really given me the tape if he knew the contents were stolen?

The professor smiled.

I continued, 'Martin Stukely received the stolen tape from Force at Cheltenham races and gave it into the temporary care of his valet while he went out to ride a horse called Tallahassee in the race from which he didn't return.'

Lawson-Young nodded. 'When Martin Stukely died, his valet, Eddie, gave the tape to you, as he knew that's what Martin intended.'

'Eddie, the valet,' the professor went on, 'was eventually one of the people that our investigators talked to and he said he didn't know anything about any stolen laboratory tape. He said he thought he was handling a tape that you yourself had made, a tape which explained how to copy an ancient and priceless necklace.'

'That's the second tape,' I said. 'It's also missing.'

'Eddie had seen your duplicate of the necklace in the jockeys' changing room. And, incidentally . . .' George Lawson-Young's smile illuminated his little office . . . 'he said your copy of the necklace was stunning. Perhaps you will show it to me one day, when all this is over.'

I asked him what he would consider 'over', and his smile disappeared. 'For me, it will be over when we find the tape of our work.'

He was aware, I supposed, that it was comparatively easy to make duplicates of videotapes. And that the knowledge recorded on them was like the contents of Pandora's box; once out, it couldn't be put back. The stolen tape itself might now show racing. The records of the cancer research might already be free in the world, and would never again be under the professor's control. For him, perhaps, it was already over.

For me, I thought, it would be over when Rose and Adam Force left me alone – but, abruptly, out of nowhere, the spectre of the fourth black-mask floated into my consciousness. It wouldn't be over for me until his mask came off.

As casually as I could, I mentioned Number Four to the professor, fearing he would discount my belief, but instead he took it seriously.

'Add your Number Four into all equations,' he instructed, 'and what do you get in the way of answers? Do you get a reason for Force to want you dead? Do you get a reason for anyone to attack you? Think about it.'

I thought that that method must be what he used in nearly all research: if I added in an x factor, an 'unknown' into all I'd seen and heard and hadn't wholly understood, what would I get?

Before I could really learn the technique, one of the young doctors came to tell me and the professor that Adam Force was standing on the pavement opposite with a thin woman with brown hair – my friend Rose. Dr Force was staring at the entrance of his former workplace as if deciding how best to storm thc Bastille. The young doctor, on the other hand, seemed to enjoy devising an escape from the fortress.

The professor said thoughtfully, 'Adam knows his way round this house and its environs at least as well as any of us. He'll have stationed the other man, the one we can't see now, at the rear door into the mews. So how do we get Mr Logan out of here without Adam Force being aware of it?'

The brilliant researchers came up with several solutions that required Tarzan-like swinging over an abyss, but with civil regard for each others' brains, they voted unanimously for the exit I actually took.

The glowingly pretty female doctor whose idea I followed gave me life-threatening directions. 'Go up the stairs. Beside the top of the staircase, on the sixth floor, there's a bolted door. Unbolt it. Open it. You'll find yourself on the roof. Slide down the tiles until you meet a parapet. Crawl along behind the parapet there, so that the man in the mews doesn't see you. Crawl to the right. Keep your head down. There are seven houses joined together. Go along behind their parapets until you come to the fire escape at the end. Go down it. There's a bolt mechanism that lets the last part of the iron ladder slide down to the pavement. When you're down, shove the last part of the ladder up again until it clicks. My car is parked in the mews. I'll drive out in half an hour. You should be on the ground there by then, out of sight of Dr Force. I'll pick you up and go to meet your driver. When I pick you up, lie on the floor, so that my car looks empty except for me.'

Everyone nodded.

I shook hands with George Lawson-Young. He gave me multiple contact numbers and mentioned with a grin that I already had the phone number of the lab. He would expect me to find the stolen tape. Deduction and intuition would do it.

I said, 'What a hope!'

'Our only hope,' he added soberly.

The author of my escape and a couple of her colleagues came up to the top floor with me in high good spirits and unbolted the door to the roof.

Cheerfully, but in whispers because of the man in the mews far below, the researchers helped me slide down the gently sloping roof tiles to reach the parapet along the edge. Seeing me safely on my knees there, they happily waved goodbye and bolted the top floor door behind me.

It was true I could have crawled along on my hands and knees, but I would have been visible to Norman Osprey waiting below. She, my saviour, being tiny, hadn't realized that I was almost double her body size. To be invisible I would have to go on my stomach, as the height of the parapet was barely the length of a forearm.

I sweated and trembled along on my stomach within the parapet's scanty cover and had to freeze my nerves and imagination to zero in order to cross crumbling bits of old mortar. It was a long way down to the ground.

Dusk gathered in unwary corners and made matters worse.

The seven houses seemed like fifty.

When at last I reached the fire escape I'd begun to think that falling over the parapet would be less terrifying than inching along so precariously behind it.

At least, I thought grimly, if Adam Force had ever been up on the laboratory house's roof, he wouldn't expect me to have gone up there myself.

My dear pretty saviour, on picking up my shaky self, remarked critically that I'd taken my time on the journey. My dry mouth found it impossible to reply. She apologized that the recent rain had drenched the roof and wet my clothes. Think nothing of it, I croaked. She switched on the headlights and the heater. I gradually stopped shivering – both from cold and from fear.

We found Jim at the rendezvous in his usual state of agitation. My saviour, handing me over, reported that the fun escape had been a great success. She wouldn't accept anything for petrol. She did accept an absolutely heartfelt hug of gratitude, and a long, long kiss.

# CHAPTER NINE

I made a detour to talk to Bon-Bon on my way home and found her tears fewer and her memory recovering. When I asked her questions, she sweetly answered. When I suggested a course of action, she willingly agreed.

By the time Jim decanted me yawning to my hill house we were both very tired and he still had a few miles to go. Far and away the most orthodox of my three self-appointed minders, he also lived nearest. His wife, he said, had told him to apply to drive me regularly until I got my licence back. I was considering the cost, and he was considering a ban on radio and music. We had agreed to let each other know.

On that Wednesday, Catherine's transport stood on its frame outside the kitchen door. Inside the kitchen, when Jim had driven away, the warm welcoming smell of cooking seemed as natural as in the past with other girls it had been contrived.

'Sorry about this.' She pointed with her elbow at half-scrambled eggs. 'I didn't know when you were coming back, and I was hungry.'

I wondered how much care had gone into saying 'back' instead of 'home'.

She gave me a careful look, her eyebrows rising.

'I got a bit wet,' I said.

'Tell me later.' She cooked more eggs while I changed, and we ate in companionable peace.

I made coffee for us both and drank mine looking at her neat face, her blonde curving hair and her close-textured skin; and I wondered without confidence what I looked like to her.

I said, 'I saw Dr Force again today . . .'

Catherine smiled. 'And was he still charming and good-looking and filling everyone with belief in humanity?'

I said, 'Well, not exactly. He quite likely meant to bump me off, if he got a chance.' I yawned, and bit by bit, without exaggeration, told her about my day.

She listened with concentration and horror.

I collected her coffee mug and put it in the sink. We were still in the kitchen, which thanks to my mother had a pair of large comfortable chairs near an efficient heater.

We sat together, squashed into one of the chairs, as much for support for the spirits as for physical pleasure.

I told her about the professor and his x-factor method of research. 'So now,' I finished, 'I go over everything that anyone has said and done, add in x and see what I get.'

'It sounds difficult.'

'Different, anyway.'

'And when you find him? Black-mask Number Four?'

'He gives me nightmares,' I said.

I smoothed her hair. She felt right in my arms, curling there comfortably.

If I added Black-mask Four into the picture when he'd first blown into my awareness of his existence I had to remember every separate blow of that encounter on the Broadway pavement and, I realized with distaste, that I had to go back and listen again in my mind to every word of Rose's.

She'd shouted, 'Break his wrists . . .'

Catherine stirred in my arms and cuddled closer, and I discarded Rose in favour of bed.

Catherine woke early and went off before dawn to her morning shift, and I walked down in the dark to Logan Glass thinking of the past two days in Lynton and Bristol and wondering, like Professor Lawson-Young, if Dr Force still possessed and could produce for sale the irreplaceable data he'd stolen.

Strictly speaking, none of it was truly the business of a provincial glass-blower, but my fast-mending skin reminded me still that not everyone agreed.

Also, strictly speaking, none of it was truly the business of a dead steeplechase jockey, but his wife and children had been assaulted by gas and comprehensively robbed of their video machines.

The dedicated professor depended, he'd hopefully said,

on my deductive abilities, but to my mind he was staking his shirt on a non-runner, as Martin would have put it.

I had come to see the hunt for the videotape as sorties up a series of roads leading nowhere: as a star-burst of cul-de-sacs. The professor believed that one of the roads would eventually lead to his treasure, and I thought of Lloyd Baxter and Ed Payne and Victor and Rose and Norman Osprey and Bon-Bon and Adam Force, all as blind alley. I thought of all they'd said and done, and the professor was right, if I could discard the lies, I'd be left with the truth.

Far more absorbing of my time and mental energy was his assertion that if I included factor x (Black-mask Four) in all my insoluble sums, I would find them adding up.

Although I arrived at work half an hour before the normal starting time, Hickory was there before me, obstinately trying again to make a perfect sailing boat. He'd made the boat itself much larger and had put in red and blue streaks up the mast and the whole thing looked lighter and more fun.

I congratulated him and got a scornful grunt in return, and I thought how quickly his sunny temperament could blow up a thunderstorm, and hoped for his sake as well as for our competent little team's that it would blow over just as fast. Meanwhile I tidied the shelves in the stock room end of the furnace room, where Hickory had set the melted glass at the working temperature of 1,800 degrees

Fahrenheit. To give Hickory his due, he handled semi-liquid glass with a good deal of the panache he would need on the way to general recognition. I privately thought, though, that he would get stuck on 'pretty good' and never reach 'marvellous', and because he understood deep down where his limit lay, and knew I could do better, his present feeling of mild resentment needed patience and friendly laughter if he were either to stay or to leave on good terms.

Irish and Pamela Jane arrived together, as they often did, and this time were arguing about a film they'd seen that had a bad glass-blower in it. They asked Hickory what he thought and embroiled him so intensely in the argument that with a fatally noisy bang Hickory's precious new sailing boat cracked apart into five or six pieces. It had been standing free on the marver table, the outer surface cooling more rapidly than the super-hot core. The stresses due to unequal rates of contraction had become too great for the fragile glass. The pieces had blown away from each other and lay on the floor.

All three of my helpers looked horrified. Hickory himself glanced at his watch and said bleakly, 'Three minutes, that's all it took. I was going to put it in the oven . . . Goddam that *stupid* film.'

No one touched or tried to pick up the fallen pieces. They were still near to their liquid heat and would incinerate one's fingers.

'Never mind,' I said shrugging and looking at the sad

bits, 'it happens.' And I didn't need to remind them that practice glass was cheap. It did happen to everyone. It happened to the best.

We worked conscientiously all morning, making swooping birds for mobiles, which always sold fast. Pamela Jane, loving them particularly, was the one who fixed their strings the following morning early and who at noon would carefully pack them in boxes in such a way that they would pull out easily to fly.

Hickory, who could make neat little birds, had recovered his good humour by the time Worthington drew up outside in Marigold's Rolls. Marigold herself, in a dramatic black and white striped kaftan, issued from her glossy car with mascara-laden eyelashes batting hugely up and down like a giraffe's. She had come, she announced, to take me to lunch in the Wychwood Dragon. She had a favour to ask, she said.

Worthington, always a step behind Marigold when on active bodyguard duty, looked the more richly sun-tanned from the skiing trip. He had spent most of the time on the slopes, he said with satisfaction, while Marigold's wardrobe had swelled by three enormous suitcases. And a good time had clearly been had by both.

Her intense vitality as usual stirred anyone in Marigold's vicinity to giggles and, as on other days, she and Hickory were soon indulging in batting a sexual ball to each other with gleeful freedom.

Marigold, with enjoyment, stayed for half an hour – a century for her – during which time Worthington drifted me with a gentle tug on the arm into the furnace end of the room, and told me with the unhappiest of expressions that the underground fraternity of bookmakers were forecasting my destruction, if not death.

'Rose is still actively prowling round here, looking for vengeance, because she can't understand why you aren't on your knees to her. They are *laughing* at her because you and Tom and I have walked away from two of her best-planned smasheroos, and there's no way she's going to put up with such a loss of face. So you just look out, because I hear that someone in Broadway has binocs on you now, reporting every twitch you make straight back to Rose.'

'Binocs?'

'Bins. Where have you been all your life? Binoculars. Race-glasses. But seriously, Gerard, Tom Pigeon says it's no joke.'

I promised to be careful, but who could live for ever in a state of alarm? I said, 'I suppose I'd better tell you, then, that Adam Force and Rose did try to do me in yesterday. At least, I think so.'

He listened grimly and asked the unanswerable, 'Where's Rose now?'

Marigold and Hickory, having enjoyed their flirting as much because of their twenty-year age difference as in spite of it, gave each other a pecking kiss on the cheek in farewell, and Marigold and I made a head-turning entrance into the Wychwood Dragon dining room. The Dragon herself swept in full sail between the tables to fetch up by Marigold's side, two splendid ladies eyeing each other for supremacy.

I counted it a draw for outrageous clothes and an easy win for Marigold in the mascara stakes, and nearly two hours slid by before Marigold, tiring of the underlying contest, told me the reason for her invitation to me for lunch.

She declaimed to start with (unnecessarily), 'I am Bon-Bon's mother!'

'Ah,' I said. I knew.

'At Christmas,' Marigold continued, 'Martin gave his wife a video camera from the children, and he was going to give her a necklace from himself as well.'

I nodded. 'But she preferred warm winter boots.'

'The silly girl has no taste.'

'But she gets cold feet.'

Marigold considered fashion far more important than comfort. 'Martin said you had made a spectacular necklace once, and that you could make the same one again. So . . . for Bon-Bon, will you do it now? As a present from me, of course. And I'd like to see it first.'

She waited an uncharacteristically long time for my answer, gazing hopefully into my face. I didn't know in fact what to say. I couldn't insult her by telling her it would cost more than the woolly boots and the video camera combined, though she would need to know, but the videotape describing how to make it and listing the detailed ingredients in grams, was not only missing but might have come into Rose's field of things to die for.

When I said I would make a necklace for Bon-Bon, I hadn't known Rose.

After too long a pause Marigold asked, 'What's the problem? Can't you do it?'

When an answer of some sort became essential I said, 'Does Bon-Bon give the necklace idea her blessing?'

'She doesn't know about it. I want her to have a lovely surprise to cheer her up. I thought of buying her something in Paris, but then I remembered what Martin wanted you to do, so will you?'

She was so seldom presented with a negative that she couldn't understand my hesitation. I put together my most persuasive smile and begged for a little time. She began to pout, and I remembered Martin, laughing, saying that the Marigold pout meant the knives were out.

Hell, I thought, I wished he were alive. He'd been dead twenty-one days and I'd found each one a quandary without him.

I said to Marigold, 'The necklace I made is in a strong box in the bank down the road here. I do agree that you should see it before we go any further.'

The pout cleared away to a broad smile of understanding, and although we could easily have walked the distance, Marigold grandly summoned Worthington, equally grandly paid for our lunch, and outshone the poor Dragon all the way to the Rolls.

In the bank Marigold had the manager bowing to the floor while minions were sent scurrying to bring my locked box into the private room where contents could be checked. I opened the metal box and laid the flat blue velvet folder containing the copy of the Cretan Sunrise onto the bench-shelf, opening it for her opinion.

I hadn't seen the antique original except lit behind glass, so I couldn't completely compare them, but in the chill light of the bank's viewing room the duplicate I'd made gleamed as if with inner life, and I gave way to such a bout of self-regard as would have caused my Uncle Ron to bury his head in his hands in shame.

Marigold exclaimed 'Oh!' in astonishment, then drew in a breath and said, 'Oh, my dear,' and couldn't decide whether or not she liked it.

The necklace designed 3,500 years ago was a matter of twenty flat pieces, each made of aquamarine-coloured and dark-blue glass streaked together with melted gold. About two inches, or five centimetres, long, by a thumbnail wide, each flat shining piece bore the imprint of a flower. When worn, the long pieces, strung loosely together round the neck by their short sides, spread out in rays like a sunrise, the imprinted flowers, outermost, lying flat on the skin. In a way barbaric, the whole thing was antiquely magnificent, and definitely heavy. I didn't blame delicate Bon-Bon for not wanting to wear it.

Marigold, regaining her breath, asked if Martin had seen it.

'Yes.' I nodded. 'He thought it would suit Bon-Bon, but she wanted the boots more.' I'd lent the necklace to him without conditions, and he'd shown it around in the jockeys' changing room. Dozens of people had seen it.

Marigold, incredibly brought again to speechlessness, said nothing at all while I re-enclosed the necklace into darkness and put the velvet folder back in the metal strong box. There were the other papers there that I checked yet again – will, insurance policy, deeds of the hill house, all the conventional paper-trail of living, but of an instructional videotape, still not a sign.

I searched carefully once more through the pile of envelopes.

There was no tape. Nothing. I reflected with irony that even if one followed the instruction tape, it wouldn't be enormously easy to fabricate. I kept it partly because of the difficult hours it had cost me.

The bank minions re-locked everything and gave me back my key, and Marigold grandly commanded Worthington to drive us all back to Logan Glass. Apart from her instruction to her chauffeur she remained exceptionally quiet on the very short journey, and also, as I'd noticed in the Wychwood dining room, her gin intake had dropped to scraping zero.

Back at Logan Glass she paraded up and down the brightly lit gallery as if she'd never been in there before, and halted finally in front of Catherine's wings before addressing all of us, Worthington, Irish, Hickory, Pamela Jane and myself, as if we'd been a junior class in prep school. She said we were lucky to be in a studio which stood so high already in the world's estimation. She was going to give us all a huge jump forward in reputation because, 'Gerard . . .' she blew me a kiss . . . 'with the help of all of you, of course, is going to make a marvellous necklace for me, which I'm going to call the Marigold Knight Trophy, and I'm going to present it each year to the winner of a steeplechase run at Cheltenham on every New Year's Eve in memory of my son-in-law, Martin Stukely . . . and *there*,' she spread her arms wide, 'what do you think of *that*?'

Whatever we thought, we gazed silently in awe.

'Well, Gerard,' she demanded, 'what do you say?'

I didn't say, 'Over the top. In fact, out of sight,' but I thought it.

'You see,' Marigold went on triumphantly, 'everyone benefits. People will flock to your door, here.'

Apart from terrible trouble with insurance the one dire probability ahead in her scheme was that someone somewhere would try to exchange the modern for the antique, with Marigold embroiled in legal pincers.

'I think it's a *beautiful* idea,' Pamela Jane told Marigold, and the others, smiling, agreed. Even Worthington raised no security alarms.

Marigold, delighted with the scheme she had thought up within ten minutes, filled in the details rapidly. She would consult the Cheltenham Race Trophy Committee immediately . . . Gerard could start work at once . . . the Press should be alerted . . .

I hardly listened to those plans. Almost anything would be a better trophy than a copy of a jewel worth a million. The obituary for Martin that I hadn't yet fashioned would be more suitable. Glass trophies were common in racing and I would be elated in general to be commissioned to make one.

Irish with enthusiasm clasped Marigold's hand and shook it vigorously, to the lady's surprise. Hickory beamed. The trophy necklace idea swept the polls at Logan Glass, but the Cheltenham committee might not like it.

The Cheltenham committee was given little time more to remain unconsulted. Marigold used my telephone to get through to an influential high-up whom she galvanized into visiting Logan Glass at once.

An hour later, Marigold, irresistible to many a powerful man, greeted the man from Cheltenham, Kenneth Trubshaw, with a familiar kiss and explained her intention even before introducing Irish, Hickory and Pamela Jane.

I got a nod from the smoothly urbane member of the racecourse's upper echelon. He knew me by sight, but we hadn't until then talked. Marigold with arms raised put that right.

'Darling, you know Gerard Logan, of course?'

'Er . . . yes, of course.'

'And it's Gerard who's made the *fabulous* necklace which you *must see*, which is down in the bank here . . .'

Everyone looked at a watch, or the clock on the showroom wall. The bank had closed its doors five minutes before and Marigold looked frustrated. Time had ticked away too quickly.

I suggested diffidently that Mr Trubshaw, so not to have wasted entirely his short journey, might care to see a few other things I'd made and although Marigold protested, 'Darling, there's more *gold* in the necklace and it's going to be a gold trophy race . . .'

Kenneth Trubshaw, though perhaps more courteous than interested, took the first few brisk uncommitted steps into the gallery. Then, to my great relief, he paused, and stopped, and went back a pace, and finished thoughtfully in front of Catherine's wings.

'How much is this one?' he asked. 'There's no price on it.'

'It's sold,' I said.

My assistants all showed astonishment.

'Pity,' commented Trubshaw.

'There isn't enough gold,' Marigold complained.

'Um,' I said, 'I did a horse jumping a fence, once. The fence was solid gold, so were the horse's hooves. The rest of the horse was crystal, and the ground, the base of the piece, was black glass, with tiny gold flecks.'

'Where is it now?' Kenneth asked.

'Dubai.'

He smiled.

'What about the necklace?' Marigold demanded, cross.

Her Kenneth appeased her gently. 'I'll come over and see it tomorrow, but this young man has more than a necklace to show us. These wings, for instance . . .' He stood in front of them, his head on one side. He asked me, 'Couldn't you make that again? If this one's sold?'

'Part of what I sell is a guarantee of one-of-a-kind,' I apologized. I wasn't sure I could, even if I wanted to, repeat the wings. The climbing powerful splendour of their construction had come from the subconscious. I hadn't even written up my notes.

Could I instead, then, he asked, make a tribute to Martin Stukely?

I said, 'I could make a leaping horse with golden streaks. I could make it worthy of Cheltenham.'

'I'll come tomorrow,' the trophy chairman said and embraced Marigold in farewell with smiling enthusiasm.

Marigold, having agreed earlier with her daughter to take me back to Bon-Bon's house, she, Worthington and I made tracks to the Stukely gravel, arriving at the same moment as Priam Jones, who was carefully nursing the expensive tyres he'd bought to replace those wrecked on New Year's Eve. Priam, Bon-Bon had reported, had after all decided not to sue the council for erecting sharp-toothed barriers overnight, but had already transferred his disgust to Lloyd Baxter, who'd ordered his horses, including Tallahassee, to be sent north to a training stable nearer his home.

Bon-Bon came out of the house in welcoming mood, and I had no trouble, thanks to her manoeuvring it privately on my behalf, in talking to Priam Jones as if our meeting were accidental. Priam looked like being the last of the cul-de-sacs.

'Bon-Bon invited me to an early supper,' Priam announced with a touch of pomposity.

'How splendid!' I said warmly. 'Me too.'

Priam's face said he didn't care to have me there too,

and things weren't improved from his point of view when Bon-Bon swept her mother into the house on a wardrobe expedition and said over her departing shoulder, 'Gerard, pour Priam a drink, will you? I think there's everything in the cupboard.'

Bon-Bon's grief for Martin had settled in her like an anchor steadying a ship. She was more in charge of the children and had begun to cope more easily with managing her house. I'd asked her whether she could face inviting Priam to dinner, but I hadn't expected the skill with which she'd delivered him to me in secondary guest capacity.

The children poured out of the house at that moment, addressing me unusually as 'Uncle Gerard' and Priam as 'sir'. They then bunched round Worthington and carried him off to play 'make believe' in the garage block. Priam and I, left alone, made our way, with me leading him through the house, to Martin's den. Here I acted as instructed as host and persuaded Priam with my very best flattery to tell me how his other horses had prospered, as I'd seen one of his winners praised in the newspapers.

Priam, with his old boastfulness re-emerging, explained how no one else but he could have brought those runners out at the right moment. No one, he claimed, knew more about readying a horse for a particular race than he did.

He smoothed the thin white hair that covered his scalp but showed pink skin beneath and conceded that Martin had contributed a little now and then to his training success.

Priam at my invitation relaxed on the sofa and sipped weak Scotch and water while I sat in Martin's chair and fiddled with small objects on his desk. I remembered Priam's spontaneous tears at Cheltenham and not for the first time wondered if on a deeper level Priam was less sure of himself than he acted. There were truths he might tell if I got down to that tear-duct level, and this time I'd meet no garden hose on the way.

'How well,' I asked conversationally, 'do you know Eddic Payne, Martin's old valet?'

Surprised, Priam answered, 'I don't know him intimately, if that's what you mean, but some days I give him the colours the jockeys will be wearing, so yes, I talk to Eddie then.'

'And Rose?' I suggested.

'Who?'

'Eddie Payne's daughter. Do you know her?'

'Why ever do you ask?' Priam's voice was mystified, but he hadn't answered the question. Eddie and his daughter had worn black masks, I thought, but could Priam have been Number Four?

I said with gratitude, 'You were so kind, Priam, on that wretched day of Martin's death, to take back to Broadway that tape I so stupidly left in my raincoat pocket in Martin's car. I haven't thanked you properly again since then.' I paused and then added as if one thought had nothing to do with the other. 'I've heard a crazy rumour that you swapped two tapes. That you took the one from my pocket and left another.'

'Rubbish!'

'I agree.' I smiled and nodded. 'I'm sure you took back to my place in Broadway the tape I'd been given at Cheltenham.'

'Well, then.' He sounded relieved. 'Why mention it?'

'Because, of course, in Martin's den, in this very room, in fact, you will have found tapes all over the place. Out of curiosity you may have slotted the tape I had left in the car into Martin's VCR and had a look at it, and maybe you found it so boring and unintelligible that you wound it back, stuck the parcel shut again, and took it back to me at Broadway.'

'You're just guessing,' Priam complained.

'Oh, sure. Do I guess right?'

Priam didn't want to admit to his curiosity. I pointed out that it was to his advantage if it were known for a certainty what tape had vanished from Logan Glass.

He took my word for it and looked smug, but I upset him again profoundly by asking him *who* that evening, or early next morning, had he assured that the tape he'd delivered to Broadway had nothing to do with an antique necklace, whether worth a million or not.

Priam's face stiffened. It was definitely a question he didn't want to answer.

I said without pressure, 'Was it Rose Payne?'

He simply stared, not ready to loosen his long-tight tongue.

'If you say *who*,' I went on in the same undemanding tone, 'we can smother the rumours about you swapping any tapes.'

'There's never any harm in speaking the truth,' Priam protested, but of course he was wrong, the truth could be disbelieved, and the truth could hurt.

'Who?' I repeated, and I suppose my lack of emphasis went some way towards persuading him to give the facts daylight.

'When Martin died,' he said, 'I drove his things back here, as you know, and then as my own car was in dock having the . . . er . . . the tyres, you see, needed replacing . . .'

I nodded without judgement or a smile.

Priam, encouraged, went on. 'Well, Bon-Bon said I could take Martin's car, she would have said yes to anything, she was terribly distraught, so I just drove Martin's car on to my home and then back to Broadway, with Baxter's bag and your raincoat, and then I drove myself home again in it. In the morning, when I came in from morning exercise with the first lot, my phone was ringing, and it was Eddie Payne . . .' Priam took a breath, but seemed committed to finishing. 'Well . . . Eddie asked me then if I was sure the tape I'd taken back to your shop was without doubt the one he'd given you at Cheltenham, and I said I was absolutely certain, and as that was that, he rang off.'

Priam's tale had ended. He took a deep swallow of whisky, and I poured him a stronger refill, a pick-you-up from the confessional.

Eddie himself had been to confession. Eddie hadn't been able to face Martin's funeral. Eddie was afraid of his daughter Rose, and Eddie had put on a black mask to do me a good deal of damage. If Tom and the Dobermanns hadn't been passing, Eddie's sins would have involved a good deal more of deep-soul shriving.

It had taken such a lot of angst for Priam to answer a fairly simple question that I dug around in what I'd heard to see if he knew consequences that I didn't.

Could he have been Black-mask Four? Unknown factor x?

Ed Payne had probably told Rose that the tape stolen from Logan Glass at the turnover of the new century was to do with a necklace. Rose had not necessarily believed him. Rose, knowing that such a necklace existed, but not realizing that the tape, if found, wasn't itself worth much and certainly not a million, may have hungered for it fiercely enough to anaesthetize everyone around at Bon-Bon's house with cyclopropane, and gather up every videotape in sight.

I had thought at the time that it had been a man who had sprung out from behind the door and hit me unconscious, but on reflection it could have been Rose herself. Rose, agile, strong and determined, would without question lash out when it came to attacking a man. I knew all about that.

Thoughtfully I asked Priam, as if I'd forgotten I'd asked him before, 'How well do you know Rose Payne?'

'I don't know her,' he replied at once, and then, more slowly, revised the assertion and watered it down. 'I've seen her around.'

'How well does she know Adam Force, would you say? Do you think Dr Force would be foolish enough to provide her with a cylinder of gas from a nursing home he visits?'

Priam looked as shocked as if I'd run him through with swords, but unfortunately from my own point of view he didn't actually flag-wave any signs of guilt. He didn't feel guilty; almost no one did.

Bon-Bon's 'early supper' proved to be just that, slightly to Priam's disappointment. He preferred grandeur, but everyone sat round the big kitchen table, Marigold, Worthington, the children, Bon-Bon, me and Priam himself. I also acted as waiter, as I often did in that house, though Daniel, the elder boy, carried empty dishes sometimes.

'Gerard,' he said, standing solidly in front of me between courses, to gain my attention, 'who's Victor?'

I paid attention very fast and said, 'He's a boy. Tell me what you've heard.'

'Is it still the same?' Daniel asked. 'Do we get the gold coins?'

'No, of course not,' Bon-Bon scolded. 'That was a game.'

'So is this,' I promised her, 'so do let's play the same way.'

I dug in a pocket and found some loose change, surprised I had any left after the twenty or more coins they'd won several days earlier.

'What about Victor?' I asked. I put a coin flat on the table and Daniel said, 'There are two things,' so I put down a second coin.

'You're teaching these children all wrong,' Marigold berated me.

Theoretically I might agree with her but Daniel unexpectedly spoke up. 'Gerard told Worthington and a friend of his that you have to pay for what you get.'

Marigold's disfavour spread to her chauffeur, but Daniel, not understanding, simply waited for me to listen.

'Go on,' I said. 'Two pieces of treasure. And they'd better be worth it.' I grinned at him.

He put his chubby hand flat over the coins and said directly to me, 'He wants to tell you a secret.'

'When did he say that?' I took him seriously, but the other adults laughed.

Daniel picked up one of the gold coins. Mercenary little devil, I thought.

Daniel said, 'He phoned here. Mummy was out in the garden, so I answered it. He said he was Victor. He didn't want to talk to Mummy, but only to you. You weren't here, but I told him you were coming for supper so he said to tell you he would try again, if he could.'

Daniel's hand hovered in the air over the second coin. I nodded philosophically and he whisked it away in a flash.

'That's disgraceful!' Marigold told me severely. 'You're teaching my grandson all sorts of bad habits.'

'It's a game,' I repeated; and one for eleven-year-olds. Bright though he was, I thought Daniel had done a good piece of work.

'Early supper' ended at seven-thirty, an hour before the younger children's bed time. Marigold, her mercurial spirits restored, gave Daniel a forgiving goodnight hug that swalllowed him in kaftan, and after coffee, three large slugs of Grand Marnier, and a giggly chat on the telephone with Kenneth Trubshaw involving the sponsorship of gold trophies, Marigold floated out to the Rolls in clouds of good will and let Worthington solicitously install her in the back seat and drive off to her home.

Priam Jones felt less than decently treated. He let Bon-Bon know, while thanking her for her hospitality, that as a racehorse trainer of prestige, and especially as her husband's ex-chief employer, he would have enjoyed more attention and consideration. He bestowed an even cooler farewell nod to me and in irritation gave his new tyres a harsh workout in his departure across the gravel. Poor Priam, I thought. It couldn't be much fun being *him*.

Victor kept me waiting a long time. Bon-Bon, going upstairs to read stories to the children, gave me a kiss goodnight and waved me to the den for the evening, but it was after eleven o'clock when the fifth caller on the line spoke with the familiar cracked voice of Taunton.

'Gerard? I'm in a public phone box. Mum thinks I'm in bed. She threw away your mobile number and I can't use the e-mail . . . Auntie Rose has taken my computer. I'm absolutely sick of things. I want to see you. Tell me where. I'm running out of money.'

There were indeed many time-over warning clicks. He was feeding small coins, I supposed, because he hadn't any others. In a short period of peace I said, 'I'll come to Taunton station, same train, on Sunday.'

'No. Tomorrow. *Please*, tomorrow.'

I agreed, and the line went dead.

'You're raving mad, that's what you are,' Tom Pigeon said at seven in the morning, when I rang and told him, 'Today's Friday. The boy should be in school.'

'That's probably why he was so insistent. He could skip school without his mother knowing.'

'You're not going,' Tom said positively, and then, a few seconds later, 'We'll get Jim to drive us. He's got an estate car for the dogs. Where are you?'

'At the Stukelys. Can you pick me up here?'

'Last Sunday, five days ago,' Tom said with mock patience, 'dear Rose tore your face open in Taunton with the tap end of a garden hose.'

'Mm,' I agreed.

'And the day before yesterday, I hear, you nearly got yourself killed.'

'Well . . .'

'How about staying at home?'

I smiled at the silly idea.

# CHAPTER TEN

By Friday Jim's wife had told him I was accursed by demons and he should no longer drive me. Our lateness on Wednesday had burned her risotto.

Jim and I however came to a mutual understanding and shook hands on it. He would drive when I needed him in bodyguard status, there would be no radio, and I would pay him double.

Despite this slightly crabby start, Jim drove Tom, me and the dogs cheerfully to Taunton and stopped in the no-parking zone outside the station. I remembered too late that the weekday timetable was different from Sunday and the expected train had come and gone, leaving Victor stranded.

He wasn't on the platform.

Giving Tom the news and receiving a promise to sit and wait, I hurried along the road until 19 Lorna Terrace was in sight. No Victor. Back to the station – and I found him there, cold and anxious, in the waiting-room.

He stood up, looking thin and stressed, my arrival not enough to bring out smiles. I'd spent part of the journey adding Victor into every event that Black-mask Four could have attended without disguise, and feeling I was nowhere near as good as George Lawson-Young at this factor x stuff, I couldn't make x fit Victor anywhere.

'I'm late because I didn't come on the train,' I briefly explained. 'What's the matter?'

'I want . . .' He sounded as desperate as he looked. He began again. 'Auntie Rose has moved into our house . . . I hate her. I can't bear her, and Mum won't speak to me unless I do what Auntie Rose says, because Mum's that scared of her. And my dad, when he gets out, won't come home while she's there. I know he won't, so where can I go? What can I do? I don't know anyone except you to ask, and that's a laugh really, considering your face . . .'

'Did you try your grandfather?'

Victor said hopelessly, 'He's shit scared of Auntie Rose. Worse than Mum.'

I said, 'Last Sunday – ' and he interrupted.

'I'm sorry. I'm really sorry about your face. I thought you wouldn't come today . . . I thought you hadn't come.'

'Forget about last Sunday,' I said. 'Concentrate on Adam Force instead.'

'He's great,' Victor said without fervour, and then with a frown, added, 'Everyone says so. He sometimes used my computer. That's how I got his letter. He thought he had deleted the file but I found it in the cache memory.'

It explained a lot.

I asked, 'How long has he known your Auntie Rose?' and this time I got an answer.

'About as long as he's known Mum. Months, that is. Mum went on the coach trip to his clinic, and he got hooked on her. He was a real cool guy, I thought. He came round for her when Dad was at work. So when Auntie Rose finds out, she goes round to the hotel where Dad's working and says if he comes home quick he'll catch them at it in Dad's own bed. So Dad goes round and Dr Force has gone by then, but Dad gives Mum a hell of a beating, breaking her nose and about six of her ribs and things, and Auntie Rose goes round to the nick and tells on Dad. So they put him away for twelve months. Then, last Sunday,' he said miserably, 'Auntie Rose takes Adam Force off Mum, which she meant to do all along, I reckon, and now he does what she tells him, and it's queer, but I'd say she *hits* him pretty hard most days, and then I've seen them kissing after that.'

He spoke in puzzlement, and Worthington, I thought, could explain a thing or two to Victor. Fatherly, steady and worldly, Worthington, a great fellow, simply *couldn't* be Black-mask Four. And Victor? Surely not Victor, though Black-mask Four hadn't been bodily substantial, like Worthington, but lithe, like Victor. But Victor *couldn't* have bashed me about then, and asked me for help now.

Not Victor, not Worthington, but what about Gina?

Was she muscular enough? I didn't know for sure and,

I decided reluctantly, I would have to find out. I'd been through almost the whole register of cul-de-sacs and failed to find anyone that fitted a factor x. Yet there had indeed been a fourth black-masked attacker. I had felt the hands. I'd felt the blows. I'd seen the eyes within the mask. Black-mask Four was real.

According to the professor, there was a question I wasn't asking, and if I didn't ask the right question, how could I expect to be told the right answer? But *what* was the right question? And whom should I ask?

With a mental sigh I took Victor out of the station and, to his obvious pleasure, reunited him with Tom and his three black canine companions. He told Tom that that day, the Sunday that we'd spent on the moor, had been one of his happiest ever. Happiest, that was, until his Auntie Rose had ruined it.

He played with the dogs, plainly in their good graces, and spoke to them instead of us. The black ears heard him say, 'I'll bet people can still run away to sea.'

After a while I said to Tom, 'I'll go round to Victor's house, and if his mother's in I'll ask her if he can spend the weekend with us.'

Tom protested, 'I'll go.'

'We'll both go,' I said, and in spite of Victor's fears we left him with Jim and, taking the dogs with us, knocked on the door of the roughly repaired entrance to 19 Lorna Terrace.

Gina Verity came to our summons and failed to close

her mended door against us fast enough. Tom's heavy shoe was quicker.

In the five days since the previous Sunday, Gina had lost her looks, her serenity and her confidence. She stared at my slashed and mending jaw as if it were one straw too many. She said helplessly, 'You'd better come in,' and with sagging shoulders led me down the now familiar passage to the kitchen. We sat, as before, at the table.

Tom and the dogs stood on guard outside the house because Gina didn't know when either her sister or Adam Force would return.

'I would like to invite Victor to stay for the weekend,' I said.

Gina lit cigarette from cigarette, as before. 'All right,' she agreed in a dull sort of way. 'Pick him up from school.' She thought it over. 'Better not let Rose find out, she wouldn't let him go with you.'

Gina's left-hand fingers were stained nearly orange with nicotine. The right-hand fingers were white. I stretched forward and lifted first her right hand and then her left, putting them down again gently. The muscles were flabby, with no tone. Too apathetic to complain, she merely looked at her own hands one by one, and said, 'What?'

I didn't reply. Black-mask Four's left hand hadn't been as intensely yellow as this one, even seen under the street lights and even while actively punching. With those strongly muscled arms, Black-mask Four had been male.

Gina had not been Black-mask Four. The certainty was unarguable.

Time to go.

Out in front of the house Tom's equivalent of my alarm whistle set up a howling, growling, barking clamour which the dogs only ever did at their owner's prompting.

Gina immediately stood and shrank away from the table, her eyes wide with unmistakable fear. 'It's Rose,' Gina said. 'She's come back. She always makes dogs bark. They don't like her. She makes their hair stand on end.'

Mine too, I thought. The deep-throated Dobermanns went on proving Gina right.

'Go,' Gina said to me, her tongue sticking on the words. 'Go out. Out through the backyard . . . and out through the gate and down the lane. Go, go. Hurry.' Her urgency was for my own safety as much as hers.

It might have been prudent to go, but I'd never been a wise devotee of the 'He who fights and runs away lives to fight another day' school of thought. Running away from Rose . . . I supposed that I'd already escaped three times from her traps, and once from Adam Force. With that amount of good luck, I thought, I might remain a bit longer undestroyed.

I stayed sitting at the table, though with chair pushed back and one knee over the other, while the front door creaked open and the purposeful footsteps came along the passage.

Not only Rose had come, but Adam Force with her. Rose had recognized Tom and his sidekicks, but the doctor was pinning his negative emotions entirely on me. He'd set me up two days ago as an insulin-dosed car crash hit-and-run victim – a scheme that had gone wrong. My presence in that house shook him.

Rose, interestingly, had bloomed as fast as Gina had faded. Her dry skin and frizzy hair seemed lubricated, and she was alight with what (thanks to Victor's run-through) I could only interpret as satisfied sex.

Adam Force, good-looking and charming though he still might be, was to my mind a con man sliding towards self-inflicted destruction. If he'd kept anywhere a copy of what he'd stolen from Professor Lawson-Young's laboratory, Rose in the end would have it. Rose would acquire whatever she set out to get, man, tape or power.

Rose had definitely worn one of the black masks, but Adam Force hadn't. He hadn't known who I was when I turned up at Phoenix House.

I said lazily, rising to my feet, 'We'll not have a repeat of last Sunday. I came to see Gina principally, but I came also to leave a message for Rose.'

They listened attentively, to my amazement.

I said, 'The fourth of your band of black-masked thugs has whispered in my ear.'

The possibility of my untruth being accurate froze Rose long enough for me to go forwards along the passage and into the Dobermanns' territory of safe keeping. Tom, eyebrows up, joined in step beside me once we were out in the road and, unpursued, we walked along and round the bend towards the station, the dogs following in silence.

'However did you manage to get out of there unharmed?' Tom asked. 'I was sure you would whistle.'

'I told them a lie.'

He laughed. But it hadn't been funny. Adam Force's sharply focused calculating assessment of me from neck to ankles had been too much like a matter of adding up the amount of deadly substance needed per kilo of body weight to finish me off. A lethal amount of insulin . . . a syringeful of 'goodbye' threat, a cylinder of cyclopropane gas, a prelude to any sort of injected extinction. Rose would inflict instant damage, but Adam Force would more deliberately kill.

In a normal kitchen, although Rose could always slash with knives, Adam Force wouldn't have to hand any poison, his weapon of choice. He would need more time than he had.

I had kept a good distance from Rose on my way out, but it was the white beard and orange socks, the gracious manners and the Phoenix House pharmacy, the hunger for a million and the belief of infallibility, these were the long-term dangers that I had most to fear.

There were two particular videotapes missing, and both had at some time been in my care. Did Rose have the one detailing the necklace? Did Force after all retain the cancer-research tape he'd stolen? I might believe the answers to be yes and no, but how the hell could I find out for sure?

On the way back to Broadway we veered into Cheltenham to call on Kenneth Trubshaw, the trophy committee man, who'd said on Jim's car phone that he would be at home. Slightly surprised by our numbers, he nevertheless generously offered the warmth of the kitchen stove to my travelling companions, plus a large tin of biscuits, and shepherded me alone into his much colder drawing room. It was a large room facing north, its daylight grey and its carpet green, a combination I found depressing.

I gave him the book I'd taken along for the purpose, which contained a series of glossy coloured eight-by-ten photographs, a long record of the work I'd done over maybe twelve years.

I explained that I couldn't in good faith repeat any of the items exactly, but I could make something similar, if he liked.

He laid the book flat on a big table and turned the pages slowly. It mattered to me quite a lot, I discovered, that he would like some at least of the pieces, even if half of them weren't suitable for racing trophies. Vases of odd shapes had recently been blown for trophies of all sorts, though. There was no ban these days on anything surreal.

Trubshaw finished turning the pages. Then he closed

the book, to my severe disappointment, and with too serious a tightening of his mouth gave me his verdict.

'If you can lend me this book I'll put it before the committee when they meet tomorrow morning. I know dear Marigold wants action. I will telephone her when the decision's made.'

I'll be damned, I thought. How did he look when he was altogether turning things down?

He said, 'The leaping horse is the one I'd choose. Can you do anything like it? And I'll need to know how high it would be overall, and how heavy. The one in the photograph looks too big.'

'Any size you like,' I promised, and told him that the leaping horse in the picture belonged to one of the Leicester Stewards and his wife.

While Kenneth Trubshaw exclaimed with surprise, I recalled minute by minute as best I could the conversation I'd had on the Stewards' guests' viewing balcony, where Lloyd Baxter had first told me about a white-bearded man stealing my money along with the much travelled videotape.

Lloyd Baxter, with his epilepsy, couldn't be factor x. His body hadn't the shape or the agility of Black-mask Four.

Kenneth Trubshaw put his hand down on the book of photos and said thoughtfully, 'Could you include enough gold to satisfy Marigold?'

'Yes. Any amount.'

'Er . . . how? And would it be . . . well . . . enormously expensive?'

'Not very expensive.'

Kenneth Trubshaw held definite reasons for concerning himself and his committee members with the subject of cost, but he hesitated for a measurable time before he waved me to a chair and, sitting himself, said, 'I don't know if you follow the background ins and outs of racing politics at all? I don't mean the form of horses or speculations about their fitness. I mean the question about whether the cost of a winner's trophy should be deducted from the prize money, as it usually has been until recently. Many owners refuse to take the trophy, preferring the whole prize to be given as money. It's being suggested that we give the whole prize *and* the trophy in every case. Ask Marigold if she is giving the trophy herself outright, or if she expects the racecourse to pay for it. Warn her the debate exists.' He stopped slowly, not proud of his shunting of his dilemma onto me.

'Well, all right,' I said, 'but don't expect Marigold to decide. She's terrific, but she leaves life's really serious decisions to her chauffeur.'

'You don't mean it!'

'Of course, I do. Her chauffeur, Worthington, is worth his weight in cut crystal ten times over.'

Kenneth Trubshaw absorbed the news manfully and then with relief went back to straight expense, saying, 'The necklace Marigold wants is very expensive, isn't it?'

I nodded. 'Very. And that necklace, if on public show, is inviting thieves. The gold is genuinely solid in that case.'

'Isn't solid gold always the real thing?' He looked quizzical.

I explained, 'Well, you can paint hot glass with molten 18 carat gold, that's seventy-five per cent mixed with other metals. You paint what you want to look gold when it's finished. Then you anneal the work for a second time, but only at 450 degrees Fahrenheit, and when it cools the second time the gold you painted on will have adhered completely to the glass, and it will look like solid gold, even if it isn't.'

Kenneth Trubshaw was fascinated, but didn't want to be considered cheap. 'Gold has to be gold,' he said. 'I want Marigold to like it, of course. That is, if we decide on this sort of thing for her trophy.'

I made murmuring agreeing noises.

He asked curiously, 'Which of all those sculptures in the book was the hardest for you to make?'

'The most difficult was the gypsy's crystal ball.'

It surprised him, as it did most people. He thought a crystal ball was blown up like a child's balloon.

'No,' I said. 'It's solid glass. And it's extremely difficult to make a perfectly round large ball of glass without air bubbles forming in it as it cools in an annealing oven.'

He wanted me to enlighten him about annealing, and

when I told him, he said, 'Could you make a leaping horse taking off from a crystal ball?'

Nodding, I said, 'It would be heavy . . . and difficult . . . but I could make sure it was unique.'

He pondered for a while, walking to his tall sash window and looking out into his sleeping winter garden.

'If we decide on giving you the commission, can you make drawings for us to choose from?'

'Yes,' I said, 'I could. But actually I'll probably make examples in glass. I'm more at home that way. Glass itself isn't expensive, and if you don't like the things I make, I can sell them in the shop.'

He smiled with irony at my frugal business sense. My chances, I judged, weren't much more than fifty:fifty.

Kenneth Trubshaw collected my crew from his kitchen and lined them up in an elegant striped nineteenth-century hall. Carefully then he looked them over. I followed his gaze and also his mind: a tubby driver in a wrinkled grey suit, a thin anxious boy, a piratical-looking vigorous man with a little black pointed Elizabethan beard, and three large black Dobermanns with watchful eyes and uncertain moods.

I said to Kenneth Trubshaw with a smile, 'They're my barbed-wire fence. Don't expect them to be pretty as well.'

He glanced my way, then said, 'It isn't enough for you and Marigold to make, pay for and give a splendid trophy to the winning owner of a race in memory of Martin

Stukely.' He stopped for reconsideration. 'At least, it's enough for that great lady Marigold, but not for you.'

He opened his front door for my guys to leave. Tom Pigeon bowed to him with ceremony, his glimmering smile making a mockery of solemnity. His dogs crowded his ankles to give him honour, and Kenneth earned Tom's allegiance for evermore by bowing back to him in return.

Then Trubshaw, hand on my arm again, made me stay while the others trooped out to the car. He said, 'Martin Stukely's darling widow may not realize that his good name is in doubt just now. Marigold certainly doesn't, nor does the racing public, nor, thank God, does the racing press. But you do, don't you? I saw it in your reaction to Marigold's enthusiasm for a race in his memory. You need, don't you, to scrub clean his honourable reputation first?'

I felt a chilled moment of disbelief that anyone else beside myself had perceived the possibility that Martin could have been knowingly dishonest.

There had been the moment when, reading through the contents of the slim hard-to-find drawer in his desk, I'd had to face the unwelcome photocopy of the letter he had written to Force. Parts of that short note had reverberated in my awareness ever since.

'. . . your formulae and methods . . . record them onto a videotape . . . and give it to me at Cheltenham races.'

Martin had known precisely what was on that tape. Had he after all known all along that the formulae and methods had been stolen? Kind George Lawson-Young had given his assured conviction that Martin had been one hundred per cent innocent in his dealings with Force. Terrible doubts all the same remained, and I didn't like finding them alive in the Cheltenham hierarchy.

I said to the racecourse trophy chairman, with a lightness I wasn't altogether feeling, 'Could you tell me what you mean?'

With disillusion, he did. 'As I understand it, on the day he died, Martin had possession of a videotape on which were recorded medical secrets of practically unlimited value. Medical secrets stolen by a Dr Force who had been known to Martin Stukely for some time. You yourself were to keep that tape hidden.'

I took a steadying breath and asked who had told him all that. 'Private investigators working for the laboratory from where the secrets were stolen interviewed all sorts of people at Cheltenham.' He looked at me curiously. 'I also heard from Marigold that you had been attacked by a pack of thugs outside your shop. The bookmakers had all heard it was the doing of Rose Payne, the racecourse valet's daughter, and she has a bit of a reputation for being violent. One of the bookmakers, a man called Norman Osprey, who looks a bit like Elvis Presley, he was boasting about the hammering they gave you. But it seems you didn't give them any tapes anyway.'

He waited for me to comment, but I didn't have much to say.

He smiled. 'Apparently, the valet thought that what he'd given you was a tape you yourself had filmed, explaining how to make a striking necklace, a copy of an antique. It seems that all the jockeys, and Ed Payne as well, had seen both the necklace and its how-to-make-it instruction tape in the changing room. Ed Payne told his daughter, Rose, that he had given you a tape and so she tried to find it by stealing every tape she could lay her hands on, including by attacking Martin Stukely's family with knock-out gas.'

'Rose herself?' I asked.

Kenneth Trubshaw didn't know. That was also the end of his up-to-dateness, except that, in the Cheltenham Stewards' opinion, Martin Stukely had very likely known that the scientific knowledge he'd promised to hide had been stolen from a research lab.

'And at present,' I said with regret, 'all those tapes are still missing. Whoever has them isn't telling.'

'I'm told you yourself are looking for them.'

'Who tells you all these things?' I really wanted to hear, but it seemed to be a matter of general supposition and logic.

'I'll tell you something myself,' I said, and I gave him Victor's latest purple homelife news.

'Dr Force and Rose deserve each other.' He laughed in his throat. 'That will do nicely for tomorrow morning's committee.' He walked with me to Jim's car. 'Give my warmest regards to Marigold. I'll be in touch.'

He shook my hand with sincerity.

He said, 'Find those tapes and clear Stukely's name.'

So simple, I thought.

When I disembarked at Bon-Bon's house, she herself with Daniel by her side came out to meet us.

'There's a message from Catherine Dodd for you,' Bon-Bon said to me. 'She has the evening free. She wants you to go to your house, if you can.'

I thanked her but she, like me and also Tom, was watching with fascination the flash of understanding between Victor, fifteen, and the four years younger Daniel. Alienation seemed more normal for that age bracket, but those two discovered immediately that they spoke computer language with a depth that none of the rest of us could reach. Victor climbed out of Jim's car and went indoors with Daniel as if the two of them were twins. Cyber twins, perhaps.

Bon-Bon would keep Victor for the night, instead of Tom, she said, amused, following the boys into the house, and Jim drove Tom, the dogs and myself back to Tom's house first, and then on to mine.

'I never thought we'd come back in one piece.' Tom left me with that bright thought and a positively jaunty wave, and I would have cast *him* as Black-mask Four if I hadn't twice owed him a rescue from crippling injury, and perhaps my life.

Catherine's motor cycle graced its customary spot outside the kitchen door, and she herself came out when she heard Jim's car arrive. There was no difficulty in interpreting her reaction to my return, and Jim drove away with a vast smile (and double cash), promising his service again, 'day or night'.

Coming home to Catherine had become an event to look forward to. I'd never asked her to take me to see her own living space, and when I did, that evening, she laughed and said, 'I'll take you there tomorrow. It's better by daylight.'

She asked me how my day had been, and I asked about hers. She frowned over Victor's troubles and was encouraging about a glass trophy horse. It was all very *married*, I thought, and we'd only known each other for three weeks.

'Tell me about the police,' I said, as we squashed companionably into one of the oversize chairs.

'What about them?' She was slightly defensive always about her job, but this time I especially wanted to know.

'The priorities,' I said. 'For instance, on that New Year's Day, you in your plainish clothes and the hobo lying on the doorstep, you were both there to frighten thieves off, weren't you, not to arrest them?'

She shifted in my arms. 'Not really,' she replied. 'We like to get our man.'

I knew better than to tease her. 'Tell me abour your partner, the hobo.'

'He's not really a hobo,' she replied smiling. 'His name is Paul Cratchet. He's a big guy but misleadingly gentle. Paul's a good detective. Many a villain has been surprised by his hand on their collar. He's known as Pernickety Paul at the station because he is so fussy over his reports.'

Smiling, I enquired plainly, 'What events get most police attention?'

'Accidental deaths, and murder, of course. Especially murder of a police officer. The murder of a fellow police officer, I'd say, gets people going most.'

'But after that?'

'Any physical assault.'

'Especially of a police officer?'

She twisted her neck and searched my purposefully straight face for levity. Satisfied, she nodded. 'Especially of a police officer.'

'And next?'

'Aggravated theft. That's when a weapon is used, or a severe physical threat, or violence as a means to achieve theft. It's called robbery.'

'And then?'

'Actually, and in general,' Catherine said, 'if someone's bleeding, then police officers will come at once. If goods are stolen, but no one's hurt, the officers will probably come in the morning after the 999 call. If cars are stolen, the police will take the registration number and promise to inform the owner if the car is found.'

'And that's that? That's all for cars?'

'More or less. It depends. They're usually found burnt out.'

'And who,' I asked mildly, 'would I go to if I found some stolen property?'

'Are you talking about those old videotapes again?'

'Yup. Those old tapes.'

'Well . . .' She let a good few seconds pass, then said, 'I did enquire about this . . .'

'It sounds bad news,' I said.

Catherine sighed. 'The tapes themselves are worth practically nothing. You said they hadn't even any covers. The information recorded on them, on both of them, even if they're totally different from each other, is called intellectual property. It has very little priority in police thinking. How to make a copy of an antique necklace? You must be joking! Industrial secrets, even medical secrets? Too bad. No one is going to waste much police time looking for them. There would be slightly more interest in your bag of cash, *if* you could identify a single note of it for sure. It would be much more likely, after three weeks, that it's been spent and dispersed. It was a fair amount to you personally, but not much in world terms, do you see?' She stopped as an entirely opposite thought struck her, then said, 'Does this dreadful Rose still believe you know where to find the tapes?'

'Don't worry about it.'

'But does she?' Catherine was insistent. 'Does she, Gerard?'

I told her, smiling, 'I now think she's had the necklace

tape almost from the beginning, and if she has, she knows I haven't got it.' And Rose knows, I thought, that I could repeat it any day.

'But the other one?' Catherine begged. 'The one stolen from the lab?'

'Yes.' I felt light-hearted. 'I could make a guess. Let's go to bed.'

I awoke first in the morning, and lay for a while watching Catherine's calm gentle breathing. At that moment, it filled me with total contentment . . . but would I feel the same in ten years? . . . and would she? When she stirred and opened her eyes and smiled, ten years didn't matter. One lived *now*, and now went along as a constant companion, present and changing minute by minute. It was *now*, always, that mattered.

'What are you thinking about?' she asked.

'Same as you, I dare say.'

She smiled again, and asked simply if I had plans for us both on her free Saturday? Relaxed, I offered the comfortable new chair in Logan Glass, and accepted a pillion ride to get there.

Hickory had again arrived before me and was again intent on a perfect sailing boat. He greeted me like the good friend of time gone by, tentatively asking if I could assist him, as he was finding it difficult on his own.

With uncomplicated pleasure I stripped down to a working singlet and helped Hickory, bringing a gather out of the tank when he needed it and holding the hot glass ready for his use. Hickory typically kept a running commentary for Catherine's sake and flirted with her mildly, and seldom, I thought, had I more enjoyed a frivolous start to the morning.

Hickory this time remembered to put the finished boat in the annealing oven, and if he accepted Catherine's unstinted praise with smugness, he had at least taken a satisfactory step forward in his training.

Irish arrived and brewed tea. Pamela Jane tidied and refilled the tubs of coloured powder that we would use during the session, to restock the shelves. The rest of the regular Saturday morning unwound in work from nine to twelve o'clock.

At a few minutes past noon, the shop embraced first Bon-Bon and the two boys, Daniel and Victor, for whom glass-blowing had temporarily become a greater draw than e-mail.

Not long after them, Marigold swooped in, batting the eyelashes, grinning at Hickory, smothering Daniel in a bright pink gold-smocked cloud-like dress and telling Bon-Bon at the top of her voice that 'Darling Trubby' would be with them right away.

'Darling Trubby', Kenneth Trubshaw, swam through the bright pink experience and emerged with lipstick on his cheek. The trophy chairman of Cheltenham races was carrying my book of photographs, and besides being apparently unnerved by the chattering din, he eyed my half-undress with a degree of disbelief and suggested that the Wychwood Dragon might be better for a business meeting.

'Darling Trubby, what a *great* idea!' Marigold's immediate enthusiasm resulted in herself, Kenneth Trubshaw, Bon-Bon, Catherine, myself and, of course, Worthington (Marigold insisted) occupying a quiet corner of the dining room to listen to the opinions of that morning's meeting of the Cheltenham Racecourse Company's trophy committee.

Irish was dispatched down the hill to fill the two boys with hamburgers and Cokes, and Hickory and Pamela Jane were left in peace to deal with that less demanding breed, the January tourist.

When six of us were neatly seated and listening, Kenneth Trubshaw began his spiel. 'First of all, dear Marigold,' he said, 'everyone on the committee wants me to thank you for your splendid generosity . . .' He gave flattery a good name. Marigold glowed. Worthington caught my eye and winked.

'The committee voted . . .' the chairman came at last to the point. 'We decided unanimously to ask you, Gerard Logan, to design and make a Martin Stukely memorial of a horse rearing on a crystal ball, like the one in the book. If it pleases Marigold and the committee – ' His final words got temporarily lost in a bright pink Marigold hug, but came out the other side with provisos about cost. To Marigold, cost was a bore. Worthington bargained, and I telephoned a jeweller who promised enough gold.

'Can you make it today, darling Gerard?' Marigold enthused. 'It's barely three o'clock.'

'Tomorrow would be difficult,' I said, 'next week would

be better. Today, I'm sorry, is impossible.' Sooner rather than later, I thought, to keep Marigold happy.

The Marigold pout appeared, but I wasn't going to help it. I needed time for thinking if it were to be a good job; and a good job was what I needed to do for Bon-Bon, for Marigold, for Cheltenham racecourse and for Martin himself.

'I'll do them tomorrow,' I said. 'The crystal ball and the rearing horse. I'll do them on my own, alone except for one assistant. They will be ready on Monday for the gold to be added, and on Tuesday afternoon I'll join them together onto a plinth. By Wednesday the trophy will be finished.'

'Not until then?' Marigold protested, and urged me to think again.

'I want to get it right for you,' I said.

And also I wanted to give my enemies time.

# CHAPTER ELEVEN

Marigold objected to my wanting no audience to the making of the rearing horse and the crystal ball. Kenneth Trubshaw understood, he said.

'Darling Trubby', substantial, grey-haired and very much a businessman, mentioned to me the one quiet word, 'Fees?'

'Worthington and I,' I said, 'will fix a price with Marigold, then you can haggle if you like.'

He shook my hand wryly. 'The Leicester Steward whose wife owns several of your things is also a Steward of Cheltenham, and he told our committee this morning that five years ago we could have bought this trophy for peanuts.'

'Five years ago,' I agreed, 'yes, you could.'

'And he said,' Trubshaw added, 'five years from now works by Gerard Logan will at least cost double again.'

Uncle Ron would have loved it. Well . . . so did I. It was surviving the next five *days* that caught my attention.

By mid-afternoon everyone had collected and split apart again. Bon-Bon and Marigold left the boys in my care while they browsed the antique shops, and Worthington and Kenneth Trubshaw developed a strong mutual regard in a stroll.

In the workshop, Victor, utterly impressed, watched Hickory show off with two gathers of red-hot glass that he rolled competently in white powder and then coloured powder and tweaked into a small wavy-edged one-flower vase. Pamela Jane expertly assisted in snapping the vase off the punty iron and Hickory with false modesty lifted it into an annealing oven as if it were the Holy Grail.

Daniel, for whom the workshop was a familiar stamping ground, mooned around looking at the shelves of bright little animals, pointing out to me the scarlet giraffe his father had promised him the day before he died. That story was most unlikely, I thought, remembering Martin's absent-mindedness towards all his children, but I gave Daniel the giraffe anyway, a gift that would have displeased his grandmother.

Giving to Daniel, though, always reaped a worthwhile crop. This time he wanted me to go outside with him and, seeing the stretched size of his eyes, I went casually, but at once.

'What is it?' I asked.

'There's a shoe shop down the road,' he said.

'Yes, I know.'

'Come and look.'

He set off, and I followed.

'Victor and I came down here with Irish, looking for

hamburgers,' he said, 'but we came to the shoe shop first.'

The shoe shop duly appeared on our left, a small affair mostly stocked with walking shoes for tourists. Daniel came to an abrupt halt by its uninspiring window.

'I should think it might be worth two gold coins,' he said.

'For two gold coins it had better be good.'

'See those trainers?' he said. 'Those up there at the back with green and white striped laces? The man with that gas, those are his laces.'

I stared disbelievingly at the shoes. They were large with thick rubber-like soles, triangular white-flashed canvas sections and, threaded in precision through two rows of eyeholes, the fat bunched laces of Daniel's certainty.

He said again, 'The man who gassed us wore those shoes.'

'Come into the shop, then,' I said, 'and we'll ask who bought some like them.'

He agreed. 'OK,' and then nodded, 'It might cost two more gold coins, to go into the shop.'

'You're an extortionist.'

'What's that?'

'Greedy. And I've no more coins.'

Daniel grinned and shrugged, accepting fate.

The shop had a doorbell that jingled when we went in, and contained a grandfatherly salesman who proved useless from our point of view as he was standing in for his daughter whose baby was sick. She might be back some day next week, he vaguely thought, and he knew nothing about previous sales.

When we went back into the street, Bon-Bon, further up the hill, was beckoning Daniel to her car, to go home. Only the fact that she had already loaded Victor, having offered him another night's computer hacking, persuaded her son to join her, and presently, when Marigold and 'Darling Trubby' had gone their separate ways, only Catherine and my little team were left, and those three, as it was Saturday afternoon, were setting things straight as if for a normal winter Sunday of no action. They departed with my blessing at four-thirty, leaving only myself and Catherine to lock up: and I gave her a bunch of keys for the future.

I also told police officer Dodd about the laces, which sent her on a brief reconnaissance only, as first of all she said she needed another officer with her if she were to question the shop owner, and second, the grandfather salesman had shut up shop and left it dark.

Catherine, like Martin before her, grew minute by minute more interested in the technical details and the chemical complexities of bright modern glass. Old glass could look grey or yellow, fine to my eyes but dingy on racecourses.

Catherine asked which I would make first, the horse or the ball, and I told her the horse. I asked her whether, even though they would not be on duty the next day, she could persuade her Pernickety Paul hobo partner to come and walk up and down Broadway with her a couple of times? She naturally asked why.

'To mind my back,' I joked, and she said she thought he might come if she asked him.

'He might be busy,' I said.

'I doubt it,' she replied. 'He seems rather lonely since his wife left him.'

We rode her motor bike to a hotel deep in the country and ate there and slept there: and I avoided Black-mask Four and explained to my increasingly loved police officer, before I kissed her, that she and the hobo might find handcuffs a good idea on the morrow. 'He always carries them,' Catherine said.

In the morning she said, 'All this walking up and down Broadway . . . is it because of the tapes?'

'Sort of.' I nodded. I didn't mention life or death. One couldn't somehow.

All the same, I woke Tom Pigeon, who woke his dogs, who all growled (Tom included) that Sunday was a day of rest.

I phoned Jim. At my service all day, he said. His wife was going to church.

Worthington was already awake, he said, and had I noticed that Sundays weren't always healthy for Gerard Logan?

'Mm. What's Marigold doing today?'

'I've got the day free, if that's what you're asking.

Where do you want me to turn up when? And most of all, why?'

I hesitated over the last answer but replied in order: 'Wychwood Dragon lobby, soon as possible, on account of fear.'

'Whose fear?'

'Mine.'

'Oh yeah?' His laugh travelled with bass reverberation. 'You'll be alone in that workshop of yours, is that it? In that case, I'll be with you soon.'

'I won't exactly be alone. Catherine and her partner officer will probably be in the town, and in the workshop there will be Pamela Jane, who's going to assist.'

'The girl? Why not that bright young man, what's his name . . . Hickory?'

'Pamela Jane doesn't argue.'

Worthington's deep voice arrived as a chuckle. 'I'm on my way.'

I made one more phone call, this time to the home of George Lawson-Young, apologizing for the eight-thirty wake-up.

'The hour doesn't matter,' he yawned, 'if you bring good news.'

'It depends,' I said, and told him what he might expect.

He said, 'Well done.'

'More to do.'

'I wouldn't miss it.' His smile came across the air. 'I'll see you later.'

Catherine and her motor cycle took me to Logan Glass,

where local inhabitants could have seen a display of affection to wag tongues for a week. I unlocked the doors, being there intentionally before Pamela Jane, and again read the notes I'd made (and filed in the locked bookcase) last time I'd tried my hand at a rearing horse.

This one would take me about an hour to complete, if I made the whole trophy, including plinth and ball. At a little less than half a metre high it would weigh roughly twenty kilos; heavy because solid glass itself weighed a good deal, let alone the added gold. Marigold had, with wide-sweeping arms, insisted on magnificence. It was to be Martin's memorial, she proclaimed, and she had been exceedingly fond of her son-in-law. Both Bon-Bon and Worthington thought this much-to-be-publicized admiration a little retrospective, but 'Darling Trubby' might think the trophy handsome in the sun.

I had filled the tank with clear crystal and put ready to hand the punty irons I'd need, also the small tools for shaping muscles, legs and head. Tweezers, too, essential always. I set the furnace temperature to the necessary 1,800 degrees Fahrenheit.

By then I 'saw' the sculpture complete. A pity they hadn't wanted Martin himself on the rearing horse's back. I saw him there clearly now, at last. Perhaps I would repeat the horse with Martin riding. Perhaps one night . . . for Bon-Bon, and for the friend I'd lost and still trusted.

While I waited for Pamela Jane to arrive, I thought about the wandering videotape that had raised so many savage feelings and, like curtains parting, the deductive faculty Professor Lawson-Young had put his faith in continued to open vistas in my mind. I had at last added in his factor x, and the mask had dropped from Blackmask Four.

Out of doors it started raining.

I stood looking at the furnace and listening to its heart of flame, looking at the raisable trap-door that kept 1,800 degrees Fahrenheit at bay. Irish, Hickory, Pamela Jane and myself were so accustomed to the danger of the extreme heat roaring within the fire-bricks that taking care was automatic; was second nature.

I knew at last the sequence of the roads in the cul-de-sacs. I listened in my mind to Catherine's list of punishable crimes and their penalties, and reckoned that Rose and Adam Force should, if they had any sense at all, just leave the videotapes where they rested and save themselves the grief of prosecution.

Thieves never had any sense.

I'd surrounded myself with as many bodyguards as I could muster that Sunday simply because neither Rose nor Adam Force had shown any sense or restraint so far, and because the making of the trophy horse left me wide open to any mayhem they might invent. I could have filled the workshop with a crowd of onlookers and been safe . . . safe for how long?

I knew now where the danger lay. I couldn't for ever look over my shoulder fearfully and, however rash it might seem, I saw a confrontation as the quickest path to resolution.

If I were disastrously wrong, Professor Lawson-Young could say goodbye to his millions. The breakthrough that would save the world in the cure for cancer would be published under someone else's name.

When my enemies came, I found it wasn't just time I had given them as much as an opportunity to out-think me.

I was still listening to the furnace when sounds behind me announced the arrival of Pamela Jane. She had entered through the side door, though usually she came in through the front.

'Mr Logan . . .' Her voice quavered high with fright, and besides, she normally called me Gerard.

I turned at once to see how bad things were, and found that in many unforeseen ways they were extremely bad indeed.

Pamela Jane, dressed for work in her usual white overalls cinched around the waist, was coming to a standstill in the centre of the workshop, trembling from a situation far beyond her capabilities. Her raincoat lay dropped in a bundle on the floor and her wrists were fastened together in front of her by sticky brown packing tape. Simpler and cheaper than handcuffs, the tape was equally immobilizing, and more effective still in Pamela Jane's case as the charming Adam Force held a full syringe in one hand and, with the other, had dragged down a clutch of female overalls to reveal a patch of bare skin inches from the needle. Thin and frightened, she began to cry.

A step or two behind Pamela Jane came Rose, every muscle triumphant, her whole face a sneer. She too came quietly, in soft shoes, and fast.

Rose, strong, determined and full of spite aimed powerfully my way, held in a pincer grip the upper arm of Hickory. My bright assistant stood helplessly swaying, his eyes and his mouth stuck out of action by strips of brown packing tape. The same tape had been used to bind his hands behind his back and also to form a makeshift hobble between his ankles.

Roughly steadying Hickory's balance loomed the bookmaker Norman Osprey, more bully beef than beauty, but arithmetically as fast as a computer chip. Just inside the side door, keeping guard and shifting uncomfortably from foot to foot was, of all people, Eddie Payne. He wouldn't meet my eyes. He took instructions steadfastly from Rose.

The actions of all four intruders had been whirlwind fast, and I had arranged little in any way of retaliation. All my bodyguards were simply to roam the street outside. Catherine and her hobo were to patrol their normal disjoined beat. Rose and her cohorts had somehow slid past them in the rain.

I was wearing, as usual, a white singlet which left my arms, neck and much of my shoulder area bare. The heat from the furnace roared almost unbearably beyond the trapdoor, if one weren't used to it. I put my foot and my weight sideways on the treadle, which duly opened the trap and let a huge gust of Sahara heat blow out over Norman Osprey's wool suit and reddening face. Furious, he made a snatch towards me, hurling me onto the trapdoor itself, but I side-stepped and tripped him, and unbalanced him onto his knees.

Rose yelled to Norman, 'Stop it, you stupid asshole, we don't want him damaged this time. You know bloody well we'll get nowhere if he can't talk.'

I watched as Rose tugged my blindfolded assistant across a good length of floor, with Norman Osprey holding him upright in a fierce grip. Hickory stumbled and fell tentatively forwards step by step until he reached the chair I'd bought for Catherine. At that point Rose revolved Hickory roughly until he fell into the chair on his side and had to struggle to turn and sit upright.

Behind me now I could hear the distressed breathing of Pamela Jane, and also the unmistakable heavy wheeze of Adam Force's asthma. He said nothing at all about his near miss with insulin at Bristol. He definitely needed an inhaler but had no free hands.

Rose said to Hickory with malignant satisfaction, 'Now you sit there, buddy boy, and it will teach you not to put your nose in where it isn't wanted.' She redirected the pleased venom back my way while Hickory tried hard to talk but produced only a throttled tenor protest.

'Now you,' she told me, 'will hand over everything I want. Or your friend here will get holes burned in him.'

Pamela Jane cried out, 'Oh no, you *can't*!'

'You shut up, you silly little bitch,' Rose acidly told her, 'or I'll spoil your soppy looks instead.'

Whether or not he was aware of Rose's speed in standing on the treadle part of the floor that raised the flap of the furnace, Hickory was unable to protest more vigorously than to shrink ever deeper into the chair. He did understand, though, the diabolical choice she was thrusting under my nose.

As if she could read his mind, she said in the same sharp tone, 'You, what's your name, Hickory? You'd better pray that this boss of yours won't let you burn. Because I'm not fooling: this time he's going to give me what I want.'

She picked up one of the long punty irons and pushed it into the tank of molten glass. Her movement was ungraceful rather than smooth with constant practice, but somewhere, sometime, she had watched a glass-blower collect a gather from a tank. She withdrew the iron with a small blob of red-hot glass on the end of it, and revolved the rod so that the glass stayed adhered to it and didn't fall off.

Pamela Jane moaned at the sight and all but fell onto the doctor's needle.

'Gerard Logan,' Rose said to me with emphasis. 'This time you will do what I tell you, now, at once.'

Extraordinarily, she sounded less sure of herself than screaming 'Break his wrists' into the Broadway night, and I remembered Worthington's judgement that as I would beat her at the tennis match of life, so she would never again face me on the actual court. Yet here she was, visibly pulling together the sinews and nerves of resolution.

I'd seen Martin summon his mental vigour when going out to race on a difficult horse, and I'd seen actors breathe deeply in the wings when the play ahead dug deep into the psyche. I understood a good deal about courage in others and about the deficiencies in myself, but on that Sunday in January it was Rose's own mushrooming determination that pumped up in me the inner resources I needed.

I watched her as she in turn watched me, and it wasn't what she said that mattered at all, it was which of us would win the desperate battle for pride.

She plunged the small, cooling ball of glass into the tank again and drew it out, larger. She swung the iron round until the molten red-hot lump and advanced it to a too-close spot under Hickory's chin. He could feel the heat. He shrank frantically away and tried to scream behind the adhering tape.

'Look out, for God's sake,' I shouted automatically and, as if surprised, Rose swung the iron away from Hickory's face until he wasn't for the minute threatened.

'You see!' Rose sounded all of a sudden victorious. 'If you don't like him burned you'll tell me where you've hidden the videotapes I want.'

I said urgently, 'You'll disfigure Hickory if you're not careful. Glass burns are terrible. You can get a hand burned so badly that it needs amputating. An arm, a foot

. . . you can smell flesh burning . . . you can lose your mouth, your nose.'

'Shut up,' Rose yelled, and again, at the top of her voice, 'Shut up!'

'You can burn out an eye,' I said, 'you can sear and cauterize your guts.'

Pamela Jane, who lived with the danger, was affected least of all in spite of her fluttery manner, and it was big Norman Osprey of the great muscular shoulders who sweated and looked ready to vomit.

Rose looked at her red-hot iron. She looked at Hickory and she glanced at me. I could more or less read her rapid mind. She had come to threaten me through my regard for Hickory and now here I was, a target again myself.

Beside Rose's powerful identity her companions' egos were pale. Even Adam Force's good looks and persuasive smile faded to second rate in her presence and I began to realize fully that her reputation in inspiring real abject terror, in men particularly, was in no way a myth. I felt the fringes myself, try though I might to counteract it. Her effect on her father sent him to the confessional at the best of times, and this being Sunday again I could barely imagine the turmoil churning in his good Catholic conscience.

To Norman Osprey no doubt one day was as good or bad as the next. His days were judged by the amount of muscle needed to achieve his own way, coupled with the fizzing ability to add, divide or multiply as if by instinct.

Adam Force's finger seemed to itch on the plunger set to activate the syringe's undisclosed contents. I wished to heaven that poor Pamela Jane would sniff back the tears and swallow the sobs, both of which seemed increasingly to irritate Dr White-Beard, and as for Hickory, stuck with wide brown bands into silence and sightlessness, and deep in the soft armchair, I thought he would be staying exactly where Rose had put him until someone pulled him out.

Impressions flashed and passed. Rose stared at me with calculation, enjoying her certainty that she would defeat me pretty soon. I couldn't swear she wouldn't. This time there were no black masks or baseball bats. But to be faced bare-armed with molten glass was worse.

Suddenly and unexpectedly Rose said, 'You came here this morning to make a trophy horse of glass and gold. I want the gold.'

Wow! I thought. No one had brought gold into the equation before. Gold for the trophy hadn't been mentioned in Rose's hearing as far as I knew. I had ordered enough for the trophy, and a little over for stock, but a quantity worth holding up the stage-coach for, it was not.

Someone had misled Rose, or she had misunderstood, and her acquisitive imagination had done the rest.

Rose was still sure that, one way or another, I could make her rich.

Adam Force was admiring her with a smile and applauding her with his eyes.

If I could use this, well . . . *golden* . . . opportunity, I could but try . . . I did need time now, and if I made the trophy horse I could slow things nicely.

I said, 'The gold isn't here yet. I'm fed up with the delay.' The carefree but complaining tone I used non-plussed Rose into lowering the tip of the punty iron for the moment.

'If I don't get the glass-horse trophy ready on time,' I said, 'the one that's ordered, that is, well . . .' I stopped abruptly, as if I'd teetered on the brink of a monster mistake. 'Never mind,' I said as if nervously, and Rose demanded I finish the sentence.

'Well . . .' I said.

'Get on with it.'

'Gold . . .' I said. 'I have to use it on the horse.'

Pamela Jane, to her eternal credit, dried her tears in mid-sniffle and in horrified disgust told me frankly across the workroom that I should be thinking of freeing Hickory, not making a trophy for Cheltenham races.

'How can you?' she exclaimed. 'It's *despicable*.'

'A car from the jewellers is bringing the gold for the hooves, mane and tail,' I said.

Rose wavered, and then demanded, 'When?'

I said I wouldn't tell her.

'Yes, you will,' she said, and advanced the hot iron in menace.

'Eleven o'clock,' I said hastily. A good lie. 'Let me make the horse,' I suggested, and made it sound on the verge of pleading. 'Then, when I've made the horse, I'll tell you where to look where I think the tape might be, and then you must promise to set Hickory free as soon as you have the gold.'

Pamela Jane said helplessly, 'I don't believe this.'

She couldn't understand how easily I had crumbled. She couldn't see that her scorn was the measure of my success.

Rose looked at her watch, discovered she would have to wait an hour for the gold to arrive and did the unwise calculation that she could afford to wait for it.

'Get on and make the trophy,' she instructed. 'When the gold comes, you'll sign for it in the normal way, or your Hickory's for the slow burn, understand?'

I nodded.

'Get on with it, then.' She looked round the workshop, assessing the state of things, and told Pamela Jane to sit deep in the other soft chair. There, while Adam Force held his threatening needle at her neck, Norman Osprey taped her ankles together.

Pamela Jane glared at me and said she wouldn't be assisting me with the horse, or ever again.

Rose consolidated this decision by telling her I'd always been a coward. I looked expressionlessly at Pamela Jane and saw the shade of doubt creep in, even while she listened to Rose pour on the disdain.

I hadn't meant to shape the trophy horse under the threat of Rose's hand on the punty irons. I had in fact mobilized the bodyguards to prevent it, and they hadn't. On the other hand a confrontation with Rose some day had been inevitable, and if it were to be *now* then I'd need to think a bit faster. I stood flat-footed, without drive.

Rose taunted, 'I thought you were supposed to be good at glass.'

'Too many people,' I complained.

She peremptorily ordered Norman Osprey and Eddie Payne to go round the half-wall into the showroom, and with more politeness shifted Adam Force round after them. All three leaned on the half-wall, watching. Having pulled out one of the punty irons that I'd put to heat beside the active part of the furnace, Rose thrust it into the crucible – the tank – holding now white-hot glass, and drew it out, a reasonably sized gather, revolving it just speedily enough for it not to fall off onto the floor.

'Go on,' she said. She shoved her lump of burning devastation towards my right arm and I retreated far enough for it not to char my skin.

It was no way to make a trophy of any sort. I needed to start the horse's body with several gathers of clear crystal and Rose, with irons loaded with plum-sized tips that would destroy whatever they touched, hovered over Hickory's and Pamela Jane's heads and threatened to melt off their ears, to make their roasting flesh smell like meat cooking if I gave her the slightest cause. I was to tell her all the time what I proposed to do next. There were to be no sudden unforeseen moves on my part. Hickory and Pamela Jane would suffer. Did I understand? Rose demanded.

I did.

I understood. So did Pamela Jane, and so did Hickory, who could hear.

I told Rose I would need to take four or five gathers from the tank, and while she had her own lump of destruction close to Pamela Jane's ear I harvested enough glass to make a horse standing on his hind legs a third of a metre high.

Pamela Jane closed her eyes.

I told Rose in advance that it was almost, if not totally impossible, to make a horse of that size without an assistant, which was partly because the body of the horse had to be kept at working heat after one had sculpted thc muscles of the neck and the upper legs while one added two pieces of glass for each lower leg and foot, and others for the tail.

'Get on with it and don't whinge,' she said. She was smiling to herself.

People in circuses could keep a dozen plates spinning in the air by twiddling sticks under them. Making that rearing horse in Broadway felt much the same: keep the body and legs hot while you sculpted the head. The resulting head wouldn't have won in a pre-school contest.

Rose was enjoying herself. The less I blocked and opposed her the more certain she grew that I was on the way to capitulation. She liked it. She smiled again, a secretive dirty-little-girl underhand twist of the lips.

I looked at that smile and abruptly I personally understood what Worthington had described. Victory for Rose was never complete without the physical humiliation of a male adversary.

Victory over Gerard Logan, which Rose now saw as gloriously her own, wouldn't be sufficient for her in that place unless it included her inflicting some depth of burn.

I might shudder at such a prospect but Rose wouldn't. I might use plain muscle power in an all-out attempt to defeat her, but I wouldn't try to wreak havoc of molten glass on Rose. Nor on anybody. I lacked the brutality.

Neither, though, could I desert my team and run.

With tweezers I pulled the horse's front legs up and its rear legs down and held the whole body on an iron within the furnace to keep it hot enough to mould.

There were still things I could do, I thought.

Honourable exits.

Exits that were more or less honourable, anyway.

I managed to juggle body and leg pieces into a headless racer.

Exits, hell, I thought. Exit wasn't enough. Defeatism never got anyone anywhere.

I held two punty irons with difficulty and transferred enough glass from one to the other to attach and shape a mane, but it hadn't the elegance necessary for Cheltenham.

Worthington opened the gallery door and began to come in from the street. His eyes widened as fast as his comprehension as he spun a fast one-eighty degree turn and was on his way down the hill before Rose could decide which had priority, chasing Worthington or keeping me penned.

When Worthington was out of anything but whistling distance she told Force and her father to lock the gallery door immediately and was furious because neither of them could find a key. I hoped to hell and back that Pamela Jane wouldn't report obligingly that she herself had a key to everywhere.

She gave me another uncertain stare and shut her teeth.

Rose stopped smiling, loaded her punty iron with a white hot golf-ball sized end of glass and held it close to Hickory.

I did my best to make and fix a tail to my increasingly non-thoroughbred creation. The tail and two hind feet formed a triangle to support the rearing horse. When I wanted a great result, this stage often went wrong. That day it all balanced like perfection.

Hickory wriggled desperately to get away from Rose's white-hot threat.

Pamela Jane saw me doing nothing to help Hickory while constructing only a toy, and went back to despising me.

I stuck the head on the neck and tweaked the ears forward. Finished, the object had four legs, head, mane and tail, and no grace whatever. I stood it upright on the marver table, where rearing, it was ready to start leaping into the future from a crystal ball.

In spite of the faults, Rose seemed impressed. Not

impressed enough, however, to lower her guard, or her punty iron beside Hickory's head.

I glanced at the workshop clock.

A minute – tick tock, tick tock – was a very long time.

I said, 'The gold will cover the hooves and the mane and the tail.'

Tick tock, tick tock.

Rose thrust her cooling punty iron back into the furnace and brought out a new white-hot gather which she again held near Hickory's head.

'How long,' she demanded, 'until that gold gets here?'

Hickory wriggled violently, trying desperately to free himself from the sticky strips on his mouth and his eyes.

Pamela Jane, eyes closed, seemed to be praying.

Two minutes. Tick tock.

'The gold,' I said, 'will come in small bars. It has to be melted, then it has to cover the hooves and the mane and the tail . . .'

Hickory threw himself forward, trying to get out of his embracing chair. Rose didn't move her punty iron far enough away fast enough to avoid him, and one of his ears did touch her waving white-hot blob of glass.

Under the parcel tape, he couldn't scream. His body arched. Rose jumped back, but Hickory's ear sizzled and now smelled of fried meat, and would never be perfect again.

Three minutes. Eternity. Tick tock.

Hickory's horror, plain and agonizing, had everyone staring. Rose should have jettisoned her iron and gone to his help, but she didn't.

Three minutes, ten seconds since I stood the rearing horse on the marver table.

Dangerous to wait any longer.

I picked up the big tweezers I'd used to form the horse's mane, and with them tore the parcel tape securing Pamela Jane's ankles. I pulled her up by her still tied wrists, and Rose turned towards me from Hickory and yelled at me to leave her alone.

Pamela Jane had no idea what she should do, and to dither could be fatal. I said to her urgently, '*Run*' and she didn't, but hesitated, looking back to Hickory. No time left. I lifted her up bodily and carried her.

Pamela Jane objected. Rose ordered me to put her down. I didn't, but aimed a bit unsteadily for the way into the showroom and shouted at the trio there leaning on the half-wall to get down behind it.

Rose came fast across the workshop after me, and drove at me, holding her hot glass-laden punty iron like a sword.

Half seeing her, half sensing the searing future, I twisted both myself and Pamela Jane roughly to let the iron miss us, like a bullfighter, but Rose in her fury dragged and stabbed and burned a long black slit through my white singlet.

No more time.

I lugged Pamela Jane round the half-wall to the show-room and threw her, screaming protests, to the ground, and I fell on top of her to pin her down.

The rearing horse had stood unannealed at maximum heat on the marver table for three minutes forty seconds when it exploded.

# CHAPTER TWELVE

The horse exploded into scorching fragments that flew like angry transparent wasps throughout the workshop and over the half-wall into the showroom beyond.

Adam Force, refusing to get down because it had been I who suggested it, had been hit twice, once in the upper arm, and once, more seriously, across the top of the cheekbone below the eye, taking away a chunk of surface flesh. Half fainting from shock, the doctor dropped his syringe. Blood reddened his sleeve, but there was no spurting arterial flood.

It was the wreck of his good looks though, I thought, that would in the end grieve him most, and if he had peered into a looking glass at that moment, he would probably have collapsed altogether. The speed and sharpness of the flying glass fragment had opened a furrow that was bound to leave an untreatable scar, and like many facial cuts this one was bleeding copiously. Adam Force bled into his white beard, which was fast turning red.

Dr Bright-Scarlet-Beard Force. Serve him right, I

thought. A pity it would wash clean. Wash clean . . . other things would wash out, too . . . an idea.

Glass cooled rapidly if it expanded and thinned. One could gently blow down an iron into semi-liquid glass so that it would expand until it looked like a soap bubble: a dollop of red-hot glass would cool to the cold shell of a brittle bubble in the few seconds it took to blow it from one state to the other.

The trophy horse though, hadn't been blown on purpose from the inside. It had split violently apart along the internal stress lines caused by the pulling and stretching as the glass cooled, the outer regions cooling faster than the inner core. The splinters had still been fiercely hot when they'd dug into the first thing they met. Adam Force had been lucky not to lose an eye.

Norman Osprey, kneeling in spite of his antipathy towards the source of good advice, had survived the shattering of the horse with his skin intact, if not his temper.

Although pale and slightly shaking, the Elvis lookalike still clung to the doctrine of 'get Logan'. In consequence he'd risen from his knees and planted his gorilla shoulders close inside the gallery-to-street door, making an exit that way a matter of hand to hand fighting and a toss up whether I won or lost. A hand-to-hand fight against that visibly dramatic strength would have been daunting always but in my tottery state at that moment, even if I'd wanted to quit the scene, which I didn't, a win would have been impossible. As long as Norman Osprey thought he was usefully stationed where he was doing me no good, however, I could count him one less trouble to deal with, and be grateful.

Eddie, who seemed not to understand what had happened, was still on his knees beside the wall. Martin's valet who, with his stubborn misconceptions, had accompanied Rose on this whole unholy tape-hunt, now looked as though he were begging absolution. To my mind he certainly failed to deserve it.

Pamela Jane heaved herself from under me in a troubled dilemma as she couldn't decide whether to thank me for saving her from razor-sharp damage since, in the chair, she'd been in a direct line to be peppered, or to revile me for leaving Hickory to take whatever came his way in the blast.

Pamela Jane, of course, had understood the physics of stress and strain in super-heated glass, and she would now be sure I'd intended to shatter the horse from the moment I'd started to make it. She would be puzzling over the nonsense of the gold delivery, both the amount and the timing because, as she confessed to me much later, it had all been so *unlike* me. She had believed every word I'd said to Rose, and now she felt a fool. 'Dear Pam J,' I contentedly said, 'you were sincerely a great help.'

That was afterwards. At the time, during the immediate aftermath of the destruction of the trophy horse, she still worried over the outcome for Hickory.

When I stood up and looked over the half-wall to see what shape Rose and Hickory were in, I found Rose bleeding down one leg but still shaking with determined fury while she shoved a clean punty iron into the tank and drew out a second one already tipped with white-hot hate.

Hickory, who had finally succeeded in flinging himself out of the chair altogether, lay face down on the smooth brick floor trying to rub the adhesive off his mouth. Tears from the pain of his damaged ear seemed to be running helplessly down inside his nose, and he was trying to deal with that by sniffing.

Sharply aware that at some point somewhere Rose had succeeded in drawing a line of fire across my own lower back ribs, I felt I'd already had enough for one morning of the unequal combat.

Rose hadn't. Rose, it seemed, had energy in stock for a third world war. As she drew her loaded iron with speed from the fire, she told me that if I didn't get back at once into the workshop the burn to Hickory's ear would be only the beginning. She could have freed him. She could at least have helped him, but she didn't.

I went round the half-wall. Hickory still lay face down on the floor, but instead of rubbing his face raw without results, he was now threshing his legs instead. Hurting and helpless, he was in no immediate danger from Rose who chose to advance on me, holding the silvery black five-foot long punty iron loaded ready to strike if I didn't dodge fast enough.

'Adam Force's videotape,' she demanded. 'Where is it?'

Short of breath from evading deep burns so long, I

managed dry-mouthed to reply, 'He said he'd re-recorded it with horse races.'

'Rubbish.' Rose advanced towards me with the white-hot ball of glass inexorably leading the way. Had we been armed the other way round I could with two cuts of heavy scissors have sliced the ball into a pointed spear. The spear, if one thrust it fiercely, would burn a path right through a body, searing, cauterizing and killing. Rose had no spear but a ball was bad enough. Its effect would be the same.

With at least some sort of plan I backed away from Rose and her deadly fire, cursing that I couldn't reach the five or six punty irons lying idle to one side – irons I could at least have used to fence with – because Hickory with his shocking wound lay suffering in my way.

Rose began again to enjoy compelling me to retreat step by backward step. Backwards past the furnace, its trapdoor shut. Backwards across the workshop, faster as she increased her pace.

'The videotape,' she repeated. 'Where is it?'

At last, *at last*, I saw Worthington again outside the gallery door, Worthington this time flanked by Tom Pigeon, Jim, Catherine and her hobo partner, Pernickety Paul.

Norman Osprey, suddenly not liking the odds, stood back to let them in and dived fast round them out into the street. I had a last glimpse of him as he set off down the hill with Tom and his three four-legged companions in pursuit.

The two plain-clothes officers, with Worthington and Jim, filled the doorway he'd left. Furiously seeing the advent of my friends as her last chance to make me remember her for life, Rose rushed recklessly at my abdomen. I side-stepped and dodged yet again and ran and swerved, and ended where I'd aimed for, beside the wide round pots of coloured powders on the stock shelves.

It was the white colour I wanted, the dust the Germans called *emaill weiss*. I snatched off the lid and plunged my hand into the open pot, grabbed as much dust as I could in one handful and threw it at Rose's eyes.

*Emaill weiss* – white enamel ground to dust – contained arsenic . . . and arsenic dust made eyes blur and water and go temporarily and effectively blind. Rose, her eyes streaming, her sight gone, went on sweeping around with her petrifying length of death-bearing punty iron.

Eddie seemingly rose from his prayers and walked around the half-wall pleading with her to be still. 'Rose, dear girl, it's over . . .'

But nothing would stop her. Blinded for a while she might be, but she lashed out with the killing iron at where she'd last seen me, trying still to penetrate my stomach or chest, then wildly slashing at where my head had been. Missing me didn't stop her being more dangerous blundering about than if she could see me and finally, disastrously, the unimaginably hot glass connected twice with living flesh.

There were screams chokingly cut off.

It was Eddie, her father, that incredibly she had hit first. She had seared the skin from his fingers as he had held them in front of his face to defend himself. There were crashes of iron against walls and a fearful soft sizzling as the worst of all calamities happened.

Pamela Jane hysterically threw herself into my arms and hid her face, but it wasn't she who had burned. From across the workshop, where the air again smelled of funeral pyre, Paul folded to the ground and lay motionless, his limbs sprawling in the haphazardness of death.

Catherine in a state of shock and anger stared hollow-eyed in disbelief. I stretched an arm towards her and hugged both girls as if I could never let them go.

Adam Force came to stand against the safe side of the workshop wall and begged Rose to stand still and let someone – like himself – come to help her and her father, with the only result that she changed direction towards his voice, lashing through the air in great sweeps of the punty iron.

Catherine, a police officer to the bone, stiffened after her first need for comfort and, with Rose following the sound of her voice, walked away from me and called her station urgently for back-up. Stifling human terror she spoke tightly on her personal radio, pushing the transit button, 'Officer down,' she said. 'Red call. Red call. Officer in need of immediate assistance.'

She reported the address of Logan Glass, and then and with less formality, and genuine, extreme emotion, added, 'Come at once. Dear God.'

She dodged Rose's rushing speed and with incredible bravery knelt down beside her silent hobo partner. The plain-clothes inhabitant of doorways, whose name to me had never been more than 'Pernickety Paul', would catch no more villains. Pernickety Paul had taken a long white-hot direct hit through his neck.

I disentangled myself from Pamela Jane and half ran across the room away from Catherine and called to Rose, 'I'm here, Rose. I'm over here and you'll never catch me.'

Rose turned half circle my way and pivoted once more when I jumped past her again and yelled at her. She turned again and again and finally began to tire enough with her blurring eyes for Worthington and Jim to reach my side and for Catherine to come up behind us, and for the four of us to grab Rose at high speed and immobilize her still slashing punty-iron arm. I wrestled the iron a good safe way away from her, feeling the heat of it near my legs, but not on my skin, and *still* she went on struggling in Worthington's and Jim's grasp.

The police side of Catherine flowed in her like a strong tide. She sought and found the handcuffs carried by Pernickety Paul on a belt round his waist. She clicked them roughly onto Rose's wrists behind her back, the metal bands squeezed tight against her skin.

Rose kicked.

'Take my belt,' Worthington shouted, and I unbuckled his pliable woven-leather belt and tied it round one ankle and knotted it to the other, until Rose overbalanced and lay on her side on the floor, still threshing her legs and cursing.

There was nothing about 'going quietly' in the arrest of Rose Payne. An ambulance with paramedics and two cars full of bristling young police officers drew up outside the gallery and filled Logan Glass, crunching the fragments of the shattered horse to dust under their heavy boots. They talked with Catherine and fetched a blanket in which they rolled Rose like a baby in swaddling clothes and, with her struggling to the end, manhandled her out through the showroom and gallery door and shoved her into the back of one of the police cars.

Spitting fury, Rose was soon joined there by the burly Norman Osprey whose muscles had been no match for three sets of canine fangs. Tom told me later that the big man had sat in the road quivering with fear, his head and hands between his legs, begging for the police to rescue him from the black snarls circling around him.

In the workshop I watched as Catherine, dry eyed, brought another blanket in from a police car to cover the silence of Paul.

More police arrived, some in uniform and others in plain clothes more suitable for a Sunday in front of the television than a trip to a fiery hell on earth. Off duty or not, some things demanded attendance. White overalls and grey plastic shoe covers were produced and soon the workshop took on the look of unreal science fiction.

I watched a policeman wearing surgical rubber gloves carefully lift the fallen syringe and place it gingerly in a clear plastic bag which he sealed.

Methodically the police began to sort and list names, and it was the Dragon across the road who offered solace and recovery with a warm heart. One of the police officers removed the tape from Pamela Jane's wrists, took her personal details, and then with a solicitous arm helped her to the hotel.

I knelt beside Hickory. I told him I was going to remove the sticky strips from his eyes and mouth. I asked him if he understood.

Hickory nodded and stopped struggling against the floor.

As humanely as possible I pulled the tape from his eyes. It came off painfully with eyelashes attached and it was several minutes before his long obstructed sight cleared and he was staring straight at me beside him.

'I'm going to take the tape off your mouth,' I said.

He nodded.

One of the young police officers stretched a hand down over my shoulder and with a lack of sensitivity simply ripped the strong tape off. Hickory yelled and went on yelling, telling the police officer to free his taped-together hands, and to hurry up.

I left them for a moment and brought the first-aid box from the stock shelves to put a dressing on Hickory's ear, and after a good deal of chat, the paramedics and the police decided together that he should go to hospital along with Eddie who was now deep in shock with hands that had already blistered badly.

Catherine stood by the ambulance's open door watching Eddie being helped aboard for treatment.

I told her other things she ought to know, extra things about Black-mask Four that had come to me during the night, that I hadn't mentioned in the dawn.

She said thoughtfully, 'Our superintendent is that man standing beside Paul. You'd better talk to him. I have to go to the station. I'll come back here when I can.'

She took me across the room, introduced me as the owner of the place and left me to deepen the frown of the top brass.

I shook hands with Superintendent Shepherd of the West Mercia police.

First of all he looked with disenchantment at my singlet, now no longer white and clean but grubby from constant contact with workshop clutter. He took in the singed piece of cloth hanging loose in the lower ribs area where Rose's relentless attentions had connected. He asked if the reddened skin beneath was painful and I tiredly said yes, it was, but I'd had worse burns in the past and would prefer to ignore it: but, I added to myself, the burns had always before been accidentally self-inflicted.

I looked down at the blanket over Pernickety Paul, the fuss-pot who had cared like a father for Catherine's safety in the violent streets.

'He was a good policeman,' I said.

The superintendent let a small silence ride by before mentioning come-uppance for the perpetrator. He would need me to proceed to the police station to make a statement which would be videotaped and in every way recorded. Judiciously he agreed I could cover the burns with dressings and restore my shirt on top, and then, reluctantly, he also agreed I could hang my coat over my shoulders so as not to freeze out of doors.

During this display of humanity George Lawson-Young arrived, and with his presence, transformed the general police atmosphere from suspicion to common sense. He was the sort of deeply respected man that other men in authority instinctively trusted. When he greeted and treated me with noticeably high levels of deference, my standing with the super took a slow drift upwards. I thought he went so far after a while as to believe what I said.

George Lawson-Young asked me as if expecting the answer 'Yes', 'Did you work out the identity of the fourth man who assaulted you outside here on the pavement two weeks ago?'

'Yes.'

He knew that answer in advance as I had told him that morning on the telephone. I had used his search-and-discard method to sort out truth from lies, and to go carefully down the cul-de-sacs, but however flatly I said the name, it would cause consternation.

The professor, tall, tidy and short-sighted, made a slow visual inspection of the damage to the most familiar of faces turned his way. No one tried to hurry him, not even the superintendent.

Adam Force, his facial bleeding down from Niagara to a trickle, had wandered dizzily into the workshop from the showroom and was standing beside Hickory, looking down on him as, on his knees, Hickory cradled his mutilated ear.

When Adam Force saw the professor, he looked as if he would prefer to evaporate rather than be in the same room as his one-time boss, and George, usually the most forgiving of men, produced a thoroughly baleful glare with no pity component for his expert practitioner of treason.

One of the policemen in white overalls asked Dr Force his name and address while another took his photograph. The flash seemed to startle him and, with a blood red rivulet still meandering down his cheek into his beard, he looked far from the assured physician I had first met on the hill at Lynton.

A spent Force, I thought ironically.

The photographer moved on, snapping under the direction of the Scene Of Crime Officer. Nothing was to be missed. Pernickety Paul would have been proud.

It was George Lawson-Young, saying he was hoping I'd done enough for him for the next thousand years, who related to the superintendent step by step how the data stolen from his research laboratory had caused me so much pain and trouble.

Naming each person in turn to identify them for the policeman's sake, and referring back to me for confirmation when he needed it, George quietly threaded his way through the complexities of January 2000.

'Adam Force,' he said pointing at Doctor Bright-Scarlet-Beard, 'worked for me but jumped ship and stole the cancer research that just may be worth millions and would certainly be to the advantage of the whole world.'

I could see the superintendent begin to be sceptical but I nodded and he focused back on the professor.

'We knew,' George went on, 'that he had stolen the information, had transferred it to a videotape and had destroyed all other records of our research. Understandably, we searched everywhere for it, even engaging private investigators, after the police had shown little interest.'

Superintendent Shepherd flinched not at all but continued listening intently.

'All our searches were in vain. We did not expect him to have entrusted the tape to the safekeeping of a jockey. Dr Force had passed it to Martin Stukely but Stukely preferred to hand it on to his friend Gerard Logan here, away from the fingers of his own children. As perhaps you know, Martin Stukely was killed at Cheltenham races on New Year's Eve. But the tape had already begun its tortuous journey by then. Adam Force tried to steal it back. Tapes were stolen from here, from Gerard's home and from the home of Martin Stukely.'

'Were we informed of those thefts?' asked the policeman.

'Yes,' I replied, 'but the theft of a few videotapes for no apparent reason hardly brought the law out like today.'

'Hmm,' replied the superintendent, knowing it was true.

'One of your officers did come round here the following morning,' I said, 'but there was far more interest in the money stolen with the tape.'

'Did Dr Force steal the money as well?' asked the super, looking at Force.

'Yes,' I replied, 'but I think that was just an opportunist theft which he might have thought would somehow smoke-screen the removal of the tape.'

Dr Force listened impassionately, his bloodied face giving away nothing.

'Anyway,' went on the professor, who did not welcome the interruption, 'somehow all the thefts failed to get back the tape they wanted and Dr Force, with assistance from Rose Payne and others, has been trying here to coerce Mr Logan to reveal its whereabouts. But he tells me he hasn't got it.'

'And have you?' asked the voice of authority.

'No,' I replied, 'but I think I know who has.'

They all looked at me. Adam Force, Lawson-Young, the superintendent and even Hickory, who had been listening with his good ear, they all waited expectantly.

Into this tableau swept Marigold, floating in emerald

silk with gold tassels and brushing aside the young constable who tried to stand in her way. In her wake came Bon-Bon, Victor, Daniel and the other children like the tail of a kite.

Marigold demanded to see how her trophy was getting along but was brought up sharply by the sight of the blanket-covered form in the workshop and the mass of evidence gatherers crawling cautiously around it on their hands and knees. Bon-Bon, realizing the enormity of the situation, swept her brood back out of the door, leaving just her mother and Victor inside, both of them stock-still, transfixed, living through their eyes.

'Gerard, darling,' Marigold exclaimed, 'what *is* going on? And where is Worthington?'

'Marigold my dear,' I said wearily, 'there's been a disaster. Please go across the road to the hotel and wait for me there.'

She seemed not to hear, her eyes steadfastly on the blanket. 'Where is Worthington?' Her voice began to rise. 'Where's Worthington? Oh my God.'

I took her in my arms. 'Marigold, Marigold, he's all right. I promise. That's not Worthington.'

She sobbed on my shoulder near to collapse.

Victor turned to me and said, his voice barely more than a whisper, 'It's not a game any more, is it?'

The question needed no answer, and presently the young constable led him and Marigold across to the Wychwood Dragon.

'So who is Black-mask Four?' asked Lawson-Young into the silence when they had gone.

'Who?' said the superintendent. 'What are you talking about?'

The professor told him. 'Gerard was attacked by four people in black masks outside his shop here. Three of them were Rose Payne, her father Eddie Payne and Norman Osprey. Gerard told me earlier today that he had worked out the identity of the fourth, so,' he turned to me and said with faith, 'who is it and where is my research?'

'I don't think Black-mask Four has the tape,' I replied.

'What!' exclaimed the professor. His shoulders dropped, his expectations had been so high and he took it now that I was leading him only to another cul-de-sac, another dead-end.

I put him right, 'My fourth assailant, Black-mask Four, was just a hired help and I'm not sure he even knew exactly what he was looking for.' But he knew, I thought, how to inflict maximum damage to my wrists. 'He is, however, a dab hand with a baseball bat and anaesthetic gas.'

'Who is it, for God's sake?' The professor was finding it difficult to stifle his impatience, as was the superintendent, yet it wasn't the easiest disclosure I'd ever made. Still . . .

'Who was the fourth man, Hickory?' I asked.

Hickory looked up from where he was kneeling on the floor still holding a dressing to his ear.

'Why are you asking me?' he said.

'You bunched my fingers.'

'Of course I didn't.'

'I'm afraid you did,' I said. 'You held my hand against a wall ready for a baseball bat to smash my wrist.'

'You must be crazy. Why would I attack you? Why you of all people?'

It was a piercing question and one with a complex answer. He didn't answer it, but we both knew what he had intended.

'Did you do it for money?' I asked.

I suspected that it was for more convoluted reasons than that. Something to do with my ability with glass-blowing and his comparative lack of it. Envy was a strong emotion and, I reckoned, he wouldn't have needed a whole lot of persuasion to oppose me.

He still refused to admit it. 'You're crazy, you are,' he said getting to his feet and turning away as if looking for some quick escape.

'The green and white laces,' I said.

He stopped dead and turned back.

I went on, 'You wore them here the day Martin Stukely was killed, and you wore them again the following day when you stole the tapes from his house, the day you hit me with the orange cylinder. Martin's eldest son Daniel saw the laces and told the police about them.'

Hickory advanced a step or two, his ear clearly hurting. His poise cracked.

'You're so fucking clever,' he said. 'I wish we *had* broken your wrists.'

The superintendent stopped leaning on the half-wall and stood up straight.

But Hickory had only just started.

'You and your fancy ways and your condescending comments about my work. I hate you and this workshop. I'm a damn good glass-blower and I deserve more recognition.' He raised his chin and sneered.

'One day,' he went on, 'John Hickory will be a name worth knowing and people will smash Fucking Logan glass to get to mine.'

Such a shame, I thought. He really did have some talent but, I suspected, it would never be allowed to develop as it should. Arrogance and a belief in skills he didn't have would smother those he did.

'And Rose?' I asked.

'Stupid bitch,' he said holding his hand to his throbbing head, 'bloody mad she is. Tie you up, she said. Use you as a hostage, she said. Nothing about frying my effing ear. Hope she rots in hell.'

I hoped she'd rot on earth.

'She promised me my own place,' Hickory said. 'Claimed she'd close you down. Her and that stupid father of hers.' He began to realize the hole he was digging for himself. 'They put me up to it. It was their fault, not mine.'

He looked wretchedly at the rapt faces around him.

'It wasn't my fault. It was their idea.'

No one believed him. It had been Hickory who had reported all to Rose. Hickory had been the 'Binocs' in Broadway.

'So where is the tape?' asked George Lawson-Young.

'I don't know,' replied Hickory. 'Rose said that it must have been in Stukely's house or in Logan's but I've sat through hours of bloody horse racing and glass-blowing and I'm telling you, there was no tape of medical stuff.'

I believed him. Otherwise, I thought ruefully, I might have been saved a couple of beatings and Pernickety Paul would still be lying around in shop doorways.

A paramedic appeared and said that it was time to take Hickory to the hospital to dress his burn. The superintendent, roused into action, arrested Hickory, 'You do not have to say anything . . .'

'Too bloody late,' retorted Hickory, as he was led off to the ambulance by a white-overalled police officer and the paramedic.

The super turned his attention to Dr Red-Beard Force who had listened in silence throughout.

He said, his speech always in the pattern of officialese, 'Well, Dr Force, can you enlighten us as to the whereabouts of a videotape containing medical research results stolen from the professor here.'

Force said nothing. It seemed that he had at least learnt one lesson from our discussion under the fir trees in Lynton.

'Come on, Adam, tell us.' The professor, I saw, still had some vestige of friendship for the man before him dripping blood from his beard onto my smooth brick floor.

Force looked at him with disdain and kept silent.

In his turn, he too was arrested and taken away for wound-stitching and fingerprinting. 'You do not have to say anything . . .' So he didn't.

In time, the gallery, showroom and workshop began to clear. The coroner's representative arrived and supervised the relocation of Paul to the local morgue. The other officers stopped work to stand and watch the sorry procession of undertakers and their highly regarded and valued burden move through the gallery to the door. There were tears in my eyes as well as in theirs. He had been a good man as well as a good policeman.

A few more photographs were taken and a few more pieces of evidence were collected. Blue and white 'Do Not Cross' tape was strung about, doors were locked and guarded, and the professor and I were gently eased out to the street into the grey appropriate drizzle.

The superintendent again asked me to accompany him to the police station to make a full statement although, this time, there was more warmth in his manner. I agreed, but first, I asked, could we all go over to the Wychwood Dragon as I was thirsty and needed a jug of tea. I looked at my cheap watch. Amazingly it was still morning though it felt to me more as if teatime must have come and gone.

They were in the residents' downstairs sitting room. Bon-Bon and her four children sat tightly side by side on the wide sofa in descending height from the right. Coca-Colas had been bought and a line of empty bottles with straws sat on a coffee table. Marigold occupied a deep squashy armchair while Worthington perched on its arm by her side. The manner in which Marigold clung to Worthington's hand reminded me of his fly-trap warning. He didn't appear to protest.

The Dragon poured tea into large millennium souvenir mugs and told us that Pamela Jane, still badly shocked, had been given a pill by the police doctor and dispatched to bed upstairs.

Victor stood by the window unable to remove his eyes from Logan Glass opposite. I took my tea over and joined him.

Without turning his head, he said, 'I suppose my Aunt Rose will be inside for a long time?'

'Yes,' I said, 'a very long time.' For life, I thought, either in prison or a secure mental hospital. Police killers didn't get early parole.

He stood in silence a moment longer, then turned and looked me straight in the eye. 'Good,' he said, 'it might give me and Mum a chance.'

I turned and took Bon-Bon out into the hotel lobby. I

needed her to do me a favour. Certainly, she said, and trotted off to the telephone booth beneath the stairs.

I went back into the sitting room to finish my tea and soon after Bon-Bon returned with a smiling nod.

I thought about the events of the morning, and wondered if there had been another way.

Punty irons in anyone's hand had to be swung around carefully. In Rose's hands a punty iron tipped with semi-liquid glass had literally been a lethal weapon, and it had seemed to me that as it was me she was after, however weird and mistaken her beliefs, it was I who ought to stop her.

I'd tried to stop her with the shattering horse and I hadn't succeeded. It had torn a hole in her lover and stoked her own anger, and I'd thought then, if I could blind her she would stop, so I'd thrown the powder, but blinding her had made her worse.

Paul had died.

If I hadn't tried to stop her, if instead I had surrendered at once to her as she'd demanded, then Paul would be alive. But, I reflected, searching for comfort, I couldn't have given her the tape she demanded as I hadn't known exactly where it was.

I'd done my best, and my best had killed.

The voice of the superintendent brought me back to the present. He said he was eager to get to the police station to interview his prisoners and also that he was less eager, but duty demanded it, to visit DC Paul Cratchet's family. 'Would the professor and Mr Logan come with me now, please, sirs,' he said.

'Another cup of tea?' I replied.

The super was not happy. 'Contrary to popular belief, the tea at the nick is quite drinkable. So, if you please.'

I needed more time.

Settling into another deep armchair, I said, 'Just a moment to sit down? I'm exhausted. How about something to eat before we go?'

'We have a canteen at the station. You can have something there.' The voice of authority had spoken and there seemed little else to do but comply.

I rose slowly to my feet and with relief found my expected guest hurrying at last through the door.

'Hello, Priam,' I said.

He looked past me towards the tall elegantly suited George Lawson-Young. He flicked a glance at Bon-Bon as much to say, 'Is this the one?'

'Priam,' I repeated, 'it's so good of you to come. Priam Jones, can I introduce Superintendent Shepherd of the West Mercia police.'

Priam turned slowly my way and instinctively shook an offered hand.

'I'm sorry?' he said, puzzled, 'I don't quite understand. Bon-Bon called me to say that she was with a potential racehorse owner and I should get down here pronto if I wanted the business. Interrupted a good lunch too, I can tell you.'

He looked around him still searching for the elusive owner.

'Priam,' I regained his attention, 'that wasn't quite the truth. I asked Bon-Bon to make that call because I needed to talk to you.' He wasn't pleased. Far from it.

'What's wrong with the bloody telephone if you needed a chat, although about what I can't imagine.' He looked down at four sets of childhood eyes staring up at him. 'Hmp . . . sorry.'

I said, 'I needed a chat about a videotape.'

'Not that bl— er . . . er . . . videotape business again,' he said. 'I have told you already, I don't have any videotape.'

Daniel said distinctly, 'I know where there's a videotape.'

'Shhhh, darling,' said Bon-Bon.

'But I *do* know where a tape is,' Daniel persisted.

I had learnt to take Daniel very seriously indeed.

I squatted down to his level on the sofa. 'Where is the videotape, Daniel?' I said.

'I think it must be worth at least three or four gold coins,' he replied.

'What *does* he mean?' asked Professor Lawson-Young.

'It's a game we've been playing,' I said. 'I give Daniel treasure if he gives or finds me information.' I turned back to Daniel. 'I think it might indeed be worth three or four gold coins.'

'A whole bagful of treasure,' said the professor, 'if it's the right tape.'

Daniel looked positively delighted at the prospect.

'It's in Daddy's car,' he said. 'It's in the pocket on the back of Daddy's seat. I saw it there yesterday when Mummy brought us to your shop.'

He looked at me questioningly and beamed when I told him, 'Ten gold coins this time if the professor agrees.'

George Lawson-Young, speechless, nodded his head until it seemed it might fall off.

Daniel said, 'I like finding things for Gerard. I'll always look for things for him.'

Priam shuffled uneasily beside me.

I said to him, 'Why did you switch the tapes?'

'I told you—' he started.

'I know what you told me,' I interrupted. 'It was a lie.' Discard the lies, the professor had told me in Bristol and I would be left with the truth. I asked again, 'Why did you switch the tapes?'

He shrugged his shoulders. 'I thought,' he said, 'that the tape Eddie Payne passed to you was one showing the hiding place of an antique necklace. Worth millions, I'd heard from someone. I found it in your raincoat that night and I thought, with Martin dead, no one would know if I kept it.'

Half truths and misconceptions had woven a path to death and destruction.

Priam went on, 'I took another tape from Martin's den, one with racing on it, and wrapped it in the same piece of paper and put it back in your raincoat pocket. When I played the original tape at home that night I discovered that it was all unintelligible mumbo jumbo with nothing about a necklace. So I just put it back in Martin's car when I drove it back to Bon-Bon's the next day.'

He looked around him. 'No harm done. You have the tape back. No need for the police.'

No harm done. Oh God, how wrong he was.

It was four days before the police would allow me back into Logan Glass.

Broadway had been the centre of a media circus. The Dragon from over the road had previously said, 'You were always news in this town, lover' and, for filling her rooms, she allowed me use of her best suite and paraded her little glass animals along a shelf in the lobby with a notice offering duplicates for sale.

Marigold, her natural competitor in the matter of saris, kaftans, eyelashes and 'Darlings', wandered in and out waiting for me to start again on her trophy. Worthington, who had been upgraded from her chauffeur to her arm-in-arm companion, was dispatched with me to collect the necklace from the bank. Marigold secured total victory over the Dragon by wearing it day and night and finally buying it from me outright at huge expense.

Rose, Norman Osprey, Dr Force and Hickory had been

remanded in custody while Eddie had been remanded in hospital, his hands a mess.

Priam, not understanding the fuss, had been given police bail, which meant that his passport had been confiscated. 'Most inconvenient,' he had declared. 'Why have I been treated like a common criminal?' Because he was one, Worthington had told him and anyone else who'd listen.

Professor George Lawson-Young had been given the tape from Martin's car. There had been a few ugly moments when the superintendent had tried to hang onto it as evidence. Having once lost the information it contained, Lawson-Young had no intention of allowing it out of his sight again. The police had reluctantly consented to him taking it away briefly to make a copy.

Catherine, cuddling in my arms every night, kept me up to date with the news from the police station.

Rose did little else but scream abuse, most of it in my direction, it seemed.

Hickory blamed, me, Rose and the world in general.

Dr Force had said a little but denied most. He had revealed, however, that Martin Stukely had not been aware that the information on the tape had been stolen. Indeed, the doctor had told Martin that he was protecting the research from others trying to steal his own work.

I was glad of that. Had I doubted it?

On Thursday we re-opened. The showroom was busier than it had ever been on a weekday in January and sales boomed. But, in truth, there was far greater interest in the bloodstains, which had proved difficult to remove from between the bricks on the floor, than in the stock.

Pamela Jane had recovered sufficiently to return in time for the weekend although she preferred to work in the showroom and made rapid transits across the workshop to her locker only when she couldn't avoid it.

On Sunday, one week after the mayhem, I set out again to make the trophy horse.

Dependable Irish had agreed to act as my assistant and this time we had an audience of one. Catherine sat in her now familiar chair and watched as I again readied my tools and stripped down to my singlet.

I stood on the treadle to lift the door to the furnace and let the heat flood into the room.

Catherine took off her coat.

'Hang it in my locker,' I said, tossing her the locker keys.

She walked to the far end of the workshop and opened a door to the tall grey cabinet.

'What's on this?' she said holding up a videotape. 'It has a label "How to make the Cretan Sunrise".'

I moved swiftly to her side. She had by mistake opened Hickory's locker and there inside we found not just the necklace instruction tape but also, tucked into a brown paper bag, a pair of bright laces, green and white striped.

I laughed. 'A tale of three tapes and one of them was under my nose all the time.'

'Three tapes?' she asked. 'Two were bad enough.'

'There were three,' I replied. 'The only really important, valuable and perhaps unique tape was the one Force made of the stolen cancer-research results. He gave it to Martin who via Eddie gave it to me. Priam swapped it, mistakenly thinking it a treasure finder's dream to millions. When he found that it wasn't, he simply left it hidden in Martin's car. That was the tape that Rose and Dr Force were trying so hard to find.'

'And the necklace tape?' Catherine asked. 'This one?'

I said, 'I had lent the necklace instruction tape to Martin and it remained in his den at his house until Hickory stole it along with all the others. Hickory kept it because, to him, the tape had some value. He thought he could make a copy of the necklace. He obviously kept the tape in his locker.'

'What's the third tape then?' she said.

'The tape,' I went on, 'that Priam took from Martin's den before Hickory's theft. He put it in my raincoat pocket and it's that tape that Force stole at midnight on New Year's Eve thinking it was his cancer tape. I would have loved to have seen his face when he played it and found horse racing instead.'

I made the trophy horse. With Irish's help I gathered the glass from the furnace and again formed the horse's body, its legs and tail. But this time I took time and care and applied the knowledge and talent both learnt and inherited from my Uncle Ron. I moulded the neck and head of an intelligent animal, prominent cheekbones and a firm mouth. I gave it a mane flowing as if in full gallop and then applied it seamlessly to the body.

I had started out to make a commercial work for Marigold and Kenneth Trubshaw and his Cheltenham Trophy Committee. In the event I made a memorial to a trusted and much missed friend. A memorial worthy of his skill and his courage.

The leaping horse finally stood on the marver table and Irish and I lifted it quickly but carefully into one of the annealing ovens. There it would cool slowly and safely allowing the strains and stresses to ease gradually. This one was not for shattering.

I went with Catherine to the funeral of Pernickety Paul, but I abandoned her at the church door to her colleagues, uniformed and not. A small bunch of plain-clothes policemen enveloped her and mourned with her and it was a thoughtful and subdued police officer who, an hour later, mounted her motor cycle, paused before starting the engine, and said blankly to her future passenger, 'The private cremation's tomorrow and there are drinks in his memory in the pub this evening. I've been given leave for the rest of the day, so where do you want to go now?'

'To bed,' I said without hesitation, and added that surely Pernickety Paul would have approved.

Catherine shed sorrow like melting snow.

I said, 'I haven't seen where you live, remember? So how about now, then?'

She smiled with a touch of mischief and then kicked down on the starter and invited me to step aboard.

Her home was maybe five minutes' walk or less than one minute's motor-cycle ride along a straight grey road from the district police station. She stopped outside a single-storeyed semi-detached bungalow in a row of identical stuccoed boxes, and I knew within a second blink that this was not the place for me. Going there had been a mistake but, as Catherine was my transport, I would smile and pretend to like it.

I actually did both, and not from politeness's sake.

Inside, the plain clothes's one-floor living space had been allied to *Alice's Adventures in Wonderland*, where a more than life-size March Hare and a same-size Mad Hatter sat at the kitchen table and stuffed a dormouse into a teapot. A white rabbit consulted a watch by the bathroom door, and a red queen and a cook and a walrus and a carpenter danced a quadrille around the sitting room. All the walls, everywhere, were painted with rioting greenery and flowers.

Catherine laughed at my expression, a mixture no doubt of amusement and horror.

'All these people,' she said, 'came to me from a closing down fun-fair when I was six. I've always loved them. I know they're silly but they're company.' She suddenly swallowed. 'They have helped me come to terms with losing Paul. He liked them. They made him laugh. They're not the same now, without him. I think I've been growing up.'

In keeping with the rest of the house, Catherine's bedroom was a fantasy land of living playing cards painting rose bushes white and strong pink against puff-ball clouds and vivid green leaves.

Brought to a standstill, I said weakly, 'Lovely,' and Catherine laughed.

'You hate it, I can see.'

'I can shut my eyes,' I said, but we pulled the curtains closed.

We made love there in Pernickety Paul's honour but, in the evening, after the party in the pub, when Detective Constable Dodd and her pillion rider climbed back on the saddle, it was to the big quiet house on the hill that they went.

It was like coming familiarly home.